MW00474345

THE
GIRL
IN THE
RIVER

BOOKS BY RITA HERRON

THE GIRL IN THE RIVER

RITA HERRON

bookouture

Published by Bookouture in 2022

An imprint of Storyfire Ltd.
Carmelite House
50 Victoria Embankment
London EC4Y 0DZ

www.bookouture.com

Copyright © Rita Herron, 2022

Rita Herron has asserted her right to be identified
as the author of this work.

All rights reserved. No part of this publication may be reproduced, stored in
any retrieval system, or transmitted, in any form or by any means, electronic,
mechanical, photocopying, recording or otherwise, without the prior written
permission of the publishers.

ISBN: 978-1-80314-963-9
eBook ISBN: 978-1-80314-962-2

This book is a work of fiction. Names, characters, businesses, organizations,
places and events other than those clearly in the public domain, are either the
product of the author's imagination or are used fictitiously. Any resemblance
to actual persons, living or dead, events or locales is entirely coincidental.

To Babette – my beautiful daughter-in law who stole my son's heart. Thanks for all your support with my writing! I couldn't be prouder to have such a brave, strong, smart and funny young woman in the family!
Love always,
Rita

PROLOGUE

SOMEWHERE ON THE RIVER

The river monsters swarmed all around her.

The little girl was seven years old and trembling as her parents led her to the motorboat at the water's edge. "I don't want to go," she cried. "I can't swim."

"We have to get out of here," her daddy said. "Hurry."

Mama stroked her hair. "Come on, baby. Daddy's right. It's not safe."

Terrified as she pictured the slimy reptiles rising in the mist, she dug her heels in. She heard the raging water slashing on the jagged rocks. Saw the river monsters that surged from the muddy depths and snatched you beneath the surface. They whispered to her at night when she slept.

The wind hissed over the water and her sneakers sank into the muddy ground. Dark clouds moved across the sky. Thunder rumbled.

Daddy climbed in the boat and her sister jumped in. The boat rocked back and forth. Then Mama scooped her up and handed her to Daddy. She closed her eyes and began to cry. She could see the eyes of the serpent watching her, teeth gnashing.

Mama climbed on board next, the boat swaying. "There,

there, baby, the life jacket will keep you safe." She slipped her arms into the shoulder straps and Mama tightened them.

The motor sounded and Daddy took off, ripping through the brown water and bouncing over the waves as they splashed and swirled. Mia hugged her knees to her chest and shivered as the spray washed over her.

Mama huddled next to Daddy as the boat zoomed into the deep part of the river. Lily pads floated past. Twigs snapped from a tree above as the wind picked up. Leaves blew across the surface.

A water moccasin slithered through the brush as they passed a bed of moss.

Fear gripped her. Thunder clapped in the distance. Lightning zigzagged across the darkening sky. Daddy looked back over his shoulder.

"Hurry, honey," Mama said to Daddy.

"It wasn't supposed to storm," Daddy muttered. He swung the boat around a curve and sped up. They zipped around a fallen tree branch, then hit a rock. She bounced and clawed at the boat's side to keep from being thrown over.

Another clap of thunder. More lightning, big yellow streaks that shot across the dark sky like fireworks. Then another sound – something pinged off the boat.

Mama screamed and ducked. Her daddy said an ugly word and swung the boat to the right. Another ping, then he swerved again. A big tree had fallen and he was heading straight toward it.

The boat spun around a curve then thunder and lightning popped again. Metal sizzled and sparks flew.

Mama screamed. Daddy tried to control the boat but smashed into the tree. The force threw her and her sister against the side. Suddenly, fire burst from the back.

Mama threw the life raft over the side.

"Get in, girls!" she shouted.

Mia was terrified but her sister took her hand. "We gotta go!"

Together they climbed into the lifeboat. Mama ran back toward Daddy, but suddenly the boat exploded. Flames shot up and then spread, catching Mama's clothes. Mama's screams flooded her ears, then Daddy's. Mia watched in horror.

Water sloshed over the side of the boat, soaking her. Her sister cried out and clutched at the seat. Mia gripped the side of the lifeboat and looked for her parents, but it was too smoky.

She wanted to get Mama and Daddy but the boat was a ball of flames. The waves grew higher, then ripped the lifeboat away. They slammed into a rock, bounced back and kept going. Her head ached. Pain shot through her back.

Then the current swept them over a rapid. River monsters lurched from the darkness. She closed her eyes as they snatched her and carried her away.

ONE

CROOKED CREEK

Twenty years later

DAY 1

A girl's wedding was supposed to be the happiest day of her life.

Detective Ellie Reeves studied herself in the mirror, adding a hint of blush to highlight her sea-blue eyes. She didn't normally wear makeup, but today was special, and she'd decided to indulge her feminine side. Her off-the-shoulder sundress accentuated her ash-blond hair which she'd styled into loose curls around her face. She pushed her feet into silver sparkly heels, a major change from her hiking boots and sneakers. She just hoped she didn't faceplant in the middle of the ceremony.

She spotted her badge and her gun on the dresser, and she ran her finger over the cool metal. She was tempted to leave them behind.

After all, Vera, her adopted mother, would be appalled to know she was carrying a weapon to a wedding. Ellie had forever balked at Vera's nudges to find a good man and tie the knot. She didn't intend to give up her badge for anyone.

Still, she felt naked without her shield and weapon, so she slipped them inside her pearl-adorned clutch.

Her new friend Mia Norman had been planning her big day for weeks now. Although Ellie had only known Mia six weeks, she didn't want anything to go wrong for her.

After the last gruesome case Ellie had worked, where she'd literally uncovered a mass graveyard, she'd decided to brighten up the exterior of her small bungalow with some curb appeal. Mia, who'd been shy and withdrawn when they'd first met, worked at the local gardening center, The Green Thumb, and had added magic to Ellie's yard with bright pockets of sunflowers, pansies and Gerber daisies – all of Ellie's favorites.

But while Mia worked in Ellie's front yard, surrounded by the beauty she was creating, sadness permeated her hazel eyes. Ellie wondered what her new friend had gone through – what she was harboring.

You're being paranoid, she told herself. A hazard of the job.

A knock sounded on the front door. Expecting her date, Special Agent Derrick Fox, Ellie rushed to answer it. Since they'd closed the last case, they'd developed a tentative closeness and she was glad he'd agreed to accompany her today.

She stumbled on her heels, then slipped them off and carried them in her hand to the door. But when she opened it, the dark look on Derrick's face, coupled with the fact that he was wearing jeans and a button down shirt instead of a suit, indicated he'd changed his mind.

Disappointment flitted through her, but she simply raised a brow. "Derrick?"

"I'm sorry," he said. "I can't go."

Ellie barely resisted thumping her bare foot in irritation as she waited for an explanation. On the job she'd learned to be patient. Silence was the most effective technique in making someone talk.

He's not a suspect, she reminded herself. *He looks troubled.* Or... maybe he'd just changed his mind about the two of them.

With a sigh, he ran his fingers through his thick brown hair. "I've been called to attend the reading of Rick's will."

Ellie's heart stuttered at the timing. In honor of Memorial Day, flags and markers of fallen soldiers who'd lived in Bluff County lined the streets of Crooked Creek. Derrick had served with his military buddy Rick. With Rick's recent suicide, the ceremonies to honor the soldiers had to be tough for Derrick. Worse, Rick's wife Lindsey seemed to blame Derrick.

Compassion welled in Ellie's chest. Derrick still harbored guilt for Rick's death and the mission they'd run together, which had taken innocent lives. "I'm sorry. I know today will be difficult," she said softly. "Do you want to come in and talk about it?"

He shook his head, his expression tormented. "I just wanted you to know the reason," he murmured.

Ellie nodded. "Thanks. I could skip the wedding and go with you," she offered.

He stepped away from her. "No, I need to do this alone."

She wanted desperately to draw him into a hug, to kiss him and assure him everything would be okay, that his friend's death wasn't his fault.

But she sensed him shutting down again.

And then he was gone.

TWO

MAGNOLIA MANOR

Today twenty-seven-year-old Mia Norman was marrying the man of her dreams.

Yet as she looked in the mirror at her reflection – the beautiful lace veil, the simple pearl earrings, the necklace that had belonged to her mother – she saw the lies hidden in her eyes.

Jesse's image taunted her.

Killing her was the hardest thing Mia had ever done. *I know you had dreams, Jess. I'm sorry I stole them from you.*

Tears laced her eyes. Her fiancé, Mark Wade, deserved to know the truth. But that was too dangerous so she kept her secrets locked away in the attic of her mind where she prayed they stayed forever.

"Mommy." Her four-year-old daughter Pixie smiled as she ran her fingers over the satin fabric of Mia's satin, mermaid-style wedding dress. "You look beautiful."

Love for her daughter filled her heart as she hugged Pixie. Everything she'd done, she'd done for this beautiful child. "So do you, sweet girl."

Pixie danced around, the tulle on her white flower girl dress swishing, her sparkly pink shoes tapping on the wood floor. A string of tiny daisies was woven in the strands of her long blond French braid, making her look angelic. And her dark brown eyes looked like chocolate drops, huge in her tiny face.

Mia's heart squeezed. She loved this child more than words.

"I can't wait to drop the rose petals down the aisle," Pixie chirped.

Mia laughed at Pixie's exuberance. She'd been so excited at the rehearsal that she'd practically run down the aisle, tossing the flowers over her head after she'd reached the gazebo where Mia and Mark would say their vows.

Still, nerves fluttered in Mia's belly. She'd never thought she'd find a nice, loving man like Mark, or that she'd ever get married. In fact, when she'd first moved to the small town of Crooked Creek in the Appalachian Mountains, she'd staunchly avoided getting close to anyone.

Especially a man.

She'd devoted herself to raising Pixie and refused to let anyone into their lives. Pixie was all she needed. She was her life.

Then one day Mark had walked into the garden center to buy fertilizer and seed, and a spark had been lit. Still, she'd run from that feeling. Sparks could get you in trouble. Charmers could be snakes beneath the act.

Yet she'd watched him patiently listen to her daughter as Pixie led him around the store pointing out her favorite flowers. He'd told her about the kids he taught and the ones he coached on the high school soccer team with such pride that it warmed her heart. Then he'd helped Old Ms. Eula, the local ghost whisperer, load gardening supplies into the back of her truck, and she decided he was a good guy.

But the first time he'd asked her to dinner, she'd balked. Getting close was playing with fire.

But his constant kindness had soon melted her resistance, and three months in, she fell for him hard.

He would make a great father for Pixie.

A knock sounded at the door to her dressing room and her coworker and maid of honor Tori James poked her head in. "Are you ready?"

Mia stood, brushing her fingers over her dress as she checked her veil in the mirror. Regret for lying to Mark threatened to steal her joy, but as Pixie bounced up and down and grabbed her flower basket, Mia nodded.

"Pixie, go potty, honey, then it's time to get lined up."

Pixie skipped into the bathroom and closed the door while Tori checked her own hair in the mirror.

Mia stepped to the window and looked out at the lilies and peonies decorating the gazebo. The sun was starting to fade with brilliant reds, oranges and yellows dyeing the sky above the majestic mountain peaks. The dozens and dozens of magnolias for which the resort venue was named still held a few blooms, white blossoms dotting the grass.

"Let's go to the river for pictures," the photographer had suggested earlier.

Mia had shaken her head. "No, I don't like the water."

A shudder rippled through her. In her mind, she heard the water angrily raging over the jagged river rocks. Saw the river monsters rising through the fog, swarming around her. Saw death and darkness and the ghosts of her parents floating in the haze, disappearing into nothing.

Sadness overcame her. She desperately wished they could be here today, along with her sister. She missed them terribly. But that was not to be.

Footsteps echoed outside in the hall, and she blinked the monsters away. Guests were congregating on the lawn. The Hintons, who owned the gardening center. Crystal Marrs, the owner of the local crystal shop, who'd suggested Mia use essential oils and herbs to calm her anxiety.

Suddenly a head of dark blond hair caught her eye. Gray suit. A tall, broad-shouldered man. Her pulse quickened.

No... it couldn't be him. She'd covered her tracks well. He had no idea where she was... None of *them* did.

And it had to stay that way. He'd kill her for what she'd done to Jesse.

THREE

Ellie spotted Lola Parks, the owner of the Corner Café, and Ranger Cord McClain as she crossed the lawn of the resort. Cord worked Search and Rescue and was a third of the task force Derrick had established under the governor's orders to tackle local crime. Dressed in a navy sports coat, button-collared shirt and gray slacks, he looked ruggedly handsome. A smile tugged at the corner of her mouth. A man of the land, he also looked as stiff and uncomfortable in dress clothes as she was in her heels.

Hushed voices whispered around her as the guests gathered. Rays of sunshine glinted off the plush lawn and shimmered off the rocky cliff where the ceremony would take place. Magnolia Manor was in Summerville, a tiny town near Blue Ridge on the Appalachian Trail which drew tourists with its scenic views and waterfalls.

Cord's dark gaze raked over Ellie, his eyes glinting with emotions she couldn't quite read. Ellie had barely seen him in the last six weeks and then only in passing. Her gaze met Lola's. Lola was usually friendly, but as Ellie waved to her, her lips pressed into a thin line.

A second later, Lola slipped her hand through Cord's arm and tugged him toward the seating area. Soft music echoed in the background as the attendees found their seats.

Shondra Eastwood, one of the deputies at Crooked Creek Police Department and Ellie's friend, walked toward her with a pretty blond on her arm. Shondra's long glossy black hair was wrapped in a gold turban today that glittered in the sunlight and accented her burnt-orange dress.

"Hey, Ellie," Shondra said. "This is Julie."

"Nice to meet you," Ellie said and meant it. Shondra had had a traumatic childhood and had overcome many obstacles to find happiness.

A singer strummed a love song on a guitar as Mark's parents walked down the aisle to the front row. Mia's fiancé Mark and his best man, Tori's husband Liam James, crossed the lawn to their places. Excitement lit Mark's eyes, although the small twitch of his hands as he clasped them indicated nerves.

All eyes turned toward the back in anticipation. Tension mounted as they waited, the guitar thrumming, a gust of wind rattling the leaves on the trees. A gray cloud moved across the sky, dimming the sun.

Seconds ticked by. Then minutes. People started to shift and strain to see if there was a problem. The guitarist began the song over again.

Mark's best man leaned over and said something to him. Mark exhaled.

Ellie turned to scan the lawn. Where was Mia?

FOUR

ATLANTA

Derrick hated to leave Ellie today. He'd never seen her in a dress and that sexy off-the-shoulder blue concoction had hugged her curves in all the right places. Dear God, she was a siren.

He not only wanted her, but damn if he hadn't started relying on her. Needing her.

That scared the hell out of him.

Flags honoring the soldiers waved in the breeze as he passed through Crooked Creek and turned onto the main highway.

He'd seen too many soldiers fall to their deaths during his stint in the service.

But the worst to swallow were the innocents. Collateral damage casualties, the government called them.

Even the soldiers who'd survived were casualties.

He flipped on the radio to distract himself and passed the high school where a banner congratulated the graduating class. Celebrations for that would be joyful.

Except he couldn't stop thinking about the kids who'd died on the mission he and Rick had been ordered to take. The innocent kids that would never receive a diploma. Never grow up and have families of their own.

And now Rick was gone... His children would not have him in the stands when they graduated.

Ellie had been his rock in the last few weeks since he'd lost his friend. Had been patient and let him talk when he wanted but she hadn't pushed, which he'd needed.

"It's not your fault," Ellie had said.

But no matter how many times she told him that, guilt ate at him like a cancer.

FIVE

MAGNOLIA MANOR

The wedding coordinator Georgia Saben approached Ellie and whispered, "I can't find the bride, her daughter or the bridesmaid. I think something's wrong."

Ellie's heart thundered. "Okay, I'll take a look."

Mark mouthed, "What's going on?"

Not wanting to panic the groom, Ellie shrugged and feigned a smile. "Sorry, folks. I'll check on Mia."

Whispers rippled through the space and Mark started toward her. "Stay here," she told Mark. "I'll be right back." *Hopefully with the bride.*

Gripping her clutch in one hand, Ellie followed Georgia down the aisle. "When did you last see her?"

"About half an hour ago," Georgia said. "She, Tori and Pixie were all in the bride's room getting dressed."

"How did Mia seem?"

"Happy. Excited," Georgia said. "I tried to call her phone a minute ago, but she didn't answer. And when I looked into the dressing room to tell her it was time, there was no sign of her. I even looked around the outside area near there, and along the path to the gardens, but she wasn't there."

Maybe Mia was having pre-wedding jitters and they'd taken a walk to calm her nerves?

In her haste, Ellie stumbled on the pavers leading to the building entrance. "Damn heels," she muttered, then slipped them off and carried them. Inside the venue, ceiling fans swirled, circulating the warm air and keeping bugs at bay, and the tile floor felt cool beneath her feet as they entered through the French doors and down a corridor lined with paintings of magnolia trees. The bridal dressing room was labeled with a gold name plate, the door ajar.

Hoping to find Mia and Tori repairing a button or the bride's hair, she paused at the door. "Mia?" Ellie called. "Tori?"

No answer, so she peeked inside. The room was empty, a chair overturned, one of Mia's silver shoes abandoned near the door.

She scanned the floor and saw a small piece of tulle stuck in the doorjamb as if it had been ripped off. A silver necklace lay on the floor. A pearl bracelet, the pearls scattered from where it had snapped.

Her breath stalled in her chest. Dammit, something had definitely happened here.

SIX

ATLANTA

As soon as Derrick entered the attorney's office, the chill in the air hit him.

Lindsey sat stiffly in a leather chair, hands clasped, her gaze fixed as if she couldn't tolerate looking at him.

The attorney shook Derrick's hand and indicated the second chair facing his large mahogany desk. "Thank you for coming, Special Agent Fox."

"Of course, I'd do anything for Rick and his family."

That earned him a glare from Lindsey that made him instantly regret saying anything. Obviously he had not done enough.

"Let us begin then," the attorney said.

Lindsey released a pained sigh, and Derrick folded his hands in his lap. Beside him, his heart ached for Lindsey. Her eyes were red-rimmed and puffy, her face pale and gaunt.

The past six weeks since Rick had been gone, she'd been left with two traumatized and grief-stricken children. She looked completely exhausted, angry and sad. And she blamed Derrick.

All understandable considering Rick had chosen to take his own life and leave her and the kids behind to deal with the fallout.

The silver-haired family attorney cleared his throat. "Rick Letterman bequeaths all his worldly belongings, the house he owned with his wife Lindsey, and all savings, financial investments and moneys to her." The attorney's gaze settled on his papers for a moment before he began again. This time his voice was solemn and regretful. "Unfortunately, Lindsey, his life insurance police was void due to his suicide."

Lindsey pressed her fist to her mouth.

Derrick went still. "I'm sorry, Lindsey, but we'll figure something out." He reached out to console her but she pushed his hand away.

"As for you, Special Agent Fox," the attorney continued. "Rick named you as his children's godfather and requested that you watch over his family. As far as monetary benefits—"

"I don't want anything financially from him," Derrick said. "Everything should go to his wife and children."

Lindsey's hot stare scorched him, but he would honor his friend's wishes. They'd gone through hell and back together and he owed him. "I agree to serve as the godfather for his children," he said, shoulders squared. "I will do anything to help this family."

Lindsey vaulted up from the chair, arms folded, bitterness in her tone. "Is that it?"

The lawyer pulled his hand down his chin. "Well, yes, that pretty much sums it up."

Lindsey snatched her purse, threw it over her shoulder and headed to the door. Derrick exchanged a look with the attorney then chased after her, catching her as she reached for the door.

"Lindsey, wait—"

She threw up her hand. "Just stop. I don't want or need anything from you, Derrick. And neither do my children."

Derrick felt as if he'd been slugged in the chest. She shot him a warning look that told him not to follow her, then yanked open the door and stomped out, her heels clicking on the floor as she put as much distance between the two of them as possible.

SEVEN

MAGNOLIA MANOR

Dread knotted Ellie's stomach. "Stay there and don't touch anything," she told Georgia. "It looks like there was a struggle."

She inched inside, careful herself not to disturb anything. A quick inventory of the room showed her: a bathrobe tossed over a velvet chair; overnight bag in the corner; a pair of slippers and flat sandals by the wall; jewelry bag on a dresser along with a makeup bag, a comb, bobby pins and hairspray; two champagne flutes and an open bottle of Moët in a silver bucket chilling on the sideboard; and a platter of assorted fruit picked over.

Various possibilities raced through her mind. She spotted a cell phone in a bright pink case on the chair, checked and saw it was Mia's. Turning in a wide arc, she looked for Tori's and noticed it wedged in the chair cushion.

The bathroom door was closed, chair jammed against it. That was odd.

The sound of water dripping echoed from within, along with another low sound she couldn't quite define. Ellie pulled her weapon and crept toward the doorway, peeking through the crack. A floral scent permeated the air. Makeup was scattered across the vanity and an overturned bottle of perfume had spilled onto the counter. A tube of soft pink lipstick was open, and a curling iron had fallen to the floor.

The hair on the nape of her neck prickled, and she set the chair aside and eased open the door. Then the sound came again. Soft. Barely discernible. Crying?

Inching closer, she slid the shower curtain open and found Pixie inside the tub, curled in a ball, knees to her chest, sobbing.

EIGHT

Ellie's chest clenched, and she knelt in front of the child and brushed her fingers over Pixie's soft blond hair. "Hey, hey, honey. It's Ellie. What's wrong?"

Pixie gulped, then slowly looked up at her, eyes brimming with tears. Fear darkened her big brown eyes. M... Mommy?"

"What about Mommy, sweetheart?"

Pixie's chin quivered. "I... wants her."

Fear made Ellie draw a quick breath. "Where's Ms. Tori?"

"I dunno."

"What happened?" Ellie asked.

"I came inside to potty and then someone shut the d-door," Pixie stuttered. "Then I heard Mommy cry and I... think there was a man..." A sob escaped her and she burst into tears again.

"Come here, honey." Ellie scooped the little girl into her arms. "Shh, it's okay now. I'll find her and Ms. Tori."

Pixie tightened her hold around Ellie's neck as Ellie soothed her.

"Did you see what the man looked like?" Ellie asked softly. "Or did he say his name?"

Pixie shook her head against Ellie's shoulder. "No... I was scared... and then it got quiet and I couldn't open the door."

Ellie patted her back. "It's all right. I'm here now." She brushed at Pixie's tears. "Let's go see Mark and I'll look around for your mommy and Ms. Tori."

Pixie sniffled and clung tight as Ellie carried her from the bathroom. Georgia stood at the doorway to the bridal room, watching in distress. "What happened?"

"I don't know. But call your security team and ask them to start searching the property."

NINE

"Stay here and make sure no one goes inside, too," Ellie told Georgia. "If Mia or Tori return, call me. I'm going to take Pixie to Mark and then I'll be back."

Worry creased Georgia's forehead but she nodded.

Ellie continued to soothe Pixie while she hurried back to the wedding site. Mark and Liam were both pacing, the guests were whispering and shuffling in their seats.

When Mark and Liam spotted her with Pixie, they hurried down the center aisle. Mark took one look at Pixie's tears and panic flickered across his face. "What's going on? I called Mia a dozen times and she's not answering."

"Neither is Tori," Liam said.

"Mia and Tori weren't in the bride's room." Ellie spoke softly, struggling not to let her own rising anxiety filter into her voice. "I need someone to watch Pixie so I can look around."

"I'll look, too," Mark said.

"No. You two stay here in case they call or show up," Ellie said. "Maybe they just went for a walk. I'll keep you posted."

Mark looked reluctant, but he agreed, then reached for

Pixie. "Come here, sweetie. You can hang with me while Ms. Ellie finds your mommy."

Pixie sniffled but allowed him to take her, and Ellie's gaze caught Cord's. He read her well; he stood and walked over to join her, Lola on his heels.

Ellie steered them to the side while Mark's parents joined him. "Something's not right," Ellie told Cord. "It's possible the bride ran off, but I think there might be foul play. Come with me, Cord."

"What can I do to help?" Lola asked.

"Watch out for Pixie. She's upset. She thinks she heard a man in the room with her mother. But I haven't shared that with Mark yet so don't mention it."

Sympathy softened Lola's eyes. "I'll see if I can distract her."

"Thanks," Ellie said. "I want the men to stay here until I figure out what's going on." She glanced at Cord. "Follow me."

Lola walked over to talk to Pixie and Ellie led Cord back to the bridal dressing room.

"What are you thinking?" Cord asked.

"The room is a mess, as if there was an altercation. The security team has been alerted to search the property. But I want to look around here in case there's some sign that Mia planned to leave."

"Any indication Mia would run out on her wedding?" Cord asked.

"Not that I know of, but I'll ask." Her stomach twisted.

"I met her a couple of times at the café with Pixie," Cord said. "She seemed devoted to her daughter."

"She was. Which is why I don't think she'd voluntarily leave without her. It doesn't make sense," Ellie murmured. "Let's examine the bride's room first. If someone took the women, we can't waste any time. For now, we treat it as a crime scene." If she determined there was foul play and not simply a runaway bride, she'd need a forensic team to go over the room.

She handed Cord a pair of latex gloves and headed inside. Using her phone, she snapped close ups of the disheveled room. Except for the overturned items, they found nothing. No note from Mia. Her suitcase and toiletry bag were still in the closet in preparation for her honeymoon.

"Pixie mentioned she heard a man's voice in here. Any sign of that?" Ellie asked.

Cord shook his head as she photographed the bathroom doorway.

"This chair was jammed against the door when I came in and Pixie was locked inside. I wonder if Mia or the man closed it."

"It doesn't sound good," Cord muttered.

"No." Ellie's nerves were getting the best of her. Today had started out with such hope for her friend. "Check with security, Cord. Maybe you can coordinate the search."

"Will do."

"I'll question Mark and Liam and ask if there's been problems in their relationships."

TEN

Ellie made a quick phone call to her boss to request a forensic team and left one of the security guards to secure the room while she returned to the main venue.

Mark and Liam rushed to Ellie, with Pixie clinging to Mark. Seconds later, Mark's parents joined them. "Did you find them?" Mark asked.

"Not yet," Ellie said.

Mr. Wade patted his son's back. "I'm sure she's here somewhere," he said, although his voice sounded less than convincing.

Mrs. Wade toyed with the gold chain of her ruby necklace. "Maybe she had second thoughts, Mark."

Mark glared at his mother. "No. Mia would never leave me or Pixie."

An odd look flitted in his mother's eyes, but she clamped her lips tight, stepped away and went to talk to two young women from the Garden Club.

Liam looked down, running his hands through his wavy brown hair. "Mark's right. Tori wouldn't leave either, not without calling me. She and Mia were so excited about today. They've been planning this for months."

The sun had completely vanished while Ellie was gone. A stiff wind had picked up, tearing flower petals from the gazebo.

Lola crossed to Pixie and Mark, holding out her arms. "Hey, sweetie, why don't we go look at the pond while Ms. Ellie and your dad talk?"

Pixie bit her lip and tightened her arms around Mark's neck.

"It's okay, Pix," Mark murmured. "Maybe you and Ms. Lola will see some fish. I'll be right here."

Tears stained Pixie's small heart-shaped face, but Mark cuddled her again, then the little girl allowed Lola to take her. Ellie watched Lola comforting Pixie and realized she'd make a good mother. Were marriage and a baby in the future for her and Cord?

Her stomach knotted although she didn't quite understand the reason. She and Cord had been together one night, but that had been years ago – she wanted him to be happy. She turned her mind back to the situation. The crowd was growing more restless by the minute, and she had to calm them. "Listen, folks," she said, "we appreciate your patience. At the moment, the bride and maid of honor appear to be missing. I need everyone to remain in this area while we search for them."

Concerned voices followed her announcement, but thankfully no one argued.

"I know you're worried, Mark, Liam, but I have to ask you some questions."

"Does my son need a lawyer?" Mr. Wade asked, his tone defensive.

Mark appeared to be taken off guard by his father's attitude. "No, Dad. Now go sit with Mom and let me talk to the detective."

A muscle twitched in the man's cheek, then he went to join

his wife.

Meanwhile, Mark and Liam followed Ellie to the back row of chairs and seated themselves, their distress palpable.

Ellie offered Mark a sympathetic smile. "When did you last see Mia, Mark?"

"Last night at the rehearsal dinner." He stretched out his hands and stared at them. "And I called her to say goodnight before I turned in."

"How did Mia seem?"

"Fine," he replied. "Excited. Why?"

"I just need to know her frame of mind. If she was upset about something or nervous about the wedding."

"She wasn't," Mark said. "In fact, we laughed at the rehearsal dinner last night. Pixie was so tickled about dropping the flower petals down the aisle that she tossed some over her head."

Ellie smiled at the affection in his voice. "Did anything else happen?"

Mark folded his hands in his lap. "No... well, just that the photographer took some candids and Mia didn't like it. From the beginning, Mia insisted she didn't want a big wedding announcement photo anywhere."

Ellie tucked a strand of her hair the wind had blown from her clasp back into place. "Why didn't she want photos?"

Mark shrugged. "I don't know. She's somewhat of an intro-vert and has always shied away from attention. When we attended the high school soccer team banquet, she stepped away from the cameras then, too."

That did seem odd.

"Do you think she might have had cold feet?" Ellie asked gently.

Mark glanced at Liam, who had his hands jammed in the pockets of his gray suit. "I don't think so. Just last night we talked about the sand ceremony we planned together."

"Sand ceremony?" Ellie asked.

"Yeah, at the altar there were three bottles of sand, each a different color. One representing me, one for Mia and one for Pixie. Pouring them into one box symbolizes we're uniting as a family."

"That's really beautiful," Ellie said.

She directed her attention toward the best man. "Liam, did Tori mention anything about Mia being upset or feeling jittery about the wedding?"

Liam's wide jaw tightened. "No. In fact, the opposite. This morning Tori called Mia and said she sounded the happiest she'd ever heard her."

Mark relaxed slightly. "We were planning for me to adopt Pixie after the wedding."

"I'm sure Pixie was excited about that."

"She was."

His comment triggered more questions. "How did Pixie's birth father feel about that? Did he relinquish his rights to her?"

"Pixie's father died before she was born," Mark said. "Mia didn't like to talk about it."

"Did she tell Pixie about him?"

"Just that he would have loved her, but he died."

So that eliminated an ex showing up to interfere with the wedding.

"Let me check in with Ranger McClain," Ellie said. "If you two think of anything else, please let me know."

The men bowed their heads in quiet conversation and Ellie phoned Cord. "Anything?"

"Not yet. Security called in a couple of extra guards. I canvassed guests at the pool and restaurant but no one has seen a bride."

"Keep looking," Ellie said. "They have to be here somewhere."

"Copy that," Cord said. "I'm going to take a look along the

riverbank."

Ellie looked out at the river. To reach the water, you had to go down a sloping hill, although a golf cart could make that trip quickly. If Mia was a runaway bride, she and Tori would have probably taken one of their cars.

With that in mind, she approached Mark and Liam again and asked about their vehicles.

"Tori drove Mia and Pixie this morning," Mark said.

"She drives a dark green 2021 Subaru SUV," Liam said, then recited the license number.

"Thanks. I'll get someone to see if it's still in the parking lot. Then I'll question the other guests." She texted the wedding coordinator and asked her to have someone search for the vehicle. While Cord and the security team continued to comb the property, she joined Mark's parents.

The cloud that had moved in earlier darkened, threatening a storm as grim as the mood of the wedding venue.

"Mr. and Mrs. Wade, how did you feel about Mia?" Ellie asked.

Mr. Wade spoke first. "Mia was a bit shy but a lovely young woman," he said. "Mark was certainly taken with her."

"He was practically obsessed with her and that child," Mrs. Wade said. "He had a chance to coach at a college but turned it down to stay in Crooked Creek because of them."

Ellie recognized disapproval in her tone. "You weren't happy about the marriage?"

The woman's eyes flickered with a chill that surprised Ellie. "I wanted my son to live up to his potential. To pursue his career to the fullest. But he wouldn't listen."

"And you thought Mia was holding him back?" Ellie asked.

Her loud exhale reverberated between them. "Well, it was *his* choice, I guess."

"Didn't you like Mia?" Ellie pressed.

"She was fine, I suppose. But there was something off about

her... She said she had no family. I felt sorry for her and offered to give them a big wedding on the river but she refused."

Mr. Wade rolled his eyes. "She said she wanted a more intimate affair with close friends. I thought it was admirable that she didn't want to accept our money or run up an exorbitant bill for a ceremony."

"Did she seem nervous to you last night?" Ellie asked.

"No," Mr. Wade said. "She and Pixie and Mark laughed and danced together."

"Mrs. Wade?" Ellie asked.

She fidgeted. "Not any more so than usual."

"What do you mean?" Ellie asked.

Her eyes flitted sideways, then back to Ellie, but Mr. Wade covered her hand with his. "Nothing," she said. "It was just... nothing really."

"Please," Ellie said. "Even if it seems trivial, it might be important."

"I said it's nothing. Now why are you asking? Do you think she abandoned my son at the altar?" the woman asked.

"I honestly don't know," Ellie said. "We have to explore all possibilities."

"Well, I hope you find her and this was just a big misunderstanding," Mr. Wade said.

Mrs. Wade nodded and squeezed her husband's hand. "Now, can we please sit with Mark? He looks absolutely miserable."

"Of course. But if you think of anything, no matter how small, please let me know."

Ellie stood and the couple rushed over to Mark, who sat hunched over with his head in his hands, body trembling.

Ellie and Shondra spent the next half an hour questioning the guests, who described Mia as a sweet, even tempered, quiet woman devoted to her daughter – exactly Ellie's impression of her.

The owners of the gardening center clung to one another. "I hope you find her and Tori," Mrs. Hinton said in a low voice.

"Did she mention having cold feet about the wedding?" Ellie asked.

"Heavens no," Mrs. Hinton said. "In fact, I spoke to her early this morning, and she was ecstatic over the flower arrangements."

"So she and Mark were happy?"

"Like two peas in a pod," Mr. Hinton said. "He stopped by the gardening center all the time to see her."

"I heard him say she was more beautiful than any flowers we carried," Mrs. Hinton said with a note of wistfulness.

Ellie smiled at the image, just as the wind picked up again, knocking Pixie's basket of rose petals over and scattering them across the lawn. Dusk had faded, the colors of the sunset disappearing as the gray sky grew more ominous. The quarter moon slithered through the clouds, beaming down on faces haunted by worry.

Thunder rumbled, and suddenly the blustery winds intensified, shaking trees and tearing the ribbon from the chairs. A few of them blew over and raindrops began to pelt the grass.

"Everyone inside!" the wedding coordinator shouted.

Ellie's gaze met Shondra's. "Keep them contained in the reception room."

Shondra nodded and began to herd the guests inside. Lola ran up with Pixie clinging to her then followed the group. Ellie's phone buzzed.

She waited until Mark and Liam were inside before answering. "Cord?"

"We found something," Cord said in a deep voice. "Meet me at the river. And, El, you might want to come alone."

Ellie's heart hammered. If Cord wanted her to come alone, it couldn't be good.

ELEVEN

Tucking her phone in the pocket of her sundress, Ellie walked briskly to the golf cart stand, waved over an attendant and flashed her shield. "Can you take me to the river?"

"Of course."

She slid in the seat and held the bar as he sped onto the cement path that curved around the resort. Azaleas, pansies, and daffodils waved in the breeze, the impending scent of the storm blending with the sweet smell of the flowers. Unlike the dilapidated orphanage where her last case had taken place, beauty filled every corner of this property.

Except now dark gray clouds shrouded the beauty – and her friend was missing.

The driver spun around the path. With the storm, the golfers had packed up for the day and shadows hovered over the land. Thick woods rose all around and backed onto the river where the current ran fast and hard downstream.

A minute later, they reached the riverbank, and she spotted Cord waving at her. The golf cart driver pulled to a stop, and Ellie thanked him and hurried down the hill. Her feet sank into the wet grass and raindrops pelted her.

The sound of the river rippling echoed a few feet away.

Worry was etched into Cord's face. "Something over there." He pointed across the river to a downed tree.

Ellie's breath caught as she spotted something indiscernible snagged onto a branch. "God. That could be fabric."

Cord had already yanked off his jacket and tie and kicked off his shoes. "I was just about to go in and check it out."

Thunder clapped and lightning grazed the tops of the mountain peaks in jagged streaks. "Be careful, Cord. The storm is getting worse."

"I've got it." Fierce determination flared on his face, then he handed Ellie his cell phone and dove into the river.

Ellie clenched her hands by her sides as she watched him swim to the other side. Cord was no gym rat, but he was strong, his strokes even and smooth, his muscular physique a testament to the fact that he spent most of his life outdoors.

The water bobbed up and down, and somewhere in the distance she heard a motorboat zipping downstream. She craned her neck to see who it was, but it was too far away.

Cord reached the tree and treaded water as he examined the netting caught on the branch.

A minute later, he shook his head and shouted, "Not good, El. We have a body."

TWELVE

Ellie gritted her teeth. Dammit. Was it Mia?

Ellie paced up and down the river bank, scanning all directions, and spotted a canoe hidden between some pines about seventy-five feet away in the opposite direction of where Cord had come. Covering her head with her hand to ward off the worst of the rain, she jogged toward it, pushed the boat to the edge of the river and climbed in it. Thankful her father had taught her how to canoe, she lifted the paddles and rowed across the river.

The boat bounced and swayed, water splashing over the edge and soaking her bare feet. The current was so strong her muscles strained as she fought to keep from being swept downstream, and the wind whistled.

The rain drilled down, soaking Ellie to the core and pinging off the surface of the water and the bottom of the canoe. Cord hung onto the fallen tree, watching as she steered it toward the bank. Her pulse hammered as she tied the canoe to the tree trunk, then leaned closer to see what he'd found.

"The lace trimmed veil with the tiny rosettes... It was Mia's. She had it in her car one day when she dropped off some plants for my yard." But the body lay face down, arms outstretched, most of it immersed in the water. Long hair swirled in all directions like snakes, streaks of red dotting the surface. Probably blood.

Ellie held her breath. "Turn her over now."

Cord scrubbed rainwater from his eyes, then eased the woman's body over. Blood streaked her face, and leaves clung to her hair and chest. Her eyes stood wide open in the shock of death, pale pink lips parted in a scream.

"She doesn't have a pulse," Cord said.

A wave of grief hit Ellie. She was definitely dead.

Only the girl in the river was not Mia. It was Tori.

THIRTEEN

"I have to call it in," Ellie said as she sank back into the canoe. Then she had to inform Liam that his wife was dead.

Her lungs strained for air, and she phoned her captain. "The bride Mia Norman is still missing," Ellie said. "Security teams are searching the property, but considering the fact that we found the bridesmaid in the river and the bride's veil was also there, Mia might be as well. Let's get a chopper to survey above and set up teams to drag the river. The current could have washed her downstream. Also, I heard a motorboat, so if this is an abduction, Mia's kidnapper and Tori's killer could be escaping via boat."

"On it."

"Ranger McClain and I are going to remove Tori's body from the river before the elements can cause more damage and wash away evidence," Ellie said. "Send the ME with a transport team. And ask Sheriff Waters and Deputy Landrum to come. Shondra is questioning the wedding guests, but we need someone to canvass everyone registered at the resort."

They hung up, then she turned to Cord. The wind was

battering the canoe, making it bob up and down wildly, rain still beating down. "Let's get her in the boat."

"Let me check and see if she's trapped by something or weighted down."

Ellie shivered as he ducked underwater to assess the situation. A minute later, he broke the surface and took a breath. "A vine is tangled around her legs. Let me cut it then we'll move her."

Ellie's mind raced as Cord dove underwater again, the river rising with the downpour. She spotted a water moccasin skimming the surface a few feet away and watched to make sure it headed away from the ranger.

While she waited, she texted the security chief and filled him in. "Do not inform the guests or groom yet," she told him. "Any sign of the bride?"

"Afraid not, but we're still searching."

She had to consider the possibility that Mia had run away, but she had a sinking feeling she'd been taken. As Mark said, she never would have left her precious daughter.

FOURTEEN

Cord lifted Tori out and Ellie reached over the edge of the boat to assist him. The woman's body was heavy with death, her pale lavender bridesmaid's dress torn and soggy.

"Poor Tori," Ellie whispered as she raked wet hair from the young woman's face. Her heart ached for her and her husband.

This day had started off with such joy. At least she imagined it had, with Tori, Mia and Pixie all bustling around getting dressed, having their hair and makeup done, taking pictures as Mia prepared for the happy occasion.

Now it had ended with one woman dead and the bride missing.

Leaves and weeds clung to Tori's dress and body. One of her diamond earrings had come off, but she still wore her wedding ring.

Meaning her death had not been a robbery gone bad.

While Cord hauled himself inside the canoe, Ellie pulled herself together and examined Tori for injuries. The gash on the back of her head was deep and wide as if she'd been struck from behind by a blunt object. Which suggested she'd been attacked.

Had that blow killed her or had she drowned?

She examined Tori's arms and legs and found a couple of bruises, which could have happened when she hit rocks or the tree. More bruises marred her wrists as if she'd been held tightly, restrained or dragged. Definitely foul play.

As she rolled Tori to her side, Ellie noted a gunshot wound to her back. Damn. Not only had she been struck on the head from behind, but her attacker had shot her in the back.

Coward.

There was no exit wound, indicating the bullet was lodged inside.

She hadn't found blood or seen a bullet casing in the dressing room, but she could have missed it. Forensics would have to conduct a thorough search there and on the riverbank.

"How did the killer get Tori down here without anyone noticing?" she asked, thinking out loud. "There were guests everywhere today."

"We found some footprints so they must have walked." Cord narrowed his eyes as he examined the property. "All the guests were at the wedding or by the pool," he said. "One of the security guards mentioned that there's a private exit from the bridal room to keep guests and the groom from seeing the bride before the ceremony. There's also a separate path leading to one of the cabins and to the river down here."

"So he could have forced Tori and even Mia out that way and no one saw them," Ellie said.

Cord gave a nod.

"Did you check out that path?"

"I did and saw some footprints but they could have been other guests, and I was looking for the women, not evidence, so you should have forensics go over it."

"I will," Ellie said. The grimness of the situation seeped through her just as the rain was soaking her clothes.

Lightning crackled, thunder roaring again as her phone buzzed with a call. Shondra. "El, you need to get back. The ME is here. I caught her before the guests or Mark and Liam could see her."

"I'll be right there."

Dread gnawed at her as she called the golf cart driver to pick her up.

FIFTEEN

Cord agreed to wait with the body for the transport team and ERT while Ellie returned to the wedding venue. Drenched in soggy clothes and dripping wet hair, she ducked into the ladies' room and quickly dried her face. Wringing the worst of the moisture from her hair, she pulled it back into a ponytail. Her dress was soaked, but she couldn't do anything about that at the moment. Taking a deep breath, she hurried to join the guests who were sequestered in the reception ballroom.

Vases of fresh flowers served as centerpieces on white table-clothed round tables. Side tables held food-laden silver trays of appetizers, and the three-tiered wedding cake stood with the bride and groom topper holding hands. Champagne flutes, wine glasses and a station for beer and a signature cocktail occupied one corner.

None of which would be enjoyed today.

Dr. Laney Whitefeather texted she was in the lobby, and Ellie rushed to meet her before the guests realized the medical examiner had been called. Sheriff Bryce Waters joined them, Deputy Heath Landrum on his tail.

"What do we have?" Laney asked.

Ellie quickly filled Laney, Sheriff Bryce Waters and Deputy Landrum in, then waved over one of the golf cart attendees and addressed him. "We found a woman's body in the river but please keep this discreet for now. Can you show Dr. Whitefeather to the river to recover the body?"

"Sure," he agreed. The driver walked outside with Laney, then Ellie turned to Bryce and Landrum.

"Shondra is with the wedding guests, but this is a large resort," Ellie said. "The killer couldn't have carried two women down to the river, so they must have walked, most likely at gunpoint since Tori was shot. There's a private path leading down to the river. But someone may have seen or heard something. Check the security cameras, Sheriff. Maybe we'll catch whoever did this on film."

"I know the drill," Bryce said, his tone clipped.

"Thanks. Deputy Landrum, get a list of all the registered guests and start canvassing them. Look for anyone who seems out of place or nervous. I'll ask Shondra to question the employees as well as the caterer and staff who were working the wedding." Ellie's mind ticked away the next steps. "Meanwhile I'll talk to the photographer."

Bryce headed to the front desk to ask to speak to security while Ellie and the deputy returned to the reception area. Quiet, worried voices echoed through the space as she entered and all heads turned to her.

Shondra met her at the door. "People are starting to panic."

"Understandable," Ellie said. "Did you learn anything from the wedding guests?"

"So far no one strikes me as suspicious. And not one person had an ill word to say about Mia, Mark, Tori or Liam."

"Go with Landrum and he'll explain what I need you to do now," Ellie said.

A minute later, he and Shondra left the room and Ellie veered toward the photographer who was standing with the wedding coordinator near the entrance. She quickly introduced herself to the young woman.

"I'm Ansley Fortner," the young brunette said.

"Did you see anyone suspicious lurking around Mia or Tori today?"

Ansley rubbed the strap of her camera. "Not really."

"How was Mia's mood? Was she excited? Nervous? Having pre-wedding jitters?"

"She was giddy and looking forward to the day," Ansley said. "I didn't sense jitters about marrying Mark at all. The only odd thing was she refused to have a photo shoot by the river which is most people's favorite setting. Something about it seemed to spook her."

Was it the river or had she seen someone she was afraid of? "Can you please send me copies of all the photographs you took today? I need those ASAP." Ellie handed her a business card from her purse.

"Sure. I'll work on that now."

"You can use my office," the wedding coordinator offered.

Ansley hurried from the room and Mark and Liam strode toward Ellie.

"Please tell me you found them," Mark said, his breathing labored.

Liam's hair was sticking out in ten different directions from where he'd repeatedly dragged his fingers through it.

"I'm sorry, Mark, but no, we haven't found Mia yet. We're still looking." Ellie gave both men sympathetic looks. "Liam, I'm afraid I have some bad news for you. Maybe we should go somewhere private and sit down."

Liam instantly threw his shoulders back. "I don't want to sit down. I've been sitting and pacing forever now. Where's Tori?"

"I'm so sorry, Liam," Ellie said quietly. "We found her in the river... I'm afraid she's dead."

Liam staggered backward, the color draining from his face.

"No... No... That can't be true. She was fine this morning. We had coffee and laughed and... and..." He broke down and covered his face with his hands.

Mark gripped Liam's arm to steady his friend. "What about Mia?"

"Her veil was in the water but we didn't find her body so she could be alive. I've requested choppers to search the river." Ellie gently touched Liam's arm. "I'm so sorry for your loss, Liam."

Liam groaned. "I have to see her. Where is she? Why would she be at the river?"

"I don't know," Ellie said. "But I promise I'll find out."

"Take me to her," Liam demanded.

"I will as soon as possible. Right now, I need to ask you some more questions."

"We've already answered your questions," Liam said tightly.

"You said Mia's veil was in the water." Mark loosened his tie as if he was choking. "But she didn't like the water. Why would she go down there today?"

"That's what we're going to find out," Ellie replied.

"Tori was a good swimmer," Liam said. "But there's no way she'd go swimming before the wedding. She paid to have both her and Mia's makeup and hair professionally done." His eyes hardened. "What aren't you telling us?"

Ellie inhaled, knowing there was no way to sugarcoat the truth. "Her death wasn't accidental, Liam. Tori was murdered. She was shot."

SIXTEEN

Tension vibrated in the air as Liam absorbed the shock. Mark helped his friend to a chair, and Liam buried his head in his hands, his body shaking with emotion.

Ellie waited, giving the men a moment, but she had to press forward. The first twenty-four hours in an investigation were key to solving the case. If someone had abducted Mia, they could already be miles and miles away. "I know this is a shock but can either of you think of a reason someone would want to hurt Mia or Tori?"

Mark shook his head. "Everyone liked Mia. All the students and our coworkers."

"Tori was a high school teacher," Liam said, pain rasping in his voice. "Sometimes students and parents got angry, but not enough to k... kill."

"You worked with Tori then?" Ellie asked Mark.

Mark gave a little nod. "She taught English."

"Any problems with another teacher or the principal?"

Mark shook his head. "She was voted teacher of the year."

"How were things in your marriage, Liam?"

Anger sparked on his face. "Good," Liam said. "And before

you go there, I wasn't cheating, and I would never hurt my wife."

His quick defense sounded sincere. "Any financial problems?" Ellie pressed.

Irritation snapped in Liam's expression. "We had some debt like everyone else. But we weren't in trouble."

The possibilities swirled around Ellie's mind. Was this a crime of opportunity? Was one of the women the target and the other collateral damage?

Mark spoke through gritted teeth, "And before you ask, my finances are solid. I'm not rich and neither was Mia, but we didn't care about money. We just wanted to be together."

Ellie's chest squeezed. "How long have you been married, Liam?"

He heaved a breath. "Eight months."

Ellie contemplated another theory. "Did Tori have a former boyfriend who might have wanted her back? Or someone who might have been following her?"

Liam knuckled tears from his cheeks. "She dated some accountant before me," Liam said. "But she said the break-up was amicable. He's married now and lives in California."

Ellie turned to Mark. "How about Mia?"

"She said she hadn't dated anyone since Pixie was born. It took me six months to persuade her to have dinner with me."

"I need to see both Mia and Tori's phones and computers."

Maybe she'd find a clue in their correspondence or social media to help explain what happened here today.

SEVENTEEN

Pixie clung to Ms. Lola's hand as they walked toward the garden with all the pretty flowers. She liked Ms. Lola because she always gave her a cookie when she went to the café. And Ms. Lola made the best cookies. Peanut butter with chocolate chips was her favorite then the sugar cookies with the frosting and sprinkles.

But Pixie didn't want to go to the garden right now.

She wanted her mommy.

Fear tickled her tummy. Something was wrong. Really bad wrong.

She looked back and saw Mr. Mark and Mr. Liam, and knew they were upset. Mr. Liam might even be crying and she'd never seen a man cry before.

Tears filled her eyes. She was s'posed to be dropping rose petals on the ground while Mama walked down the aisle in her pretty white dress. But now everybody was whispering and shaking their heads and looked worried.

She wiped at her face. She'd been scared when she heard that mean voice outside the bathroom. Then she'd heard that chair scraping and the door was locked.

She tugged at Ms. Lola's hand. "Where's Mommy?"

Ms. Lola stopped by a bench and patted the seat. She sat down, and Ms. Lola did, too, then she put her arm around Pixie and pulled her close. "I'm not sure, honey. But Ms. Ellie will find her."

Pixie bit her lip. Ms. Lola was saying one thing. But her nose was all wrinkled up with a frown.

And that made Pixie even more scared.

EIGHTEEN

Ellie's phone signaled a text.

> Laney: *Estimated time of death based on liver temp and lack of rigor was sometime between four-thirty and six. The fact that Tori's watch stopped because it was crushed indicates she was attacked at 5:21.*

Just before the ceremony was supposed to take place. That fit with the wedding coordinator's story.

> Laney: *Called an ambulance for transport.*

Ellie sent a return text.

> *Husband wants to see her. Let me know when he can view.*

> Laney: *Will do.*

"What's going on now?" Mark asked. "Did they find Mia?" Ellie shook her head. "I'm sorry, no word yet, Mark." She turned to Liam, giving him a compassionate look. "The medical examiner is transporting Tori for an autopsy. She'll make contact when you can see her."

"I can't believe this is happening," Liam said, choking on the words.

Worry deepened the frown lines beside Mark's eyes as he looked at Liam.

"I'm so sorry, Mark, but I have another question," Ellie said. "Where were you two between five and five-thirty?"

Mark clamped his jaw tight, and anger flared on Liam's face. "In the groom's dressing room," Mark snapped. "Getting ready to meet my bride."

"And you, Liam?"

"With Mark. We had a toast after the pictures and walked over here together." Liam fisted his hands, and Ellie noticed a scratch on the back of his hand that looked fresh. "How did you get that cut on your hand, Liam?"

His gaze shot to the red jagged line. "I fell on the rocks during the photography session at the river."

Ellie arched a brow. "So you *were* down at the river?"

His expression bordered on panic as he realized he'd just placed himself at the crime scene. "Like I said, we took pictures there."

"We did," Mark said. "And Liam slid on a rock."

"Did you see anyone else down there? Maybe someone in the woods or on the property?" Ellie asked.

"Not anything suspicious," Mark said.

"There were guests roaming all over," Liam pointed out.

Hushed voices rumbled around them, the guests growing more antsy. Emily Nettles, the head of the local prayer group The Porch Sitters, sat with Lola, who was rocking Pixie in her arms. The little girl clung to her, looking terrified.

"Is there any other family we need to contact?" Ellie asked.

"Mia had no one," Mark said. "Except Pixie."

Liam swiped a hand over his eyes. "Sweet Jesus, I have to call Tori's mother."

"Do you want me to do that?" Ellie asked.

He shook his head. "No, I'd rather her hear the news from me. She's going to be devastated."

Ellie's heart ached for him.

Just then, Mark's parents strode toward her. "Are you going to tell us what's happening?" Mrs. Wade asked.

Her accusatory tone set Ellie's teeth on edge. "I was just about to make an announcement." Ellie walked over to Lola and Emily and asked them to take Pixie aside.

They didn't ask questions but took the child to the dessert table and let her choose a cookie before the staff began boxing them up. Then they disappeared into the foyer with benches overlooking the gardens.

Ellie stepped up to the podium reserved for the celebratory speeches. She felt sick that she was imparting this news on a day that was meant to be full of joy. "I'm sorry to have to inform everyone, but the bride is still missing. We suspect foul play."

Gasps reverberated through the crowd. In the last two years, crime had escalated in the area, and just when the town of Crooked Creek was feeling safe, now this had happened and would trigger fear again.

Knowing she had to calm the guests, Ellie continued, "Teams are searching the property and river now. If you saw or heard anything suspicious, no matter how trivial it seems, please let me know. That said, you all are free to leave, but please stay in town in case we need to question you further."

Frantic looks and whispers drifted through the room as the guests began to disperse. Ellie turned back to Mark and Liam. "Before you go, I need to see your hands."

Mark's eyes narrowed and Liam's mouth curled into a scowl. "What for?" Mark asked.

"To check for gunshot residue."

"I told you I'd never hurt Tori. I loved her," Liam said, his expression full of angst.

"This is simply protocol," Ellie assured them. "In order to eliminate you as a suspect, I have to verify there's no gunpowder residue on your hands."

Mark extended his hands. "Go ahead. I have nothing to hide."

Liam jerked his hands toward her. "Neither do I. Instead of giving us a hard time, I'd think you'd be looking for whoever killed my wife."

Ellie bit her tongue, then quickly checked their hands. She didn't spot residue but would have Shondra swab their hands to make certain.

NINETEEN

Mark Wade did not like the questions the detective was asking. As if she thought he might have done something to his beloved fiancée.

The argument he and Mia had had the other night haunted him. Sure, they'd made up, but she'd been acting off ever since. Quiet. Secretive.

He'd found a key that looked as if it belonged to a safety deposit box. But when he'd asked her about it, she'd said she'd stored copies of Pixie's baby pictures inside for safekeeping. Then she'd changed the subject quickly.

He'd had the uncomfortable sense that she was lying.

Had she been having second thoughts?

He didn't want to believe that.

And his mother had created tension. She'd always been nosy about his relationships and she'd drilled Mia to the point that he'd worried she'd drive her away.

He glanced at Liam. Liam had lied about not having problems with Tori. There had been rumors...

But surely there was nothing to them.

Another disturbing thought rattled him. Though they'd

been together most of the day, Liam had disappeared for a few minutes after the pictures. When he'd shown up again in the groom's room, he'd been winded, his face flushed. He'd also sensed tension between him and Tori last night at the rehearsal dinner. Mia said Tori was crying and she'd asked Liam about it, but he'd told her everything was fine.

Only nothing was fine. Tori was dead and Mia was gone.

TWENTY

Ellie saw local reporter Angelica Gomez fly into the room, her cameraman in tow. She dashed to her, determined to warn the tenacious journalist about what she could report and what was off the record.

Angelica tossed her dark hair over one shoulder, the red highlights shimmering. "I heard the bride is missing from Sheriff Waters," Angelica said. "Is it true Tori James was murdered?"

"Yes, but I didn't announce that yet. I know you have a job to do, but this is a difficult time and I need you to be discreet," Ellie said. "You can't report on the murder until the family has been notified."

"Understood," Angelica agreed, smoothing down her black pencil skirt. "But you know getting word out about Mia could help bring in a lead."

"True." Although it could also trigger false leads, which only wasted time and divided manpower. She motioned to the sheriff to join them.

"Take the interview," she told Bryce.

He straightened and spoke to Angelica while Ellie crossed

to Mark. He stood holding Pixie now, patting the little girl's back. "Still no call from Mia or anyone who might want a ransom?" she said softly.

He shook his head.

"The sheriff is going to talk to the press now," Ellie said.

"I want to say something," Mark said. "Maybe offer a reward. If Mia was kidnapped, I'll find a way to pay."

"I wouldn't do that just yet," Ellie said. "Offering a reward could attract greedy people who'll lie and take advantage of your emotions to make some money."

A muscle ticked in his jaw indicating he didn't like it, but he would do as she advised.

"Also, Mark, we're withholding the news about Tori for now until Liam can contact her mother."

He nodded and carried Pixie as Ellie walked with him to join Angelica.

Sheriff Waters' jaw was set firmly as he spoke into the camera. "If anyone has seen Mia Norman this evening or has information about her whereabouts, please call the sheriff's office or the Crooked Creek Police Department."

Ellie indicated to Angelica that Mark wanted to speak. Pixie was still clinging to him, her arms wrapped tightly around his neck.

"Come here, Pixie," Ellie said. "Let's let Mark talk to the reporter."

Pixie looked up at her with wide eyes, then ducked her head back against Mark's shoulder. Mark stroked her back, comforting her.

Tom captured the scene on camera, and Mark gestured to Angelica that he was ready.

Angelica gave him an encouraging smile. "We're here now with Mia Norman's fiancé, Mark Wade," Angelica said. "Mr. Wade?"

Mark's expression was dark with turmoil. "Mia and I were

supposed to be married tonight. She would never leave her daughter behind. Please, if you know where she is, help us bring her home safely to her little girl."

He paused for a breath and Angelica wrapped up by listing the phone numbers for Bryce's office and the police department. Ellie just hoped it brought them a lead and not the crazies.

TWENTY-ONE

Cord detailed how he'd found Tori's body to the ERT and Laney. The rain still drizzled down and lightning illuminated the sky, making it more dangerous for the team to be in the water.

But time was of the essence.

Flashlights and underwater cameras in hand, divers dove into the river to search for evidence. The choppers were holding off until the lightning died down, which meant they were losing precious time. Dr. Whitefeather remained beside Tori.

A medic team had arrived at Laney's request and Cord met them. They jumped out, dressed in rain gear and carrying a stretcher.

"She's down here," Cord said. "Detective Reeves and I managed to get her in the canoe."

The medics set the stretcher beneath a large oak for cover and followed Cord down the hill.

Laney looked up from where she'd stooped by Tori's body, her tone all business. "Gunshot wound to the back," Laney told them. "Dead on arrival. I'll know more about the bruises on her body when I get her to the morgue."

"We've got it," one of the medics said.

Cord steadied the canoe while the medics climbed in and lifted Tori. He stepped to the edge and helped them onto the ground, then they carried Tori to the stretcher and the ambulance.

"I'll text Ellie and tell her we're on the way with her." Laney stood, water dripping from the hood of her rain jacket as she followed the medics up the hill.

Cord's phone rang. He figured it was Ellie but saw Lola's name instead.

"Hey," he said.

"I'm leaving. Get a ride with Ellie."

Thunder clapped and he started to ask her to wait, but Lola hung up. Dammit, she sounded upset with him. Again.

TWENTY-TWO

Tears blurred Pixie's eyes. She squeezed them shut and hoped when she opened them her mommy would be back.

But when she did, all she saw was the messy room and the rain outside and how the pretty decorations were all torn and ripped away in the storm.

Mr. Liam was slouched in a chair crying. And Mr. Mark was pacing around and running over to Ms. Ellie every time he saw her. Ms. Lola had left and now she was sitting with Ms. Emily. She was Mommy's friend and Pixie had play dates with Ms. Emily's little girl, Norah.

"It's okay, honey," Ms. Emily said. "Ellie will do everything she can to find your mother."

Pixie wanted to scream no, it wasn't okay.

But her throat hurt too much from crying so she bunched herself into a ball like a crybaby.

Ms. Ellie, who she knew was a cop, walked over with a sad face, and Pixie suddenly felt like she couldn't breathe.

"Hey, sweetie," Ms. Ellie said. "Hi, Emily. I sent the other guests home but need to ask a favor."

Emily clasped Pixie's hand. "Of course."

"Mark offered to carry Pixie home with him, but under the circumstances I wondered if you could let her spend the night with you."

"Sure," Ms. Emily said. "She can play with Norah in the morning." Ms. Emily rubbed her hand. "Is that okay, sweetie?"

Tears caught in Pixie's throat. Tonight, they were supposed to be dancing and laughing and eating that pretty cake with the pink roses on top. Mommy let her pick the icing and pink was her favorite color. But the people in the black outfits had already wheeled the cake away.

"Pixie?" Ms. Emily said.

"I wants Mommy," Pixie whispered.

"I know, honey." Ms. Emily brushed her fingers over Pixie's cheeks. "But it's getting late and tonight we have to let Ellie do her job. Let's have a slumber party at my house and you can have chocolate chip pancakes with Norah and the boys in the morning."

Pixie didn't want pancakes. She wanted the cake with the pink roses on it, and Mommy said there was going to be a s'mores table.

Ms. Ellie patted Pixie's hand. "It'll be all right, sweetie. Get some sleep tonight, Pixie. I promise I'll try to find your mom."

But it wasn't all right. Nothing was right. The cake was gone and the decorations were torn up in the rain and there was no music or her mommy here dancing.

Grown-ups just said *that* when things were bad and they didn't know what else to say to make you feel better.

TWENTY-THREE

Ellie couldn't erase Pixie's little heartbroken face from her mind as she and the teams finished for the night. Mark and Liam had both reluctantly left although she knew neither one of them would get much sleep.

She just hoped she had good news for Mark and Pixie in the morning.

The team gathered to confer before they left.

"Choppers had to hold off until the worst of the lightning passed, but they've been at it for nearly an hour now," Cord said. "So far nothing. But they'll look again at first light."

Ellie sighed. "Thanks for coordinating, Cord." Although they both knew that every hour that passed decreased their chances of finding Mia, much less finding her alive.

Even if she had escaped Tori's killer, if Mia was in the river, she couldn't survive the strong current and frigid temperature.

Abraham Williams, the chief of the ERT reported next. "There were drag marks on the riverbank and we got a partial footprint. Looks like the shoe was a loafer."

Ellie frowned. A loafer meant the killer might have been dressed up, that he could have been a guest at the resort or wedding or even an employee. And it definitely pointed to a male.

One who might have hidden in plain sight.

"What about the bullet casing?" Ellie asked.

"We found one in a patch of weeds. It looks like it came from a thirty-five-millimeter. We collected a button that appears to have come from a man's shirt. A few feet away, we found a diamond ring. Silver heels were tossed in the bushes as well."

He held up the evidence bag, and Ellie's stomach knotted. "That's Mia's engagement ring. And most likely her shoes."

"We did a thorough search in both the bride's and groom's dressing rooms and dusted everything for prints," Williams said.

Ellie's mind flashed to the bride's room. What if the perpetrator had sent the champagne and drugged it with something to subdue the women? "Did you collect the champagne and glasses?"

"We did. Everything is on its way to the lab."

"Thank you. Be sure and have them test the champagne for drugs."

"It's already on the list."

Ellie turned to the ME. "Dr. Whitefeather?"

"I scraped beneath Tori's nails and will send it to the lab. The victim sustained bruises on her wrists and arms that are consistent with a struggle. The gash on her head was deep and wide, but I'm not sure it was severe enough for her to lose consciousness."

"Is it possible it was made by the butt of the gun?" Ellie asked.

"It's possible. I can tell more when we get her on my table."

"He shot her in the back. Was she dead before she went into the water?" Ellie asked.

"I can't say until we check her lungs," Laney answered. "And I'll run a full tox screen as usual."

"Thanks. Please keep me posted on the forensics and

autopsy results." She dismissed the ERT and Laney, then turned to the others. "Tell me what you learned from the wedding guests." She desperately wanted a suspect, someone besides Mark and Liam.

"Not much," Shondra said. "Mark's mother gave me the impression she wasn't thrilled about the marriage, but I also sensed she's the type who wouldn't be pleased with anyone taking her son from her." Shondra lifted a finger to make a point. "The wedding coordinator mentioned some tension between Tori and her husband last night. But said it's not abnormal for tensions to run high during a wedding."

Ellie would have to ask Liam about that.

"Maybe Mia was a Godzilla bride?" Bryce asked.

Ellie glared at him. Bryce would go for the negative about the woman. "Mia was not like that."

"I obtained a list of the staff," Deputy Landrum said. "No one claims to have seen anything suspicious. The caterer said the couple appeared to be happy and agreed on all the details. Although the wedding coordinator did mention a moment when Mia got teary and said she wished her family could be there."

"That's understandable since all her family was gone," Ellie said. "Anything else?"

"Nothing that stood out," Landrum answered.

Bryce made a low sound in his throat. "I issued a missing persons report on Mia and am circulating her photo. Gomez is doing the same. When can we report the James woman's murder?"

"After Liam notifies Tori's mother," Ellie said. "Let's give them the night before they see the harsh reality on TV. What about security cameras?"

"Footage was mostly of the guests arriving," Bryce replied. "Photographer taking pictures on the lawn and by the river."

So that confirmed Liam and Mark's statement about the pre-wedding photography session.

"The cam overlooking the path to the section of the river where the bodies were found wasn't working," Bryce said. "Looks like it was shot out."

Dammit. "Sounds premeditated. I want all the footage sent to my office," Ellie said.

Bryce tensed. "You second guessing my work?"

Ellie and he had clashed before, although she'd thought they'd reached a more even keel recently. But he still sounded defensive. "No. But there might be something that seemed insignificant at first sight that could lead us to a clue." She wanted to study body language, behaviors, relationships between the couples and family, attendees and staff. She also wanted Derrick to see them.

"Forensics collected Mia and Tori's phones," Deputy Landrum said. "I looked through but didn't find anything suspicious."

"Dig deeper in the morning. Check social media as well. We'll confiscate their computers when we search their homes." Ellie's muscles ached from the strain of the evening. "I guess we should call it a night. Maybe tomorrow will bring some answers."

She just prayed Mia didn't end up like Tori.

TWENTY-FOUR

Cord replayed Lola's terse phone call in his head as the team dispersed.

On the way to the wedding, she'd pushed him again about moving in together. He still hadn't answered her.

Now he sensed she was pissed that he'd abandoned her to lead the search, but that was his job and his work drove him. It was the one thing that had kept him sane over the years when his demons crawled from the grave to drag him back to hell.

Ellie was the bright light in the darkness. Earlier tonight she'd taken his breath away when he'd seen her in that sexy sundress and heels.

Now she looked totally exhausted. Rain had drenched her, but she hadn't let the bad weather deter her from helping to rescue Tori's body from the muddy river.

His admiration for her rose with each case they worked. But he couldn't tell her how he felt. She and Agent Fox were together, and all he wanted was for Ellie to be happy.

And safe.

Now she was chasing another killer. He wouldn't let her do that alone.

"What a mess," Ellie muttered with a shake of her head. "Are you ready to go?"

"Yeah, but I can come back and help tomorrow if you need."

"I'll let you know. Let's hope tomorrow we find Mia. Her little girl needs her mother."

His chest tightened as they headed outside. The wind had died down, although leaves, and branches had been ripped from trees and littered the manicured land. The fresh flowers decorating the venue had been destroyed. Golfers would have to wait tomorrow to hit the greens so the staff would have time to clear the course.

But that was the least of the resort's worries. No doubt having a murder occur on their property would deter guests and put a kink in holiday weekend plans.

He studied the rising peaks and ridges of the Appalachian Mountains in the distance as he and Ellie climbed in her Jeep. So many places in those woods for a predator to hide.

The darkness of his own past threatened to rise from the bowels of hell again, a constant reminder of his foster father's cruel and demeaning treatment when Cord was a kid.

He should be immune to violence by now. Knew that it could strike at any time. Could strike anyone.

But he wasn't immune. Especially when innocent women and children were involved.

"Lola was wonderful tonight with Pixie," Ellie said, cutting into his thoughts. "She obviously loves children."

Lola's caring smile when she'd talked to Pixie flashed in his mind. She would make a great mother.

But her child needed an equally good father. Lola needed a good husband. And he had no idea how to be either.

TWENTY-FIVE
BLUEBERRY HILL

Sylvia Wade shivered as she sipped her third glass of sauvignon blanc and looked outside over the holler from her vantage point on Blueberry Hill. Her husband Bill had stayed around the resort to make certain Mark arrived home safely. They were both worried to death about him and how he would handle what happened tonight.

But she'd retreated back home to escape the questions.

Bill had bought the blueberry farm a few years back and hired workers to take care of it. She'd rather have lived in the city but she had to admit she liked the peacefulness and beauty of the countryside.

She drained the glass and poured herself a fourth, her nerves raw. All she'd ever wanted was for her son to be happy.

He'd insisted that he'd found that with Mia.

At first she'd thought so, too. She'd embraced the girl. Had felt sorry for her because she had no family of her own.

But then she'd sensed something off about Mia. Mark was naïve and too trusting. He'd been fooled by another woman before.

Sylvia had been terrified that Mia was just like her.

And then... well, she'd been right.

Her hand trembled as she lifted the glass to her lips. She didn't dare tell anyone what she'd done tonight.

Mark would never forgive her.

The wind battered the glass panes of the Victorian house where she and Bill had lived now for fifteen years. The tornado a while back had ripped off shutters, shattered windows and knocked a tree into the roof. The water damage had been extensive both inside the house and the yard, which had flooded.

She pushed her guilt over the evening aside. They had rebuilt their home just as Mark would rebuild his life without Mia.

TWENTY-SIX

CROOKED CREEK

Although it was late, Ellie drove by Mia's house on the way home.

"Her car is in the drive," Cord said as she parked.

"Tori drove her to the wedding venue. All the lights are off." Still, she pulled her gun, climbed out and scanned the property. As expected, Mia's yard held beautiful flower beds and greenery. A small pink bike was parked beneath the carport. Hummingbird feeders hung from a tree.

Ellie slowly headed up the path to the front door while Cord walked around outside. She knocked on the door and rang the doorbell, then waited. Stepping to the side, she tried to look through the window but the curtains were drawn. The house was dark, the property silent except for the rain dripping from the awning.

Her rational mind told her that Mia was not here. That she hadn't run away and come back home. But in the morning she'd return with a warrant.

TWENTY-SEVEN

Derrick was wiped out by the time he reached Crooked Creek. He'd spent the journey trying to devise a plan to help Lindsey and her children when she wanted nothing to do with him.

The flags adorning the town, celebrating fallen soldiers, ridiculed him. No one could bring Rick back or alleviate the pain of losing him. His children would grow up without a father.

The thunderstorm he'd battled since he left Atlanta had forced him to a crawl, and the wind beat at his vehicle, tires churning through the rainwater accumulating on the streets. The traffic light swung back and forth but at least the storm had people turning in early and the streets were deserted.

He wanted to see Ellie. But he checked his watch and realized it was way too late to disturb her.

To distract himself, he flipped on the radio and listened to the news. Angelica Gomez was reporting.

"This evening, wedding plans at Magnolia Manor took a drastic turn when the bride, twenty-seven-year-old Mia Norman, disappeared. Mia is approximately five-four, one-hundred and thirty-five pounds with brown hair. Police suspect foul play and are asking that you be on the alert for Ms. Norman. If you spot her or have information on her whereabouts, please call the local police."

Derrick's pulse jumped, and he changed direction, steering his car onto the street toward Ellie's. All the lights in the house were burning bright indicating she was still awake. The wedding party had obviously turned into a criminal investigation.

Regret for not being with her struck him. Ellie could have used his help.

But he was here now.

He pulled into the drive and cut the engine, debating whether to go inside. She was most likely exhausted. So was he.

He should probably allow her to get some sleep, and he should do the same.

But the evening had taken its toll, and instead of listening to reason, his need to see Ellie drove him to climb out.

TWENTY-EIGHT

RED RIVER ROCK

"Mia Norman disappeared from her wedding today around five-thirty p.m. under suspicious circumstances," Angelica Gomez stated on the late-night news. "This footage was taken earlier this evening at Magnolia Manor where Ms. Norman was supposed to marry local high-school teacher and coach Mark Wade."

A dark-haired man held a little girl who was curled against his shoulder, crying. "Mia and I were supposed to be married tonight. She would never leave her daughter behind. Please, if you know where she is, help us bring her back to her little girl."

Kevin Moon's fingers tightened around the curve of his high ball glass so tightly he thought it might shatter between his fingers.

A picture of the missing woman flashed onto the screen, and he stared at the dark-haired Mia, his gut in a knot.

Swirling his scotch around in his tumbler, he glanced at the photo of Jesse, the love of his life. Jesse had been so beautiful, with her long blond hair and twinkling sky-blue eyes. Her heart-shaped face and porcelain skin were a picture of sweetness, hope and purity. She'd had ambition and a creative spark that he'd admired. Her lips tasted like honey, her body was a temptress. He closed his eyes, remembering the way her fingers glided over his body with feather light touches, arousing him as she teased him with her touches.

Then she'd gone missing. Suddenly. Their future – in shambles.

Hatred bubbled inside his soul. Mia Norman had destroyed it.

She'd taken Jesse from him.

He'd spent the last five years looking for Jesse. Loving her. Mourning her.

Trying to move on.

But the need for revenge ate at him.

TWENTY-NINE

Ellie ran her fingers through her damp hair, rolling her shoulders to alleviate the tension straining her muscles. As she'd showered, her mind had been plagued with images of Tori floating in the river.

At the sound of the doorbell, she glanced at her clock. Who would be here this late? Maybe one of the deputies or Bryce with some information?

She tightened the drawstring on her pajama shorts and hurried to the door. Always cautious, she checked the peephole and was surprised to see Derrick standing on her porch. His dark hair looked mussed, frown lines tugged at his forehead, and his jaw was clenched.

Obviously, his day hadn't gone well.

As she opened the door, tension radiated from his rigid posture. "I didn't expect to see you tonight," she said softly.

"I didn't expect to come," he said gruffly.

She reached for his hand. "Come in, Derrick. I'll pour us a drink."

He gave her a look of gratitude, followed her inside and

closed the door. "I heard Gomez's report about the murder on the way back from Atlanta. Mia Norman is missing?"

"Yes, what started out to be a happy occasion turned into a nightmare." Ellie poured herself a vodka on the rocks and Derrick two fingers of Maker's Mark, handing it to him. She opened the French doors to let the fresh air inside, the sound of crickets chirping filling the silence as she led him to the couch. "There's more. The maid of honor was murdered. We didn't report that on the news yet in order to give Tori's husband time to notify her mother."

Derrick swirled the bourbon around in his glass as he seated himself. "Must have been a rough evening. Any suspects?"

"Not yet. The groom and Tori's husband were together at the time of Tori's death. So far nothing indicating their relationships were anything but happy." She sighed and looked into her own drink as if it might hold answers. "We'll hit the ground running tomorrow. I'm having security footage sent to the station and requesting search warrants for the women's homes and computers."

"Cause of death?" Derrick asked.

"Laney will perform the autopsy tomorrow. But Tori was struck on the back of the head and shot in the back."

Derrick sighed. "In the back. Geesh. She must have been running away."

"Exactly," Ellie said.

"Sounds like you're covering all the bases."

"We're just getting started."

For a long moment, they lapsed into silence, simply sipping their drinks and allowing the dust of the day to settle.

Finally, she broke the quiet. "Do you want to talk about what happened in Atlanta?"

He sniffed his drink then turned it up and downed it. Ellie knew opening up was difficult for him, so she rubbed the back of his neck.

He moaned softly, rolling his shoulders as he leaned into it. "Rick appointed me godfather to his kids."

Ellie stilled for a second, wondering what that would entail. Would he move back to Atlanta permanently? *Don't be selfish, Ellie.* "That means he trusted you to watch over them, Derrick."

He shrugged, then spoke through gritted teeth. "Lindsey sure as hell doesn't. She doesn't want me anywhere around them."

After draining her vodka, Ellie set her glass on her farmhouse coffee table. "She's grieving right now. She'll get past it, Derrick. Just give her time."

"I don't think so," he said in a pained voice. "Besides, I don't blame her. I let Rick down. Her children need someone she can trust, someone who won't disappoint."

Ellie cupped his face between her hands. "Listen to me, you are a strong, brave wonderful man. Those kids, *any* children, would be lucky to have you in their lives. Rick never would have chosen you as their godfather if he didn't believe that."

"Rick didn't know about Kim. Maybe he would have felt differently if he had."

Indecision and hurt warred in his eyes. Ellie couldn't stand to see him in such agony. He blamed himself for his little sister's death years ago.

"You can't save everyone," Ellie said under her breath. Just like she couldn't.

She just prayed Mia didn't turn out to be another one she lost.

THIRTY

SOMEWHERE ON THE AT

Hard work and pure grit had made Ronnie who she was. She'd built her own empire here along the river and ran it like she wanted.

No damn body could take that away from her.

She was a survivor. The poor girl in the whiskey barrel was not. Course that was her own stupid fault.

While the acid ate her flesh and bones, she would remain here tucked away in the mountains with the others. It was tempting to put her in the river and let it carry her body far away, but it made Ronnie antsy. Her boys had made that stupid mistake of dumping one years ago and now, with the police crawling all over the mountain, she was scared shitless it would turn up.

She picked up the Mason jar full of corn liquor and swirled it around. A long slow drink washed away the taste of the blood on her hands. She'd trained her two knucklehead sons to do what she said but they had another job tonight, so she'd had to take care of the bitch herself.

A laugh crept out. Not that she minded getting her own hands dirty. Growing up in these parts where the river churned around her day and night, and the water moccasins and rattlesnakes slithered up to her porch in the dark, she'd thrived on the rugged wilderness.

She was bred from this land and would die here one day. But not today.

Weeds, bushes and the thick trees of the Appalachian Trail hid what she was doing from the folks that floated by in their canoes and kayaks, happy as pigs at a trough.

A mosquito buzzed around her face and she slapped at it, wiping the dead bug off her skin as a log bobbed up and down and the current dragged it into the dark ahead.

Wiping her hands on her shirt, she pulled her phone and texted Chester.

Is it done?

She tapped her boot on the rickety floor of the dock while she waited. The scent of wet moss and a dead animal swirled around her. The sound of water crashing onto the bank and the hoot of an owl echoed in the silence.

Finally, the response came.

Taken care of for now.

She smiled and took another swig of liquor.

THIRTY-ONE
CROOKED CREEK

DAY 2

Early morning sunlight streamed through the window of Ellie's bedroom as she stirred, and for a moment she allowed herself to curl into Derrick's arms. He stroked her hair and held her close, his breathing steady.

Last night had been intense, both of them purging emotions and frustrations from the day. In spite of the fact she'd only slept a couple of hours, she felt calmer with him beside her.

But her phone buzzed, and when she saw Mark Wade's name, reality shattered that calm.

She kissed Derrick gently on the cheek, then slipped from his embrace to answer it. He moaned and looked up at her. "Don't go."

"Mark Wade is already calling." And Tori James needed justice.

"Right." Derrick pulled her back for a long slow kiss that made her want to crawl in his arms and hide for the day.

But Ellie Reeves did not run from trouble. She ran straight into the fire when she saw the cinders spark to life.

Hoping Mark was calling with news that he'd heard from Mia, she snagged her phone from the nightstand and answered. "Detective Reeves."

"Any word on Mia?" Mark asked, his voice hoarse with emotions.

"Not yet. Have you heard anything?"

"No, dammit. Where is she?"

"I don't know but I will find out, Mark. I need to look around Mia and Tori's houses this morning. Do you have a key to Mia's?"

"Yes, I'll meet you there. I'll do whatever I can to help find her." Determination laced his voice.

"Forty-five minutes?"

"Sounds good."

She would be a few minutes early to make certain he didn't go inside first.

By the time she'd got ready, Derrick had dressed and brewed coffee, the rich pecan scent filling the air and calling to her. Dark stubble grazed his jaw but his hair was damp indicating he'd showered. Maybe she'd suggest he leave a toiletry kit at her place?

Or... no. That was too soon. Especially now he was godfather to two children in Atlanta.

He handed her the coffee, his eyes black with turmoil.

Ellie checked the clock. "I'm meeting Mark Wade at Mia's in half an hour."

"Let's drop my car at the station and I'll go with you."

The May sun was beating down as they left the house, grass and flowers sagging beneath the weight of last night's storm. With a breeze rolling off the mountains and more clouds moving in, a chill had settled in the air. The Corner Café parking lot was filled with locals and tourists, and stores were opening their doors for the day.

As they passed the monuments of the soldiers lining Main

Street, she noticed Derrick clenching and unclenching his hands.

A parade was planned for the next day, a service at the local church afterward.

They dropped Derrick's car at the police station. Deputy Landrum had texted that the camera footage from the resort had been sent over, so they went inside to quickly review it before driving to Mia's.

Armed with more coffee, she and Derrick watched the reels of film. Bryce was right. The footage captured excited guests arriving. Employees arranging the tables, the florist decorating, wedding planner coordinating with everyone. Mark and Liam arriving, happy and joking, sharing a beer before pictures, then the photographs at the river. Mia turning up with Tori, both women smiling and welcoming the hair stylist and makeup artist. Pixie dancing around animatedly. No sense of trouble on the horizon.

The scenes inside the bridal room were not filmed, but Ellie leaned forward, her interest piqued as something caught her attention: Mark Wade's mother entering the bridal room. Several minutes passed before the woman emerged again.

Ellie stiffened, noting Mrs. Wade's body language. Arms folded, shoulders rigid, eyes darting around the hallway as if she was nervous. What had happened between them?

Minutes later, Ellie drove toward Mia's with Derrick staring out the window.

As she parked in the drive, everything was quiet. Squirrels skittered up the trunks of the tall pines and birds twittered as if welcoming the day.

Yesterday had started off bright and sunny, too. Except it had ended in death.

Were there answers inside Mia's house?

Five minutes later, Mark pulled in behind Ellie and stepped from his gray Forerunner. He looked rough around the edges as if he hadn't slept, pain heaped with anger in his expression as he strode toward them.

Ellie and Derrick met him at the path to the door and walked to the porch in silence. With a shaky hand, Mark handed Ellie the key, and she unlocked the door. As soon as it swung open, she went still.

Mark gasped behind her. "What the hell?"

Ellie's stomach twisted. The house had been ransacked.

THIRTY-TWO

BABBLING CREEK RANCH

Pixie jerked awake with a scream. Where was she? Where was Mommy?

"Shh, honey, it's okay."

Her mind felt fuzzy and her eyes hurt. The bright light in the room blinded her.

"Mommy?" Pixie whispered.

Soft fingers brushed across Pixie's forehead, and she blinked hard, but tears filled her eyes. "It's Ms. Emily, sweetie."

"Where's Mommy?" she cried.

"Ms. Ellie is looking for her. You had a sleepover with Norah, remember," Ms. Emily said. "We're making pancakes right now."

Norah slipped up beside Ms. Emily and pressed one of her dolls into Pixie's arms. "Here, hug Dolly. You can bring her to breakfast, too. We got chocolate milk."

Pixie buried her face against the soft cuddly rag doll with red hair. But she couldn't think about pancakes right now or chocolate milk. All she could do was think about was her mommy and if she'd ever come back.

THIRTY-THREE

CROOKED CREEK

Cord stopped by the Corner Café for breakfast and coffee.

It had been too late to call Lola last night and apologize for abandoning her at the wedding. And... frankly he wasn't ready to get into it about the whole moving in proposition.

When he walked into the café, he saw her serving coffee and breakfast to Sheriff Waters and Mandy Morley, who he now knew was Bryce's daughter. That had been a shocker.

He slid onto a barstool, his stomach growling as he waited on Lola, but she took her time chatting and laughing with Bryce and bringing Mandy some kind of fancy coffee drink with whipped cream that all the teenagers were crazy about now.

Bryce's folks, his snotty mother and the mayor, entered yet they walked right past Bryce and Mandy, raising his curiosity.

Then whispers and stares rippled through the room as Liam James entered with an older woman who looked teary-eyed. She must be Tori's mother. Poor Liam looked sullen and angry, with bloodshot eyes as if he hadn't slept all night.

Cord checked his phone, wondering if Ellie had made any progress finding Mia Norman. Or Tori James' killer.

Lola stopped to speak to Liam, then patted his shoulder and

walked back toward the bar. She gave Cord a quick glance, then gestured for the young teen waiting tables to take his order while she poured coffee for Liam.

She was definitely giving him the cold shoulder this morning.

He ordered ham and eggs with red-eyed gravy and drowned himself in coffee, then wolfed down his meal while Lola completely ignored him.

She asked you to move in with her.

But he hadn't responded.

Maybe she'd assumed his silence was his answer.

His phone buzzed with a text. SAR. They'd been dragging the river for Mia. And they'd found something.

He tossed some cash on the bar and headed outside. When he looked back from the doorway, Lola was wiping tears from her eyes. But work was calling.

And Ellie needed his help finding Mia.

THIRTY-FOUR

Ellie's senses jumped to full alert as her gaze swept the entrance to Mia's house. Someone had been here. Were they still inside?

"Mia!" Mark started to rush inside, but Ellie held up a warning hand to prevent his entry.

"Wait here, Mark."

"I have to see if she's here!"

"Agent Fox and I will look for her," Ellie said, vying for calm. If Mia was in the house, injured or dead, she didn't want Mark to be the one to find her.

"It may be a crime scene, man," Derrick explained. "We don't want to contaminate evidence."

"I don't give a damn about evidence." Hysteria sharpened Mark's voice. "I just want to find my fiancée."

Ellie squeezed his arm. "I understand and so do we. So please let us do our jobs."

Her rational tone seemed to seep through his panic, and he heaved a breath then leaned against the doorjamb.

Ellie and Derrick both pulled their weapons, and Ellie led the way, inching inside. The interior looked light and airy, appearing to be empty. The small entryway led into an open-concept living room and kitchen decorated in a farmhouse style with reclaimed shelving, a whitewashed brick fireplace, white cabinets and a stone countertop.

A beautiful home for a family.

Except it had been defaced.

Books, magazines and furniture had been tossed across the room as if someone was looking for something. The corner desk drawer stood open with papers strewn on the floor and shattered picture frames, glass fragments dotting the wood floor.

The couch cushions had been ripped, batting spilling out, and the smell of fresh ashes drifted from the fireplace. She saw paper scraps on the floor by the refrigerator, walked over and studied them. They were RSVPs to the wedding.

"Someone was angry about the marriage," Ellie said.

She and Derrick exchanged looks, and she turned down a small hallway while he veered in the opposite direction to search the rest of the house.

She found a small bedroom, which was obviously Pixie's. Lavender walls, a white iron twin bed covered in a princess comforter, and a doll house in the corner. Books, toys, shoes and a little girl's clothing filled the closet. Nothing here had been destroyed.

The neighboring room, Mia's, told a different story. The white comforter had been tossed into a rumpled pile, lamp overturned, dressers rifled through with clothing overflowing and littering the beige carpet. More shards of glass from broken picture frames lay on the floor.

Ellie peered at the torn photos and realized they were of Mia and Mark.

Her pulse stuttered. This read like a crime of rage targeting Mia. Someone who hated the sight of her and Mark together?

She quickly scanned the room for blood, but thankfully didn't find any.

When had this place been violated? She hadn't seen a smashed window or door lock.

Had the perp come here looking for Mia, discovered she'd left for the resort and flown into a rage? Or did the intruder break in last night after Mia disappeared?

Ellie called a crime team as she joined Derrick in the living room. "ERT is on their way. Pixie's room is untouched, but Mia's was ripped apart."

Derrick's brows creased as he plucked burned debris from the fireplace. "No sign of a struggle outside. No blood either." He lifted a partial piece of charred paper. "Looks like it was a picture of Mia at the gardening center."

"Someone either had a grudge against Mia or they were looking for something," Ellie said. "The question is what?"

THIRTY-FIVE

Ellie phoned Captain Hale to request an ERT while Derrick spoke with Mark. "There was definitely foul play," she told her boss. "I think Tori's murder might have been about Mia. Her place has been tossed. I'm going to look around myself."

"I'll get them right out there," Captain Hale said.

"Ask Shondra to talk to the owners of The Green Thumb again, where Mia worked. Maybe there was someone, even a customer or other employee, that seemed especially interested in Mia."

He agreed, and she hung up then returned to the living room. The sight of the burned photos was especially disturbing. She went to the desk in the corner and found bills, bank statements and confirmation that Mia had joined the local YMCA and had signed Pixie up for an art camp. Not an indication that she planned to leave Crooked Creek.

Ellie dug into the drawer and found a brochure on a resort for families. Mia had mentioned she and Mark intended to do a family honeymoon.

Her heart tugged as she looked at the vision board above the desk. Photos and details of the wedding planning, then scraps of paper littered the desk in ruins. Next, she found a calendar noting upcoming jobs Mia had lined up for the summer. She'd blocked off the next week for the honeymoon.

The remainder of the summer was full. Judging from the number of personal clients requesting home consultations, Mia intended to stay in Crooked Creek.

THIRTY-SIX

Derrick forced himself to keep an open mind where Mia's fiancé was concerned. At the Bureau, he'd dealt with enough criminals to know that some only appeared to be concerned, charismatic individuals. Love, devotion and shock could all be faked.

Although the man slumped on Mia's front steps looked anything but charismatic. Nothing like a con artist or a killer.

But the devil often appeared in disguise.

"What did you find in there?" Mark asked in a whisper.

Derrick had to be a straight shooter. No sense lying.

"Her house has been ransacked," Derrick said. "It looks like an intruder here. He destroyed furnishings and photographs of you and Mia."

Granted, if Mark had problems with Mia, he could have done that in anger.

Mark's gaze swung to him. "What? Who would want to destroy pictures of me and Mia?"

"I don't know, man," Derrick said. "You tell me."

"How the hell should I know?" Mark said. "We were happy. We've been planning our wedding for weeks. And...

Pixie... She was so excited." He dropped his head into his hands.

"I don't understand why this is happening. What will we do if we don't find her?"

Derrick allowed a beat to pass as he studied Mark.

"Try to think positive," Derrick said quietly. God knows, he'd been there, terrified when his little sister disappeared years ago. The not knowing could eat at your soul. "Were you two having any problems?"

"No. I already told Ellie all of this." Anger edged Mark's tone. "Now stop wasting your time on me and find out if someone took her."

His defensive tone could be a protective measure, but Derrick's gut told him Mark was for real. "We're going to do that," Derrick assured him. "Just think hard. Did Mia mention anyone bothering her at work? That she saw someone following her or watching her?"

Mark shook his head with a groan. "If there was, she didn't tell me about it."

An engine rumbled, and the crime scene van rolled up, three ERT investigators climbing out. Ellie appeared at the door, her expression solemn, and Mia's computer bagged in hand.

"What's happening?" asked Mark.

"Mia's house is a crime scene now," Ellie said. "Mark, we're going to have to ask you to leave."

He stood, rubbing a hand down the back of his neck. "I want to stay. Help you find her."

"The best way you can help," Derrick said, "is to go home and wait. And don't leave town."

Anger rolled off him again. "Don't worry. I'm not leaving. I want to be here when Mia comes home."

"I promise to keep you updated. We'd like to put a trace on your phone," Ellie said.

"Jesus, you still think I did something to her?" he replied, his frustration spilling out.

Derrick used another tactic to diffuse Mark's anger. "No, but if someone abducted Mia, he might contact you. If we trace the call, maybe we can catch the bastard."

THIRTY-SEVEN

Mark gave a resigned nod and passed Ellie his phone so she could copy his number. She took a minute to scroll through his recent calls and texts but found nothing from Mia since yesterday morning when she'd messaged that she loved him.

"What's going to happen to Pixie?" Mark asked, his voice gruff.

"Emily Nettles is a foster parent and also does respite care. For now, Pixie will stay with her." Ellie tried to soften the blow. "At least Pixie knows Emily and has had playdates with her children."

"She must be so scared. Can I see her?"

Ellie and Derrick exchanged a look. "I think we can arrange that," Ellie said. If Mark was a comfort to Pixie, she couldn't deny him a visit for the little girl's sake.

He jammed his hands in the pockets of his jogging pants, his body a ball of tension.

"There's something else I need to ask you, Mark," Ellie said.

"What?" He shuffled sideways. "Anything to help?"

"Did your mother and Mia get along?"

A tense second passed before he answered, "Yes, why do you ask?"

"The security cam footage from the resort showed your mother visit Mia before the wedding was supposed to start. When she exited the room, your mother looked nervous, as if something was wrong."

"That makes no sense," Mark said. "You must have misread things. Mom knew Mia was alone and had no family so she probably just wanted to make sure she was okay."

That could explain things, Ellie thought. But she would ask Mrs. Wade nonetheless.

Mark glanced back at the house then headed to his SUV, shoulders slumped. "Please find her, Detective."

Ellie squeezed his arm. "I will, Mark."

Meanwhile, Derrick was talking to Abraham Williams, the leader of the ERT. "We confiscated her computer," Derrick said. "Someone tore the place up. Maybe they left prints or DNA."

"Be sure to send a toothbrush or hairbrush to Dr. White-feather for DNA comparison," Ellie said.

"Copy that. We'll be thorough," Williams assured her. *Whether she's dead or alive.* His team joined him and Ellie turned to Derrick.

"Let's go to the James' house and talk to Liam," Ellie said.

While they drove, she called Shondra and filled her in. "I realize it's summer break for schools but get a list of the teachers and talk to each one of them. I'm almost certain Mia was the target here, but she might have confided something to Tori."

"On it," Shondra agreed.

As she hung up, Derrick arranged for the trace to be placed on Mark Wade's phone. Ellie just wished she could hear his conversation when he called his mother. Because she knew for sure that he would.

THIRTY-EIGHT

LITTLE CREEK

Morning sunlight shimmered off the asphalt, the temperature heating up as Ellie and Derrick drove toward Liam's. They passed SUVs and trucks loaded with canoes and kayaks heading into the mountains for the day, and mini vans holding families flocking to the area for the holiday weekend.

Liam and Tori lived outside town by Little Creek, a narrow ribbon of water that fed into the river further south. Small cabins and bungalows had been built on quarter acre lots with views of the towering mountains. At the house, a small yard with a rock bed island held assorted flowers.

Liam's black Lexus sat to the side. Ellie braced herself as she and Derrick walked up and knocked on the door. Shuffling sounded from within and a minute later, Liam opened the door, his face ruddy, hair disheveled, eyes bloodshot. He'd obviously had a rough night and probably a rough morning with Tori's mother at the café.

"Hi, Liam," she said, then introduced him to Derrick. "Can we come in?"

His mouth thinned into a hard line, but he stepped aside and allowed them in. Moving to the sofa, he sat, picked up a coffee mug and sipped before speaking. "Tell me you found out who killed my wife."

A heartbeat passed, Liam's labored breathing rattling in the silence.

"Not yet," Ellie said.

He ran a hand through his hair. "And Mia?"

"We're still looking," Ellie said. "But that's one reason we're here." She quickly glanced around his living room but there were no signs an intruder had trashed the place. "We just came from Mia's house. Someone ransacked her things. Did you see signs of an intruder here when you got home last night?"

His eyes narrowed. "No. Nothing like that. Why would someone trash Mia's house?"

"I don't know yet." Ellie chose to be direct. "We think Mia was the target. This intruder destroyed photographs of her and Mark, burning them in the fireplace."

Liam set his coffee mug down with a thud and sank back against the sofa. "So you think Tori was killed because she was with Mia?"

"That's one theory."

"Jesus, this is so screwed up," Liam said angrily. "When can I see her? I... have to make arrangements..." His voice cracked.

"I'll talk to the medical examiner and let you know," Ellie said.

"We're going to do everything we can to find her killer," Derrick added.

Liam's anguished gaze lifted to them. "It still won't bring her back."

"No," Ellie said, her heart cracking. "But we will get justice for her, Liam. I promise."

THIRTY-NINE

BLUEBERRY HILL

After leaving Mia's, Mark was so shaken his mind was a mess. The detective's question about his mother nagged at him as he parked at his parents' house.

His mother had always been a bit of a hoverer, had never really liked any of the women he'd dated. Always found something lacking. Said he was naïve.

And maybe he was. But he preferred to see the good in people. And Mia was all good.

Except...now ...now she was suddenly gone.

She needs you to believe in her now. To be strong for Pixie.

He punched the doorbell just to announce his presence, then opened the door and went inside. The house smelled of bacon and coffee, and he pictured his father stirring eggs over the stove while his mother poured coffee in those tiny china cups she liked so much.

He preferred big sturdy mugs like the ones Mia owned.

"Mom? Dad?" he called as he crossed the foyer to the kitchen where he found things just as they always had been.

That alone felt oddly disconcerting considering what had

happened the night before. Their routine went on as usual while his life had been turned upside down.

His father paused at the stove, the scrambled eggs nearly done, and his mother set the coffee pot down and rushed toward him.

"Oh, sweetheart, how are you?" She enveloped him into a hug, her floral perfume almost overpowering him. A tight squeeze then she pulled back, cupped his face between her hands and studied him. "Did you get any sleep?"

"Is there word?" his father asked, spatula in hand, thick brows furrowed with concern.

"No." Mark lifted his mother's hands from his face and took a step back. "I just met Detective Reeves at Mia's. Her house was torn apart."

His mother gasped, and his father set the spatula down. "What?"

"Someone ransacked her house." He swallowed hard. "Mom, Detective Reeves said that you visited Mia before the wedding ceremony was due to start. That you looked tense when you left." He hardened himself. He knew how his mother could be. "Did something happen between the two of you?"

She stumbled back at the obvious censure in his tone.

"Mark?" his father said, his tone a reprimand.

"I need to know," Mark said. "Tell me, Mom. What did you say to her?"

She released a weary sigh, running her fingers over the edge of the counter. "I heard her tell Tori the night before that she wished her mother was there. So I went in to check on her and tell her that I was there for her. That's all."

Mark waited, sensing there was more. "What happened then?"

"She got teary and cried for a minute, then I hugged her and left."

That could be true. After all, Mia had no family.

But when his mother turned and started setting plates out as if everything was all right, he saw her hand tremble.

He knew she wasn't telling the truth.

FORTY

BABBLING CREEK RANCH

Derrick opened Mia's computer and booted it up while Ellie drove toward the station. The lack of a breeze this morning left the air stagnant and muggy, and her shirt was already sticking to her skin as she navigated the winding mountain road.

Ellie's phone rang. Seeing it was Emily Nettles, she connected and put her on speaker.

"Do you have any word on Mia?" Emily asked.

"No," Ellie said, "but it looks like someone may have taken her. How's Pixie?"

"Pretty scared," Emily replied. "I finally got her to eat a little breakfast and she's coloring with Norah right now. But she keeps asking me about her mom and I don't know what to say."

"I was hoping she might remember hearing something more concrete," Ellie said. "Has she mentioned anything?"

"No, but she had nightmares last night. I have some experience in forensic interviewing with children, so I'll work on it, but I'll have to tread carefully."

"Understood."

Tension stretched over the line for a long second. "There's something else though," Emily finally said.

"What is it?" Ellie asked.

"Can you stop by the house?"

Ellie's pulse jumped. "Of course. I'll head there now."

She spun the Jeep around and wove through town, battling the growing traffic. Tourists were already crowding the streets and stores.

Derrick looked up from his computer. "What do you think that was about?"

"I have no idea, but it sounds like Emily might know something." She glanced at the computer. "Anything there?"

"I'm only getting started. Doesn't look like she was on TikTok, Snapchat or Instagram."

"That is odd, especially in this day and age," Ellie agreed. "Although Mark mentioned she was shy so she probably didn't want pics on social media. Or maybe she was setting an example for her daughter."

The town disappeared behind them, the road twisting into farmland. She'd never been to Emily's house but knew the Nettles lived and worked on a ranch that served as a home for troubled children and teenagers. Emily's husband Andy was the resident pastor of the ranch, which offered counseling and housing with the goal to steer kids back on track and reunite them with their families.

They passed cows grazing in green pastures and a horse stable, and Ellie had to slow as deer crossed the road. A flock of blackbirds flew in formation, then landed on a power line above them.

She pulled down the drive, passing a schoolhouse, then up a hill past the chapel and veered onto a path that looked as if it disappeared into the forest. A mile down the road, she came to a rustic ranch with a porch swing, rockers and playground.

Emily's three boys were shooting hoops at the basketball goal. She waved to them as she got out, swatting at a fly buzzing around her.

"Nice place here," Derrick said.

"This couple is a godsend to the area," she said.

Together they walked up to the door and knocked. Emily met them and stepped outside onto the porch.

"Thanks for coming."

"No worries. What is it? Do you need me to talk to Pixie?" Ellie asked.

Emily shook her head. "It might be more upsetting if you do. Give me a little time with her. She and Norah are drawing pictures now. Sometimes art helps children express their feelings." She shuffled back and forth, obviously laboring over what to do.

"What is it, Emily? Do you know something about Mia?"

Emily lowered her voice, moving closer. "Three months ago, Mia came to me for counseling. I can't really divulge our conversation but she seemed nervous."

"I understand about confidentiality, Emily, but if she was afraid of someone and you think it's connected, you can tell me."

"I know... She never talked about anything like that or anyone specific, but she gave me this." Emily pulled an envelope from her back pocket and offered it to Ellie. "She told me if anything ever happened to her, to give it to you. I thought about giving it to you yesterday but it was so late and I hoped she'd turn up. But since she's missing..."

Ellie's mind spun, jumping to a worst-case scenario.

Derrick leaned over her shoulder as she unfolded the piece of paper and read the message.

Ellie, if something happens to me, please take Pixie to Jo-Jo and Seth Pennington. They will explain everything.

Sincerely,

Mia Norman

Ellie swallowed hard. There was no doubt that Mia had been afraid of something – or someone.

FORTY-ONE
MOSQUITO COVE

Cord hated mosquitos. The damn insects were the bane of his existence during the humid summer years back when he'd had to live in the woods in order to survive. Night after night he'd swatted and slapped at them, rubbed natural herbs over his skin to ward them off, and clawed at the bites that covered him.

This place, Mosquito Cove, was known to house the biggest insects in the area, and at night they clogged the air in clusters so thick you could barely see your own damn finger in front of your face. The muggy heat and the weeds choking the riverbank bred them just as the river bred the cottonmouth water moccasins that slithered through the tangled weeds and vines. This was their home and the tourists were invading it. They defended their territory and fed on unsuspecting flesh.

He sprayed his arms, ankles and even his socks, then patted his cheeks with the stinking stuff, hiking along the path to the cove where the rescue and recovery team had been dragging the river.

Water crashed violently as the current carried debris from storms and visitors downstream.

The sun shone hot and bright, reflecting off rocks and toads sunning on lily pads.

Voices sounded from ahead, and he picked up his pace, waving off flies and gnats circling his eyes. He slashed at the overgrown brush choking the land, climbed over a fallen tree and trudged through the muddy sections until he reached the riverbank edge.

There, he found an SAR team standing over a whiskey barrel. "Over here!" one of them called out.

He broke into a sprint and crossed to them, breaching the clearing by hacking away another cluster of weeds and briars.

"Chopper spotted it and thought we should check it out. We haven't opened it yet," Milo, his coworker said.

Cord zeroed in on the find. The whiskey barrel was stuck in the mud.

He approached cautiously, a knot of fear seizing his gut. This area was about eight miles directly downstream from Magnolia Manor, where Mia had disappeared.

Was Mia's body inside?

FORTY-TWO

BABBLING CREEK RANCH

With a frown, Ellie contemplated the message Mia had left in the envelope.

A breeze stirred, bringing the scent of honeysuckle and farm animals. Behind them, Emily's boys shouted, the sound of the basketball hitting the goal post echoing over and over.

"Mia made plans for her daughter," Derrick said in a low voice.

"She did." Ellie's mind raced. Why leave this to her and not Mark or an attorney?

"What does it say?" Emily asked.

Ellie folded the page and slipped it back into the envelope. "She asked me to take Pixie to a couple named Jo-Jo and Seth Pennington. Do you know who they are?"

Emily massaged her temple with her fingers. "No, she never mentioned them to me."

"I know your counseling services are confidential," Ellie said, emphasizing her earlier comment. "But if Mia mentioned someone she was afraid of, you have to tell us."

"I would tell you," Emily said. "But she honestly never said anything. She mostly talked about her fear of the water. Apparently, her parents died in a boat accident when she was young and it traumatized her."

"Maybe Pixie knows who these people are," Derrick suggested.

Emily bit her lower lip. "We'll have to ask her. But she might be overwhelmed if we all go in together."

"I'll wait in the car and dig into the Penningtons," Derrick said. "Mia may have had contact with them through email or her phone."

"Good thinking." Ellie followed Emily through the screen door. As they entered, she saw a brown mutt curled on the sofa, and Pixie and Norah at the kitchen table with crayons and paper. Norah was singing as she drew, but Pixie sat quietly, fingers curled tightly around a purple crayon.

"Mommy, look," Norah chirped as they approached. "I drawed Snickers, the new baby goat doing goat training."

"Great job," Emily said with a warm smile. "I like the flowers you hung around his neck."

Pixie looked up, her eyes big with fear when she spotted Ellie, making her wonder if she should have stayed outside with Derrick. "Hi, honey," Ellie said.

Pixie opened her mouth to speak, but nothing came out, tearing Ellie's heart in two.

Emily slid into a chair beside the little girl and pointed to her drawing. Where Norah's had been bright, with the sunshine gleaming down on the yard where the goat was climbing a rock, Pixie's drawing was dark, with grays and blacks and lightning zigzagging around the treetops. She had drawn giant raindrops on the windows.

Or perhaps they were tear drops, Ellie thought.

"Pixie, Ms. Ellie is still looking for your mother," Emily said softly. "I need to ask you something though."

Pixie's fingers curled around the crayon so tightly that it snapped. She gasped softly and looked up at Emily.

"Don't worry about the crayon," Emily said softly. "We have buckets of them."

Norah covered her mouth and whispered to Pixie, "It's okay. I breaks 'em all the time. My mama says don't sweat it."

Norah was trying to be sweet, but at the mention of her mother, Pixie's little face wilted again.

Emily brushed Pixie's blond bangs to the side. "Listen, honey. Do you know a woman named Jo-Jo?"

Pixie's nose crinkled with a frown then she shook her head.

"She might have been one of your mommy's friends," Emily prompted. "Or maybe she's part of your family like your grandmother."

Pixie's lower lip quivered. "We don't gots any family. It's just me and Mommy... and Mark... Mommy said he was gonna 'dopt me and be my daddy."

Ellie's heart splintered. Why hadn't Mia included Mark's name in the letter?

Emily waited a beat. "How about a man named Seth? Seth Pennington? Does that ring a bell?"

Pixie shook her head back and forth, her hair swinging over her shoulders.

If Pixie didn't know these people, why would Mia ask Ellie to take her to them?

FORTY-THREE

A few minutes later, Ellie gave Pixie a quick hug. "I have to go, sweetie. But I'll be back." Hopefully with good news. If this couple had a connection to Mia, they might have answers.

Emily walked her to the door. "What do you think is going on?"

"I don't know. But it looks like Mia was afraid something would happen to her. You said she gave this to you three months ago?"

Emily nodded.

Ellie contemplated the timing. Something must have spooked her. "Just watch Pixie. Maybe Mia revealed some information without Pixie even realizing it."

"I understand. I'll try some art therapy with her." Emily gave her a small smile. "And don't worry. She'll be safe here with us."

Ellie nodded, another thought occurring to her. "Thanks. If Mia was scared and escaped Tori's killer, she may have gone to the Penningtons and is waiting for me to bring Pixie to her."

"Then go find them," Emily murmured. "I hate to see that child suffering."

"So do I." Ellie squeezed Emily's arm. "Thanks for your help. I don't know what we'd do without you."

"Just find Mia," Emily said. "And bring her back to that precious girl."

Ellie hoped she could. But she'd lost so many victims along the way that she was afraid to make promises she couldn't keep.

The humidity had turned sweltering, perspiration beading on Ellie's skin as she made her way back to the Jeep where Derrick was waiting with all the windows open. He sat hunched over his laptop.

Ellie slid onto the driver's seat. "Pixie doesn't know Jo-Jo or Seth Pennington. Not family or friends. She said it was just her and her mommy and Mark."

"I didn't discover any communication between Mia and them on her computer or phone records. But I found out where they are." Derrick angled his computer to reveal an obituary notice. "Pixie didn't know them because the Penningtons are dead. They were murdered four years ago."

"Murdered?" Ellie's heart thundered as she started the engine and drove from the ranch. "How were they killed?"

"A home invasion," Derrick replied. "Or at least that's what the report says."

"Did they find the killer?" Ellie asked.

"No. Let me look and see what I can dig up on it."

Pockets of rain clouds dotted the sky, promising another summer storm. While she headed toward the station, Ellie called Mark.

"Detective," Mark said, his voice anxious. "Did you find her?"

"I'm sorry but not yet. Did Mia ever mention a couple named Jo-Jo and Seth Pennington?"

"No, why? Who are they?"

"That's what I'm trying to figure out. Apparently, Mia left a note with Emily Nettles stating that if anything happened to her, to contact the Penningtons to take care of Pixie."

"I don't understand," Mark said, hurt lacing his voice. "We agreed that I was going to adopt Pixie."

"I don't understand either. But I'm going to find out their connection to her."

"Maybe they know where Mia is." Hope flickered in Mark's voice.

Ellie's chest tightened, but she decided not to reveal that the couple had been murdered until she knew more. "I'll keep you posted."

As soon as she hung up, Derrick looked up from his computer. "According to this article, the Penningtons lived in Dawsonville. The couple were in their early forties. The wife was a website designer, the husband an accountant. No children. And no surviving family."

"Mia must not have been aware of their deaths or she wouldn't have left that directive," Ellie said.

"Small town news," Derrick said. "Looks like there was a major accident on the interstate that same day that stopped traffic for several hours involving multiple casualties. Drunk driver ran and police had to chase him down across counties where he crashed into someone's house and caused another death."

"Good heavens," Ellie muttered.

Derrick nodded. "Considering the fact that the Pennington case was ruled a B&E, their story probably got buried beneath all that drama."

"Got it. Tell me more about what happened with the Penningtons."

Derrick drummed his fingers on his thigh. "Police stated that a lawn company showed up and discovered the home had been broken into. Police discovered the wife and husband tied to chairs, beaten and shot in the head."

"Sounds like overkill, not just a B&E," Ellie said. "Was it personal? Did they have any suspects?"

"Doesn't say. Just that a detective named Mathis investigated and left the case open."

"We need to talk to him. Let's head there now."

They drove north about forty miles, passing more farmland, and Derrick called ahead to set up a meeting with the detective. Tourists and families flocked to Amicalola Falls in Dawnsonville for hiking and to enjoy the natural beauty of the area. As a kid, Ellie had visited the pumpkin farm here in the fall and spring was strawberry picking season.

The town square was crowded with people milling around and visiting the tourist hot spots. She parked in front of the sheriff's office and, as she climbed out, the humidity made her hair stick to the back of her neck.

Derrick tugged at the collar of his shirt, too, as if he felt it as well, then the two of them entered the building. A deputy greeted them, and Derrick introduced them. "I called about seeing Detective Mathis."

"Right," the middle-aged brunette said. "He's expecting you. I'll buzz you on back."

She pressed a button and the door to the right opened. Ellie led the way and a minute later they were seated inside the detective's office.

Detective Mathis was a tall, broad-shouldered man who looked as if he might have been the town football hero once. Stark features, thick salt-and-pepper hair and tanned skin from being outdoors. Probably a hiker or fisherman.

He crossed his arms and leveled his gaze at them. "Regina said you had questions about the Pennington case."

"Yes," Ellie said. "Their names came up in one of our cases. We're aware they were murdered. Can you tell us about the investigation?"

"Sure enough." He opened his desk drawer, pulled out a file and spread it in front of him. "That one bugged the hell out of me. Ain't never seen anything like it."

"What do you mean?"

He shrugged. "This is a little town where everyone's

friendly. Well, except when they dip into the moonshine too much. We have a domestic here and there, kids breaking and entering to steal electronics or jewelry they can sell at the pawn shop, but nothing like this murder."

His jaw hardened as he removed crime scene photos. "Everyone who knew the couple said they were real nice. Church going. Helped out in the community and volunteered at the soup kitchen. No trouble financially or with their businesses. Coworkers liked them. Neighbors liked them. Darnedest thing I ever seen."

Ellie sensed he was deeply troubled about the way he'd found this couple. "Tell us more about the crime scene."

He turned the stack of photos to face them then spread them out. "It was brutal. Both of them were tied to the kitchen chairs, beaten to a pulp. No DNA."

"This doesn't look like the work of teenagers or a B&E," Derrick added.

"Sure as hell don't." Mathis' sigh rent the air, then he dragged his fingers toward another set of photographs. "House was ripped apart. They tore up the cushions on the couch, destroyed furniture, slashed open the damn mattresses and broke and burned pictures in the house." Ellie's pulse raced as she stared at the images. The destruction was similar to the scene at Mia's.

"Did you find forensics?" Derrick asked.

"Not a damn thing. Which tells me this was premeditated."

"And perhaps personal," Ellie said. "A crime of rage against the couple. But why?"

"That's what stumped me," Detective Mathis said. "Never found a motive."

"The killer was looking for something," Ellie said, thinking out loud as she considered a possible connection. "Maybe information. That's why he beat them, to make them talk."

FORTY-FIVE

Detective Mathis' chair rocked backward. "What's your interest in this case?"

"Mia Norman disappeared from her wedding yesterday under suspicious circumstances," Ellie said, retrieving a photo of Mia. "In the event anything happened to her, she left word that her daughter was to go to the Penningtons."

"I see." Mathis worked his mouth from side to side. "You looked for the Penningtons and that led you here."

"Exactly." Ellie tapped Mia's picture. "Do you recognize her?"

Mathis leaned forward to study it, then shook his head. "No. But if the Penningtons were dead, why would she leave her daughter to them?"

Ellie raised a brow. "She was obviously unaware of their murders. But their deaths and the fact that her house was destroyed in a similar manner to the Penningtons makes me wonder if her disappearance is connected to this case."

"Did either the wife or husband have family?" Derrick asked.

Mathis flipped back through the file. "The husband had a

brother who lives abroad. I checked him out and he was in London at the time of the murders. He came back and handled the funeral arrangements."

"How about the wife?" Ellie asked.

"Parents died when she was young and she and her sister were raised by the grandmother who passed about six years ago. I searched the house for papers, but like I said the place was torn apart. One of Jo-Jo's coworkers said her sister died a long time ago. She had no other family."

"Maybe she and Mia were friends," said Ellie.

"I'll re-question the neighbors and their workers and ask if anyone heard of Mia Norman," the detective offered. "This is one case that's haunted me for years now. I don't like not having answers."

"Me neither," Ellie said. She understood the way an unsolved murder could get under your skin.

FORTY-SIX

Before they drove back to town, Ellie and Derrick stopped at a little place called The Catfish House for lunch and seated themselves at an outdoor picnic table. As they ordered shrimp po'boys and fries and drank sweet tea, the river gurgled behind them, blending with the sound of children laughing and families chattering.

Ellie's phone rang. Laney. She connected and put her on speaker. "Are you finished with the autopsy?"

"Yes," Laney said. "As we thought, Tori James died of blood loss due to the gunshot wound. The blunt force trauma to the back of the head was not severe, and it could have occurred while she was trying to escape an attacker."

"He shot her while she was trying to run away."

"That fits," Laney said. "I also have some lab results that are puzzling."

Ellie tensed. "What do you mean?"

"About the champagne. I found traces of Rohypnol in the bottle."

"So Mia and Tori were drugged."

"Yes, I found traces in Tori's bloodstream as well. But

there's something else. The DNA from the glasses. Tori's matched one of them. But DNA from the second glass is confusing."

"How so?"

"It matched DNA from the system belonging to a woman named Jesse Habersham."

Ellie's head spun. "I don't understand. Unless Jesse Habersham was in the room with Mia and Tori... Then she could have had something to do with Tori's death and Mia's disappearance."

"I suppose that's a possibility," Laney continued. "But here's the odd part. Just to be precise, I ran it against the DNA from Mia's toothbrush the ERT sent over, and it also matches that DNA."

Ellie rubbed her temple. "Are you sure?"

"I ran both of them three times myself just to verify," Laney said. "And I'll compare their dental records when I get them."

"How is that possible the DNA is the same?" Ellie asked.

"Well, if Mia and Jesse were twins, their DNA would match."

"As far as I know, Mia had no family," Ellie said, her thoughts racing. "Unless Mia and Jesse are the same person." Or she'd lied about not having a family or being a twin. But why would she do that?

"That would explain it," Laney agreed.

What the hell was going on? "Thanks, Laney. Let me know if you get any new information."

"Will do."

After hanging up, Ellie washed down the lump in her throat with another swig of tea.

The waitress came over with their food, and Derrick waited until she was finished delivering their order before relaying what she'd learned.

"Sounds like we need to find out more about Jesse Habersham." Derrick wiped his mouth with a napkin. "Maybe the fiancé knows."

"I don't like it," Ellie murmured. "If she had a twin, then she lied about not having family. And if she and Jesse are the same person, then she's hiding something." She stewed over that possibility. "She must be running from something," Ellie said.

"Or she committed a crime," Derrick suggested.

That was definitely motive for running and changing her name. "Let me see your laptop."

He pushed it toward her and scooped up a forkful of coleslaw while she entered the name Jesse Habersham into the computer's search engine. The name did not appear in the criminal databases, nor did she have an arrest record. Ellie found three Jesse Habershams in the DMV database – one was sixty years old, the second a middle-aged teacher, and the third a pretty blond with bright blue eyes. Mia had hazel eyes. Jesse was thin too, 110 pounds, which was at least fifteen pounds less than Mia.

Ellie leaned closer, studying the shape of her face; although Mia's cheeks were fuller, the dainty nose and high cheekbones were the same.

"Did you find her?" Derrick said as he finished his sandwich.

"Mia *is* Jesse," Ellie said, as she showed him the DMV picture. Her hair color was different, and she was obviously wearing contacts and had gained weight but it was her. "Let me see what else I can find out about her."

Clouds started hovering overhead, stirring a much-needed breeze. Ellie wiped perspiration from her forehead as she researched Jesse Habersham. A Google search turned up several articles.

The first was a human-interest piece featuring a small clothing boutique she owned. "Listen to this, Derrick. Jesse was a waitress turned clothing designer who designed her own line and sold it in a little boutique called Moonbeams. It was located in the town of Red River Rock."

Derrick's gaze swung to her. "That's only half an hour or so from here, where the Penningtons lived."

"Interesting."

In a photo, Jesse looked hip in her outfit and stilettos with her blond hair in a chignon, nothing like Mia in her jeans, flannel shirts, and a ponytail. Ellie scrolled to the next article and Derrick studied it with her. "She was engaged. Here's the announcement." In another picture, Jesse stood in a sparkly red dress beside a tall, handsome man named Kevin Moon.

"Moon is the name of the local businessman who owns half of Red River Rock," Derrick said.

"This must be his son." Ellie pointing out a photograph of Kevin and his father Armond.

Ellie wiped her face as a raindrop pinged off her cheek. Thunder rumbled and people began to pack up their leftovers and hurry inside before the storm hit.

Intrigued, Ellie found another article dated five years ago, with images from the wedding day. Pictures of the happy couple and family and friends on a riverboat created a montage.

But the headline made her lose her breath.

WEDDING OF PROMINENT GROOM KEVIN MOON TURNED TRAGIC WHEN A FIRE BROKE OUT ON THE BOAT. BRIDE JESSE HABERSHAM THOUGHT TO HAVE DIED IN THE EXPLOSION.

FORTY-EIGHT

FOGGY MOUNTAIN

A frisson of unease skittered up Ellie's spine. Jesse was thought to have died at her wedding and Mia had disappeared from hers. How odd was that?

Stomach churning, she pushed away her food basket. "Before we talk to Mark, I say we take a little trip to Red River Rock."

Lightning lit up the sky, popping off the tops of the mountain. Derrick grabbed the laptop and they made a mad dash for the car as the gray clouds unleashed. She slammed the door and they sat for several minutes while the rain pounded the car.

"While we wait out the worst of the storm, see what else you can find on Jesse Habersham's disappearance," Ellie said.

Derrick consulted his computer. "There was an investigation by local sheriff Kincaid, but Jesse's body was never found."

"Because she didn't die," Ellie said. "She assumed another identity."

Seconds later, Derrick snapped his fingers. "Six weeks after the explosion, a woman's body thought to be Jesse surfaced."

"But we know it wasn't her," Ellie said. "Does the article identify her?"

"Dammit," Derrick muttered. "The battery just ran out. We need to charge the laptop."

"Then let's get going." Ellie started the engine and pulled away from the restaurant, grateful the rain was starting to slacken. The sky was still dark though, casting a gloom over the beautiful scenery, and Ellie's mood as she considered what they knew so far.

Ellie pictured Mia's smiling face as she and Pixie planted sunflowers outside her house, and her head was reeling. Had Mia planned her own escape or was she creating a pattern of being a runaway bride?

The Mia she knew didn't seem to be capable of that, but apparently she didn't know Mia at all.

But she would find the truth. Her gut told her that Mia – Jesse – had left because she was afraid of something.

The downpour dwindled to a drizzle, but cars were still driving at a snail's pace, and with the wet streets she turned her focus to the road. The weather would curtail water sports for a while, ruin holiday celebrations, and if rain rolled in again, make the creeks and river rise and possibly flood, creating treacherous conditions on the AT.

The next twenty minutes, she and Derrick lapsed into silence as she navigated the road's curves. A red mist had formed above the cliffs, forming a hazy fog and blurring the view of the ridges and peaks. Locals dubbed it Foggy Mountain and there were legends about people disappearing into the haze and never being seen again.

A giant boulder at the edge of town sported a sign reading *Welcome to Red River Rock* in red letters.

"Hmm, it's obvious who owns this town," Derrick commented, as they noticed all the storefronts boasting the Moon family name. Moonbeams, the clothing boutique Jesse had owned, a restaurant/brewery on the river named Moondoggy's, another bar Moon Stillery, an antique store called Moon Gems and a diner called Moon's Roadkill Café.

"Yeah, interesting."

Now the rain had eased off, a ray of sunshine shot through the fog, nearly blinding Ellie as she parked at the sheriff's office. She had a feeling the truth was somewhere in this town. Small towns had secrets. Time to start uncovering the ones on Foggy Mountain.

Questions fired through Ellie's head as she and Derrick entered the police station. Like most rural areas, the facility was unimpressive. A desk with a sergeant manning it, an open bullpen area with a couple of metal desks, double doors leading to what she assumed was the holding cells and another door that probably led to the sheriff's office.

She introduced themselves to the desk sergeant and asked to speak to the sheriff, Larry Kincaid. Five minutes later, they were escorted to his office. He was a balding chuffy man, with a dark mole on his chin and looked to be mid-fifties. The buttons on his wrinkled beige shirt looked like they were about to pop and his uniform pants hung low beneath his belly.

"Sheriff Kincaid," Ellie began. "I'm Detective Ellie Reeves and this is Special Agent Fox."

He chomped on a peppermint as he lumbered up from his swivel chair. "What can I do for you, folks?"

They seated themselves. "We'd like to ask you some questions about a case you worked five years ago. The disappearance of Jesse Habersham."

A flicker of surprise caught in his eyes. "What about it?"

Ellie decided to share, hoping he'd return the favor. "We believe she survived the fire on the boat on her wedding day and has been leading another life."

"You know where she is?" A muscle ticked in his jaw.

"Not at the moment," Ellie said. "But that's the reason we're here. Can you tell us about the case?"

He picked up a paper clip and rubbed it between his stubby fingers. "She married Kevin Moon, Armond Moon's son. The Moons built this town up. Moon has a big houseboat where they held the wedding. But a fire broke out after the ceremony and Jesse was thought to have fallen overboard and drowned."

"You never found her body?"

He shook his head, then finished crunching the mint in his mouth. "Kevin was devastated. He loved that girl more than anything."

"What caused the fire?" Derrick asked.

"Something in the kitchen," Kincaid responded. "Spread like a wildfire. Everyone ran to escape, but Kevin went to look for his wife and couldn't find her. We searched the river and surrounding property for days, then had to assume the current carried her downstream."

Ellie crossed her arms. That story sounded eerily familiar. "Did you suspect foul play? That someone set the fire and abducted Jesse?"

He shrugged. "I investigated, questioned everyone at the wedding and her coworkers." His Adam's apple bobbed as he swallowed. "But this is a close-knit community. Folks around here take care of each other. No one saw anything and no one had a reason to hurt Jesse."

"What about her and Kevin? Did they have problems?" Ellie asked.

He jerked his head back with a stunned look. "Hell no. I told you he loved her more than anything. He even helped her launch her boutique."

"Were there any issues with the business?" Derrick asked.

Kincaid tapped the paper clip on his desk. "Nah, Jesse was excited, got some write-ups in the local paper and Kevin said she was starting to sell well online through her website." His chair squeaked as he leaned back in it. "After a few days we assumed she was dead. Then six weeks later a body washed up down near Byrne Hollow. At first we thought it was Jesse. Kevin was there holding his breath. The body was burned badly and already deteriorating from the elements. But she was wearing the wedding ring Kevin gave her."

"But it wasn't Jesse?"

"Nope. ME did an autopsy and said it was a woman named Stella Carnes. She died in a house fire but her body was donated to the Body Farm in Knoxville, Tennessee where students train in crime scene investigation."

"Then what did you do?" Derrick asked.

"Decided she was either kidnapped or ran off. Kept the missing persons file active. But... it's been five years, so again we assumed she was probably dead."

Jesse could have been abducted five years ago, then escaped her kidnapper and gone into hiding. But who put her ring on the cadaver's finger? If her abductor had and Jesse escaped, why wouldn't she have gone to the police or come back to Kevin?

Unless she was running from *him*...

FIFTY

"Sheriff, we need to talk to Kevin Moon," Ellie said. "Where can we find him?"

The big guy cut his eyes over Ellie. "Probably at the real estate agency he and his father own. Kev takes care of the sales, listing and mortgage side while his dad oversees the other businesses they support."

"Then we'll stop by there," Ellie said.

Sheriff Kincaid's ruddy cheeks flamed. "Now, I helped you. You gonna share what you think you know?"

Ellie and Derrick traded a look, then Ellie spoke. "Like I said, we think Jesse may have been living under an assumed name."

His brows climbed his forehead. "Are you talking about that missing woman on the news, Mia Norman?"

"We are," Ellie said.

"That woman didn't look nothing like Jesse."

Ellie couldn't argue with that. But DNA didn't lie. "She could have easily altered her appearance."

"That still don't make sense," the sheriff said. "Jesse had a good life, a great job and Kevin. Why would she disappear and take on a new name? You think she was in trouble before she came to Red River Rock?"

"Good question," Ellie said. "Did you look into that theory?"

The chair squeaked again as he shifted. "I did but didn't find anything." He leaned forward, eyes boring into Ellie. "Except Kevin's dad told me she skimmed money from the boutique before she left. Maybe that was her plan all along. Then she set up a new identity so we wouldn't find her and arrest her."

Ellie pressed her lips together, shocked by the accusation. He painted Jesse as a calculating, cold-hearted thief. But stealing money didn't fit with the Mia she knew. Then again, Ellie was finding out all kinds of things she didn't know about her friend.

"We'll definitely explore that angle," Derrick said.

Ellie stood. "Thank you for your help, Sheriff." Now she really wanted to talk to Kevin.

He clicked his teeth. "Sure enough. You let me know if you learn anything," he said. "That family suffered a lot when Jesse disappeared. I'll do whatever I have to do to bring them closure and protect them."

Something about the way he worded that statement made the hair on the back of Ellie's neck prickle. He definitely sounded loyal to the Moons. "What would you have to protect them from?" she asked.

He made a low sound of disgust. "Gossip. Accusations. Poor Kev was put through the ringer. You know how small towns are."

She did indeed.

Gossip. Rumors. Secrets. Lies. Alliances.

What would she find in Red River Rock?

FIFTY-ONE

FOGGY MOUNTAIN REAL ESTATE

Red River Rock centered around a small town square, situated on one of the higher parts of the mountain offering majestic views of the lower valley, hollows and river.

Moon's Foggy Mountain Real Estate was on the edge of town, perched on a hill. The building was an impressive two-story log house with stacked stone, a front porch with wooden rockers, a porch swing and a whiskey barrel holding a checker set.

"Looks like the Moons are doing well for themselves," Derrick commented.

They climbed the wooden steps and entered through the screened door to an open lobby with a station, a reception desk, and a large area filled with brochures for activities in the area. One wall held a diagram of two new local developments with the plans for community gatherings, a pool, clubhouse, golfing and lots for sale. A second offered information on cabin rentals along the river. Another wall held an artistic mural depicting the town in its original state decades ago with horse drawn carriages, a saloon and the original Roadkill Café.

Ellie felt as if she was in a time warp. Glass casings enclosed three offices. A slender brunette dressed to the nines sat in one cubicle talking to a middle-aged couple. The second office was empty at the moment, and another woman with auburn hair was on the phone, her arm full of bracelets glinting beneath the lights.

At the sound of a voice, Ellie turned to see a staircase leading to a second floor. "His office is probably up there."

Derrick gestured for her to lead the way. Along the stairwell were black and white photographs of businesses in town which the Moons must have owned. Just as they were nearing the office where some voices were coming from, a robust man in overalls lumbered out, a scowl on his face. He darted past them and strode down the steps with barely a glance at them.

The bronzed sign on the door read Kevin Moon, Mortgage Broker.

Ellie knocked on the door and poked her head in. A tall, fair-headed man wearing a suit was facing the window.

"Mr. Moon? May we come in?"

He pivoted, and Ellie had a glimpse of a handsome, in-shape man with a charming smile. "Yes."

Ellie identified them and he motioned for them to sit while he moved to his desk chair. "Sheriff Kincaid called," he said, his gaze level. "You're here about Jesse's disappearance?"

Ellie nodded while Derrick dove into observation mode. "We believe her disappearance is linked to a case we're working involving a missing woman named Mia Norman from Crooked Creek."

"Sheriff Kincaid explained that, too," Kevin said. "I can't believe Jesse is alive after all this time."

She should have asked the sheriff not to give Kevin a heads-up. But he was loyal to the Moons and she doubted he would have done so.

"I'm sure this is painful for you," Ellie said, using a sympathetic voice to cater to his emotions.

"It is," Kevin said, his voice laced with disbelief. "Are you certain they're one and the same?"

"DNA confirmed it," Ellie said.

Another tense second passed. "Did she really change her name to Mia and was she engaged?"

"That's what we think," Ellie said. "We're sorting things out, trying to determine if this time she disappeared intentionally or if she was abducted."

His brows shot upward. "Why would you think she was abducted?"

"Because there were signs of foul play in the bridal dressing room." Ellie studied his reaction. "And her maid of honor was murdered."

For the first time since they'd entered the room, unease darkened his eyes. "How was she killed?" he asked quietly.

"I can't discuss the details at this point. But I need you to tell me everything you can about Jesse Habersham."

His shoulders went rigid. "Listen, Detective, Special Agent Fox, I went through hell when my wife disappeared. Not only did I lose my wife, the love of my life, but people actually thought I might have done something to her." His voice rose an octave. "I've had to live with that. Grief over the loss of my wife, plus rumors. Strange looks. Suspicions. But now you're telling me she's alive..." He crossed his arms, gaze steady. "Are you here to accuse me of kidnapping this Mia woman? I mean, Jesse."

"We're here for information," Ellie said. "Where were you yesterday between the hours of five and six p.m.?"

He tunneled his long, tanned fingers through the layers of his well-groomed hair. "With my father discussing a business deal."

"He can verify that?" Ellie asked.

"Of course."

"Was anyone else there?" Derrick cut in.

"No." He reached for his phone. "Now, I think I should call my attorney. I don't want to be ambushed like I was before."

"We're not here to ambush you," Ellie said. "Just for answers and to help you. I thought Kincaid was loyal to your family. Did *he* ambush you?"

Kevin's nostrils flared. "No, he knows I wasn't capable of hurting Jesse, that I loved her with all my heart. But reporters and tabloids revel in smearing reputations of successful people. And I don't want them invading my life again."

"You do want to know what happened to Jesse, don't you?" Ellie pressed. "If you loved her so much, I mean. You want answers."

Pain wrenched his face. "Of course I do. I don't believe for a minute she left me of her own volition. And if she's in trouble, I'll do whatever I can to help find her." He ran a hand down his chin. "Was she okay before she vanished?"

Ellie schooled her reaction. "She appeared to be," Ellie said, thinking of Mark.

Mark, who claimed to love Mia just as Kevin claimed to love Jesse.

FIFTY-TWO
MOSQUITO COVE

Cord pulled on rubber wader boots, suit and gloves and joined Milo at the edge of the river. Humidity plastered Cord's shaggy hair to his neck and he waved away flies and gnats as he grabbed the crowbar he'd brought and stepped into the water.

Mosquitos buzzed as the current sloshed loose twigs and sticks along the riverbank. The air smelled stagnant with wet moss, wild mushrooms and the pungent odor of lichen.

Cord waded knee-high until he reached the whiskey barrel, then checked the top to see if it would open. But nails held it together.

He tapped on the exterior to see if it was hollow; it wasn't.

Milo wiped sweat from his forehead with the back of his arm. "I tried to move it to shore, but it's too heavy and weighted down by mud and sludge. Thought it might be from the stillery around here, but there's no markings to indicate that. Still, it could contain moonshine from an illegal still or drugs."

"Hopefully that's all it is," Cord said. "Only one way to find out."

Milo used a tool to loosen the nails, and Cord worked to pry the lid off. Seconds ticked by. Somewhere in the distance, a motorboat rumbled, a three blade propellor chopping through the river water.

The afternoon sun beat down, slicing through the edges of the trees and creating pockets of light among the muddy surface. Cord's arms strained as he worked the crowbar around the edge.

An acrid odor seeped from the barrel as he pushed the top away from the side. His pulse thundered as a rancid smell assaulted him.

A body had been stuffed inside, the charred remains unrecognizable.

FIFTY-THREE

RED RIVER ROCK

Derrick had interviewed countless suspects, witnesses and victims in his days at the Bureau. He'd learned to analyze body language for signs of lying. For grief, pain, rage and guilt simmering below the surface.

But he hadn't gotten a good read on Kevin Moon yet. The man could be honestly devastated and confused.

Or... he could be a sociopath.

Derrick never made snap decisions. The truth was in the wait. The watching. Being patient. Even sociopaths revealed their true colors at some point.

"Mr. Moon, why don't you walk us through your relationship with Jesse Habersham, how you met, became business associates, your engagement?" Derrick asked.

The man inhaled a sharp breath as if it pained him to talk about Jesse. "Jesse came to town with a vision. I think she'd heard that our family liked to support small businesses and she was in the midst of designing her own clothing line." A smile curved his lips. "The first time I laid eyes on her, she was wearing this red off-the-shoulder sheath she'd designed and made herself. It was exquisite." He closed his eyes as if he was in the moment. "I fell in love with her at first sight. She looked like an angel with a spark of mischief and ambition and so much talent that I asked her out. We went to dinner a few times and we just... clicked. She loved living in the small town, said people here treated her like family." He hesitated, breathing hard now. "We bonded over that, too. Her parents were dead and I'd just lost my mother a few months before."

"I'm sorry for your loss," Ellie said.

"Thank you," he murmured. "Anyway, Jesse wanted to start her own boutique and there was a small building that was empty so I offered to back her. By then I was in love with her and on board with her vision. I helped her set up the boutique, renovate the space, hire workers to manufacture her designs, and we launched Moonbeams."

"And it was a success?" Ellie asked.

"We started a little slow, but I arranged publicity, created a website and a catalog for the store, then it really took off."

Jesse must have been excited, Derrick thought. And probably felt indebted to him.

"She was so proud." Kevin wiped his hands over his eyes as if emotions were overcoming him. "It was perfect. Then we got engaged and planned the wedding. We even talked about starting a family..."

Derrick nodded, although doubts trickled in. If everything was as picture perfect as he painted it to be, why had Jesse disappeared from her wedding and never contacted Kevin again?

FIFTY-FOUR

Ellie's phone vibrated on her hip. A quick glance at the number and she saw Cord's name. Knowing he was spearheading SAR's search for Mia, she excused herself to answer it and stepped into the other room.

"Hey, Cord."

His gruff voice echoed back, "SAR found a whiskey barrel in the river. I met Milo out here to check it out and we opened it."

Ellie's fingers tightened around the phone. "What is it, Cord?"

"A body," he said. "It's been burned beyond recognition."

"Where was it found?" Ellie pinched the bridge of her nose. It could be Mia.

"A few miles downstream from Magnolia Manor," he replied.

"I'll call Dr. Whitefeather and an ERT. We'll need to transport the remains and the barrel to forensics."

"I'll wait here and take a look around," Cord offered.

"Send me the GPS coordinates and I'll meet you."

Ellie quickly filled him in on what they'd learned about

Mia, Jesse Habersham and the Moons. "Keep this between us," she said. "I don't want details leaked until we investigate further."

"Copy that."

"And don't move the body until I get there."

"I know the drill, El."

She thanked him and hung up, her stomach roiling as she called her boss to request assistance.

FIFTY-FIVE

Ellie scrutinized Kevin as she returned to his office and sensed he meant what he said. He seemed sincere. So did Mark.

So had Mia.

Someone had to be lying...

"You have had no contact with Mia Norman the last five years?" Ellie asked.

"I never even heard of her until Sheriff Kincaid called earlier," Kevin said. "To be honest, I'm in total shock right now over what you've told me." He took several deep breaths. "I'm trying to process the fact that my wife is still alive."

"How would you account for her not contacting you?" Ellie asked.

He tilted his head sideways in thought. "I've being going over this again and again since the sheriff called. I honestly don't understand."

"How did she seem the few days before the wedding?"

"Excited," Kevin said. "We were madly in love, and we'd been planning the service for months. She even designed her own wedding dress and the maid of honor's dress."

"Nothing happened to upset her?" Ellie asked.

He shook his head. "There were a few minor kinks with the flowers and we were worried it might rain, but nothing major."

"She didn't have any trouble with the boutique? Maybe with a lender or customer?"

"No, the business was stable. I went through all this with Sheriff Kincaid at the time. He checked security cameras around the store but found nothing."

So he'd said. "Did Jesse have family?" Ellie asked.

"Not that she ever talked about. I think that was why she was drawn to mine so much. Because she felt so alone."

That fit with what Mark had told her as well. But if Mia had loved Mark's family and Kevin's, why wouldn't she turn to them if she was in trouble?

FIFTY-SIX

Kevin thought the detective and fed would never leave. Talking about his precious Jesse was the kind of torture he'd never known existed. He loved her with every fiber of his being.

Until death do us part. He'd meant every word of it.

The day they said their vows flashed through his mind, drawing him back to the moment she'd walked down the aisle. He'd never forget it.

He could hardly breathe as he waited to get a glimpse of her. Then she appeared at the doorway in that stunning white off the shoulder sequined dress. His heart pounded as he soaked in her beauty.

Her gorgeous silky blond hair was twisted in a fancy chignon at the nape of her neck with a glittery jewel comb, and the dangling teardrop diamond earrings he'd given her the day he'd proposed sparkled against the sunset. They matched the engagement ring he'd had handmade just for her because she deserved to be decked in diamonds and precious stones. The wedding march began and she floated toward him like an angel longing to be in his arms.

The next few seconds blurred as he cradled Jesse's hand in his and they exchanged promises. The air stirred with the scent of her perfume and the roses she'd carried.

"You may kiss the bride," the pastor murmured.

She smiled up at him with adoration and he cupped her heart-shaped face in his hands and drew her toward him for a long slow kiss.

Cheers and clapping erupted. The music signaled their exit and they faced their guests as husband and wife. He danced her down the aisle and the wedding party began their parade.

The deck grew crowded as his family rushed to congratulate them and the guests were being ushered to the top deck for pre-dinner drinks and hors d' oeuvres.

The next few minutes passed in a haze as pictures were taken and they smiled at the camera, hands clasped, the air bubbling with excitement. As they finished the photographs, Jesse whispered she needed to visit the ladies before she joined the guests. He kissed her tenderly and promised to wait. Then she disappeared down the stairs to the bridal dressing room.

Above, guests were milling around, enjoying the signature cocktail Jesse had chosen and nibbling on crab-stuffed mushrooms and caviar.

Suddenly someone screamed from below deck where the kitchen was housed. Smoke curled and began to fill the main level deck. The alarm blared. One of the staff rushed out and screamed, "Fire!"

Guests cried out and began to stampede down the stairs, running toward the exit and boat ramp, crowding each other in their panic to escape.

Panic ripped through Kevin. His father yelled at him to get off the boat, but he couldn't leave his wife. He pushed through the guests and staff as they raced from the lower deck and he rushed down the stairs, yelling Jesse's name. "Jesse! Where are you?"

The smoke grew thicker, clogging his vision and he coughed

but charged through it to the bridal room. Flames were starting to eat the cabin and the kitchen was engulfed.

He grabbed a towel from a serving cart and covered his mouth as he pushed through the smoke. "Jesse! Jesse, where are you?"

The bridal room was empty. Terror bled through him, and he raced down the narrow hall to the other cabins, checking them one by one. No one was downstairs.

Praying she'd made it upstairs, he plunged back through the fog of smoke, batting flames as he jogged up the steps. Outside the upper deck had cleared. His father stood at the edge of the boat ramp, looking panicked.

A fire engine roared up and firemen descended. His father grabbed his arm and yanked him toward the ramp. "We have to go, son."

"But Jesse!"

"She probably got off with the crowd," his father said as he yanked him onto the dock.

Kevin stumbled, coughing, tears from the smoke and fear blurring his eyes.

"Jesse!" he screamed as his father dragged him onto the shore.

Jerking back to the present, he picked up the photo of their wedding kiss and dried his wet cheeks with the back of his hand.

He'd never stopped loving Jesse. He had to get her back.

FIFTY-SEVEN

SOMEWHERE ON THE RIVER

Mia stirred from unconsciousness, her stomach turning. Where was she? What had happened?

She was so dizzy she could barely lift her head. Her mouth felt dry, like cotton balls had been stuffed inside. Her head swam. A noise sounded, constant. Water? The river?

Panic zinged through her as she realized she must be on a boat. How had she gotten here?

She rolled to her side to get up, but the room tilted and bile climbed to her throat.

Squeezing her eyes shut, she lay her head back down and inhaled to keep from throwing up. The boat rocked, bouncing up and down as it crashed over rocks. Outside thunder crackled, taking her back years ago to when her parents had been killed.

She had been on a boat with them, racing away. But lightning struck and fire burst from the stern. Then her parents were screaming and she and her sister were clinging to each other, terrified and crying.

Fear had made it hard to breathe then. It made it hard to breathe now.

She inhaled another deep breath and racked her brain to

remember what had happened, why she was here. She'd been dressed for her wedding... Pixie and Mark were waiting...

The boat lurched forward. Nausea built. Darkness beckoned again.

She fought to stay awake and looked down. Fear choked her. She was dressed in a thin cotton T-shirt and shorts, not her wedding dress.

She felt her hair; the veil was gone too. And her ring... She checked her hand. Missing.

Tears burned the backs of her eyelids. Pixie... Where was her daughter? Was she here, too? Was she okay?

Images flashed through her mind. A scream sounded in her head. Her own scream. *Tori's... They were running. Then Tori... He caught her. Tori stumbled. She turned to help her, but a gunshot blasted the air. Tori stumbled forward and collapsed.*

Mia tried to help her, but she staggered. The trees were spinning, turning upside down. Then something slammed against the back of her head and light disappeared as she fell into nothing.

She blinked her surroundings back into focus and glanced up at the tiny window in the cabin, forcing herself to crawl to it. Sucking in a breath to steady herself, she peered through it. In the distance, lightning zigzagged across the tops of the trees. A red mist rose from the river just as the legends said.

All she could see for miles and miles was water. And the river monsters swarming like piranhas.

FIFTY-EIGHT

FOGGY MOUNTAIN

Another storm was starting to brew as Ellie and Derrick left the real estate office. "Cord called, Derrick," Ellie said as they got in the Jeep. "SAR found a body in a barrel in the river."

"Mia?"

"Don't know yet. I hope to God it's not... Apparently it was burned. I want to take a look. We also need to ask Mark if he recognizes the name Jesse Habersham."

"Let's talk to Kevin's father first," Derrick said. "He owns this town. Maybe he knew something about Jesse that his son didn't."

"True. Although Kevin has probably already spoken to him."

"Or the sheriff called and gave him a heads-up," Derrick said.

"He'll either be prepared to help or have his story ready."

Derrick looked up from his phone where he'd been scrolling for information. "Kevin's father's name is Armond. I have an address."

He plugged it into the GPS system and Ellie drove onto the country road leading out of town toward the peak of Foggy

Mountain. All around her, the mountains climbed, trees shivering in the building wind. In spite of the cloud cover, the temperature was rising, the fog thickening.

"Have you been here before?" Derrick asked.

"My dad and I camped on Foggy Mountain a couple of times and ran the river," Ellie said. She didn't mention that she and Cord used to go rafting together here when she was young. "Maybe we could go sometime."

"Yeah. Maybe when this case is over."

Ellie shivered. Would she be able to save her friend before it was too late?

She reached a fork in the road where signs pointed toward various cabin rentals, a campground and a water park. Veering left onto a private road, she climbed the mountain. Wildflowers exploded everywhere adding pops of purple and yellow, and oak trees and pines flanked the private drive.

Knowing the family owned the town, Ellie wasn't surprised that the Moons' home was a stunning estate sitting in a clearing with an expansive view of the river and mountains. White columns and a wide porch gave it a stately feel and flower beds added color against the lush greenery.

"Who knew small-town businesses were so profitable?" Ellie said beneath her breath.

A second passed as if Derrick was contemplating her comment. "Must be the real estate and tourism."

A detached garage to the right held a black Mercedes and a shiny silver BMW convertible. She parked and climbed out and they walked up the stone path to the front porch. Ellie rang the doorbell while Derrick checked out the property.

"Nice boat dock and boat," Derrick said with a whistle.

Ellie nodded, and the door opened, revealing a man who looked very much like his son although silver streaks laced his hair, his nose slightly more prominent. "Mr. Moon?" Ellie said before she identified them.

"Yes. My son called and said you'd probably be stopping by." His deep voice held no emotion and his eyes lacked Kevin's charm.

"May we come in?" Derrick asked.

"Of course." He led them past a study with judge's paneling and a giant cherry desk, then into a smaller sitting room with dark brown leather furniture. The décor was definitely upscale and masculine. They seated themselves in the chairs flanking the brick fireplace.

"What's this we heard about you finding Jesse?" Mr. Moon asked.

Ellie said, "We didn't exactly find her. We believe a woman named Mia Norman, who disappeared from Crooked Creek, is Jesse."

Mr. Moon straightened his tie. "Tell me everything," he said. "And don't spare the details. That woman nearly destroyed my son's life. She needs to answer for it."

FIFTY-NINE

The venom lacing Mr. Moon's voice was consistent with a protective father. But was there more to it?

Ellie used a soothing pitch to relay the circumstances that had led them here. "We understand she disappeared after her wedding to your son," she said.

"Of course she waited until they said '*I do*' before she ran off. That way she could legally have access to his money."

"And did she?" Ellie asked.

His gaze remained level. "Kevin admitted that she skimmed money from the boutique. He said she just took her salary, but I think she took more and he was too ashamed to admit he was a fool. I also assumed she'd try at some point to get more."

Again, Ellie was shocked at the accusation. "But she didn't. She disappeared and Kevin claims he hasn't heard from her since."

"True," he admitted quietly.

"I understand another woman's body was found a few weeks after Jesse went missing, one thought to be Jesse, and that she was wearing Jesse's wedding ring. What do you think happened?"

"How should I know?" He drummed his fingers on his leg. "Kevin insisted someone must have abducted her. He waited and waited for a ransom call. But... one never came. Now you're telling us she was alive and living in your town with a new name," he said in disbelief.

"It appears that way, although I don't know yet what happened between the time of her wedding to Kevin and when she arrived in Crooked Creek."

"She must have planned the entire thing herself. Pretty devious," Mr. Moon said.

"Did you like Jesse?" she asked Kevin's father.

Mr. Moon raised an eyebrow. "Do you have children, Detective?"

Ellie bit her lip. "No."

"Then you can't understand. She broke my son's heart. That was difficult to watch."

"I'm sure it was. Tell us what you thought of her before she disappeared. Did you notice anything off with her? Did she seem nervous or scared or like she was having cold feet?"

He picked up a pen and began to click it. "At first I was impressed with her ambition. She was talented and had no family so we embraced her." He crossed his legs. "And no, I didn't notice anything strange going on. She and Kev were happy and excited to start their lives together. They discussed expanding the boutique and traveling." He ran his hand over his tie again. "But apparently she changed her mind or was lying to all of us." Mr. Moon heaved a sigh. "Now tell me about this woman, Mia."

Derrick pulled up a photo of Mia on his phone. Age lines crinkled around Mr. Moon's eyes as he studied it.

"That can't be Jesse," Mr. Moon said. "Her hair's all wrong, so is her eye color. Plus, Jesse was slender and well dressed. That woman looks like some kind of country farmer."

Ellie would hardly say that. "DNA confirms they are one and the same," she said matter-of-factly.

Mr. Moon twisted sideways as if struggling to absorb the news. "What was she doing in Crooked Creek?"

"She worked at a gardening center," Ellie explained. "She had a knack for floral arrangements and landscaping."

He made a derisive sound. "You said she went missing from her wedding there. How could she marry someone else when she was married to my son?"

"All questions we need to answer," Ellie replied.

"Who is this guy she was engaged to?" Mr. Moon asked. "Maybe they planned this together and Jesse deserted Kevin to be with him."

"If that was the case, why go ahead with the wedding to Kevin?" Ellie said, thinking out loud.

His frown deepened. "I'm at a loss. My son gave her everything. They were happy together. I can't imagine why she'd possibly leave him, not unless she was cheating."

"I knew Mia personally and she didn't seem the type. She told me about meeting her fiancé at the gardening center. He said it took him months to convince her to go out with him. She spent most of her time with her daughter."

Mr. Moon stiffened, the pen clicking again. "Her daughter?"

"Yes."

"Was this man the father of the child?" Mr. Moon asked, his tone cold.

Ellie's heart thundered. She should have withheld that information but Mark had been holding Pixie when he'd spoken to the press the first night Mia disappeared. If they'd seen the news, she assumed Mr. Moon or Kevin would have noticed that.

"Was he?" Mr. Moon asked again.

Ellie shook her head. "According to Mia, the little girl's father was dead."

She saw the wheels turning in Kevin's father's head, and Ellie's mind connected dots that might or might not be linked.

Jesse disappeared from her wedding to Kevin five years ago. Pixie was four years old.

Mia had lied about who she was. Had she lied about Pixie's father?

SIXTY

Mr. Moon cleared his throat. "Where is this child now?"

"In a temporary foster home," Ellie replied.

"Where?" he demanded.

"I'm sorry but I can't divulge that information during an ongoing investigation."

"If she's Kevin's child, he has a right to know," Mr. Moon said.

"We don't know that she is his," Derrick said. "Jesse could have met someone after she disappeared and he might be the father."

"Or she had an affair and got pregnant. That's why she left Kevin," Mr. Moon said with a look of disgust.

"We will find out the truth," Ellie said. "And I'll keep you and your son abreast of everything we learn."

Derrick stood and Ellie rose, laying a card on the side table. "Thank you for your time. If you think of anything else, please give us a call."

Ellie's head was reeling as she and Derrick walked to her Jeep.

"Do you think Mia lied about Pixie's father?" Derrick asked.

"I don't know. She lied about so many things that I suppose we can't rule out the possibility."

Ellie liked Mia, had trusted her, had never doubted a word she'd said. She'd seemed like one of the most humble, sincere people she'd ever met. Could she have got her so wrong?

"We should request a DNA test," Derrick said. "Judging from Mr. Moon's reaction, he and his son will want one."

"If Jesse was carrying Kevin's baby," Ellie said, "she must have had a good reason for leaving."

"And a reason for keeping Pixie away from her father," Derrick added.

"It's plausible that Jesse faked her disappearance because the baby was Kevin's and she didn't want him to know."

"Which means she was afraid of him," Derrick said. "Although from what we've heard the family welcomed her and Kevin doted on her."

"Maybe too much..." Ellie said, searching. "Let's dig deeper and see if the Moons are the upstanding citizens they appear to be."

Ronnie hung up the phone, fury boiling through her like a summer storm raging through the forest. Her stupid boys were going to be sorry. They didn't have the sense the good Lord gave a gnat.

She picked up a hammer, then stormed outside to the dock where the sorry ass dimwits were yacking. River water sloshed onto the bank and waves rippled as a fishing boat churned through the water across the way.

"Did you see that pair of tits?" Using his hands, her youngest Lloyd squeezed as if he was fondling them. "They be the size of cantaloupes."

"That bitch can twirl them tassels," Chester said with a belly laugh.

A stream of black juice shot across the water as Lloyd spit a black stream of chewing tobacco. "I bet she squeals like a heifer when you ride her."

Chester reached for his jar of apple pie. "Just like that bitch did when you whacked her upside the head."

"You dip shits," Ronnie spat. "I told you to do the job and get out without making a stink."

Both her boys scuttled backwards like scared river rats. "We just took care of things like you said," Lloyd replied.

"What you getting your panties in a wad for anyway?" Chester said with a smirk, which told her the liquor had gone to his head and made him even more stupid. Her boys knew better than to talk back to her.

The dock swayed as she crossed to him, grabbed his hand and twisted his fingers.

He howled like a banshee, but she pushed his hand to the floor of the dock then slammed the hammer down across his fingers. Bellowing in pain, his face turned beet red and tobacco trickled from the corner of Lloyd's mouth as he jerked his hands into his lap.

"We got the job done, Mama," Lloyd said in a tiny voice.

Lloyd was the ass sucker. "You done brought the law around town, that's what you stupid shits done." She shoved Chester backward and he rolled on the dock, writhing in pain as he sucked his fingers.

"You two better lay low and keep your traps shut," she growled. "Or else you'll end up at the bottom of the river just like the others."

SIXTY-TWO
MOSQUITO COVE

The ME and ERT showed up just as Ellie and Derrick did. Ellie also received a text from Laney confirming that the dental records for Mia and Jesse matched.

Although the sun was fading slightly, the temperature had climbed into the mid-eighties, the humidity zapping Ellie's energy as they hiked down to the river edge.

Bugs swarmed around them, the sound of waves crashing melding with the sound of wildlife in the cove. Brush crackled beneath her boots, weeds clawing at her legs.

She skidded down the hill on the wet grass, then spotted Cord and his coworker Milo on the bank. The team followed her and Derrick, gathering by a pine tree that had fallen across the narrow part of the water.

Ellie snapped some pictures of the area and the whiskey barrel before stepping closer. She climbed on a bed of rocks, then shined her flashlight inside the barrel. Her stomach revolted at the grisly sight and putrid smell. She covered her nose with her hand and breathed out to stem her nausea.

Cord was right. There were charred remains inside, bones and ashes, maybe burned skin.

"Let's move the barrel onto the shore so Dr. Whitefeather can examine the remains," Ellie said.

"My team will start combing the woods for forensics," Abraham Williams said.

Ellie nodded. While Cord, Milo and a member of the ERT worked to free the barrel from the weeds and haul it onto the bank, she and Derrick checked the shore for footprints. The cove was secluded, overgrown and known to be a hotbed of insects, making it an undesirable site for campers and hikers. Given that, the victim could have been killed elsewhere then put in the barrel and dumped here, although that would have been no easy feat. You might need an ATV or truck but there was no sign of tire prints that she could see, unless the rain had washed them away.

Most likely whoever was inside the barrel had been murdered, then stuffed inside and pushed into the water somewhere upstream. The killer probably thought it would sink and no one would ever find it, but it had floated to this spot. The recent storms had ripped up trees and brush, trapping it from floating further away.

"I don't see signs anyone else has been here," Derrick said. "Except for a couple of boot prints in the mud."

"Probably Cord's and Milo's," Ellie said. "We'll take prints for elimination purposes."

Cord and the team finally managed to haul the barrel onto the dock and Ellie, Derrick and Laney stepped closer. The stench of charred bones was so strong Ellie had to step away for a second to draw breath. Derrick muttered a curse, and Laney exhaled and pulled on a mask before peering deeper into the barrel.

"Charred body will make identification harder," Laney said. "But we should be able to pull DNA from the bones and compare to Mia's and Jesse's."

Ellie twisted her hands together, fear pressing against her chest.

Laney agreed and stepped away from the barrel for a deep breath.

The ERT fanned out to search the surrounding property and Ellie took a moment to calm her raging emotions then dialed Sheriff Kincaid's number. "It's Detective Reeves."

"Yes, Detective?" the sheriff growled.

"Sheriff, a murder victim has been found in the river near your town."

A heavy pause then he cleared his throat. "Where?"

"Mosquito Cove," Ellie said. "Dr. Laney Whitefeather, the ME from Crooked Creek, and an ERT are here now."

"Don't do anything until I get there," Sheriff Kincaid said. "This is my jurisdiction and I want the body transferred to the ME in Red River Rock."

Ellie turned away from the ghastly site and looked across the river. She didn't like Kincaid's demanding tone. If this was Mia, she wanted her home in Crooked Creek.

"Sheriff, it's possible this victim could be our missing woman," Ellie said firmly. "Which means I want her autopsy performed in Crooked Creek."

"It's not up for debate, Detective. She was found near my town. If I must, I'll talk to your superior."

"Then call him," Ellie snapped. "Because I want it done right and I trust my ME to do it."

"Are you implying you don't trust me?" Sheriff Kincaid barked.

Ellie was still straddling the fence on that. "I'd just think you'd want to uncover the truth."

"I worked both cases to the letter of the law," he said angrily.

"I understand," Ellie said. "But it never hurts to have fresh eyes."

"Do not move the body," he replied. "I'll be there in twenty."

The line went dead as he hung up on her.

SIXTY-THREE

That damn sheriff was giving Ellie a hard time, and Derrick didn't like it. She was an insightful detective with incredible instincts that had led her to solve several major cases. He had to be in her corner now. "What was that about?"

Ellie rolled her eyes, looking frustrated. "Sheriff Kincaid wants to take charge of the victim. He's probably talking to Captain Hale right now. But... I want Laney on the case."

Derrick lifted his phone from his pocket. "Let me talk to him." He was sick to death of small-town sheriffs bullying their way into shutting out other law enforcement, just like Bryce Waters had ever since they'd met. Sure, they were territorial but the bottom line was getting the bad guy, not who got credit. He'd long ago learned to set that part of his ego aside for the betterment of a case.

He punched Kincaid's number and paced over to a bed of river rocks that created a natural path from the water to the sloping hill above. The phone rang three times, but Kincaid didn't respond. He tried again and got no response as the forensic team examined the exterior of the barrel and the recovery team discussed lifting it into the van for transportation.

A siren wailed, and minutes later Sheriff Kincaid pushed his way through the weeds toward them. He blustered over, a firm set to his jaw.

"Dammit," Ellie muttered.

Derrick went stone still.

Sweat dotted Kincaid's ruddy face as he stopped by the barrel.

Ellie crossed her arms, impatience in her expression. "The charred remains of a person are inside," she said, pointing to the barrel.

"I can damn well see that for myself," Kincaid grumbled. "Who found this?"

"Ranger McClain," Derrick said then gestured toward Cord. "He works SAR and consults with us on the task force ordered by the governor."

Sheriff Kincaid dug his heels in. "Thanks for the call. I'll take it from here."

"No," Ellie said. "It's possible this body may be related to our case. Our ME will handle the autopsy."

Kincaid gave a shake of his head. "The body was found in my town and I demand it stay here, too." He scrubbed a hand over his chin. "I finish what I start."

"I get it," Derrick said. "But since these cases involve multiple jurisdictions, the FBI will oversee them. If I need to call the governor and the chief of the Bureau, that can be arranged."

Kincaid muttered a curse. "Just like a fed. Always trying to wield your power."

"Just stating the facts, Sheriff. I won't allow you to stonewall our case." Derrick silently called the man a few choice words but remained tight-lipped. He was a negotiator after all. "Let's just work together and find the truth. I'm sure you want that, don't you?"

A boat sputtered somewhere in the distance, the wind

wheezing through the bushes. "Of course I do," Kincaid groused. "But my ME will work with yours. You can't hide details or evidence from me. I won't have it."

Derrick bit back a sarcastic comment. If anyone was hiding something, it was this Podunk sheriff. "Then we're in agreement that we'll coordinate efforts," Derrick said. "Our ME will work with yours and we share information."

"Fine," Kincaid replied. "But the body is to be transported to our morgue in Red River Rock. Your ME can assist with the autopsy. Take it or leave it."

Derrick was not above requesting the governor's involvement, especially since Kincaid's reticence definitely raised his curiosity. But he'd put an end to this pissing contest. He'd keep his eyes on Kincaid and find out the real reason he wanted the body to stay in Red River Rock. But he trusted Dr. White-feather not to allow any details to slip past her.

The sooner they got the autopsy done, the sooner they'd know if the body was Mia's.

SIXTY-FOUR

SOMEWHERE ON THE RIVER

The constant rocking of the riverboat kept lulling Mia into a deep, dark sleep. Except the sleep was anything but restful.

"There are no river monsters," Mama had said.

But there were. They were lurking all around her, stalking her, the scent of her fear tempting them. They rose through the fog like scaly sea creatures emerging from a ghost ship, tearing through the crashing waves.

Mia curled into the blanket on the narrow cot, willing them to disappear. But she sank deeper into the endless abyss, the monsters pecking at her bare skin, their sharp fangs drawing blood. All her life, she'd run from the creatures that skulked in the riverbed where they gathered like beasts hungrily staking out their next meal to feed to the devil.

The river is a breathing entity that gives life and takes it, the legend says. It runs deep and wide and you should fear it.

She did fear it.

The scaly serpents slithered along the surface, hiding behind the cypresses and in the moss and weeds, waiting for the right moment to pounce.

And she knew they were coming for her.

SIXTY-FIVE

CROOKED CREEK

Before leaving Red River Rock, Ellie and Derrick arranged for Laney to stay at the Moonlit Inn in town, another place named after the Moons. Laney had already placed a call to the ME in Red River Rock, a doctor named Chatterman. They agreed to meet and perform the autopsy together at seven the next morning.

Ellie was still irritated at Kincaid, but at least Derrick had negotiated a joint autopsy.

The sun had come and gone a long time ago, fatigue wearing on Ellie as she parked at Mark Wade's house. But her instincts urged her to not waste time. If Mia was alive, and not the body in that barrel, she needed his help.

Ellie braced herself as she and Derrick knocked on Mark's door. He opened it in seconds as if he'd been waiting with bated breath for them to return. She wanted to offer him hope, but she couldn't at the moment.

"May we come in, Mark?" she asked.

He nodded, a wariness replacing that sliver of hope.

"Coffee?" he asked as if to delay the inevitable.

"Sure," Ellie and Derrick replied at the same time.

They followed him to the kitchen where he filled three mugs. "Cream and sugar are on the table."

They seated themselves and Ellie stirred sweetener into the dark brew, stalling.

Derrick spoke first, "I'm afraid we have disturbing news."

Mark made a strangled sound. "Oh, God... Is she..."

"Not that we know of," Ellie jumped in, reading his mind. "But we do have some information."

Derrick cleared his throat. "Mark, have you ever heard the name Jesse Habersham?"

Mark shook his head. "No, should I know her?"

Ellie and Derrick traded a look. "I hate to tell you this," Ellie said. "But we believe that Mia was using an assumed name. DNA reports proved that her real name is Jesse Habersham."

The color drained from Mark's face and he blinked as if trying to absorb that information. "What? Jesus, you can't be serious."

"I'm afraid I am," Ellie said, gauging his reaction. He seemed genuine, the pain raw. "Jesse was a clothing designer and owned a boutique called Moonbeams in the small town of Red River Rock."

Derrick laid a photograph of Jesse on the table, and Mark cradled his head in his hands as he scrutinized it.

"She changed her hair color and she may have been wearing colored contacts," Ellie explained. "But it's the same woman."

Mark looked as if he was going to be ill. "Why... would she change her name?"

"That's what we wanted to know, so we drove to the town to talk to people who knew her as Jesse," Ellie continued.

Confusion clouded his eyes, impatience in his voice. "For God's sake, just tell me what you learned."

"Jesse Habersham was engaged to a man named Kevin

Moon. He's a real estate broker in Red River Rock, and his family owns most of the town."

"Mia was engaged before?" he asked, his voice cracking.

"Yes," Ellie said. "In fact she disappeared on her wedding day shortly after she and Mr. Moon exchanged vows."

"I don't believe this." Mark started shaking. "If she was already married, why would she agree to marry me? Why would she buy a dress and flowers and pick a venue and... why wouldn't she have told me about all this?"

"All questions we need to answer." Ellie reached out and squeezed his shoulder. "It's possible she was running from something. Or someone. That she was afraid."

Mark suddenly stood, anger sharpening his eyes. "I need to be alone right now." His voice broke, and Ellie and Derrick stood.

"I understand this is disturbing," Ellie said softly. "But if you think of anything that might help, something Mia may have mentioned, no matter how small, please give me a call."

She and Derrick started toward the door, but Mark's voice stopped them. "Did you talk to this other man? Mia's hu... husband?"

Ellie slowly turned to face him. "We did."

"What did he have to say about this?"

"He seemed just as shocked as you that Jesse had taken another name," Ellie said. "That she was even still alive."

She knew Mark well enough to believe him. But she didn't know Kevin Moon at all.

SIXTY-SIX

RED RIVER ROCK

Kevin Moon stared at the river running behind his custom-designed house, watching the water ripple and crash.

He'd built this home for Jesse and the family they'd longed for.

Now she had a daughter.

He curled his hands into fists. Ever since his father had called the night before and told him about the child, he'd been tormented.

Was the little girl he'd seen on TV his daughter? If so, why would Jesse keep her from him? Why had she run away? He'd loved Jesse with every fiber of his being; this was tearing him apart.

The fact that she'd been living in another town and seeing another man made his head want to explode.

This little girl was four. Jesse had run out on him five years ago. Had she been pregnant at the time?

He picked up their engagement picture and traced his finger over her face, remembering her gorgeous eyes. The silkiness of her hair. Her soft pliant lips. Her adoring smile.

Time swept him back to the day that other girl had been found in the river.

He'd fallen to his knees and sobbed like a baby, thinking it was his Jesse. Looking at her had been impossible. So painful he'd thought he'd die himself.

The days he waited on the autopsy had been excruciating.

Then the call with the results. He and his father rushed to the morgue and met the ME Dr. Leonard Garrett.

"The woman is not Jesse," Dr. Garrett said. "Her name is Stella Carnes. She was dead long before she was put in the river."

Kevin staggered backward with relief and hope. If this woman wasn't Jesse, then she might still be alive.

The wind hurled a branch from the tree and banged it against the window, jarring him back to the present. He squeezed the photograph in his hand so tight the glass shattered. Sharp fragments jabbed his skin, blood dripping from his hand.

He stalked to the kitchen, grabbed a hand towel from the drawer and wrapped it around his bloody palm.

Tomorrow, he'd call the PI he'd used before and have him locate the little girl. If the child was his, he'd find out. Then he'd go to her rescue. Make sure she knew her father was very much alive.

SIXTY-SEVEN
CROOKED CREEK

DAY 3

Pixie bit her bottom lip to keep from crying again as Norah decorated her pancake with a smiley face made of chocolate chips.

"Make an emoji face," Norah said with a toothless grin.

Pixie didn't feel like it, but Norah was so excited and kept bopping up and down in her chair, twisting her long red hair around her finger.

"Pixie?" Norah tugged at her arm. "It can be any kind of face. Make it silly."

Pixie wanted to smile at Norah, but her mouth wouldn't turn into one cause all she could think about was her mommy and how she hadn't come back. She liked sleepovers, but she didn't have her own clothes here or her special blanket and even though she liked Ms. Emily's cause there was always kids to play with, she didn't feel like playing.

But Norah had let Pixie sleep with her big stuffed teddy bear and had snuggled up to her last night when she woke up crying. So she picked up a chocolate chip and made one eye, then another, then a triangle for a nose. Then she lined them up to make a mouth, only this one was turning down.

Her chest hurt and her throat felt weird again and she dribbled the syrup to make teardrops below the chocolate chip eyes. Her pancakes were crying, just like she was inside.

SIXTY-EIGHT

Determined to find some answers today, Ellie stopped to pick up breakfast at the Corner Café and slid onto a bar stool beside Cord. The morning crowd was steady with locals and tourists, the air filled with aroma of cinnamon rolls, bacon, sausage and country fried ham.

The gossipy biddies in town led by Maude Hazelnut hovered, eyes darting around for any juicy tidbits for their next brood session. Crystal Marrs entered, her silky caftan sweeping the floor, tiny bone earrings dangling to her shoulders as she walked breezily to a table and seated herself. Families were decked out in red, white and blue in honor of the Memorial Day weekend, the kids chattering excitedly about the parade.

Cord sipped his coffee while Lola set a plate of eggs and country fried ham in front of him and left Ellie a cup of coffee.

"Thanks, Lola," they said at the same time.

"Sure." Lola gave Ellie a chilly look. "I'll get your food in a minute. Gotta take care of Bryce and Mandy."

Ellie nodded, wondering what had Lola off today. She seemed on edge. Then again, maybe she was just busy with the breakfast crowd. Memorial weekend had brought them in in droves. Good for Crooked Creek's economy, especially considering that the recent crimes had taken its toll on tourism. She'd even heard a few locals were moving out of town, touting that Crooked Creek was too dangerous a place to raise a family. That it was happening under her watch hammered guilt even deeper into Ellie.

Cord watched Lola while he chomped a piece of ham, his expression troubled too. What was going on with the two of them?

Not your business, Ellie. Your friend is missing.

Still, she studied Lola as she stood laughing and chatting with Bryce and his daughter – her niece – Mandy. The teenager had struggled a couple of months ago when she and her friends had discovered the bones of several children at an abandoned orphanage. Ellie had rescued Mandy and was glad she and Bryce seemed to be forging a relationship. Mandy needed him.

And he needed her. She'd begun to see a change in Bryce since he'd learned he had a daughter.

Cord sipped his coffee and angled his head toward her. "You sleep last night?"

She shrugged. "Some. But I keep thinking about Mia and wondering if she's okay or if... she was in that barrel."

"That sheriff didn't seem very cooperative."

"He wasn't. He insisted the autopsy be performed at his morgue. Laney stayed in Red River Rock last night so she can assist with it."

Cord forked up a bite of fried egg. "You don't trust the sheriff?"

Ellie made a harumph sound. "I don't trust anyone." A little smile tugged at her mouth. "Well, maybe except for you. And Derrick. And Shondra. Laney, too." They made a good team.

He chuckled. "Happy to be among that list."

"You've earned it, Cord. I know you'll always be honest with me."

His eyes flickered with some emotion she couldn't quite define as he locked gazes with her. A second later, it disappeared and he looked down into his plate, picked up his biscuit, slathered it with peach jelly, and ate half of it in one bite.

The air suddenly stilled in the café, voices dying and heads turning as Mark Wade and Liam James walked inside.

Ellie gripped her coffee mug, the atmosphere in the room causing even the tourists to quiet.

Aware people were staring at them, Mark and Liam stopped at the door, both tensing. When they saw Ellie, they headed toward her, patrons gawking at them.

Ellie swallowed hard, stood and met them, ignoring the stares and whispers, then herded them outside away from prying eyes.

SIXTY-NINE

"We went to the police station to see you," Mark started when they were outside. "But they said you weren't there. Then I spotted your Jeep here."

"What the hell is going on?" Liam barked. "Mark said Mia wasn't really Mia, that she was some woman named Jesse."

She forced herself to remain calm. Both men had reason to be upset. Both had lost women they loved. One whose wife had been murdered in cold blood.

"That's where the investigation has led," Ellie said. "We matched DNA from the scene at the wedding to a woman named Jesse Habersham who disappeared from Red River Rock five years ago. Her DNA also matched Mia's. Special Agent Fox and I have spoken to the sheriff who investigated Jesse's disappearance."

Mark's labored breath rattled in the air. "And?"

"I don't know the reason she disappeared, yet. If it was foul play or if she planned it," Ellie admitted. "But I'm headed back to Red River Rock today. I understand this is difficult for both of you but bear with me. I will get to the bottom of this."

Liam shot her and Mark a furious glare. "So what you're

saying is that my wife was murdered because Mia was a damn liar?" He gripped Mark's shirt. "Did you know who she really was?"

"Of course not," Mark said defensively.

Ellie rushed to diffuse the situation. "Listen, both of you. Don't do this. Don't blame each other. I suspect this situation is far more complicated than we think. There had to be something really wrong for her to lie to all of us."

Liam released his friend with a little shove and Mark took it without pushing back.

Ellie gave them a moment as two more vehicles pulled into the parking lot. A family unloaded from the van and strolled into the café.

The tension was palpable as they waited until the people stepped inside before continuing.

"You said Mia..." Mark's voice wobbled. "That Jesse disappeared from her wedding to a man named Kevin Moon. Do you think he had something to do with this?"

Ellie did not want to incite suspicions to the point Mark might attempt to find answers for himself. "I honestly don't know. But I have to warn you that when his father realized Mia had a child, he questioned whether or not the child was Kevin's. I'm just telling you in case they try to reach you."

Worry dimmed Mark's eyes. "Oh, my God. What if Pixie's his daughter?"

SEVENTY

Of course both men would question the identity of Pixie's father. Ellie was wondering herself.

"We'll run a DNA sample to determine paternity," Ellie said. "Although Mia could have met someone and had a relationship after she left Kevin."

"Or she could have cheated on this guy Kevin and had that man's baby," Liam said, his voice bitter.

With more questions than answers, Ellie could not argue at this point. "Again, we'll compare DNA to determine that."

She had to cut this short and get moving. "Sorry, guys, I have a press conference in a few minutes. I promise to keep you updated on anything I learn."

Mark cleared his throat. "Please, Ellie, find her. I know she lied to me, but... still..."

She squeezed his arm. "I won't give up until I do. She was my friend, too." Mia's smile as she planted sunflowers in Ellie's yard taunted her. Mia had looked so happy and at peace. There was no way Ellie could have been that wrong about her. Whatever had happened, Mia was in trouble and needed her.

The sun poked through gray clouds, the heat rising to the

mid-eighties and the cloying humidity making it hard to breathe. It was going to be a scorcher today.

She ducked back inside to get her to-go order and saw Bryce paying his bill and Lola still talking to him. Cord looked sullen as he watched them, arousing her curiosity again. When Lola spotted her, she rushed to the kitchen then returned a minute later, handing over her food.

Ellie thanked her, paid cash, then left, knowing Angelica would be waiting. She'd already given her the green light to report on Tori's murder.

SEVENTY-ONE

RED RIVER ROCK

He watched the press conference in Crooked Creek with a football-sized knot in his gut. The lead detective, Ellie Reeves, was a pint-sized ash-blond woman with a ponytail and soulful blue eyes. She looked harmless. But he knew different. She was a storm to be reckoned with. She'd plowed through multiple cases, brought down vicious serial killers, and was still standing.

She's never dealt with the likes of you though.

Another curse rolled off his tongue, and he blotted the sweat on his forehead with a handkerchief as she spoke into the camera.

"We are still searching for Mia Norman, who has been missing now two days, and working the investigation into Tori James' murder, which we believe is connected." The detective lifted her chin as she continued, "In more news, late yesterday the body of another woman was found in a whiskey barrel near Red River Rock. At this point, the remains have not been identified and we don't know if her death is related to our current investigations or not. We're working in conjunction with the Red River Rock Police Department to determine what happened. Again, we implore anyone with information regarding these cases to call our office."

"There you have it," the reporter Angelica Gomez said. "We'll keep you abreast of any developments in these stories as soon as information becomes available."

He punched off the television with a curse then snatched his phone and made a call.

"Did you see the news? That damn ranger discovered a whiskey barrel with a body in it. How the hell could you be so sloppy?"

"It should have sunk to the bottom by now," came the reply. "I can't help it if the weather knocked down a tree and it got caught up in it."

"The last thing we need is a slew of damn cops crawling all over Foggy Mountain." Their town had its secrets and he'd managed to keep them hidden for years.

"Don't worry. If she gets too close, we'll take care of her."

"A fucking fed is with her, too," he bellowed. "You mark my words. No one is going to ruin what we have going here. And if you screw it up, you'll end up in a damn barrel yourself."

He didn't wait for a response. He hung up, knowing his message was received. Others had tried to betray him before. And they had learned their lesson.

There were some deaths that came easy. Some more painful. Some begged to end their lives and stop the suffering.

Ellie gathered the information they had and met Captain Hale, Deputy Eastwood, Deputy Landrum and Bryce in the conference room at the police station while Derrick remained in her office and made some phone calls. Everyone shuffled in with coffee, tea and water, gathering around the table.

"How'd the press conference go?" Bryce asked.

Ellie was surprised he hadn't seen it. He usually basked in the media attention. "Short. Can't report too much at this time. How's Mandy doing?"

"Better," he said with a small smile. "She's starting to see her friends again. And she calls me sometimes."

"Good," Ellie said. "Even if she doesn't act like it, she needs you, Bryce. Every girl needs her father." She saw Pixie's face in her mind and hesitated. Pixie loved Mark like a father. But if Kevin Moon was her birth father, would she live with him? And how would that affect the little girl?

A sheepish look crossed Bryce's face, and Ellie smiled. Bryce had come a long way from his drinking days.

Ellie laid the folder containing the photos they'd assembled on the table. Her boss tapped his watch to indicate they should start and Ellie crossed the room. First, she tacked Mia Norman's picture on the whiteboard and wrote her name below it. Everyone in the room knew what had happened but sometimes laying it all out triggered something to click in their minds.

"Our case started with the disappearance of Mia Norman on her wedding day. There were signs of a struggle in the brides' dressing room." She added the crime scene images. "I found her four-year-old daughter Pixie locked in the bathroom, leaving us to believe that either Mia locked her inside to keep her safe, or if Mia was abducted, that her kidnapper did."

"Did Pixie see anything?" Shondra asked.

"No," Ellie said. "She was pretty upset and heard a man's voice but didn't recognize it." Next, she added pictures of Mia's house. "When Special Agent Fox and I went to Mia's house, it had been ransacked. Most interestingly, photographs of Mia and Mark had been destroyed."

Bryce lifted a finger. "Do you think Mark destroyed them out of rage because she left him at the altar?"

Ellie breathed out. "That is a possibility, I suppose. But I was with him when he saw the place and he seemed stunned. He's also a model citizen and teacher in the community. At this point, he's not high on the suspect list."

She paused, then added a photo of Tori James. "While we searched the resort for Mia, Ranger McCord found the body of Mia's maid of honor in the river." Crime photos of the scene and Tori's bloody body went up next. "She was shot in the back, suggesting she was running from her attacker. We questioned Mia's fiancé, Mark Wade, and Tori's husband, Liam James, who both appeared devastated. They were together all day so we've eliminated them as persons of interest."

She tensed, another thought striking her. Mark may have seemed genuinely shocked at the possibility that Mia had lied about Pixie's father, but what if he'd discovered that fact prior to the wedding? That would have been motive for him to call off the wedding or to hurt Mia.

But no... not to kill Tori. And she still couldn't imagine Mark as a killer...

"Do you have *any* suspects?" Captain Hale asked.

Ellie shrugged. "Nothing definite. There's a new development though. Mia left instructions that if anything happened to her to contact a couple named Jo-Jo and Seth Pennington. Agent Fox and I searched for them and learned they were murdered four years ago." She placed a picture of the crime scene at their house. "At first, the detective who investigated thought it was a home invasion but there were signs that the couple were tortured. Their house was ransacked, just like Mia's. Somehow they're connected but we don't know how yet."

Derrick looked up from his computer. "I'm working on that."

"Who is this woman?" Bryce asked with an eyebrow raise.

"That's what we're going to figure out," Ellie said.

Next, she tacked a picture of Jesse Habersham beside Mia's. "Now meet Jesse Habersham. She owned a small clothing boutique in Red River Rock."

A rumble of recognition echoed through the room. "They're the same," Shondra muttered.

"They are." Ellie gave them a moment to let that sink in. "It gets even stranger – five years ago Jesse Habersham disappeared from her own wedding to a man named Kevin Moon. We spoke to him and he also appeared shocked that she was alive and using the name Mia Norman. He talked about how much he loved Jesse and claimed to know nothing about where his wife was or why she left."

"She enjoys leading men on then jilting them," Bryce said.

Shondra let out a sound that sounded like disgust. "Or she's running from something or someone."

SEVENTY-THREE

Questions nagged at Derrick about what they'd uncovered so far. He pulled the copy of Detective Mathis' notes on the Pennington case and thumbed through it, studying the pictures of the crime scene at the Pennington's house. It was so violent. Brutal.

Either a psycho intending to inflict pain or someone wanting answers. Had they gotten what they'd wanted before they killed the couple?

They'd been murdered four years ago. If it was about Mia and they'd learned her whereabouts, why hadn't they come for her before now? Unless the couple hadn't folded...

The second question needling him was why Mia would want to turn her child over to complete strangers? There had to be a reason. She trusted them for some reason.

Mathis had mentioned that Seth Pennington had a brother. He shuffled the papers and found the man's number then stepped from the room and called it. The phone rang five times then rolled over to voicemail. *"This is Steven Pennington. I'm currently unavailable. Please leave a message and I'll get back with you as soon as possible."*

"This is Special Agent Derrick Fox. Please call me when you have a minute." He left a number and asked him to return his call.

While he waited, he returned to the conference room, took his seat again and looked up the birth certificate for Jesse Habersham. Two women by that name cropped up, but only one fitting the age he had.

Jesse Habersham, seven pounds, two ounces, nineteen inches long, born to parents Helen and Douglas Habersham, May 25 in Cumming, Georgia.

Mia/Jesse said she had no family so he searched death certificates next and found copies for Helen and Douglas Habersham. Both deceased on the same day.

Curious about how they'd died, he ran a search on them and found an article about their death.

Helen Habersham, age thirty-five, and Douglas Habersham, thirty-seven, died in a tragic accident during a storm on the Chattahoochee River, August 27. The couple were survived by daughters Jesse, age seven, and her sister Jo-Jo, age eleven.

Derrick drummed his fingers on the table. That was the connection. Jo-Jo was Jesse's sister.

SEVENTY-FOUR

"I think you're right, Shondra," Ellie said. "I think Jesse was running from something. Agent Fox and I are going back to Red River Rock today to dig deeper. We suspect Jesse was afraid of someone there."

"What about that woman they found in the barrel?" Landrum asked.

"I'm waiting on her ID. Dr. Whitefeather is there now assisting with the autopsy. Due to the state of the remains, it may take some time." She inhaled. "This is what I need from you."

Captain Hale signaled he wanted to say something. "I need Deputy Eastwood here to cover in town. What with all the tourists and the Memorial Day festivities, we can't leave our own unguarded."

Ellie knew he was right, although Shondra didn't look pleased that he'd assigned her to the more routine tasks. But Landrum had been here longer and had rank. Besides, he was a techie and good at digging up information behind the scenes.

"Please go on," Hale said.

Ellie nodded. "Red River Rock's sheriff insisted the autopsy be performed there which makes me wonder if he's hiding something. Bryce, why don't you use your contacts and find out what you can on Kincaid?"

"Glad to."

"Deputy Landrum, I'd like you to see what you can find out about Armond Moon. He and his son Kevin own most of Red River Rock."

"Copy that," Landrum replied.

Derrick raised a finger. "I know the connection between Mia and the Penningtons."

Ellie gave him the seat. And?"

"Jo-Jo Pennington's maiden name was Habersham. She and Jesse were sisters."

Ellie made a clicking sound with her teeth. "That makes sense now, that she'd want her sister to have Pixie. Although according to Kevin, Jesse had no family. Mark said the same."

"They could have been estranged," Derrick suggested.

"Or she lied to Kevin and Mark," Bryce said.

"Or Kevin Moon could have lied," Deputy Landrum pointed out.

Ellie nodded. "Mia must not have known her sister and brother-in-law were dead. It fits that whoever killed the Penningtons was looking for Jesse."

She turned to Shondra. "Go by Mia's and collect Pixie's toothbrush or hairbrush and get it to the lab. We need to find out if Kevin Moon is Pixie's paternal father."

"You think he'll want custody if she is?" Shondra asked.

Ellie twisted her mouth in thought. "I have a feeling he will. All the more reason we dig deep into him and see if he had anything to do with Jesse's disappearance and her sister and brother-in-law's murders." If he did, little Pixie could be in danger.

SEVENTY-FIVE

SOMEWHERE ON THE RIVER

Mia was so weak she could barely lift her head. She wished she could keep her eyes open and summon enough energy to break down the door to this cabin. But her lids felt heavy, her stomach queasy and her body limp.

She tried to reach the bottle of water on the tiny end table, but her hand was trembling so badly she dropped it and water soaked her clothes. A frustrated sob caught in her throat and her eyes drifted shut as the tears fell.

The boat rocked and dipped and she was thrown back in time again, back to when she was Jesse.

Her parents were dead and gone. They had been for years. The river had taken them. The monsters had come for her as she and Jo-Jo had been swept away by the current.

Now she and Jo-Jo were standing at her grandmother's grave. Wind hurled dead leaves across the brittle grass and clouds gathered, raindrops falling like tears onto the tombstone. The people who'd come to the graveside started rushing toward their cars. Engines fired up and she and her sister were left alone with the memories and the emptiness.

"I'm going to find out what happened to Mama and Daddy," Jesse said.

Jo-Jo was four years older than her but she acted like she was Jesse's mother. "No, Jess. Grandma said not to ask questions. That it was too dangerous."

"That's just it," Jesse said. "I'm not a kid anymore. I remember things..."

Jo-Jo clenched her arm. "What kind of things?"

Jesse pressed a hand to her mouth to stifle a sob. "We were trying to get away. And someone was after us." She tugged at Jo-Jo's hand. "What do you remember?"

"Same," Jo-Jo admitted. "I... think it had something to do with me," she said in a raw whisper. "But I don't know what. And... I'm not sure I want to know."

Jesse dug her heels into the wet earth, wiping raindrops from her face as they splattered her. "Well, I do. And I'm going to Red River Rock to get some answers."

Jo-Jo pleaded and begged her not to go, that she was afraid for her.

But the next morning, she packed her bags and went anyway.

The memories receded and Mia blinked, battling nausea and fear as footsteps pounded outside the cabin door. Her body shook with tears and rage. That day was the beginning of the end for Jesse.

Ellie called Laney as they drove into Red River Rock. Just like Crooked Creek, the town was decked out for the holiday.

"Hey, Ellie," Laney said, her voice slightly muffled as if she didn't want anyone to hear her. "I'm at Dr. Homer Chatterman's office. The medical examiner is working on the remains now."

"How's it going?" Ellie asked.

"He's made it plain and clear that he doesn't want me here or assisting at all," she said. "Sheriff Kincaid was talking to him this morning when I arrived and they got all hush-hush when I showed up." A heartbeat passed. "I don't know what's going on. But I insisted on being in the room and documenting what I saw, and neither of them are happy about it."

Was the small town ME simply protective of his own morgue or... was he covering for someone?

"If he poses a real problem, let me know and Agent Fox will call the governor. And make sure he sends DNA to the lab so we can ID the victim."

"Don't worry, Ellie. I'm not backing down. I'll get copies of the autopsy results and oversee every test he runs. The last case taught me that anything can happen in a small town and not everyone in law enforcement can be trusted."

Laney was referring to the former sheriff of Crooked Creek who'd murdered her mother years back and tried to kill Laney to protect himself.

"Thanks, Laney. I know the last few months have been difficult."

"Hey, I survived thanks to your good work and I won't let you down on this one. If Dr. Chatterman tries to withhold evidence, I'll handle it."

Unexpected emotion overcame Ellie. "Just be careful. And I mean it – call if you need anything."

"Of course."

As they hung up, Ellie had a bad feeling in her gut. The only reason she could think of that Kincaid and the medical examiner would want to derail their investigation was if they were involved in Jesse's disappearance or Mia's, or if they were covering it up.

Sheriff Larry Kincaid gripped his phone with a curse as the man on the line shouted at him.

"What the hell is going on? I thought you had things covered there in Red River Rock. You swore—"

"Calm the hell down. The situation is under control." He ran a finger over the mole on his chin, which was bugging the shit out of him. He needed to see the dermatologist but who had time for self-care when the world was blowing up all around him?

"How can you say that? I saw that detective on the news. She's had her ass into every crime that's happened in these parts. She might look like a little darling, but that's the last thing she is. She'll bury us all." He wheezed a breath. "And she's working with a goddamn fed. That's trouble."

"Just keep your cool. We talked about this. There is nothing for them to find." Kincaid unlocked his desk drawer and opened it, then pulled a file from inside. The one that held the truth.

"I've handled everything. Just take care of your part."

Cursing the day he got involved in all this, Kincaid gathered the papers that could expose the rotten lies and fed them into the shredder, watching the evidence spew out in mutilated pieces.

Their secrets were safe. At least for now.

But he needed to warn Doc Chatterman to stay the course.

SEVENTY-EIGHT
POSSUM POINT

Ronnie set the iron skillet with the red-eyed gray on the table, then scooped up a spoonful and poured it over the mashed taters she cooked to go with her fried chitlins.

Her boys were already chowing down on the crunchy pig intestines, licking their fingers. Gravy ran down Lloyd's chin and Chester chewed with his mouth open while he reached for a shot of moonshine.

She shot him a don't-you-dare look. "You got too much to do today to get knee-walking before noon," she snapped.

"What's today, Mama?" Chester said through a mouthful of taters.

"Make the rounds. Let everyone know to keep their mouths shut or else."

Lloyd grinned at the *or else.* He was brawny and sadistic and enjoyed putting the fear of God in the dumb nuts around town who got themselves in a mess.

Ronnie scoffed down her ham then shoved her plate aside. "Clean up when you finish. I got stuff to do today."

Chester sopped gravy up with his biscuit. "Where you going, Mama?"

"To make sure our business is safe."

She'd made a pact with the devil a long time ago. And she had to keep it.

SEVENTY-NINE
MOONBEAMS

"Let's talk to some locals," Ellie said as she parked in the center of Red River Rock. "See what they have to say about Jesse and the Moons."

Derrick looked up from a text. "The Bureau has nothing on Kincaid. Maybe someone in town can shed some light."

"Good point." Ellie and Derrick walked toward Moonbeams, the boutique Jesse had opened. No surprise that a moon-shaped sign adorned the shop and colorful dreamcatchers hung around the space, a crystal windchime tinkling when they entered.

The shop looked eclectic with areas holding earrings, purses, and hats. Cowboy boots filled a tall wall, along with hot pink, yellow, and purple glittery knee-high boots.

Racks of clothes lined two walls and a circular rack in the center of the room offered one-of-a-kind, trendy designs. Two teens were oohing and aahing over the pieces they'd selected as they ducked into the curtained-off dressing rooms.

"This place may be in the mountains but it's designed for fashionistas." Ellie wrinkled her nose. She couldn't reconcile these designs with the down-to-earth gardener she knew as Mia.

A twenty-something young woman with a pink streak in her black shoulder-length hair and a row of earrings sparkling along her ears looked up and smiled. "Welcome to Moonbeams."

After they crossed the room, Ellie introduced them. "We'd like to talk to you about Jesse Habersham." The girl's nametag read Missy. "Did you know her?"

Missy began folding a stack of scarves. "No, she ran out on her husband a few years ago. Don't know why. Kevin Moon was a catch."

"So you know the Moons?"

She laughed. "Everyone on Foggy Mountain knows the Moons. They own the boutique and most of the businesses around here."

"Were you living here when Jesse disappeared?"

The girl's eyes remained focused on the scarves. "Yeah, but I was in community college and didn't have the money to shop in this store."

"We know Jesse designed her own line of clothing. Did she design the merchandise you carry now?"

"We still have a few pieces," Missy said. "But most of it is stuff I chose. I'm the buyer now and styles change, you know."

"Yes, I know," Ellie said, although she wasn't into fashion herself. Jeans and flannel shirts suited her better.

"So what do you think happened to her?" Ellie asked.

The girl shrugged. "Lots of gossip went around. First off, people thought she was kidnapped. Then they found that other girl in the river and people thought she stole money from the boutique and ran off with another man."

Ellie leaned against the counter. "Did people speculate about anyone in particular? Another friend of Jesse's?"

"Not really. It was just gossip. I mean, why else leave Kevin?"

"That's what we're trying to figure out," Ellie replied.

"Any talk that Kevin cheated on Jesse?" Derrick interjected.

"God, no," Missy said.

"Would he possibly have hurt her?" Ellie asked.

"No way. He worshipped her. Even found a company to produce her designs so she could expand. She should have been grateful."

Maybe, Ellie thought. But there had to be more to the story.

"Sounds like you think a lot of the Moons," Derrick said. "Are they hands on with the running of the boutique?"

"Kevin takes care of the books, but he pretty much lets me do the buying and we've started carrying my own designs. Has them made for a bargain to increase profit." No wonder she was singing his praises.

Missy's cell phone buzzed, and she glanced at it then gestured for them to wait. Turning her back to them, she answered the call, then spoke in a low whisper.

"I am, don't worry," Missy said. "I'm handling it. I can't talk right now. I'll call you back."

A second later, she stuffed the phone back in her pocket and sighed. "Listen, I got some new merchandise I need to put out for the holiday. We done here? 'Cause if you want me to badmouth the Moons, it's not going to happen. I owe them."

Knowing she had all she'd get from the young woman, Ellie laid her card on the counter. "If you think of anything that might help us find out what happened to Jesse, please call me."

Missy eyed the card but didn't pick it up.

"That was interesting," said Ellie, once they were outside.

"Yep. She's not going to badmouth the family who's buttering her bread."

"I wonder who that call was from," Ellie said glancing back at the store. "She certainly shut us down right after it."

She glanced through the window. Missy finally picked up the card, then she tossed it into the trash and snagged her phone again. Her dark lips curled into a frown and she paced back and forth behind the counter, clearly upset.

What had she meant when she said she was handling it? Was she talking about the business? Or was she referring to them?

EIGHTY

Ellie and Derrick walked from Moonbeams to the souvenir shop, Moondust. T-shirts boasting the name of the town catered to tourists with shelves of trinkets, natural stones and gems. Small vials containing fake moondust were also a commodity.

The store manager was a robust woman who also praised the Moons. "Wouldn't have no job without that family," she said as she motioned to another clerk to take over the register.

"I do remember Jesse," she said, her eye twitching. "Always thought her designs were ahead of the times for these parts, but they weren't as wild as Missy's."

"Do you know anything about Jesse's disappearance?" Derrick asked.

"Just what the Moons said. She ran off and left poor Kevin." She clucked her teeth. "Boy was all busted up for months."

They chatted for another moment before leaving, passing the coined-laundromat, which was empty, then stopping in the convenience store. Hunched behind the checkout counter, a scrawny gray-haired man in overalls squinted through coke-bottle glasses. His name tag read Buster and an opened can of Pabst Blue Ribbon sat behind the counter.

Derrick introduced them, then asked about the Moons. The man coughed into his hand, eyes darting around the store as if to make sure they were alone.

"People round here owe 'em," Buster said.

"Does that include you?" Ellie asked.

His wrinkled face twisted into a scowl. "Yeah. Fell on hard times but Moon asked me to run this place. Ain't glamorous but keeps the lights on."

And him in beer, Ellie thought.

"Did you know Jesse Habersham?" Derrick asked.

"Seen her around, but never talked to her."

Just then, a short beefy guy with a scraggly beard in overalls entered, his eyes cutting to Buster, his teeth stained from chewing tobacco.

As the man veered toward the back by the cooler, Buster ducked his head and his hand trembled as he reached for his PBR.

Ellie left her card with him and they exited, but her anxiety was mounting. They visited two more shops with the same response each time. Everyone owed the Moons.

"Let's go into Moon Pies then head to Moondoggy's for lunch." Cafés were always a hub of gossip and conversation.

"I haven't had a Moon Pie since I was a kid," Derrick said.

"These are homemade," Ellie said as they entered. "Look, they even have RC colas." One of her favorite Southern treats when she and her dad went camping was an RC cola and a Moon Pie.

A bell rang as they entered and Ellie saw a woman behind the counter handing over Moon Pies to three children and another two to the parents with a smile. She was as wide as she was tall and her apron was dusted with flour and dotted with chocolate stains.

When she saw them, her smile faded.

Ellie smiled and introduced them as they stepped up to the

counter, asking her name. Always better to appear friendly and non-confrontational.

"Name's Opal Dean," the woman replied, "but folks around here call me Ms. Opal," she said, as if she was proud they respected her.

"Hi, Ms. Opal. Your Moon Pies look great. We'll take a couple to go," Derrick said.

The woman wrapped two pies and put them in a bag, but her eyes kept shooting to the door. The same reaction Buster had had.

"Did you know Jesse Habersham?" Ellie asked as she picked an RC cola from the glass case next to the counter.

The woman shuddered then glanced up at the corner. A security camera hung from the wall, making Ellie wonder if Opal Dean was sending her a message.

"Didn't know her. So got nothing to say."

The truth dawned on Ellie. The camera was not there for Opal Dean's protection. The woman had nothing to say because someone was watching.

EIGHTY-ONE

The sun was blinding as Ellie walked outside to her Jeep. Children ran through the splash pad at the park, laughing and squealing. Birds twittered and a flock of geese gathered around the pond.

"Did you notice Ms. Opal looking at the security camera?" Ellie asked as they climbed in her vehicle and headed toward Moondoggy's, the local restaurant on the river that boasted they served the best fried catfish and hushpuppies in the South.

"Yes," Derrick said, pulling on Aviator shades. "She looked nervous."

"So did Buster and Missy," Ellie said. "I saw cameras in the other stores, too. At first, I thought they'd been installed for the owner's protection, but now I'm wondering—"

"If someone is monitoring the storeowners," Derrick finished.

Their gazes locked. "Exactly. Something's not right in this town, Derrick. I feel it."

"I know what you mean. Everyone seems too hush-hushed and indebted to the Moons."

"As if the Moons hold the power and everyone protects them no matter what."

Using his tablet, Derrick began to search for information. "You've heard of the Redneck Mafia. What if this is something like that?"

"Could be," Ellie said, driving past the sheriff's office. "Moonshining, stills, and meth labs are common in the mountains."

Derrick focused on researching the Moon family while Ellie turned onto a winding road that led to the river. Wisteria and honeysuckle dotted the untamed land, the sharp curves shadowed by evergreens. Two miles later, they reached a section called the Riverwalk.

"Look at this," she muttered in awe. "This was countryside when I was little. But now it's filled with businesses. Looks like they've taken advantage of the river location."

Derrick gestured to the land. "The Moons own all of this, too. They brought the property and developed it from the ground up."

Unease skittered up Ellie's spine. "Which means they run this part of the mountain as well." And could be knee-deep in whatever illegal activities might be going on.

EIGHTY-TWO

MOONDOGGY'S

Kevin spotted his father at his usual table in Moondoggy's, the restaurant and bar they'd bought a while back.

His father sat in the rear by the window overlooking the water outside but facing the door so he could keep an eye on the employees and everyone who entered.

The tension in Kevin's body made it almost impossible to breathe. His father was on the phone, his head bent, deep frown lines creasing his tanned face.

Armond Moon was a cutthroat businessman and Kevin had learned everything he knew about the real estate business from him. Life was about money and power and his father reveled in it.

He'd also tried to micromanage Kevin's personal life, which had its fair share of problems.

He hung up abruptly when Kevin sat down.

"What was that about?" Kevin asked.

"Just confirming things are on track." A cold look flashed in his eyes. "With that detective and fed nosing around, we have to be careful."

Didn't he know it? They fell silent for a moment while the

waitress brought his father a scotch and lifted a brow in question toward him. "The same?"

He nodded and waited until she returned to the bar, then spoke, "They said Jesse has a little girl. She's four years old, Father. Did you know?"

Armond rocked back in his chair, anger deepening the lines around his eyes. "How would I know?"

"Because you know everything," Kevin said under his breath. "I know you hired someone to investigate Jesse when we were together and after she disappeared."

The ice in his drink clinked as he sipped his scotch. "I had to protect our interests, ensure she was a solid investment. Unlike you, I don't make decisions with my dick."

A muscle ticked in Kevin's jaw, but he ignored the jab. "I hired a PI to find out where the child is. If she's mine, I'm going to get custody."

"What will you do with a child?" his father asked.

Kevin grinned. "Use her to get Jesse back."

His father cursed. "Fool."

Kevin let that comment roll off his back, too. All his life he'd tried to please the old man. Done everything he'd asked, even when he knew he was handing his soul to Satan on a silver platter.

But Jesse was his wife. She'd promised to love him until death do us part.

He intended to see that she kept that promise.

EIGHTY-THREE

Ellie parked at the rustic wood restaurant and bar, which had been built on the river. The parking lot was full of SUVs and trucks carrying locals, tourists, and adventure seekers hauling their kayaks and canoes to the put-in spot.

Trees shuddered in the wind that blazed through the mountains, branches sagging. The river had risen from the recent rains and the current tossed water onto the bank, only inches below the dock. Turtles and fish splashed along, children gathering to watch.

Inside the décor was just as rustic, with one wall showcasing license plates from various states, another paddles and photos of rafters. Country music echoed from an old-fashioned juke box. The place was packed, noisy chatter and laughter surrounding them. A chalkboard hung on the wall listing the daily specials.

The hostess, a college-aged girl in a tie-dyed tank top and shorts greeted them. "Table for two?"

"Please," Ellie said.

She seated them by a window overlooking the water and mountains, and a tall middle-aged woman with a bad perm sauntered over with a pencil tucked in her hair.

"Hey y'all. I'm Thelma. What you having today?"

"The catfish with the collards and tea," Derrick answered.

Ellie scanned the menu on the chalkboard and spotted a security camera in the corner. "Barbecue chicken with mashed potatoes, and I'll try that blackberry lemonade."

"Sure enough." Thelma fluttered her hand. "Be right back."

"Kevin Moon and his father are here," Derrick said, tilting his head to the rear.

Ellie glanced their way. "Looks like they're arguing," Ellie said. "Wonder what that's about."

After a few minutes, Thelma brought their drinks and food, sliding them onto the table. "Y'all enjoy."

"Can we ask you something, Thelma?" Ellie asked. "We're investigating Jesse Habersham's disappearance. Did you know her?"

She pursed her lips. "Why you asking about her? She ran out on poor Kevin five years ago."

Everyone in Red River Rock seemed to believe Kevin was the victim. "Her disappearance may be related to another case," replied Ellie. "What can you tell us about her?"

Thelma cut her eyes toward the Moons then gave Ellie a crooked smile. "She seemed real nice, that is until she broke Kevin's heart."

"I take it the Moons own this place," Derrick said.

"You'd be right about that," Thelma said.

"Did Kevin and Jesse have problems?" Ellie asked.

A frisson of alarm glinted in Thelma's eyes. "How would I know?"

Ellie offered her a smile. "Small town. People talk."

"Not in this town, they don't," Thelma said. "I mind my own business." Lifting her chin stubbornly, she turned and headed to another table, but Ellie thought she saw fear darken her face as she glanced at the Moons again.

"Everyone is either really loyal to the Moons or they're afraid of them," Ellie said. "So what exactly are they afraid of?"

EIGHTY-FOUR

Two redneck guys in baggy jeans and wifebeater shirts lumbered in. The chubbier one lifted bandaged fingers to scratch his bearded face, and she recognized the other man from Buster's convenience store. When they spotted the Moons, they swerved to the bar, heads ducked as if avoiding the men.

Ellie and Derrick surveyed the crowd as they ate.

They were just finishing when Kevin and his father walked toward Ellie, bypassing the two men without a glance.

Derrick stood. "I'm going to talk to the bartender."

Ellie nodded. Maybe he'd talk.

As Derrick made his way to the bar, Kevin and his father stopped at Ellie's table. "Any word on Jesse?"

"Not yet," Ellie said as she sipped her lemonade. "But we're still looking."

Kevin's mouth tightened. "What about the little girl? I want a paternity test done."

"She's safe," Ellie said. "And we will run a test. But it may take time."

"Speed it up," Kevin's father ordered. "We need to know if she's a Moon."

Obviously expecting her to obey like everyone else in this town, they stalked away. Ellie gritted her teeth. She didn't take orders from anyone. She *would* find out the truth about Pixie's paternity, only she'd keep the results to herself until she discovered what happened to Mia. If Kevin was Pixie's father, she'd sure as hell make sure the Moons weren't dangerous before any introduction was made.

Just then, a hunched over white-haired women with a cane hobbled by, dropping her purse. Ellie bent to pick it up and hand it to her. The woman leaned over as well, and their hands brushed. "Be careful, dear. There's bad blood around here."

Her voice was so low, for a moment Ellie thought she'd misheard, but the woman trembled as she hobbled away. Thelma appeared a minute later with the check.

Ellie paid in cash then took the receipt and saw a name scribbled on the back.

Patty Lasso.

Ellie quickly tucked it away then looked up to ask Thelma who Patty was, but the waitress had already hurried to another table as if it had never happened.

EIGHTY-FIVE

SOMEWHERE ON THE RIVER

Mia crawled to the tiny cabin window, her stomach lurching with the movement of the boat. All she could see for miles was water and more water. Shadows darted across the gray sky, a few leafy trees slipping into view in the distance as the boat glided along, blocking out the sunlight.

Fingers of dread tiptoed across her skin. All she could think about was the legends of the river she'd heard growing up from her grandmother.

Gram's voice taunted her: *Far into the woods in the deep, deep South, the murky river water breeds monsters. Big scaly creatures, amphibian-like lizards with eyes that pierce the night, following its prey until time to attack. Just before their fangs sink into you, they release a feral roar that echoes off steep mountain walls and rings for miles and miles.*

Flesh-eating insects, poisonous serpents and the wet earth can suck a body below, like quicksand burying you so deep you might never be found.

Then the Devil's door opens and swallows you as if Satan called you home.

Trying her best to banish the legend from her mind, Mia

glanced around the small room, blinking things into focus. The bed, a chair with a small table where a new water bottle sat. She had no idea where she was or how she was going to escape.

"You're mine forever," Kevin had said the first time he'd kissed her.

She'd smiled and thought it was romantic.

She had no idea what was coming next...

She dropped back down onto the bed with renewed determination. No matter what the legend said about the monsters, she would fight.

She'd done it once before to save her daughter. She'd do whatever it took now to survive and make sure Kevin Moon never got his hands on her.

EIGHTY-SIX

CROOKED CREEK

Calvin Plummett slid onto a stool at the Corner Café, sizing up the crowd. Not much different from Red River Rock and most small towns in these parts. Town decorated for Memorial Day, tourists flocking in, locals gathering for lunch and little old women huddled in gossip.

If he didn't learn what he needed to know here, he'd hit the Beauty Barn next, the best place to get the scoop on the sins of those up to no good behind closed doors.

Like the Moons.

But family was family. Some secrets had to be kept no matter what.

He popped an antacid and swallowed hard against the bile in his throat. Every now and then, he let what he had to do get to him.

He was indebted to the Moons. And they owned him. End of story.

He couldn't change the past. And he didn't have the energy or the willpower to go against them. God forbid. He knew what would happen if he did...

A pretty young thang named Lola poured coffee into a mug

for him and gave him a smile that made him feel like he was
somebody. Then again, she treated everyone the same. Such a
sweet Southern gal.

He hoped he didn't have to hurt her to get what he wanted.

Dumping sugar into his coffee, he grinned right back at her,
angling his head so his droopy eye didn't stand out. Girls in high
school had made fun of it and he'd dropped out.

But he wasn't a total dumbass like Ronnie's boys. He had
some smarts.

"What can I get you?" Lola asked.

You, he wanted to say. But she was way out of his league.
Besides, he was here for information and couldn't draw attention to himself. "What's good, darlin'?"

"The salads are great but ..." She eyed him. "But you don't
look like a salad kind of guy. How about the roast beef sliders
and some peach cobbler?"

"Perfect." Man he wished he had a darlin' like her around to
cook for him. "You do all the cooking?"

"I make the breakfast and pastries and plan the menu," she
said. "Got a nice lady named Ms. Ellen who bakes the pies."

She beamed and called out the order then went to another
customer, leaving him to keep an ear out. The old women at the
table in the corner were tittering about some kooky cat café next
door.

The one they called Maude leaned onto the table, half-
covering her mouth as if whatever she had to say was to be kept
between them. "Y'all hear about that little child Pixie's mama
run off and left her?"

"I can't believe it, Mia seemed like a sweet girl," the one
they called Betty said.

Maude whispered, "Just goes to show you – you don't know
anybody these days."

"You sure enough don't." This from the woman he'd heard
them call Edwina. The mayor's wife.

"What do you think will happen to Pixie?" Betty asked.

Maude made a tssking sound. "I heard she's in foster care. Probably with Emily Nettles. She takes in all the strays."

Calvin grinned as he pulled out his pocket note pad and scribbled down the name. Moon wanted him to find the little girl.

Now he knew where to look.

EIGHTY-SEVEN

BABBLING CREEK RANCH

Pixie pumped her legs back and forth in the swing, the metal rungs creaking as she looked up at the clouds. One looked pretty and white like a cloud a magic genie would ride on. But there were other gray ones that formed shapes. She and her mommy liked to name them. A lion. A bear. A bird. A shark.

Shivering, she made herself look away. Norah and her three brothers were building a fort in the backyard and were covered in mud and pine needles. Their dog Debbie was running wild, digging in the dirt. But Ms. Emily didn't seem to mind the mess. She said she'd just hose 'em all off.

Pixie curled her fingers around the ropes and pumped her legs harder, making the swing fly higher and higher, so high she wished she could fly back to her mommy's house and be in her own backyard with her and Mr. Mark.

She didn't want to play in the fort right now although she liked Norah and her brothers and the dog and the two guinea pigs and parakeets they had inside. On the ranch they even had horses and goats that were silly and ate everything in sight. Norah's daddy sang goofy, made-up songs that didn't make sense but made everyone giggle, and Ms. Emily had the kindest blue eyes and always had snacks and hugs and Band-Aids for boo-boos.

Only she wasn't Mommy and now she was starting to wonder if her mommy was ever coming back. Ms. Emily just gave her a hug and a sad smile when she asked like she wanted to make her feel better but that she didn't know either.

She bit her lip. That worried her the most.

Maybe Ms. Emily knew something she wasn't telling her. And why hadn't she seen Mr. Mark? He'd said he wanted to be her daddy.

Had he changed his mind? Didn't he want her anymore?

Tears filled her eyes and made the clouds look blurry. She blinked and started to cry again. Her legs were tired from pumping and she let them hang, the swing slowing down and her toes dragging the grass.

She pushed her fist against her eyes to stop crying, then saw a black car drive by and slow down. The car stopped on the street by the fence but she couldn't see who was inside.

Then the window rolled down and she saw a man with a camera aiming it at the yard. She thought he took some pictures of her or maybe of Norah and the brothers.

Her heart stuttered and she had a bad sick feeling like when Mommy told her not to speak to strangers.

She jumped off the swing and started running back to the house to tell Ms. Emily. But the car engine roared up and the car sped away before she made it to the house.

EIGHTY-EIGHT
MOONDOGGY'S

"What did the bartender have to say?" Ellie asked when Derrick returned to the table.

"Not much to offer," Derrick replied. "He just moved here a few months ago so he didn't know Jesse. Like everyone else around here, he said the Moons run the town. He hangs out with a lot of the raft guides at the company next door. Didn't seem to care for Kevin. Kevin runs in different circles."

"Maybe we should talk to the raft guides," Ellie said, then lowered her voice. "And I want to find out about this woman named Patty Lasso."

"Who?"

"Thelma scribbled her name on the back of the receipt and left it. But she didn't give me a chance to ask about her."

"My guess is she probably wouldn't have, not with the Moons watching," Derrick said. "She looked nervous as hell."

"A lot of people here do," Ellie said. "Another little old lady whispered to me to be careful, that there's bad blood around here."

"Interesting. They want to talk but are paralyzed with fear," Derrick said.

"I think so. Why don't you talk to the folks at the outfitters store while I look into Patty?"

"Good idea. Maybe one of the raft guides knows her."

The afternoon sun was blinding as they left, flickering through tall pines, oaks and cedars. Birds flew from branch to branch, the sounds of summer filling the air as people lined up for the raft tours.

Ellie took her laptop to the deck overlooking the water while Derrick headed inside the outfitters to question the owner. She booted up her computer and entered the name Patty Lasso, first checking DMV records.

Patty was a pretty brunette in her twenties, five-three, 130 pounds. According to her license, her address was not in Red River Rock, although the license had been issued ten years ago and had not been renewed.

Her skin prickled. Why hadn't she renewed it?

Curious, she googled Patty's name to see what came up and she found an outdated Facebook page, with no posts in five years. Her search for an Instagram and a Twitter account ended with nothing as well. Finally, she found a LinkedIn page. It was short but indicated Patty worked in retail and was an assistant manager at Moonbeams five years ago. Nothing since.

Her gut clenched and she googled Moonbeams' website. It took a few minutes to navigate the pages which catered to the millennials and Gen Z's. She checked the names of the staff, but Patty Lasso was not listed anywhere on the site.

A bad feeling stirred inside her and she decided to search death certificate records. That took another few minutes but she didn't find one for Patty.

The timing of everything hit her – if Patty worked at Moonbeams, she must have worked with Jesse. She might know what had happened to her.

She pulled up Sheriff Kincaid's phone number and called him. His voicemail kicked in, and she left a message. "Please

call me, Sheriff. I'd like to talk to you about a woman named
Patty Lasso."

EIGHTY-NINE

RED RIVER ROCK OUTFITTERS

Derrick watched the visitors listen to the raft guide's instructions and smiled at their excitement. Twin boys who looked to be about twelve years old were strapping on life vests with an exuberance that indicated it was their first time.

They reminded him of Rick and Lindsey's son, Evan, who was only nine. He was too young to take the trip yet, but he would be old enough soon. Only Rick wouldn't be here to take him.

Maybe you can.

Grief and guilt tightened his chest. He'd be happy to do that but Lindsey wanted him nowhere near the kids.

Maybe that would change. Maybe not. He didn't blame her for how she felt. She was in pain and so were those children.

"You here for a tour?" the thirty-something guy in jeans and a T-shirt sporting the logo for Red River Rock Outfitters asked.

Derrick eyed the posters on the wall. "Not today, but one day." Maybe he'd bring Evan. *Or maybe a child of your own.*

He shook his head in surprise at his own thoughts. What in the hell had made that idea pop into his head? He'd failed his sister. And Rick. Lindsey didn't want him to have anything to do with her kids. He didn't deserve to have one of his own. He'd probably just screw that up, too.

"Sir?" the young guy said.

Derrick shook off his thoughts and steered his mind back to the case. "Actually, I'm a federal agent. I wondered if you could shed some light on the Moon family."

The guy's eyes twitched as he glanced around the store. Derrick saw the security cams and silently cursed. "Don't know them personally but heard they help folks in trouble around here."

"How so?"

"Give them loans to support the businesses," he said. "Although we're doing fine with the raft company. The tourists keep us alive."

"I can see that," Derrick said with a smile. "Did you know Jesse Habersham?"

The guy tilted his head toward the two rednecks he'd seen inside who'd followed him into the store, then shook his head. "Naw, heard about her. Ran that boutique in town." He motioned around the store. "More of an outdoor guy myself."

"I hear you. How about a woman named Patty Lasso?" Derrick asked.

The guy shifted, picked up a T-shirt from the counter and rang it up. "Cash or credit card, sir?"

Derrick took the hint and pretended to be a customer buying a souvenir shirt. "Cash." He handed the guy a twenty-dollar bill from his wallet.

"You might want to talk to Reggie, one of the guides. He's our best and gives you just the kind of ride you want."

Derrick took his change and T-shirt and headed outside. He couldn't help but notice the men hovering by the section of souvenir shot glasses watching with narrowed eyes.

Ellie spotted Derrick walking down to the river, stowed her laptop in her bag, and hurried to join him. All around her, visitors chatted excitedly, lining up to climb into the rafts. The wind barreled off the mountain, the sun blazing.

Derrick stood by a stand with a guide who was organizing the tours. "Anything yet?" Ellie asked quietly.

"Maybe. Clerk inside told me to talk to Reggie. He's just gotten in from a trip and will be here in a minute. You?"

"Patty Lasso was the assistant manager at Moonbeams when Jesse was there. Can't find anything on her in recent years."

They halted conversation as a dark-blond dude in a bathing suit and sunglasses approached. It was obvious he'd taken a dive into the river and had been doing this a while. Muscles bulged in his arms and his skin was tanned.

"Phil said you wanted to talk to me," he said, shaking water from his hair.

Derrick was suddenly aware the two guys from the store were eying them. Damn, they had a tail.

"Pretend we're talking about setting up a trip," Derrick

murmured as he gestured at the rafts. "I'm Special Agent Fox and this is Detective Reeves. What do you know about a woman named Patty Lasso?"

The guy's friendly demeanor turned wary, but he motioned across the river as if telling them about the guided tour. "Patty and I dated a while back. She just up and left one day. I talked to the sheriff, was afraid something happened to her, but Sheriff Kincaid said he went to her house and found a note on her counter to the super. Said she needed a change and was leaving town."

Derrick nodded and Ellie curled against Derrick as if they were a couple of tourists.

"Did you have any idea she was leaving?"

He gave a small shake of his head.

"Did you think something happened to her?" Ellie asked.

Reggie shrugged. "That last week before she left, she seemed jittery and anxious. When I asked what was wrong, she said nothing, only that she might have to leave town."

"Have to?"

"Yeah. I got the impression she'd heard something she shouldn't, that she was scared to talk about it." He hefted two paddles over his shoulder. "Then she was gone."

Clearly, a lot of people in Red River Rock were afraid to talk. "You didn't hear from her after that?"

He pushed his wet hair from his forehead. "No, odd since she was friends with Jesse. Then... you know Jesse disappeared two days later."

Apparently Reggie suspected something had happened to Patty. It was too much of a coincidence for her to leave one day and then Jesse two days later.

"Did Patty have family?" Ellie asked.

"I think she had a brother but she didn't like to talk about him. Not sure about his story. But I got the impression he'd gotten jacked up with the law, maybe drugs."

"Was she afraid of him?"

His jaw clenched. "Like I said, she wouldn't talk to me about him. Maybe she was afraid. Could have been why she left town."

A group of people walked by then, and he looked back to the river.

"Reggie, if you know something please tell me."

"I told you what I know." He pointed toward the booth in front of the outfitters' store and raised his voice in case they had an audience. "You can sign up for the next trip up there. I'm done for the day."

Derrick gave a nod of understanding.

Ellie tucked her hand in Derrick's arm and scooched next to him, still in pretense although it felt damn good to be that close to him.

"What do you think?" Derrick asked.

She feigned a smile as they walked up the hill and they passed the same two guys she'd seen before. Turning to the river with lit cigarettes, the men did a piss poor job of concealing the fact they were following her and Derrick.

"I'm going to ask Laney to request Patty's medical and dental records and compare to the remains in the barrel along with Mia's," Ellie said.

She just prayed those ashes didn't belong to Mia.

NINETY-ONE

SOMEWHERE ON THE RIVER

A constant buzzing, droning sound echoed in Mia's ears. Low voices. Footsteps. Machines.

The boat was rocking again, up and down, jamming into rocks, scuttling through the water and taking her farther and farther away to God only knew where.

A whistling echoed through the walls, sending a chill through her. She'd heard that same whistling sound before. Over and over and over – "Down in Dixie".

She hated that song. That whistle took her back to the nightmares of the river monsters. And some big room in the woods.

It was so hot her clothes were sticking to her skin and her hair dripped with sweat. She and Jo-Jo had snuck inside to hover in front of the fan but it felt like hot air blowing in her face. It made her so sleepy she could barely keep her eyes open. The room was a foggy blur of people and steam from the irons, women and young girls rushing through rows of bundled garments stacked so tall she couldn't see over them. Country music echoed from the speakers as the buzzing hummed on. One of the records was scratched, causing the line "Hello, Darlin'" to repeat as if it was on a constant loop.

A whistle blew – or was it the wind outside? – and she blinked and saw her mama at the cutting table, pinning the pattern, then using the shears to cut the material. One by one, she cut then stacked the pieces until they were a mile high.

Then she slid behind the sewing machine and began to stitch. The droning sound went on and on...

Outside, a noise jolted her back to reality. She banged on the door. "Please let me out..."

But no one came. Only the whistle transformed into laughter and she knew she was trapped.

NINETY-TWO

Since Sheriff Kincaid had not returned her call, Ellie decided to stop by his office.

"I'll be inside in a minute," Derrick said, his phone in hand. "I'm going to check on Rick's kids. That is if Lindsey will talk to me."

Ellie gave him a sympathetic look. "Good luck."

"By the way, did you notice those two burly guys at Moondoggy's that were watching us?"

Ellie gave a little nod. "You think they're keeping tabs on us?"

"Looks that way," Derrick said. "When I went to the bar, I managed to take a photo of them. I want to find out who they are."

She agreed, left him in the Jeep and made her way into the police station. A deputy named Jimmy Stancil was at the front desk. He was lean with a long face and high forehead, brown eyes and hair somewhere between wheat and a dirty brown. "I need to see Sheriff Kincaid."

"Sheriff ain't here right now," the deputy said, his gaze raking over her. "You that detective from Crooked Creek?"

"I am. Maybe you can answer our questions," Ellie said. "Has he explained what we're doing here?"

Deputy Stancil shifted the toothpick in his mouth to one corner. "Course. Said Jesse Habersham not only ran off but she was using a phony name." He gave a low whistle. "Didn't see that coming."

Ellie tilted her head to the side, studying him. "What did you think happened to her?"

"No idea. Couldn't imagine her leaving a big dog like Kevin Moon. All the women around here throw themselves at him."

"Do you think he accepted their advances?"

"You mean was he a cheater?" The deputy chuckled. "Hell if I know. I'm just hired help." He twirled the toothpick with his teeth. "But if he did, he'd expect her to put up with it. He watched that girl like a dog guarding his bone."

His comment stirred questions in Ellie's head. If Kevin had cheated, perhaps Jesse threatened to leave him and he got angry. But why go through with the wedding?

Good question. "Did you know a woman named Patty Lasso?" she asked.

Just then, the door opened and Sheriff Kincaid entered, a hiss escaping him as he spotted her. "I'll take it from here, Jimmy."

"Sheriff," Ellie said, watching as the deputy shut down.

Kincaid ignored her and motioned to the deputy. "Need you to make some phone calls for me. You can use the back office."

Annoyance flickered in Jimmy's look, but he took his phone with him to the back.

Ellie crossed her arms. "Did you get my message?"

"Yes, but I still have a town to run. You wanted to know about Patty Lasso?"

Ellie nodded. "She worked with Jesse, but I heard she left town two days day before Jesse went missing."

He worked his mouth from side to side. "She did. Her boyfriend got worried so I went out to her apartment, but she'd packed and gone. Landlord said she left a note saying she was moving but didn't say goodbye."

"Did you try to find out where she went?" Ellie asked.

"Didn't see no reason to," Kincaid said. "It's not a crime to move, Detective."

"No, but since Jesse disappeared two days later, didn't you think it was too much of a coincidence?"

"Not really," he replied. "I can't keep up with everyone who comes in town and leaves. Heard she wanted more say in the business so figured she got a job somewhere else."

"Maybe so. Although I haven't been able to find anything on her the last five years."

Kincaid ran his finger over his belt. "I don't know what to tell you then. Maybe she got married and changed her name."

That was also possible. But Ellie still didn't like the timing. Her phone vibrated and she glanced at the number. Laney.

"This is the ME," Ellie said. "I need to take it." She turned her back to him, her pulse racing as she answered.

"Dr. Chatterman received the medical records we requested," Laney said. "The remains in the barrel are not Mia, Ellie. They're a woman named Patty—"

"Lasso," Ellie finished.

NINETY-THREE

FOGGY MOUNTAIN REAL ESTATE

Flexing his hands to alleviate tension, Kevin gazed through the giant floor-to-ceiling window in his office, crafted to give an expansive view of the widest part of Foggy Mountain and the river flowing behind the property.

Pride puffed up his chest. He and his father owned this town – and the people. If they crossed them, they knew what would happen.

Jesse had definitely crossed him. She'd humiliated him and made a fool out of him by abandoning him and starting another life.

A life with a different man. Even more despicable, if the child was his, by denying him his daughter.

She would pay for that.

He found a photo of Mark Wade on his computer. Damn man was nothing but a high school teacher and coach. Kevin made more on one sale than the bastard did in an entire year. Photos of him and his winning soccer team occupied the front page of the paper from when they won the county championship. Another article showed him accepting an award for Coach of the Year.

Jesse – Mia – was not in any of the photos. Disgust rolled through him in waves. He knew the reason. She didn't want anyone to find her.

But he'd vowed not to give up until he did.

Feeling more motivated than ever, he found Wade's address and pinpointed it on a topographic map.

It took him a few minutes, but he located the man's house, a little red brick craftsman with a small yard near the high school where he taught. Not shabby but definitely not the fabulous mountain home he'd built for him and Jesse.

An image of Wade talking to that reporter the night of his wedding mocked him. The man looked devastated and in shock.

"I know how you feel, buddy."

A grin curved his mouth. Fitting that Mia Norman disappeared from her second wedding. That Mark Wade should know the pain and the bitterness of betrayal he'd suffered for the last five years. Holidays and birthdays and trips and... his honeymoon. All time he'd never get back. Instead of those memories, rage and the agony of wondering if Jesse was alive and safe or if she'd been mutilated by some crazed serial killer had dominated his thoughts.

His phone rang and he pulled it from his pocket. His PI, Calvin. Tension thrummed through him as he answered. "Kevin."

Calvin's breath rattled out. The old geezer needed to quit smoking and lay off the fried chicken.

"I found the child," Calvin said.

"Were you discreet? I don't want this coming back to me."

"Hell, it was a piece of cake. Didn't even have to ask around. Bunch of old biddies in that Podunk café live for gossip."

Kevin's pulse jumped. "Where is she?"

"Some broad named Emily Nettles takes in fosters. I got her address, drove by and saw the girl in the backyard." Calvin wheezed again as if struggling for breath. "Sending you pics now. You want me to bring her to you?"

"Not yet," Kevin said. "I have to play this just right. I'll let you know when to make a move. What's the little girl's name?"

"Pixie Ann," Calvin said. "She was born at Bluff County Hospital February 2, 2018. Seven pounds, six ounces, nineteen inches long."

Kevin quickly calculated the timing. February 2, 2018 was almost exactly nine months after Jesse disappeared from their wedding.

Emotions slammed into him. His gut told him Pixie was his, that Jesse had stolen her from him. He had missed her birth, her first step, her first words, the first four years of her life.

"Mr. Moon?"

"Thanks," he said. "I'll get back to you."

Calvin agreed and Kevin hung up. He grabbed his keys and headed down the steps to the receptionist. "Cancel my appointment this afternoon and reschedule. I have to go."

"Sure, Mr. Moon."

She batted her eyelashes at him as if she wanted more than just a job, but he didn't have time for her. After all, he was still a married man.

When he found Jesse, he'd remind her of that.

For now though, he wanted to see the little girl himself. He had a feeling he'd know just by looking at her if she was his daughter.

NINETY-FOUR

FOGGY MOUNTAIN FOREVER GARDENS

Thelma Coonts, the waitress at Moondoggy's, parked at Foggy Mountain Forever Gardens where silk flowers struggled in the wind and birds twittered above the tombstones, as if they were singing a soft melody to the dead. Tears burned her throat and she checked over her shoulder as she climbed from her Honda and wove through the rows of graves to her daughter's.

For a moment she thought she could see her girl's angelic face floating through the red misty fog, smiling at her. Only she hadn't smiled that last year she was alive.

Clenching the fresh daisies in her hand, Thelma stooped down, removed the plastic ones she'd left last week and arranged the daisies in the vase attached to the base of the marker.

Carrie Coonts, loving daughter, in my heart forever.

It was her fault Carrie was dead. She'd made mistakes and broken promises and sneaked around where she shouldn't have been sneaking. And Carrie had paid the price.

The pain in her daughter's young face had ripped at Thelma and she'd tried to change things, but it had been too late. By then Carrie's days were numbered.

She ran her fingers over the gravestone and sang the lullaby she used to sing to Carrie when she was a baby. Right before she'd died, her daughter had asked her to sing it again and Thelma had barely managed to get the words out for the hot flow of tears choking her.

She swiped at her eyes now and let her anger take root. She was sick and damn tired of this town and everyone in it. Secrets had been kept too long, things had spiraled out of control.

She wanted to run from this like she figured poor Jesse had, but every time she thought about it, she remembered she couldn't take Carrie with her and she couldn't leave her either. Not here alone.

Damn the Moons.

She didn't know everything. But she knew enough. Knew the Moons were everywhere watching everyone. That folks who'd fallen on hard times turned to the Moons and the family swept in like fairytale heroes, spreading fake magic dust and then turning into ferocious vultures.

The only reason she'd stayed here so long was that she owed them. Then she'd lost her beloved girl Carrie and she'd stayed to fight for her and the other helpless girls just like her.

Other than the strip club and the Moon Stillery, Moondoggy's was the best place in town to keep her eyes and ears open. She didn't have enough yet worth risking her life over, but one day she would.

Then she'd help blow up this evil-infested county and everyone in it.

NINETY-FIVE

"Sheriff," Ellie said. "That was the medical examiner. They've identified the body in the barrel as Patty Lasso."

Kincaid steeled his jaw from reacting. Detective Ellie Reeves was a shitload of trouble. The moment he'd met her, he'd known she wouldn't stop digging until she found something. "What was cause of death?" he asked.

"Fire complicated things. Still waiting on the ME to determine that," Detective Reeves said, her gaze intently studying him. "We found no record of her anywhere in the last five years. Most likely she was murdered the night she supposedly left town or shortly thereafter. So who wrote that note and left it for her landlord?"

"I don't know. Perhaps she was leaving and was attacked on her way out of town?" He tugged at his uniform shirt, tucking it in.

"The timing is still too coincidental. Did you keep the note Patty left?"

He shook his head. "Didn't see no reason to. I can ask the landlord if he did."

"Let me," she said. "Maybe he can tell me more about Patty. What's his name and where are the apartments?"

Kincaid ground his teeth, then scribbled the information on a sticky note.

"Can you think of anyone who'd want to hurt Patty?" the detective asked.

He shook his head. "I didn't know her very well, but she seemed friendly. Hung out with that raft guide that came to me worried about her when he couldn't reach her one night. They could have had a fight and he killed her."

"True," the detective replied, although she didn't sound convinced. "But I think there's more to the story. Jesse could have witnessed Patty's murder and run out of fear."

He squared his shoulders. "If she had, she could have come to me and Kevin. We would have protected her."

"Unless she was running from Kevin."

His eyes narrowed to slits. "I wouldn't go around making accusations like that, Detective."

She gave him a cold stare. "I'm going to find the truth," she said firmly. "Mia is still missing and her daughter needs her. If you learn anymore about Patty, you'll let me know, won't you?" She finished with a challenging smile, tension reverberating between them.

"Of course. She died in my town. I'll be conducting my own investigation," he stated. "The locals don't always trust strangers. They'll talk to me before they would you."

Annoyance deepened in her eyes. She knew he was right. "Then we'll be in touch." She strode from his office with an air of determination. He waited until the door closed behind her and he walked to the window, watching as she got in the car with the fed and drove off. His deputy's footsteps pounded the floor as he joined him.

"That one's a spitfire," his deputy muttered in admiration.

Kincaid crossed his arms. "What the hell did you tell her?"

"Nothing," his deputy said. "Trust me, I know how things work around here."

"Good. Don't you forget it." He stormed back to his office, where he found his contact and made the call.

"The ME identified the girl in the barrel as Patty Lasso. Reeves is a damn cyclone ready to tear up this town to get what she wants."

"Just make sure she doesn't find out the truth. We need time to tie things up."

He rubbed his hand over his face, wiping away sweat. The situation was already out of control. If she kept pushing, she'd end up in a barrel just like Patty.

NINETY-SIX
MOON STILLERY

The minute Ellie and Derrick entered the bar, she knew it drew a local boisterous crowd. Country music rocked full blast, the décor offering a mountain vibe with river photos, deer heads on the wall, and bar tables made of whiskey barrels. Bear skin rugs covered the floor, and corner booths offered a more private gathering spot. To the left, she saw a curtained-off area which she suspected hid some sort of side business.

She and Derrick wove through the crowded room to the bar where they perched on stools and ordered beer.

"I can't do moonshine," Ellie said.

Derrick grinned. "I learned that lesson a long time ago. An uncle... don't ask."

Ellie smiled, forgetting for a second they were working a case.

The bartender, a wrestler type, leaned toward her, beefy arms on the counter.

"Name's Al. What'll you have, sweetheart?"

She tried not to take offense. Everyone called everyone honey and sweetie in the South.

"Vodka on the rocks. Kettle one if you have it."

"Sure thang." He cut his eyes to Derrick. "You?"

"IPA. Whatever you have on draft," Derrick said.

Ellie scanned the crowd of beer guzzlers and good old boys downing moonshine and playing darts. She spotted the same two rough-looking guys she and Derrick had seen earlier, the ones they thought were keeping tabs on them.

"Wonder what's behind curtain number one," Derrick murmured, gesturing to a black curtain to the right. A busty blond in booty shorts and a crop top ducked inside, boobs bouncing.

"Strippers for hire," Ellie said. "Interested?"

He took a sip of his IPA and gave her a teasing smile. "Jealous, Ellie?"

"Hardly." She rolled her eyes.

Derrick laughed but pivoted on his stool as a noise sounded from the opposite end of the bar. She peered around a group of young men who looked as if they'd come straight from rafting and spotted the two burly guys again, this time arguing with a blockish-figured woman with curly short hair and leathery skin dragging them by the shirts to another room.

The bartender slid her vodka in front of her with a grin. "Double on the rocks."

Ellie's instincts roared to life. "Who are those guys and that woman?"

Al straightened and handed Derrick his IPA, then leaned over the counter and lowered his voice. "Ronnie and her boys Chester and Lloyd. She owns the stillery. Trust me, you don't want to get on their bad side."

Ellie feigned an innocent smile. "Thanks for the warning. By the way, did you know Jesse Habersham or Patty Lasso? They used to live around here."

His flirty smile faded and his eyes pinged to the room where Ronnie and her sons had disappeared. "Just that Patty left town. I don't know what happened to Jesse. Just heard talk, but..."

Ronnie came out of the curtained room, and the bartender clammed up, darting to another customer. Judging from his reaction and his warning, Ronnie and her boys were dangerous.

"Did you notice those whiskey barrel tables are similar to the one Patty was found in?" Derrick asked as they sipped their drinks and studied the patrons.

"Yeah," Ellie said. "The bartender hinted that Ronnie and her boys are dangerous. What if they're connected to the Moons?"

NINETY-SEVEN

BABBLING CREEK RANCH

Kevin parked on the corner of the street near Emily Nettle's house facing the backyard, hoping to get a glimpse of Pixie. Through the window, he saw a slender sandy blond-haired woman in the kitchen with kids running all around her as she juggled plates into the dishwasher.

He didn't see Pixie, but he would tonight. The need to know the truth was making him crazy.

While he waited, he retrieved the photos Calvin had sent. He'd used a wide angled lens to view a close-up of the little girl.

Her face was heart shaped like Jesse's, her blond pigtails the same golden silky shade as well. And those big brown eyes...

Jesse had blue eyes.

His were brown.

His breathing turned raspy as he swiped to see another photo – this one of the little girl sitting alone in a swing, her face downcast, with tears running down her cheeks. Other children were playing in the yard, but she was all alone.

He traced a finger over the photograph. "Are you my baby girl?" he whispered.

Chest tight, he opened the photo album he'd brought from

home, the one chronicling his early years that his mother had made for him before she'd died. Unlike most folks these days, she'd insisted on storing his baby pictures and other photos in an old-fashioned album. She called it scrapbooking or something like that.

As he thumbed through, he found a picture of himself where he was four, the same age as the little girl Pixie.

Anger nagged at him at that silly name. He'd had no say in that choice. Although he could always change it when she came to live with him.

He zeroed in on the details of himself as a child – his hair had been blond when he was young but turned darker to a light brown by his twenties. He focused on his eyes – the same dark chocolate as Pixie's. He felt as if he'd been sucker punched.

The back door opened and three boys raced out and ran to the trampoline, shouting as they began to jump. Following them came a red-headed girl with freckles then Pixie, both the girls carrying popsicles over to the swings. They climbed in, the redhead giggling and licking. Pixie nibbled at hers with those big sad eyes, haunted and quiet. As she gripped the rope swing, he noticed a tiny little birthmark on her hand.

He looked down at his own and lost his breath. He had the same birthmark.

In that very second, he knew without a doubt that she was his.

Damn Jesse for robbing him of his daughter. Damn her to hell.

He would have his daughter and raise her. He felt like running to her now and telling her the truth, that her mother was a liar and a thief, and that he was her daddy.

His hand reached for the doorhandle, then he paused, common sense bleeding through his rage and pain.

Although the sun was fading, it was still light. He had to play it smart. Wait until the right moment.

NINETY-EIGHT

LIZARD CREEK

Night had fallen, the sun only a memory as dark clouds moved in to end the day in a dismal gray. As Thelma wound around the switchbacks, she kept thinking about that detective and federal agent, hoping they could do something about the bad blood on Foggy Mountain.

Some said the red mist was caused by mineral deposits in the soil but she believed it was tears of blood rising from the graves of those who'd been living in fear for so long. Her tears for her lost daughter were among them, falling now, her gut wrenching with such pain she felt like she was literally bleeding inside.

Lights flickered behind her as a car crept up on her and she slowed, hoping he'd pass as she reached a wider section of the road and crossed the bridge over Lizard Creek. That creek always gave her the shivers. She'd heard stories about the Tegus lizards that could grow up to four feet long. Normally seen in southeast Georgia, some said they were migrating here and were destroying the wildlife.

She hadn't driven this way in ages because it led her to the horrible place that had stolen her soul, but tonight she had it on her mind and wondered if there was something she could do to save the others.

The car sped up, riding her tail as she neared a ravine, and a frisson of alarm crept up her spine. Night shadows danced around her, a tree limb cracking and snapping off in the wind. The branch hit her windshield and bounced off, but it startled her and she swerved right slightly. Her tires churned on the graveled shoulder of the road and she tried to right herself, but the vehicle behind her sped up and rammed into her.

She screamed and clenched the steering wheel with clammy hands, struggling to stay on the highway, her car skidding. Branches broke like matchsticks as she sailed through the trees and the windshield shattered, glass spraying. The car bounced and bumped, diving toward the ravine.

Pain knifed through her body and for a moment the car hung, suspended in the air, teetering between two trees. She heaved a breath, trembling with fear as she forced herself to be still. The last thing she wanted was to dive into Lizard Creek and be covered in the reptiles.

One hand slid to the seat to find her phone but even that movement rocked the car and the branches broke, sending her plunging to the ravine below. Her lungs felt crushed as the air bag exploded and the front of the car slammed into the woods below. Her head hit something. The dash crumpled, crushing her legs, and a shard of glass stabbed her throat.

Tears blurred her eyes as she reached up to rip the air bag but when she touched her neck, she felt blood spurting, and the world started tilting and fading. Carrie's ghostly face floated in front of her... A second later she saw the creek water rising as the car was sinking.

She closed her eyes, body jerking as she struggled for a breath that didn't come. Resigned to her fate and knowing they'd finally won, she reached out for her daughter's hand to take it.

"You sorry shits," Ronnie bellowed as she guided the boat across the choppy water.

"You brought the law down on us bad. Now we have to make sure they don't find out about what we're cooking back here in these parts." She slapped both her sons across their dumbass noggins and smiled as they cowered in fear, eyes bulging.

"Mama, we just did what you said," Lloyd whimpered.

She sped up, soaring around the dark place where most folks around these parts got lost.

River Bottom was perfect for her business because no one came the hell out here to camp or hike and there wasn't no damn waterfalls or scenic trails or sightseeing crap. Only woods and bugs and the river, the place that fed her soul. Some talked of the river monsters, but she intended to keep them alive, knowing the legends scared folks away.

She slowed the boat, cutting the engine and coasting through the coves until she reached her destination.

Docking the boat, she peered at the warehouse. It was dark and no one had followed her. The place was locked down for the night, the cargo safely tucked inside where no one knew the wiser.

"Out," she ordered her boys. "And you better make damn sure none of 'em git away tonight. If word got out the law was around, someone might try something."

"Whatever you say, Mama," Chester said, rubbing at his bandaged hand like some big-ass baby.

"Yes, Mama," Lloyd said. "They'll be locked in tight."

Ronnie slapped them both upside the head again, just for fun this time. "They better be. If even one gets loose, you're in that river with the bloodsuckers."

ONE HUNDRED

SOMEWHERE ON THE RIVER

Mia fixed Pixie's sweet face in her mind for motivation, her energy returning slightly since she'd been rationing the water. She realized whoever had taken her had drugged her to keep her sedate. She was trying not to drink much but her mouth was cotton dry, her tongue thick, and she took a tiny sip.

Head spinning, she crawled to the cabin door and banged on it. "Let me out. At least show your face and tell me what you want!"

She leaned her head against the cold wood, battling nausea, and waited. But all she heard was the lapping of the river against the boat.

"Who are you?" she cried. "Where are you taking me?"

She closed her eyes at the silence but Kevin's face appeared in her mind. Was he behind the door? Had he hired someone to take her?

Her head lolled and memories rose from the darkness, making her dizzy as if she was on a tilt-a-whirl.

"You're beautiful, Jesse. I can't wait to make you my wife. Forever."

She shivered. He'd been so charming and romantic when

they'd first met. Had played the hero by saving her fledgling business. Had doted on her with flowers and candy and fancy dinners out. Had promised her the *moon*.

Then one evening she hadn't worn the dress he'd wanted and she'd questioned him about a discrepancy in Moonbeam's financial records in front of his father. That night... he'd morphed into a monster. One slap across the face and she'd tried to get away. Had told him the engagement was off.

Standing up to him had been a mistake. He wouldn't allow it.

She rubbed her wrist where he'd squeezed it so hard he'd broken it. The bruises on her face had forced her to call in sick at work the next two days.

While he'd slept, she'd sneaked into the bathroom and called her sister, spilling everything. "Don't marry him," Jo-Jo said. "I had a bad feeling about him when we met."

Jo-Jo *had* warned her he was trouble from the beginning. But she'd been too blind to see beyond the package. At the time, she'd argued with her sister and stopped calling her, certain she was walking into paradise.

But that first slap had changed everything.

The next day Kevin apologized, brought her a diamond necklace and promised it would never happen again.

She'd lied to herself and they'd fallen back into a nice rhythm, planning the wedding. Only he wanted a lavish ceremony on the riverboat his father owned.

"Please, you know I'm scared of the water," Jesse had begged. "Let's do it on land."

"No, baby, it's all planned. And it's going to be so beautiful."

The next week she'd noticed a beefy guy with tats on his arms following her. Patty had seen him too, said he'd been in the shop and gave her a creepy vibe.

"I think something's going on with the books," Patty said. "Things aren't adding up, Jess."

Jesse took another look at them and agreed. Thinking his accountant might be cooking the books, she pointed it out to Kevin, in private that time. He'd promised to take care of it.

Then he'd become more possessive. Even paranoid. She'd found him checking her phone. Heard him talking to his father and saying he had her under control. Heard him telling her sister, "Stop calling, Jo-Jo. I told you Jesse wants nothing to do with you anymore."

Jesse had known then what she had to do. Get away from Kevin and Red River Rock.

Only getting away meant lying and pretending. She needed help. It was only a week until the wedding and she had to make a plan...

ONE HUNDRED ONE
CROOKED CREEK

Dark clouds had rolled in for the night as Ellie drove back to Crooked Creek. If it rained overnight, maybe it would cool things off and still allow holiday plans not to be canceled. Not that she would be celebrating anything until Mia was found.

"How did the call with Lindsey go?" she asked as she parked beside Derrick's sedan at the police station.

"She didn't answer," he said. "I'm not surprised. But I do worry about the kids, especially with the memorial services this weekend."

"I'm sorry, Derrick. I'm sure she just needs time," Ellie said softly. "And she knows you're there. That's all you can do, just be there for her when or if she does need you." She brushed her fingers over his hand. "You want to come over?"

"I'm tired, Ellie. It's been a long day and I think we've only scratched the surface of what's going on in that town. I'll see you tomorrow." He leaned forward and gave her a kiss on the cheek, and she swallowed hard.

A sadness had washed over him, and she knew he was still mourning his friend. There was no time limit on grief.

She had to take her own advice, be patient and be there for him.

He slid from the passenger seat and got in his sedan, and she turned onto the road and drove to her bungalow. At this late hour, the diner and all the shops were closed for the evening. Her shoulders ached as she pulled into her drive.

She hesitated, her pulse quickening. She always left the porch lamp and the light in the kitchen burning, but the outside light was off. Unease splintered her calm and she ignored her aching muscles as she grabbed her gun and climbed from the Jeep. She eased the door closed, examining her property, senses on alert.

The wind whistled through the trees like a siren, and barking dogs echoed in the distance. Lightning zigzagged across the sky, illuminating the mountain ridges behind her bungalow.

She inched toward her home and thought she detected movement at the side of the house. The flowers in the beds Mia had planted were drooping, the brisk breeze tearing newly budding leaves from the trees and tossing them around like confetti.

There was the movement again. So quick she thought she'd imagined it.

Someone was on her property.

Cursing a blue streak, she pulled her weapon and moved to the right, holding her gun at the ready as she moved forward. She crept past the crepe myrtle and the azaleas, hugging the corner of the house as she rounded the corner, then searched across the side yard toward the woods.

Suddenly a loud growl broke the silence, then a hulking, masked figure grabbed her and threw her to the ground. She screamed and tried to fire a round, but he knocked the gun from her hand, then flipped her to her stomach. Something hard slammed into her kidney.

A fist.

She struggled to push herself up, but he was heavy and used his body weight to pin her down as he pummeled her over and over. It took every ounce of her energy to buck him off and she rolled to the side, her chest aching as she raised her legs to kick him. He blocked the kick and punched her in the face. Blood filled her eyes as she clawed at his dark mask.

She reached one hand sideways to find her gun or a rock, anything to use as a weapon, but he grabbed her arm, twisted it until pain wrenched her shoulder. Then he flipped her over and straddled her again.

Another blow to her back and pain ricocheted up her spine and down her legs. She tasted dirt and blood as her face dug into the ground and he beat her.

Minutes later, the darkness swept her under.

ONE HUNDRED TWO

CROOKED CREEK

Cord had spent the day searching for a lost boy and dog on the trail, grateful they'd finally found them trapped behind a waterfall although the kid had been trembling and terrified. A smile curved his mouth. The boy had been so brave, hugging the dog and reassuring it that someone would find them. He'd driven by Lola's to share the news and make up to her for whatever the hell he'd done wrong, but her lights were off.

So here he was driving by Ellie's. *Fool. Fox is probably with her.*

But the fed's car was not in the drive. And the light was not burning in the front, which Ellie always left on.

His skin prickled. Something felt off.

He parked in front of the house then called Ellie's number, but there was no answer. Maybe she was in the shower and for some reason had turned off the porch light. But as he got out and passed her car, he noticed her purse was still inside. He checked the door. Unlocked.

His pulse hammered. Dammit, he always worried about her. He had to know if she was all right before he went home. Keeping his eyes peeled for trouble, he walked up to the front door. Locked. He rang the doorbell, his ears craned for a noise inside. The shower. TV. Music. Ellie on the phone.

But only the whir of the wind and the sound of thunder broke the quiet. He rang the bell and knocked again but nothing. His anxiety mounting, he looked around the front then decided to check the property. Maybe she was out back on her deck?

Tension buzzed through him as he eased to the side of the yard, past the flowers and the bushes, his gaze shooting to the woods beyond. Tree limbs bowed and leaves fluttered in the wind. Pulling his flashlight from his inside his jacket, he shined it around the corner, then halted.

A low groan broke through the wheezing wind, and he turned to the left. The groan again. Then he saw a hand reaching out from under the red tip bushes.

Panic clenched his insides, and he darted to the bushes, then stooped down and parted them.

His heart stalled, his breath trapped in panic. Ellie was lying in the brush, face down, groaning, half unconscious.

ONE HUNDRED THREE

Derrick glanced around the interior of the cabin he'd rented and decided he needed different furniture if he was going to make this place home. The oak bed was old and worn, the carpet in the bedroom a faded beige, the kitchen outdated.

Not that he was into decorating, but when he visited Ellie's he felt instantly comforted. Her bright colors, white paint and throw pillows made the house feel homey, not just a place to crash at night.

Or maybe it was the fact that she was there, brightening his spirit with her fierce determination and the loving care she freely gave to others.

He rolled his shoulders and walked outside to the back deck, the one plus side of this cabin and the reason he'd signed the lease. The mountains rose in the distance like stairs to heaven, the trees so tall at the peaks that they almost looked like they touched the clouds.

He was dog-tired from the long day or... maybe it was the stress over Lindsey not answering his calls. He had a feeling he wouldn't sleep. Rick wouldn't let him.

He kept thinking about Rick's three-year-old little girl,

Maddie, who he'd doted on and his son, Evan, who turned nine last month and would miss having his daddy at his baseball games.

The attorney's words echoed in his ears: *Rick asked you to be his children's godfather.*

Tonight, as he watched the trees tremble in the wind and smelled the sweet scent of honeysuckle, Atlanta and its city life seemed a million miles away.

But he was close enough to make it to some of Evan's ball games and the kids' birthday parties. Evan and Maddie might even like to go camping in the mountains and see the waterfalls.

The memory of losing his sister on a camping trip haunted him. It was his fault she'd been kidnapped and murdered.

Rick had it all wrong and Lindsey had it right. He didn't deserve to be around those children.

His phone buzzed and he pulled it from his belt. Cord McClain.

Instantly his pulse jumped, and he punched Connect. "Fox."

"Ellie was attacked," Cord said as if he was out of breath.

Fear bolted through Derrick and he stormed back inside to get his keys. He had to get to Ellie. Dammit, he never should have left her.

ONE HUNDRED FOUR

Cord's first instinct had been to scoop Ellie up and drive her to the hospital himself. But his training kicked in and, knowing he could cause more damage by moving her, he'd called an ambulance.

"How serious?" Derrick asked over the phone.

Cord stroked Ellie's hair. He didn't think she had any broken bones, although it was possible. Also possible that she had internal injuries. "She was half-conscious when I got here and passed out now but breathing. Looks like she took a beating."

Derrick cursed. "I'll be there in five. Tell her to hang in there."

"Don't worry, I won't leave her." Emotions thickened his voice as he hung up, and he cradled Ellie's hand in his, wanting her to know she wasn't alone. Her skin was cold and clammy, her breathing shallow, her pallor gray.

"El, listen to me," Cord said. "You are the strongest woman I've ever known. You fight, you hear me." He choked as fear threatened to rip his guts out. He could not lose her. Not now. Not ever. "Please... You have to be okay." *I... need you.* But he bit back the words. He couldn't put that on Ellie. She was with Fox now.

Only where had the bastard been tonight? Not here when she needed him.

A siren wailed, lights twirling as the ambulance careened into the driveway. "Help is here, El. I'll be right back." Cord kissed her hand, then stood and jogged around the side of the house to meet the paramedics. Fox's car skidded in beside the ambulance and he jumped out, looking panicked.

"She's around back," he told the medics and the fed.

Leading the way, Cord ran back to Ellie.

"What happened?" Fox asked as the medics knelt beside Ellie.

"I don't know. Someone must have ambushed her."

Cord heard her groan, which he read as a good sign. Maybe she was rousing back to consciousness.

One of the medics took her vitals while the other called into the hospital. "Female, pulse thready, appears to be severely beaten. Transporting to the hospital now."

Fox's breathing was choppy as he stood by and watched the medics secure Ellie's neck before loading her onto the stretcher. Then the fed stepped over to her, brushing her hair from her face. "Hang in there, I'll meet you at the hospital."

Cord gritted his teeth as the fed patted her hand, then turned to him. "What were you doing here?"

"I just drove by to ask about the case," he snapped. "I saw her car and the porch light was off, then realized she wasn't in the car or the house so I decided to look around." He crossed his arms. "Where were you?"

Fox rubbed a hand over his face. "At my place," Derrick said. "I—"

"Should have protected her," Cord said, unable to bottle his anger.

Ellie groaned and opened her eyes as the medics lifted her

onto the stretcher. "Shut up, you two. You're giving me a headache."

Both Cord and Derrick went still. "I'm sorry, Ellie," Derrick said. "He's right. I should have been with you."

"I said shut up," Ellie growled. "Just look around, get a crime team out here and find some evidence to nail this bastard."

ONE HUNDRED FIVE

Ellie was so pissed she saw red. Her attacker had come out of nowhere. How could she have let him get the jump on her? She'd known he was there, had seen movement. Still, he'd pounced and he was so strong and heavy he'd pinned her to the ground like she was an ant.

The lull of the ambulance rocked her back into unconsciousness yet pain splintered her body, agonizing and intense. The whining of the siren echoed in her ears, tires bouncing over the ruts in the road, making it worse.

"We're almost there, Detective Reeves," the medic said.

She nodded or at least she thought she did. The movement hurt just like her bones did.

She must have passed out again and, when she came to, she was being wheeled into the ER. She heard Cord's voice asking if he could stay with her, but she didn't want anyone hovering.

"Sir, let us examine her and run some tests, then you can see her."

Ellie sighed in relief. Being poked and prodded was humiliating enough without having an audience.

The next two hours were excruciating as she underwent an

exam, a CAT scan and MRI. All she could think about was that she hoped Derrick and the ERT found something at her house to identify her attacker.

Head throbbing, she closed her eyes, begging for sleep, yet a half-dozen doctors and nurses paraded through, each pressing her belly and back and asking questions.

Finally the results were in and the doctor cleared his throat. "Detective, can you hear me?"

"Yes..." she mumbled, although her voice sounded slurred from exhaustion.

"Good news here. You definitely sustained bruises and will be sore for a few days, but thankfully there's no broken bones or internal bleeding."

Her head felt so heavy she tried for a nod but failed. "Go... home." She managed to eke out the request.

"Not tonight," he answered. "We're keeping you in for observation." He patted her shoulder like she was a dog. "Now get some rest."

She heard the door squeak open, then footsteps. He was leaving. But then Cord was there.

"You okay, El?"

"Peachy..."

His chuckle felt like a hug that she needed. "Did you see who did this to you?"

She shook her head but the movement hurt too much and she couldn't keep her eyes open any longer.

ONE HUNDRED SIX

RED RIVER ROCK

DAY 4

Morning sunlight fought through the clouds as Kevin stormed into his father's house. He strode straight to his study, gave a hard knock on the closed door with his fist then burst inside. His father was on the phone, a scowl deepening the grooves around his eyes.

"Let me call you back," his father said. He ended the call and rocked back in his chair, eyes narrowed to slits.

"Did you know about the little girl?" Kevin asked. "Tell me the truth this time."

"That Jesse had a child?"

"Yes, Father," he said through gritted teeth. "Did you know?"

His father gave a shake of his head, although he didn't quite meet Kevin's eyes. "You hired the PI to find her. Didn't he tell you?"

"No," Kevin said. "But I think she's mine. And I'm not going to let Jesse get away with this. She's already made me miss four years of her life."

"I told you that woman was trouble," his father said, his voice full of disapproval. "I'm tired of cleaning up your messes so don't do anything stupid."

The jab hit home. "You're talking about the other woman who lied to me, aren't you?"

"You good and damn well know I am. And now the cops are all up our asses about Jesse and they found that girl Patty. Everything we've got going on is in jeopardy."

"I can't let it go," Kevin said. "She deserves to suffer for what she's done."

A long tense minute vibrated between them. "Do you really mean that?"

Kevin couldn't believe his father doubted him. "Of course I do. She made a fool out of me, cheated on our marriage and stole my baby from me."

"Why don't you let me handle this?" his father said coldly.

"No," Kevin said. "You said you were tired of cleaning up my messes." He clenched his hands. "I want to do this myself so I can see her face when I punish her." Grinning as he imagined her expression when she saw him again, he strode from the room, his keys in his hand.

He would go back to Crooked Creek to get what was rightfully his: his daughter. And no one would get in his way.

Ellie moaned as she stirred from sleep. Every part of her body was throbbing.

She struggled to open her eyes and saw a blur of people in the room. Bright lights. The beep of a machine. Hushed voices echoing around her like a pack of angry wolves circling each other.

Oh, God. The night before rolled back in vivid tidbits. Driving home. Her porch light off. Someone on her property. On the ground, being beaten.

She licked her parched lips and tried to focus on who was in the room. Derrick. Cord. Her father. Bryce?

No... this couldn't be happening. All the men she knew in one place. All seeing her at her worst. Seeing her weak.

"The doctor said she'll be okay," said Cord, his voice gruff and deep. She remembered him finding her, calling the medics.

"Who did this?" Bryce, this time. Demanding. Angry.

"Where were you, Fox?" her father barked. "You're supposed to be her partner. If you aren't watching her, then go the hell back to Atlanta."

Silence. Then Derrick, "Sir, I'm sorry. We had no reason to

believe Ellie was in danger."

"She's in danger with every case she works," her father shouted. "Sometimes I wish she'd listen to her mother."

More noise. A door opening. A nurse shushing them.

Ellie opened her eyes. "Stop," she said, then threw up a battered hand. "Either behave or get out."

The room grew quiet immediately. Her vision was blurry but she saw the men stammering and looking at each other as if they had no idea what to do.

"She's so stubborn," her father growled.

"Tell me about it," Cord muttered.

"Won't let anyone help her," Bryce grumbled.

"I want her off the case," her father said.

Cord next. "She'll never go for that."

"No, she won't." Derrick.

Finally, two of the men agreed in this pissing contest. "Sir, I won't leave her alone again," Derrick said.

If her head wasn't throbbing like a mother, she would have rolled her eyes, gotten up and stalked right out.

"Be quiet," she said in a strangled voice. "Now someone get the doctor, the discharge papers and my clothes. I'm leaving."

"No, honey, you need to rest," her father replied.

"I can handle the case," Derrick said.

Cord pleaded, "Please, El."

Bryce now: "Let me take this one."

She felt as if she was going to blow a gasket and hissed, "I said stop it."

Another hushed silence fell, then she heard footsteps again and the door closed, as she squeezed her eyes shut.

She had no idea which of the men had followed her orders, and she didn't care. She had a case to work and she needed a shower or a hot bath.

Then she was damn well going to find Mia and nothing, not even a beatdown, would stop her.

ONE HUNDRED EIGHT

CROOKED CREEK

"As Memorial Weekend activities fire up, the temperature outside is heating up as well," local meteorologist Cara Soronto reported as Derrick drove Ellie home from the hospital. "Remember your sunscreen, folks, especially if you're on the water."

Cara's voice died as he cut the engine. Puffy white clouds danced across the sky, the morning sunlight shimmering off the asphalt. The humidity was cloying and made Ellie's hair cling to the back of her neck as she got out. Derrick took her elbow but she shook him off.

"I'm fine. Just a little sore. We've got work to do."

"You need to stay home and rest today," Derrick said. "Trust me to take care of things."

"It's not about trust," Ellie quipped as they entered her house. "It's about finding Mia. And if some son of a bitch thinks he can beat me into giving up, he's an idiot."

Derrick's frustrated sigh punctuated the air. "I know you won't, but you can delegate. Whoever attacked you last night is still out here. Let me find them and keep you safe."

Ellie turned to him as he closed the door. "I appreciate your concern, Derrick, but I don't intend to take this lying down. If he did this to me, just think what poor Mia might be going through."

"Do you know who assaulted you?" Derrick asked. "I thought you didn't see his face."

"I didn't, but I could tell he was a man. All this has to do with Mia and the Moons and that creepy town. Now..." she pressed her hand to her ribs as she inhaled. "Let me clean up and then I want to talk to Mark. We owe him an update."

Derrick's jaw tightened, but he didn't argue. "I'll wash up in your extra bathroom," he said. "Then I'll drive you."

Ellie conceded to that. After last night, she needed back-up. And a driver. Her body hurt like hell and she realized Derrick and Cord probably hadn't slept much either. Maybe she'd cut Derrick some slack.

But she didn't intend to sleep the day away when Mia needed her.

Kevin slowed as he neared Emily Nettles' house, then parked on the curb across the street. Through the window, he saw the kids running around but he didn't spot Pixie.

He reminded himself to be patient. But he'd already missed so much time with her that it took every ounce of his restraint to keep from walking up to the door and demanding to have his child.

While he waited to get a glimpse of her, anger seized him. How unfair was it that he had to skulk around and watch her from afar?

That he hadn't gotten to name her? For a minute, he mulled over girl names. Maybe Sarah after his mother. Or Tiffany, he liked that. Or... Holly...

He'd have to fix up a room for her, too. Maybe they could pick out some furniture together and he'd take her shopping and let her choose some toys. Little girls liked dolls, didn't they? And colors like pink and purple and what was it – teal? Or fuchsia?

She'd need hair ribbons, too, and patent leather shoes and dresses. His daughter was going to look like a princess!

The door opened and the kids ran to the van in the drive, piling in. They were dressed in bathing suits and bright colored crocs, and he assumed they were going to the local pool. The woman, who must be Emily, hauled a giant beach bag outside and stuffed it in the back, then ducked back inside and returned with a small cooler.

A seed of worry darted through him. Children drowned every summer. Did Pixie know how to swim? Would the woman watch her carefully or would she be too distracted with her own children to really pay attention?

The boys were rowdy, shouting about a cannonball contest. But Pixie dragged her feet as the redheaded little girl tugged at her hand. Then she paused for a second and glanced across the street at his car as if she knew he was there.

He ducked low so she wouldn't see him and hoped she didn't say something to Emily. It took another few minutes for Emily to get everyone buckled in and he inched his head up enough to see Pixie's little face pressed against the window looking at him. She looked scared and sad and... like she needed her daddy.

His pulse quickened. "Soon we'll get to meet, my little one. Soon."

An hour later, Ellie forced herself not to think about her aching body as she knocked on Mark's door. He looked miserable when he answered, his hair disheveled, his sunken eyes filled with worry.

His brows rose in question. "What happened to you?"

"She was attacked last night," Derrick cut in.

Mark's face turned ashen.

"I'm sorry, we haven't found Mia yet," Ellie said. "But don't give up hope yet."

He gave a pained nod, a heavy silence falling between them as she and Derrick followed him to his kitchen. A box of half-eaten pizza sat on the counter and she spotted a few crushed beer cans in a trash can.

He poured a mug of coffee and offered them one but she declined. Derrick accepted, the faint lines around his eyes a tell-tale sign of his fatigue. She'd already had two cups at the house and figured she'd get a to-go one for the road as they headed back to Foggy Mountain.

"Do you have *any* information?" Mark asked, his tone desperate as he leaned against the counter.

"Some," she said. "We suspect something happened in Red River Rock that scared Jesse Habersham into running. We think it has to do with her former fiancé and that there's something strange going on in that town."

Mark jerked his head up. "You think that guy hurt her?"

"I don't know yet, Mark. But it would explain why she came here and assumed a new identity. If not him, there may have been someone else in Red River Rock who threatened her."

He pinched the bridge of his nose. "If she was scared, why didn't she tell me? I would have protected her."

"Maybe she wanted to protect you," Ellie countered softly.

He grunted a sound of disbelief. "If she loved me, really loved me, she wouldn't have lied to me." His chest rose and fell with an uneven breath. "Besides, if she was already married, our marriage wouldn't even have been legal."

He had a point, one that had obviously kept him up all night.

Ellie gave him a minute then continued, "Mark, we found out who the Penningtons are. Jo-Jo Pennington was Jesse's sister."

Mark gaped at her. "But she told me she had no family."

"Maybe she was trying to protect them, too," Ellie speculated.

"Only it didn't work," Derrick added. "The Penningtons were murdered a few months after Jesse disappeared from Red River Rock."

Mark dropped into the chair. "I don't understand."

Ellie sighed. "We're guessing Jesse went into hiding and her sister and her husband were murdered in an attempt to learn where she was."

Mark sat shaking his head, obviously struggling to make sense of these revelations.

"Mark, did Mia ever mention anyone by the name of Patty Lasso?"

His brows pinched together. "No. Who is she?"

"She was Jesse's assistant at the boutique where she worked."

"Boutique?"

"Yes, she designed clothing and opened her own store in Red River Rock. Did she mention an interest in fashion or designing?"

He shook his head again, then a flicker of something registered in his eyes. "She did make her wedding dress, though, and Pixie's dress for the wedding. I... remember being surprised that she knew how to sew but she said her grandmother taught her." He rubbed his hand over his forehead.

"The change in careers could have been another ploy to disguise her identity. If whoever was after her looked for a designer, they wouldn't think to look for her at a gardening center."

Mark looked up bleakly. "Or she left me so she could start over somewhere else."

"You don't believe that and neither do I," Ellie said softly.

"I don't know what to think," he said, sounding defeated.

"Believe that Mia wouldn't leave Pixie," Ellie said.

He nodded. "I do believe that."

"The woman I mentioned, Patty Lasso," Ellie continued. "Her body was discovered in a whiskey barrel in the river yesterday. We suspect she was murdered about five years ago. When I questioned the sheriff and Patty's landlord, they said she left town two days before Jesse did."

Mark's gaze locked with hers, the wheels starting to turn.

"It's possible Jesse knew who killed Patty. She may even have witnessed her murder and she's running from the killer. If she thought he'd found her, she could have left you and Pixie to protect you or—"

"Or he got her," Mark muttered in a raw whisper.

"We can't give up on her, Mark. She needs us."

ONE HUNDRED ELEVEN

LIZARD CREEK

Cord's nerves were raw from worrying about Ellie, his eyes gritty from lack of sleep. He tried to take a nap when he got home but images of her lying in those bushes beaten to a bloody pulp refused to let him rest.

Just like he knew she'd refuse to turn the case over to Sheriff Waters.

On some level, he understood. She was friends with Mia and if whoever assaulted Ellie had taken Mia, the young woman was in serious danger.

If she was still alive.

Besides, he didn't know if Waters was all that competent. Certainly not as competent as Ellie.

His phone buzzed with work. "Got a call about a possible car crash around Lizard Creek. Not sure yet if it's a rescue or recovery mission but gather a team and head up there."

"Copy that." He ran his fingers through his shaggy hair, snagged his keys and hurried outside to his truck, grateful for work to distract him. Traffic was thick with the holiday crowd and big kick off for the whitewater rafting season, slowing him as he left town and drove toward Lizard Creek.

Fifteen miles north of Red River Rock, the place was not a popular tourist spot because of the stories about the river lizards that inhabited the marshy banks. The creek fed into the river, inciting tales about monsters hiding in the murk who preyed on other animals and children.

He didn't believe that last part but smalltown folklore had a way of taking on its own life.

He passed an outfitters store and headed onto the country road leading north of Red River Rock, not surprised that traffic had thinned out. By the time he reached the coordinates his boss had sent, Milo, two other SAR members and a medic team were there.

Shading his eyes from the blinding sun with his hand, he joined them.

"Does look like a car down there," Milo said. "I've already called a tow truck to haul it from the water."

Cord nodded as he eyed the situation. The only visible part of the vehicle was the rear bumper which was barely sticking out of the water. He gestured to the other SAR workers.

"Search the area for the driver in case he or she survived and got out." It was doubtful but miracles sometimes happened. "Milo and I will go down and take a look." He indicated to the medics. "You may as well stay here until we see what we're dealing with."

The team agreed, and Cord and Milo put on their waders, then grabbed goggles, flashlights and crowbars in case they needed to pry open the car door. The force of the water and mud could have glued it shut. Depending on how long the car had been submerged, water might have leaked in.

"There's a trail around here," Cord said. "We'll follow it instead of repelling."

He led the way, hacking at weeds and swatting flies as they plowed down the hill and wove through the rough terrain. He kept his eyes trained for snakes, scanning the path in case the driver had gotten out. If they had, they'd probably sustained injuries from the crash. Or depending on the timing of the crash, they could have succumbed to injuries or the elements, and the team might find a body instead.

His breath heaved out as he listened for a voice or a scream as he pushed on through, winding around the trail and wiping sweat from his face. When they finally reached the creek edge, he and Milo assessed the situation.

"Creek must be about four or five feet deep here," Cord said. "Maybe even a little deeper. I'll go in and see if the driver is still in the car."

Milo gave a nod, then walked up and down the riverbank, searching for signs someone had escaped the vehicle. Cord pulled on rubber gloves, adjusted his goggles and waded into the water. Beavers had built a dam to the right, and he saw a lizard sunbathing on the log. Muddy water sloshed up his waders and the scent of rotting moss and lichen rose around him.

He felt the car's bumper but it was cold, suggesting the car had been here for a while. Taking a deep breath, he ducked below the water. Just as he expected, the car had nosedived in, probably at such a rate that it had gone deep and the mud sucked it down farther.

He swam to the driver's door and used his flashlight to see inside. Though the water was muddy, he pressed his face to the glass and panned his light across the interior.

A woman was inside, head face down over the steering wheel.

ONE HUNDRED TWELVE

CROOKED CREEK

Ellie laid her head back against the headrest, her mind spinning as she and Derrick left Mark's.

"I'll drive you home to rest," Derrick said. "You look like hell."

"Thanks a lot," Ellie grumbled. "But I'm fine. A few bruises won't stop me from finding Mia. Time may be running out. I can feel it in my bones."

"That's the beating talking, reminding you to take care of your body."

Ellie chuckled, then cursed. "Don't make me laugh. I want to find Patty Lasso's brother. Maybe he had something to do with all this."

"I figured you were going to say that," Derrick said. "So while you had your beauty sleep at the hospital..." He gave her a wry look. "I did some digging. Patty's brother's name is Chuck. He's got a sheet for petty crimes. Mostly drug-related. He did a few months in prison about five years ago."

The hair on the back of Ellie's neck prickled. "Interesting timing. Where is he now?"

"Foggy Mountain," Derrick said with a twitch to his mouth. "Drives a delivery truck for Moon Stillery."

Was Patty's brother in the Moons' pocket? Ellie winced at the sun beaming through the windshield and covered her eyes with her hand. God, her head felt like it was going to blow right off.

"I want to—"

Derrick squeezed her hand. "Sleep, Ellie. We're heading there now."

ONE HUNDRED THIRTEEN
SOMEWHERE ON THE RIVER

Mia was so weak she could barely lift her hand to collect her water bottle. Whoever the monster was who'd taken her had left her nothing to eat but crackers. Was his plan to starve her to death? Or keep her so weak and disoriented she wouldn't have the energy to run even if she had the chance?

She already felt that way. Trapped, like she had five years ago. Haunted by wondering what had happened to her parents. Then... Patty...

Dear God, it was her fault Patty had died. And Tori.

She curled into the pillow and let the tears fall as memories of the day she came to Red River Rock floated back to her.

Her parents had been murdered. The boat accident was no accident at all.

Oh, Jo-Jo, where are you?

Surely by now the police were investigating her disappearance. Ellie would talk to Emily and Emily would give her the envelope about Pixie and her sister. Her daughter was in safe hands. Relief mushroomed inside her. Even if she wasn't safe, at least her daughter was. That was all that mattered.

Hope even budded inside her for moment.

Jo-Jo would explain everything to Ellie and take care of Pixie while Ellie hunted for her. And she knew Ellie wouldn't give up.

If only she'd listened to Jo-Jo in the first place and never gone to Red River Rock.

The boat bounced against the current, the sound of water crashing resurrecting her nightmares of the monsters lurking in the shadows.

Only there were real monsters here now.

ONE HUNDRED FOURTEEN

FOGGY MOUNTAIN

The warmth seeping through the window, coupled with the motion of the car, lulled Ellie into a deep sleep. When she woke up, Derrick had stopped at Moon Pies for coffee and pastries.

She stretched, already anticipating the gooey chocolate and marshmallow Moon Pies and the pecan roasted coffee.

In the café, while he ordered, Ellie ducked into the restroom, gripping her side as she splashed cold water on her face to clear her head of the mustiness of sleep.

Derrick was paying at the counter when she returned. "Did you know Patty Lasso?" he asked Opal Dean.

Ms. Opal tucked two Moon Pies into individual plastic sleeves and cut her eyes to the camera again. "She came in a few times. Liked my special caramel Moon Pies. Why you asking about her? Heard tell she moved away a few years back."

"Her body was found in the river," Derrick said. "According to her boyfriend she'd been acting skittish the last few days before she disappeared."

"Well, I declare." The woman pressed a wrinkled, trembling hand to her pudgy cheek. "I'm sorry to hear that."

"Did she ever mention her family?" Ellie asked.

The woman busied herself filling a napkin dispenser. "No, Detective. I'm not a gossip barn here. I just sell Moon Pies."

The bell over the door tinkled, a family of eight trickling in.

Ms. Opal waved them off to tend to her customers.

"I just sell Moon Pies, my ass," Ellie said, the effects of her headache making her edgy as they stepped outside into the muggy heat.

"Just like everyone else in town. They're scared to talk," Derrick said. "Let's see what Patty's brother has to say. Maybe his little stint in the pen taught him to be fearless."

Ellie winced as she lifted her hand to accept her coffee. "Maybe. Or... maybe he's working for the people who killed his sister."

ONE HUNDRED FIFTEEN
MOON STILLERY

The stillery was hopping with the lunch crowd, but Ellie felt a stillness in the air as she and Derrick entered. Several patrons at the bar turned to stare at them, then looked away and whispers rumbled.

Her body throbbed with every step and she had to grit her teeth to keep from moaning as she climbed onto a bar stool beside Derrick. The rustic décor suited the mountain location, the scents of burgers, fries and wings wafting through the room, blending with the smell of beer and whiskey.

Derrick gestured to the bartender, and they ordered beers and burgers. Normally she wouldn't drink on the job but one beer would help dull the pain and wouldn't incapacitate her like the painkillers the doctor had prescribed.

She noticed the burly guy with the bandaged hand talking to his mother Ronnie. The conversation looked heated, then Ronnie pulled him into a corner.

The bartender Al slid the beers in front of them. "Food'll be up in a minute."

"Hey, Al," Ellie said, feigning a light smile. "Last time we were in here, we asked about Patty Lasso. Why didn't you tell us her brother worked for the stillery?"

A muscle ticked in his jaw. "You didn't ask."

Just like everyone else, he wasn't volunteering any information.

"Is he around?" Derrick asked.

"Haven't see him," Al muttered. "He made a delivery last night so he's probably sleeping in today. I'll get your burgers."

He hurried to the opposite side of the bar where a waitress had set their orders, and Ellie scanned the room. Ronnie was watching them.

"I'm going to talk to Ronnie," Ellie said.

Derrick touched her hand as she started to get up. "No way. We'll get her to come over here."

Ten minutes later, Al returned and delivered their food, and Derrick asked, "Al, can you tell Ronnie we need to talk to her?"

His nostrils flared and an uneasy look passed over his face. "I told you not to mess with them."

"Listen to me," Ellie said, irritated. "We're investigating a woman's disappearance and a murder. It's my job to mess with people."

He tossed the rag he used to wipe the counter aside. "Suit yourself. But I warned you."

Ronnie started through a side door, but Al caught her just in time. A moment later, she glared at them then stalked over, arms crossed. Her skin looked as rough around the edges as she did, her face square and unforgiving. She looked like a mountain woman that had grown up in these parts.

Derrick introduced them, but Ronnie cut him off. "I know who you are. So does everyone in town."

"Ronnie, this is a great bar. You own this place?" Ellie said.

She grunted. "Don't be a kiss ass. I know you been asking about Jesse Habersham and that girl Patty. But they ain't my kind of people and I don't know nothing."

"Well, Patty's brother works for you," Ellie said. "And we need to talk to him."

Ronnie patted the pocket of her flannel shirt, which held a pack of Camels. "He ain't here and won't be back till night."

"You must have his home address in your employee records," Derrick said, flashing his credentials. "We need that."

She rubbed a scarred hand across her ruddy cheek. "Guess I don't got no choice."

"No, you don't," Ellie said. "Get it for us." She didn't bother to say please or else she'd get the kiss ass comment again.

Ronnie's glare said she didn't like it, but she walked toward the side door and disappeared through it. Ellie and Derrick started on their burgers while they waited.

A few minutes later, Ronnie returned with a sticky note with an address on it.

"You knew about his prior arrests when you hired him?" Ellie asked.

Ronnie's smile revealed a mouthful of crooked yellowed teeth. "Just tryin' to be a good guy. Ain't no law against that."

Ellie simply stared at her. No use replying. She didn't believe Ronnie was a good guy for a second. In fact, she might have hired Patty's brother *because* he had a record for selling drugs, and she needed help moving her own illegal product.

ONE HUNDRED SIXTEEN

BASS HEAD TRAIL

Chuck Lasso lived in a shack in the woods near Moon Docks. The narrow dirt road named Bass Head Trail drew fisherman onto the river. An old beige Chevy was parked in the drive and a hound dog lay basking on the porch. A shed to the right appeared to hold fishing gear, a cleaning station, and a wood-work table.

The place was isolated, off the beaten path, but they'd passed several other fishermen's cabins after they'd turned off the main road.

Derrick parked, and Ellie bit back another groan as she stepped from his car. The scent of pine trees burst to life, the sun beaming down onto the patchy grass. Derrick held her elbow as they made their way up the graveled drive and for once she swallowed her pride and leaned on him.

The stairs creaked as they climbed them and she dodged a rotten spot on the landing. The dog's snore rumbled, but at the sound of the squeak he lifted his head and opened one droopy eyelid. Derrick offered his hand for the dog to sniff, and a second later, the hound dropped his head back down and the snoring started all over again.

It took three knocks before the door opened. A scrawny guy wearing baggy jeans and a Grateful Dead T-shirt rubbed his hand over his eyes with a yawn. His ratty brown hair was sweaty and sticking in all directions.

"Chuck Lasso?" Ellie asked.

"Yeah, why you wanna know?" He tugged a cigarette from his pocket and rolled it between his fingers. Fingers that bore scars – from gutting fish or woodworking or... maybe prison?

He didn't have the body of a fighter and had probably had a tough time in lock-up.

Derrick introduced them. "Can we come in? We need to talk."

"Am I in trouble with the law or something?" he grumbled. "I keep up with my parole officer. If she says I don't, that bitch is lying."

"*Are* you in trouble?" Ellie asked.

His face contorted as his defenses rose. "No, hell, no. I follow all the shitty rules they give me. Got a job and pay my rent."

Gnats swarmed around Ellie's face. "Let us step inside, sir. Please. It's important."

He muttered a foul word but waved them in and sauntered to a living room with furniture that looked as if it came from a junkyard. Either Ronnie wasn't paying him very well or he was doing something else with his money.

He slumped onto a plaid sofa and Derrick and Ellie claimed seats in the two ladderback chairs, the only furniture in the room besides the fifty-inch smart TV. Apparently the man had priorities. "Mr. Lasso, I'm sorry to have to tell you this but your sister's body was found."

He pulled a lighter, flicked it and lit up. He shifted his eyes away for a second, took a drag and blew out the smoke. Ellie barely resisted coughing as the stagnant air clouded.

"Yeah, sheriff done talked to me."

Why hadn't Kincaid told them?

"Do you have any idea what happened to her?" Ellie asked.

"How would I know? I was locked up on some bogus charges when I was told she'd left town. Didn't bother to visit or write me. I figured she just went off on some adventure."

"Why would you say that?" Derrick asked.

"She was one of them dreamer types. A do-gooder too. Thought she'd make the world a better place." He blew smoke rings in the air and for a moment, rubbed his eyes as if he was battling emotions. "I figured she decided she was better off not having a loser like me around."

"Were you two close before you were incarcerated?" Ellie asked.

He shook his head. "Not really. Old man used to beat me, doted on her. Pretty little Patty could do no wrong. You know how it goes." He coughed, obviously realizing he sounded bitter. "But she didn't deserve what they did to her."

"Do you have any idea who killed her or why she was murdered?" Ellie asked.

"Told you, I was locked up."

"Why did you say the charges against you were bogus?" Derrick pressed.

Chuck tapped ashes into a Mountain Dew can. "Forget it. I did my time. Didn't do no good to say anything back then. Won't now either."

Derrick frowned. "Do you think someone framed you?"

Chuck's bony shoulders jabbed upward. "Don't know. I admit to smoking a little weed and doing coke a few times. But I sure as hell wasn't no drug mule."

"Did you have enemies?" Ellie asked. "Someone who might have hurt Patty to get to you?"

"Look, I'm small potatoes around her. Maybe *she* was into something illegal or got mixed up with a bad seed." He stubbed the end of his cigarette in the can. "Why you care about Patty anyway? Sheriff in Red River Rock said he'd find whoever done that to her."

Ellie gave him a short version. "Because we think her death may be connected to Jesse Habersham's disappearance. And if Jesse is still alive, that she's in danger."

He studied the scars on his hands. "Like I said, I don't know anything."

Frustration knotted Ellie's stomach. She laid her card on the table. "If you think of something that might help, please call me."

She and Derrick stood and walked to the door, then let themselves out.

"If someone did frame him," Ellie said, "they may have wanted him out of the way. Hyping up drug charges would have done that."

"Or it's possible he met another con in the pen and was so pissed off at his sister for abandoning him, that he hired someone to take care of her."

"Yeah, but the fact that she worked with Jesse and they both disappeared can't be a coincidence." Ellie's phone rang, and she yanked it from her belt and answered. "Hey, Cord."

"I'm outside Red River Rock where a woman was found dead in her car. It went over the edge into the ravine at Lizard Creek."

"An accident?"

"I don't think so," Cord said. "Sheriff Kincaid is here now. They've just pulled her car from the water."

"Any ID on her?"

"Yeah, her name was Thelma Coonts."

Ellie dug her nails into her palms. "Damn."

"Did you know her?" Cord asked.

"We met at Moondoggy's. She's the waitress who told us about Patty Lasso."

ONE HUNDRED SEVENTEEN

ATLANTA

While Pixie was at the pool with that Emily woman and her brood, Kevin drove to Atlanta to do some shopping. Red River Rock and Crooked Creek had a couple of boutiques for adults and some outlet stores, but he would have nothing but the best for his little girl.

First he'd buy her some clothes, then toys. He already had a vision in his mind for her room. A white princess bed with pink and yellow tulips, frilly curtains and unicorns on the walls. It would be like her very own princess castle.

On the way to Lennox Square, he considered calling the designer he'd used in the house and asked her to draw up some plans for a playroom. Then he thought again and decided to wait. If things didn't go smoothly with custody and he had to leave with Pixie for a while, he didn't want anyone to get suspicious.

But he did make a call to his attorney.

"I have a daughter," he told him then explained about Jesse being alive and having stolen his little girl from him. "I want you to start formulating a strategy against her mother so I can obtain legal custody of my child."

Maybe they'd take a trip somewhere. Disney would be fun for Pixie, then a beach trip. A smile tugged at his lips as he imagined her in a cute little pink bathing suit and jellies, the two of them collecting seashells. He could hear the ping of them as she dropped them into the bucket and saw her little footprints in the sand, her tiny hand in his looking up at him with adoration.

She'd be a daddy's girl in no time!

"Certainly," his attorney agreed.

Oh, how he loved his authority. Everyone in Red River Rock respected him and his father.

Jesse would learn that, too. The hard way.

Shaving a few pounds off her would restore her beauty and a hair stylist could turn her back into the beautiful woman he loved, not the dirty country bumpkin he'd seen in the pictures of Mia Norman.

He exited the freeway, battled his way to the shopping mall parking lot and glanced around at the Mercedes, BMWs, and even saw a Rolls and a Bentley. This was his kind of place.

He pulled up to the valet section, got out and handed the man the keys to his Range Rover. "Do not park this near anyone else. And no taking it out for a joyride. I will be checking the mileage." He pulled a hundred-dollar bill from his wallet and waved it around. Long ago, he'd learned that you couldn't trust everyone. People took advantage. "Understood?"

"Yes, sir," the guy in uniform said, his voice jittery.

"Great. This is yours if I come back and my vehicle is just as perfect as it was when I handed it over."

The young man took the keys with a nod, and Kevin straightened his suit tie and went inside the exclusive Lennox Square. Designer stores were everywhere. The marble floor gleamed beneath the lights. Women dressed in high fashion, decked out with jewels. Just the way he'd liked seeing Jesse.

He'd already researched the mall and made a list of shops to visit. He headed straight to Little Princesses to pick out some sparkly dresses. But a jewelry store caught his eye. He veered toward it, remembering the extravagant engagement ring and wedding band he'd bought Jesse.

Bitch.

Moving to the window, he glanced at the display in the glass encasement and practically jumped up and down with excitement at the necklace – the beautiful delicate gold chain held a tiny half-moon with a glittering diamond chip in the corner. It was the perfect gift to welcome his little girl into the Moon family.

He ducked into the store with a grin. They'd be like two peas in a pod, and she'd forget all about her deceitful mother.

ONE HUNDRED EIGHTEEN

LIZARD CREEK

Ellie phoned Sheriff Waters on the way to the accident. "Bryce, can you look into a man named Chuck Lasso?" Ellie explained about Patty and her murder. "Chuck served time in the pen for drug trafficking, but he claimed the charges were bogus."

"They all say that," Bryce said. "Don't you know? Everyone in prison is innocent."

Ellie rolled her eyes as Derrick parked behind Cord's truck at Lizard Creek. "I know, I know. Just talk to the prison warden, ask about his mail or visitors, if he had contact with anyone while he was there. We're in Red River Rock now. If someone framed Chuck, maybe they did so to get him out of the way so they could kill Patty. Jesse could have seen something, even Patty's murder, and that's the reason she ran."

"On it," Bryce said. "I have a buddy in the DEA. Maybe he knows something."

"Good idea." Ellie winced as she reached for the door handle. "Thanks, Bryce. Keep me posted."

"Same."

She clipped her phone back onto her belt as she and Derrick walked to the edge of the road and looked down at the car which the rescue workers had recovered from the creek. "I need to see Thelma," Ellie said as she took off to the trail that wound down to the ravine.

"Damn, Ellie. Can't you wait till they bring her up?" Derrick snapped.

"No. Thelma was probably killed because she gave us Patty's name. And I don't trust Kincaid or anyone in this town."

She skidded on the muddy terrain and Derrick took her arm. Together they followed the trail until they reached Cord and Kincaid and the rescue team.

The minute she saw the woman's car, she spotted black paint on the bumper. Thelma's car was gray, which suggested another car had hit her from behind.

Her gut instinct screamed that this was no accident. That Thelma had been murdered.

ONE HUNDRED NINETEEN
CROOKED CREEK

Mark studied the picture of himself, Mia and Pixie that they'd taken at the county fair last month. Pixie had squealed as they rode bumper cars and ate cotton candy, and he'd won her a giant panda bear. Then they'd visited the petting zoo and she'd laughed at the baby goats and begged for a puppy. He and Mia had decided to surprise her with one for Christmas.

That night, Mia had tucked her arm in his and whispered that she was thrilled for the three of them to become a family.

Had she been lying about that?

No... She'd seemed so happy and content. She couldn't have faked it.

Ellie was right. Something bad had happened to her.

Every hour that passed felt like an eternity and his fear that Mia was never coming back mounted. He missed her and he missed Pixie. He walked to his back patio and stared out at the woods. There had been so many murders in Bluff County the last two years. Was his darling Mia going to be another?

How could he go on without her? Without the little girl he loved like a daughter? And what would happen if Mia didn't come back and that man she'd married demanded to have Pixie?

A knock sounded at the door and he hurried to it, hoping it was Ellie Reeves with answers. But his mother stood on the stoop, holding a casserole dish in one hand.

Her eyes crinkled with worry as she raked her gaze over him. "You look terrible, honey."

He didn't bother to argue. She stormed past him, her heels clicking on his wood floor as she made her way to the kitchen. He followed, his mind already ticking away an excuse to get rid of her.

She set the dish on the counter with a smile. "I made you a roast with those tiny little potatoes and peas that's your favorite."

"You didn't have to do that, Mom."

She pinched his cheek with her fingers like she did when he was a little boy. "Your color is bad, too. Have you eaten *anything* the past few days?"

He released a wary sigh. "I haven't exactly been hungry. I keep worrying about Mia."

"I'm so sorry, darling," she murmured. "Have you heard anything?"

He hadn't told her everything yet. And he sure as hell didn't feel like getting into it now. "Nothing concrete," he said. "I did find out she had a sister, and she and her husband were murdered. Detective Reeves thinks it might be connected to Mia's disappearance."

His mother gasped and shock glazed her expression. "Do they know who murdered them?" she whispered.

He shook his head, his chest hurting with the effort to breathe. "Not yet. But they think it may be linked to a man named Kevin Moon. They're investigating him now."

His mother swayed slightly then caught hold of the counter for support. "Oh, honey. I... don't know what to say."

ONE HUNDRED TWENTY

LIZARD CREEK

Guilt seized Ellie as she realized Thelma might have died because she'd pointed them toward Patty. Sheriff Kincaid spoke to the rescue worker as they pulled her from the car, his body rigid, jaw clenched. Cord stood back with his SAR team member while Derrick circled the muddy car that had been dragged from the water, analyzing it.

"I met Thelma at Moondoggy's. She seemed like a nice lady. Did you know her personally?" Ellie asked the sheriff.

"Not well. She was a good waitress," Kincaid answered. "Friendly to everyone."

Ellie crossed her arms. "You realize this was no accident, don't you?"

"Why do you say that?" His mouth thinned into a frown.

"I saw the black paint on her rear bumper." She arched a brow. "Don't tell me you didn't."

Sheriff Kincaid walked to the back of the car and peered at it, then gave a nod. What else could he do? She wasn't stupid, nor did she intend to let this slide.

"I'll have a forensic team process the vehicle and look into the accident."

"Not an accident," Ellie said again.

"She could have been hit by a car at another time or she may have backed into someone else's vehicle herself before she crashed here."

"Sure, that could have happened. But it's suspicious. First Jesse's disappearance five years ago. Then we find Patty's body and we know she was murdered. Now Thelma."

He adjusted his Aviator sunglasses. "What did Thelma say to you when you talked to her?"

She decided to toss out some bait. "Nothing really. But she may or may not have mentioned Patty Lasso."

He went so still Ellie wasn't sure he was breathing. "Listen to me," he said in a menacing whisper. "This is my town and I have things under control. Do not interfere, Detective."

"If you have things under control, then why are bodies piling up? Why is everyone in this town afraid to talk? Including you?"

His lip twitched as if he was biting back a threat. "I believe you've had your own share of murders in your town, Detective Reeves. You weren't able to save everyone, were you?"

Ellie's heart thundered. "No, but I certainly didn't cover up the truth. I did what I could to get justice."

"And so will I," Sheriff Kincaid said. "Now, get out of my county."

She shook her head. "No way. My medical examiner will join yours for the autopsy."

Furious, she turned and pulled her phone to call Laney.

ONE HUNDRED TWENTY-ONE

SOMEWHERE ON THE RIVER

Mia's stomach roiled, her mind a tornado of emotions. What was her kidnapper planning to do to her next?

He was torturing her, letting her die a slow death and keeping her away from Pixie.

Thank God Kevin didn't know about Pixie and she was safe.

She nibbled on the dry crackers, anything to give her energy, and prayed they'd stopped drugging her water. Her past life drifted back to her, a memory of when Patty had first come to her, upset, and raised alarm bells in her head.

"Jess, something's wrong. Last night I noticed a discrepancy with the books and asked Kevin, and he... he scared me."

"What do you mean?" Mia – Jesse – had asked.

"He ordered me to do my job and let him take care of it. But... I followed him outside and heard him talking to someone and... he told them he'd take care of me and stop me from asking questions." Patty burst into tears. "I'm scared, Jess. I think someone's been following me all day."

That night she'd asked Kevin what was going on. He'd

wrapped his hands around her throat, squeezed her neck and she'd thought he would strangle her to death.

ONE HUNDRED TWENTY-TWO
CROOKED CREEK

Pixie hugged her beach towel around her as she trailed Norah and her brothers from the van. The boys ran to the trampoline again and Norah chased after them.

Pixie trudged behind them. She didn't feel like jumping, just like she hadn't felt like swimming today but she had climbed on the big pink flamingo float with Norah and for a few minutes she laughed and forgot that her mommy wasn't coming back for her.

Tears bubbled in her throat and she swiped at her eyes.

"Come on, sweetie," Ms. Emily said as she put her arm around her. "You want to play outside or watch a show?"

"I want Mommy," Pixie cried. "And Mr. Mark."

Ms. Emily scooped her up and carried her to the backyard then they sat in the glider for a minute, rocking back and forth. Pixie looked up for a minute and saw the black car she'd seen before slowing as it drove by.

She buried her head against Ms. Emily and cried and cried. Finally her tears dried up and she settled down.

Then she heard Ms. Emily talking on the phone to Ms.

Ellie. "I think it might be good for Pixie to see Mark. Is that okay?"

Pixie clenched her hands as she tried to hear what Ms. Ellie had to say, but she couldn't hear.

Then Ms. Emily said, "Okay, I'll set it up."

Ms. Emily patted her back. "I'm calling Mark now."

Pixie nodded and brushed at her eyes as Ms. Emily made the call.

"Do you want to meet up at the park and have a visit with Pixie?"

Pixie held her breath. Mommy was gone. Did Mr. Mark not want to see her? Didn't he want to be her daddy anymore?

"Okay, see you in half an hour," Ms. Emily said. She hung up and stroked Pixie's hair. "Mr. Mark is meeting us at the park, Pixie. He loves you and misses you and your mommy."

Pixie bobbed her head up and down but she couldn't talk for the tears in her throat and the snot running down her nose. Maybe Mr. Mark would tell her when Mommy would be back and why she'd left them at the wedding.

Or maybe he'd know where to find her and they could go look for her together.

ONE HUNDRED TWENTY-THREE

RED RIVER ROCK

Ellie had no intention of leaving the investigation in the hands of Sheriff Kincaid.

Bryce called as Ellie and Derrick got in the car, and she put him on speaker. "I checked with the prison where Chuck Lasso was incarcerated. Confirmed that his sister never visited him. Warden said the guy insisted he'd been railroaded into jail on trumped up charges. Was assigned a court-appointed attorney who encouraged him to accept a plea. Judge's name was Kotter."

"Where was he tried?" Ellie asked.

"Red River Rock," Bryce said. "And get this. He was arrested a week before his sister was murdered."

"So he didn't kill her, but his arrest could have been connected."

"If the judge knows Kincaid, he could be in the sheriff's pocket," Ellie suggested.

"It's possible, I guess. One more thing," Bryce said. "I looked into Jesse's finances and Mia's accounts. She earned a modest salary with no heavy debt. Lived within her means and had a little savings but not enough to indicate she'd stolen money from Kevin Moon." He paused for a beat. "Melvin Kramer at the bank told me she has a safety deposit box there. He has no idea what's inside, but under the circumstances thought we should know."

Ellie's pulse jumped. "It may contain something important like her will or... something about her past that can help us." She rubbed at her shoulder which was throbbing. "Go by her house and see if you can find the key. And bring a warrant for us to open it."

"Copy that. I'll call a judge on the way."

She thanked him and hung up and spoke to Derrick. "Let's talk to Kevin Moon again. Push him and see what he knows about Patty and her brother."

ONE HUNDRED TWENTY-FOUR

SOMEWHERE ON THE RIVER

Mia looked out the cabin window again and saw the monsters chasing her. They bobbed up and down in the water, eyes peering back at her, tongues slithering in and out. Gray storm clouds gathered above, a rumble of thunder making her flinch. Lightning highlighted the sky in the distance.

It was storming the night her parents died.

"What happened to them, Grammy?" she'd asked dozens of times. *"Why were they running?"*

"Don't go asking questions," Grammy said. *"They're gone and nothing good can come of you poking around."*

But Mia couldn't let it go. By the time she'd reached her twenties and once her grandmother was gone, she'd had to know. Even Jo-Jo pleaded with her. "Please, Mia. I can't lose you, too."

Mia had grown angry at her sister then. "Do you know what happened?"

Jo-Jo looked down at her knotted hands. "Don't you remember what Grammy said when we first came to live with her? It's dangerous to ask questions."

They were keeping secrets from her and the questions constantly nagged at her. But she wasn't a child anymore. So she'd driven to Red River Rock, looking for answers.

Then Patty... The week before the wedding. Patty had been nervous. Had suggested they go to the police with her suspicions... Two nights before the wedding came Patty's frantic call. "I'm scared, Jess. Meet me at the docks...."

And she had.

She'd tried to blot out the memory of what happened that night, and wanted to go to the police, but the threats stopped her. She'd just learned she was pregnant and known she had to leave town. Get away from Kevin. Protect her unborn child.

And now... she had a bad feeling she was going to die because of it.

Suddenly she heard voices outside. A man, the one who'd taken her. Then a gruffer voice.

"I want to see her now."

Panic zinged through Mia. The other voice... one she'd never wanted to hear again.

Then the door opened and terror shot through her.

Kevin. He was behind this just as she'd feared.

"Hello, sweetheart," he said with a menacing grin. "Did you really think you could leave me?"

"You did this? You had that man kidnap me and lock me in here?"

"Actually, that was my father's doing. He wanted to clean up the mess you made. I just figured it out." He chuckled. "And how perfect it was. To have you taken from your wedding just like you disappeared from ours."

Don't show your fear. He revels in it.

"Kevin, please. Don't do this. Let me go home."

"And where would that be?" His voice was icy cold. "To the home I built for us? To be with me – your husband?"

Mia choked back a cry. She had to stay calm. Appeal to his logical side.

"You know the reason I left," she said. "I had to."

"Why? Because I didn't give you everything you wanted? Everything you could possibly need?" He walked toward her, a sinister look teeming in his brown eyes. "I gave you the boutique. And diamonds. And a car, a damn Mercedes. We had a bright future." His voice turned to gravel. "And I gave you my love. *All* my love."

"You don't know what love is," Mia said, unable to refrain from speaking her mind. "Your love is cruel, obsessive. To you, love means controlling someone, smothering them and locking them away." She gestured around her. "Just like you're doing now."

His body went steely straight, hands fisting by his sides. "You humiliated me and let me believe you were dead. Do you have any idea how I felt thinking you'd drowned? Terrified that someone had abducted you? That someone might have tortured or killed you?" He paced to her, gripped her face in one hand and squeezed so hard she thought he was going to break her jaw. "You're my wife. We said vows," he shouted.

Mia whimpered at the pain shooting down her jaw.

"And now I find out we have a daughter that you kept from me. That you never told me about." Rage made his face beet red. "What did you tell her about me, Jesse?"

Mia felt her world completely crumble. Dear God... he knew about Pixie. "I had to protect her from your family," she whispered.

"From her own father?" He released her jaw so hard her head snapped back. "I would have given her everything," he growled. "I *will* give her everything. And now you and your lover will know exactly how I felt. You'll know the agony of not seeing your child."

Tears blurred her eyes. "No, Kevin. My daughter is safe with my sister and her husband. I made sure of that."

A manic laugh boomed from him. He yanked his phone from his pocket, scrolled for a minute, then flipped it around and shoved it in her face.

She gasped as she realized what she was looking at. Her sister and brother-in-law's obituary.

ONE HUNDRED TWENTY-FIVE

Kevin smiled at the horror on Jesse's face.

No, the woman looking at him didn't look like the woman he loved at all. She was Mia and Mia had killed his Jesse.

He should do as his father wanted when he'd told him where she was and just get rid of her…

But not now. Not yet. She had to suffer first. He reached for the door to leave.

"Where are you going?" she cried.

His heart burst as he pictured his precious little girl. "I have things to do to prepare for my daughter. I want everything perfect when she meets me."

"Please, Kevin, you'll scare her…"

He smiled again then stepped from the room, locking it. The fear in her eyes spiked his blood as he climbed to the main deck and made his way to the captain's seat. Below deck, he heard her banging on the door and screaming for him to let her out as the wind shifted.

He had to let the storm pass before he got off. Until then he'd savor the sound of her screams.

Now he was here, he wanted to draw out the pain. He

could still feel the aching emptiness in his chest from those days she was missing and he'd had no idea where she was. But each day that passed, he'd become more and more determined to find her.

That had been a challenge, but now he finally had.

The boat rocked with the force of the current. The river water splashed onto the deck as the storm raged around them. Lightning flashed and thunder boomed, the constant swaying a reminder of the night Jesse had first disappeared.

The river had swept her away just as it was sweeping them into the safety of the mountains now. There, darkness thrived and secrets could be buried forever.

The river monsters Jesse had been terrified of crawled all around them. Poisonous spiders spun invisible webs, then slunk into their hiding holes waiting to trap their prey. Cotton mouth water moccasins slithered along the surface, blending in with the sticks and twigs brought down by brutal winds rolling off the sharp ridges, and hungry mosquitoes buzzed in the night, nibbling on flesh and spreading diseases.

He could still hear his Jesse crying from that very first time he'd taken her to his father's riverboat. Screaming that she hated the river.

But the river was his home. And now it would be hers forever.

ONE HUNDRED TWENTY-SIX

CROOKED CREEK

Derrick and Ellie had stopped by Foggy Mountain Real Estate where they learned Kevin had taken an out-of-town business trip for the day. Bryce called with the warrant for Mia's safety deposit box so they met him at the bank in Crooked Creek.

"When was the last time Mia came to the box?" Ellie asked the banker, Mr. Kramer.

He consulted the log on his computer. "Three weeks ago," he answered as he removed a set of keys from inside his locked desk.

Sheriff Waters handed over the warrant, and the man examined it. "Looks in order. Follow me."

A few patrons stood in line at the teller window and another office held a financial consultant. They followed Kramer through a set of doors, then down a hall to another locked door. He unlocked it and they stepped into a rectangular room lined with safety deposit boxes.

He located Mia's on the third row and handed Bryce the key, who opened it. Kramer stepped away to give them privacy as Derrick removed two folders and a manilla envelope, carrying them to a table in the center of the room.

He handed Ellie the envelope and he examined the first folder. "It's a copy of Mia's will."

Ellie hoped to God she didn't need it but was glad her friend had one. While Bryce skimmed it for details and Derrick studied the second folder, she pulled a stack of photographs from the envelope.

The first ones were shots of the boutique and shops around Red River Rock. There were others of the mountains and the river. Why would Mia keep these pictures in a safety deposit box?

Bryce cleared his throat. "According to the will, Mia left everything to her sister. She also had papers drawn up giving her custody of Pixie."

"Is there a birth certificate for Pixie?" Ellie asked.

Bryce nodded. "But she didn't list the father's name."

"There had to be a reason she didn't want him to know about Pixie." She glanced at Derrick. "Anything in there?"

"Yeah. Articles about her parents' death. She also scribbled some notes. She went to Red River Rock to find out what happened. She suspected they might have been murdered. She wrote in a journal as well," Derrick said. "Said she suspected the Moons had something to do with it. That the day she realized she was pregnant she knew she had to get away from them."

"It's starting to make sense now." Ellie dug through more photographs and saw one of Moon Stillery and then a riverboat shrouded by thick trees. Finally she came to several shots of the woods and what appeared to be a warehouse of some kind tucked back into the foliage. A cargo van sat parked nearby.

There were two other pictures that made her instincts scream. The photos were of Ronnie's sons slinking into the building.

Had Jesse or Patty discovered an illegal still? A drug

running business? Was that what had gotten Patty killed and forced Jesse to go into hiding?

ONE HUNDRED TWENTY-SEVEN

MOONDOGGY'S

In an effort to learn if Thelma had talked to any of the other waitresses about Patty, Ellie and Derrick revisited Moondoggy's.

The place was rocking with the holiday crowd, loud jukebox music filling the air, families chattering and patrons imbibing.

As she entered, she scanned the room for Ronnie or her sons but didn't see them. Another waitress named Delilah popped over, her wavy blond hair the color of butter. She looked to be in her late twenties.

"What can I get y'all?"

Ellie ordered the pulled pork sandwich and Derrick the brisket, then Ellie introduced them. "Did you hear that Thelma Coonts was killed?" Ellie asked.

Delilah cut her eyes around the room, then fiddled with the moon-shaped pendant dangling on a gold chain around her neck. "I did. Poor Thelma, she was a hard worker."

"Did she ever mention a woman named Patty Lasso?"

Unease splintered her expression and she shifted and

tapped her order pad with her pencil. "Don't know that name," Delilah said. "I'll put your orders in."

"Did you see the moon-shaped necklace?" Ellie asked Derrick after the waitress headed off.

"Yeah," Derrick replied. "You think they sell them in town?"

"Maybe. Or maybe it's a sign that the Moons own her."

Derrick stood. "Going to talk to the bartender again. See if he knows anything about an illegal still or meth lab around here."

Ellie nodded and while he went to the bar, she phoned Detective Mathis, the cop who'd investigated the Penningtons' deaths.

"I figured I'd be hearing from you again," he said in a deep voice.

Ellie filled him in on Patty Lasso's and Thelma Coonts' murders. "When Jesse Habersham, AKA Mia Norman, disappeared from Red River Rock, I believe she tried to fake her death out of fear because she and Patty discovered illegal activities in town. My guess is either money laundering or they're running drugs. But she needed help to fake her death." She hesitated, a scenario playing out in her head. "I think it could have been her sister and her sister's husband helping her. At least someone with access to the Body Farm where they use cadavers to teach crime scene investigation."

"That would have been Mr. Pennington," Detective Mathis said. "His step brother worked there."

"Did you question Pennington's coworkers about his death?"

"I did but got nowhere. If he took the cadaver, which would make sense, then he did it on his own."

"And whoever killed the Penningtons thought the couple knew where Jesse was." Her heart felt heavy. "They died trying to protect her."

Derrick returned as she ended the call. "I showed the bartender the photo of that warehouse. Said he didn't know what they were doing up there, but he and a buddy were hiking once and came on it. One of Ronnie's boys ran them off with a shotgun."

ONE HUNDRED TWENTY-EIGHT
SOMEWHERE ON THE RIVER

Mia screamed and beat on the door until her hands ached and her throat was raw. "Let me out, Kevin! Please don't go after Pixie!"

She had no idea if he could hear her over the storm or if he was just ignoring her. Or maybe he'd left her alone on the boat.

She pictured Jo-Jo's face, grief and anguish overcoming her. All this time she'd stayed away from her sister and her husband to keep them safe. She'd missed holidays and birthdays and hadn't contacted them once, although she missed her sister every day. But she'd prayed eventually they'd be able to connect again.

And she'd trusted that if anything happened to her, Pixie would live with her aunt.

Pain, raw and deep, ripped through her. Then came the guilt. She never should have asked for their help. She'd put them in danger. They were dead because of her.

And she hadn't even known it. Hadn't been able to say goodbye.

Tears clogged her throat. The night she'd called Jo-Jo for help flashed back.

Patty had come to her. "You have to see what the Moons are doing," she'd said urgently. "Someone has to stop them."

She and Patty snuck up to their warehouse, hid in the shadows, and snapped pictures. Those mean boys of Ronnie's were guarding the place with shotguns. She and Patty waited in the woods until the men dipped into the moonshine and passed out.

Or at least they thought they had. They started toward the warehouse but suddenly one of the brothers stirred and attacked. Patty screamed and Jesse searched for something to use as a weapon. But the other one grabbed her and put her in a chokehold. Sweat from his shirt soaked her back. His heavy breathing bathed her neck. He smelled like corn liquor and cigarettes, nauseating her.

She cried and screamed in horror as the other one beat Patty until she went limp.

"No, stop..." Terror filled her as they stuffed Patty into a barrel...

Mia rubbed her eyelids to blot out the memory. Watching Patty being murdered had been terrifying. She'd thought about the baby she was carrying, the one she hadn't told Kevin about.

Paralyzed with fear, she'd known she had to run when she got the chance.

The loss of her parents when she was young had sent her to Red River Rock. She'd lost her grandmother. Lost Jo-Jo. Tori.

And now, Pixie... she couldn't lose her precious child. Not to the Moons. Pixie could not grow up with those monsters.

ONE HUNDRED TWENTY-NINE
CROOKED CREEK

Kevin left Jesse on the boat alone to stew over the fact that he'd found his daughter. After deserting him, it was fitting that she should suffer and face her worst fears in the place that terrified her most.

He cleaned up, then drove to Crooked Creek and parked near the drive by Emily Nettles' house, his nerves on edge as impatience set in. Emily and the kids were home. She'd sent them to the backyard to play while she whipped up an early dinner. Her husband came in and kissed her, and she looked at him in adoration.

The Nettles were the perfect American family.

But his daughter was not one of them and never would be. She was *his*.

And he would love her to the moon and back. Laughter bubbled in his chest at his own witticism.

The family finished burgers which the saintly husband had grilled and then cleaned up, and the man, the boys and the little redhead went for a bike ride. Emily took Pixie's hand and they walked out to the van and got in.

Kevin's heart stuttered. Maybe he should take his daughter now. Emily... She would be collateral damage.

But then he thought of her other kids and the little redhead with the freckles. He couldn't do that to them. She looked like a good mother, the kind he wished he'd had as a kid. One that took him places and laughed with him and made apple pie and didn't mind if you played in the mud.

Besides, it wasn't like he was a monster.

Making sure she didn't see him following her, he stayed two cars back as they drove for a couple of miles until they reached the park. He pulled into a space a few rows behind her beneath a shade tree her, then trailed her, maintaining a safe distance and glancing at his phone pretending to be in conversation.

The park was fairly empty this evening. He paused at a bench, watching as a man approached Emily and the little girl.

The child – his daughter – lit up with a smile, then squealed and ran to the man. Hot rage heated his blood as the man scooped her up, hugged her and swung her around.

A litany of ugly words raced through his head. It was Mark Wade.

And the bastard was holding *his* daughter.

ONE HUNDRED THIRTY

RED RIVER ROCK

Ellie and Derrick asked the waitress and a few patrons at Moondoggy's about the warehouse but if they knew its location, they weren't saying. She spotted one of Ronnie's sons, the one they called Chester, speak to the bartender, then he disappeared out back.

She and Derrick left through the front door, eying the parking lot for the guy.

"That beat up pick-up truck," Derrick said, pointing to the vehicle Chester was climbing into.

Ellie rushed to his sedan and Derrick got in, started the engine and eased from the parking lot. Chester opened the driver's window and hung his arm out. Through the rear window, she saw smoke curling from his cigarette.

He seemed oblivious that he was being tailed, although Derrick took precautions by not getting too close and occasionally turning onto a side street then catching up a couple of blocks over. They left the town center and turned onto a country road winding along Foggy Mountain. With the recent rain and night setting in, the mist rose in thick waves, like steam oozing from a tea kettle.

They passed another outfitters store, a restaurant called Goats on the Roof, and signs for scenic trails for hiking to Red River Rock Falls. A deer darted in front of them and Derrick slowed as a family of four raced across the road. SUVs and trucks hauling canoes and kayaks passed, done for the day.

Chester turned down a dirt road that looked like it disappeared into the mountain.

Three miles in, swallowed by the wild landscape, they made a couple more turns then Chester stopped at a chain-link fence. Derrick cut his lights and pulled into some bushes several hundred feet away.

Chester got out, snagged a metal ring of keys from his pocket and unlocked the chain. After opening the gate, he drove through and relocked it. His lights faded as dust whipped up behind him.

A few moments later, she and Derrick slipped from his sedan, climbed the fence and followed on foot. Ellie's body still ached, side splitting as they hiked up a hill then through the pines and aspens. The area was fraught with overgrown weeds and briars that clawed at her legs as she pushed through the dense foliage. Insects hissed and buzzed around them and in the distance she heard the drone of an ATV chopping through the woods.

A mile in and she spotted the old warehouse and a van parked beside it.

Her foot slipped on a branch and it cracked, then suddenly gunfire rang out.

ONE HUNDRED THIRTY-ONE

Kevin was so crazed with anger that he was shaking. He slid his hand into the pocket of his dress slacks where he'd stowed the .38 he kept for his own protection. His father's lectures about people targeting those with money and power echoed in his head. Predators, jealous lovers, business associates, and disgruntled employees would stab you in the back if you dropped your guard.

The injustice of that drove him to purchase a gun and visit the shooting range regularly. The feel of the smooth, cold steel beneath his fingers calmed his nerves as he watched Mark and Pixie kick a soccer ball back and forth.

Pixie laughed when she missed the ball and ran in circles around Mark, then he swung her around and around while she giggled.

How dare that Emily woman leave his little girl alone with that man? He was nobody to Pixie, and never would be.

Night settled in, the sun dipping below the horizon, a quarter moon peeking from behind the cloud cover.

Finally, the bastard collected the ball and they walked toward the parking lot, swinging hands.

A scream of protest burned through him and he started after them.

What if Mark was taking her back to his house? What if she called him *Daddy*?

No! No! No! He couldn't allow that. Mark was not her father. Never would be.

Pixie was *his* just like Jesse had been. His to love and hold and keep forever.

They were *Moons*.

He closed in on them as they reached a dark gray Range Rover. The man opened the trunk and tossed the ball inside then he and Pixie walked to the back door.

Sweat beaded Kevin's skin and suddenly he couldn't breathe. His body shook. His lungs strained for air.

He couldn't let that stranger have his little girl.

Moving quickly, he inched closer, scanning all directions to make certain no one was watching. Mark leaned forward to open the car door, and Pixie started to climb in.

Kevin slid the .38 from his pocket then jammed it into Mark's back. "Step away from her."

Mark jerked his head up, eyes stretched with shock, then he threw up an arm as if he planned to fight. The gun went off, bullet hitting Mark, and his body jerked. Blood soaked his shirt as he collapsed.

Pixie screamed from the back seat as he reached for her. "Shh, sweetie. I'm your Daddy."

Her eyes widened, huge in her face.

"It's okay," he said, desperate and trembling as Mark groaned and grabbed at his leg.

Kevin kicked Mark's back, causing blood to gush, then pulled Pixie from the SUV and scooped her up.

She cried out for Mark, incensing him even more. "Shh, it's okay." He stroked her hair, tucking her face into his shoulder as another car turned into the parking lot.

"Don't cry, honey," he murmured. "I'm going to take you to your mommy."

Heart hammering, Ellie peered through the dark and realized there was more than one shooter in the woods. Bullets pinged by her head and Derrick fired a round, motioning to the right. She pivoted and released a shot, but it was so dark and with the damn fog, she could barely see a foot in front of her.

Her phone rang and she checked the number. Bryce.

Hunkering low while Derrick continued to fend off the shooters, she answered in a hushed tone.

"It's Bryce. 9-1-1 call just came in. Mark Wade was shot at the park, and someone took Pixie."

No... not Pixie. "Did you issue an Amber Alert?"

"Done."

Her mind raced as another bullet flew past. "How's Mark?"

"On his way to the hospital," Bryce answered. "I looked for witnesses but the park was deserted this time of night. A group of teens showed up to hang out and found Mark by his car, unconscious, but they didn't see the shooter. One of my deputies is staying to supervise the ERT as they process the scene."

Leaves rustled as Derrick crept toward her. In the distance she heard bushes parting and dogs barking as if in attack mode.

"We'll be there ASAP," Ellie whispered into the phone. "If you talk to Mark first, ask if he knows who took Pixie. My guess is Kevin Moon or someone working for him."

"Already planning on it."

"Find out what kind of car Kevin Moon drives, too, and issue an APB for it."

"I know how to handle this," Bryce said staunchly.

"Just thinking out loud," Ellie said. She hung up and pocketed her phone, praying Pixie was okay. "Let's come back at daylight when we can see what we're dealing with," Ellie whispered. "Mark Wade was shot and Pixie abducted."

Derrick muttered a sound of frustration. "You're right. If Moon took her and we find him, we can use kidnapping charges as leverage to persuade him to tell us what's going on out here."

They stayed crouched low as they maneuvered the terrain back to the road and climbed the fence. A coyote howled from somewhere in the woods. By the time they reached Derrick's sedan, she was sweating buckets and her ribs throbbed.

As she crawled into the car, she pushed aside the pain. Saving Pixie was all that mattered.

ONE HUNDRED THIRTY-THREE
CROOKED CREEK

Pixie cowered in the back seat, frozen like one of the ice statues she and Mommy had seen at Christmas.

Stranger danger, Mommy always said. *Yell, stranger danger!*

But she hadn't. She just stood there like a big baby and her voice wouldn't work.

Then she'd seen Mr. Mark fall. And there was blood, she was pretty sure of it. And he didn't get up. And now this stranger was swerving, driving like a crazy man, throwing her across the car, the tires screeching.

Don't ever get in a car with a stranger. Mommy told her that all the time. But she was in the car and now what was she going to do? She couldn't reach the door handle or the lock and even if she could, if she jumped out, she might get runned over.

"I'm your daddy," the stranger said. "I'm taking you to your mommy."

No... he couldn't be her daddy. Mommy said her daddy was dead.

He swerved around another car and honked his horn, shouting bad words, and she covered her ears with her hands and squeezed her eyes closed. Sniffling back tears, she pictured her mommy waiting for her.

But she had a bad tickle in her tummy and she thought the man might be a big fat liar. That he wasn't really taking her to her mommy. That he was the kind of stranger Mommy warned her about.

Derrick swung into the ER parking lot, tires screeching, Ellie's anxiety at peak level. Laney texted:

> With the ME in Red River Rock. Autopsy confirms Thelma Coonts died of internal bleeding sustained from the crash. Tox screen negative.

Ellie quickly replied thanks then filled Laney in on Pixie's kidnapping. She'd fretted the entire drive, her mind venturing to dark places she didn't want to visit where Mia or Pixie were concerned.

Her phone call to Sheriff Kincaid raised her anxiety even more. He hadn't answered so she'd left a frantic message, demanding his help. "Mia – Jesse's – daughter has been kidnapped and Mark Wade, Mia's fiancé, shot. Find the Moons and see if they're responsible for this. A little girl's life is at stake." Her breath rushed out. "And dammit, call me when you do."

Derrick threw the sedan into park and they jumped out,

rushing into the hospital. Bryce stood in the waiting area, a frown tugging at his mouth.

"Any word?" Ellie asked. "How is he?"

"Not good. A gunshot wound to the back," Bryce said. "They're not sure if it severed his spinal cord. He's in surgery now."

Oh, God. Ellie swallowed hard. "Did you call his parents?"

A grim look flashed in the sheriff's eyes. "They're on the way. Meanwhile, the Nettles are here."

Ellie's heart hammered as she spotted the couple holding hands, heads bowed in prayer. "Was Emily there when it happened?" *Please don't let her children have witnessed this.*

"No. She met Mark at the park and left Pixie with him for a visit."

Ellie silently chastised herself. She should have anticipated Kevin might try something and placed Pixie in protective custody.

She and Derrick crossed the room to the Nettles, but in reverence to their prayer, she waited until they finished and looked up.

"Mark is hurt and Pixie's gone," Emily said, huge tears swimming in her sea-blue eyes. "I... I'm so sorry."

Ellie sank onto the chair beside her while Derrick and Andy walked over to the coffee machine to talk.

"This is not your fault, Em," Ellie said. "So don't even go there. Just tell me what happened?"

Emily inhaled a deep breath and twisted her hands together. "Pixie was so sad," Emily said in a low voice. "I found some drawings she made of Mia and Mark, and I sensed she felt like her mother and Mark both abandoned her. That's when I called you, then Mark. We met at the park."

A hitch caught in her voice. "I should have called you or maybe the sheriff and had someone watch them but I... didn't think..." Tears laced her words as she trailed off.

Ellie took Emily's ice-cold hands between her own and rubbed them. "Listen, you had no way of knowing she was in danger. No one knew where Pixie was staying."

"Then how did this person find her?"

Ellie's mind raced to catch up. "I don't know. He must have hired a PI or have contacts somewhere. If the Moons did this, they have connections."

"You have to find her," Emily cried. "That poor baby. She must be so terrified."

"I know," Ellie said. "And we will, Emily. Just keep praying."

A second later, Angelica Gomez raced into the hospital with her cameraman. Ellie appreciated the reporter's tenacity and her willingness to help, but Ellie's emotions were raw.

The ER doors swished open and Mark's parents rushed in, both looking scared to death. Ellie sped over to cut them off before they approached Emily. She didn't deserve to deal with Mark's parents' emotions, which understandably were running high.

Mrs. Wade had been crying, and Mark's father had his arm around her in an effort to calm her although judging from her hysteria it didn't seem to be working.

"Where's our son?" Sylvia Wade demanded.

"In surgery," Ellie said.

"Who did this to him?" Mrs. Wade cried. "Who would shoot Mark?"

Derrick joined them, his jaw rigid, but his voice remained calm. "We don't know yet. Maybe Mark can tell us when he regains consciousness, ma'am."

"This is about Mia running off, isn't it?" she said, her voice angry.

"Mrs. Wade," Ellie said, tightening a leash on her temper. "I'm certain it is. But it's also about Pixie and finding that child is our priority now. She was kidnapped by the person who shot your son."

The color drained from Mark's mother's face and her legs buckled.

"Let us know if we can help," Mr. Wade said as he guided his wife to a chair.

A strained silence filled the room as the wait began to see if Mark would make it.

Bryce motioned Ellie over to where he and Angelica stood. As much as she hated press conferences, she had to give one. Pixie's life might depend on someone coming forward.

ONE HUNDRED THIRTY-FIVE

Ellie's phone rang before she started the press report. Seeing it was Sheriff Kincaid, she answered. "Tell me you have news."

"I went by Kevin Moon's house but he wasn't home. I'm on my way to talk to his father now," he said. "What makes you think Kevin took the little girl?"

"Because it's possible that he's her birth father," Ellie said. "We're waiting on DNA results, but the timing of Jesse's disappearance and her daughter's birth fits."

"Who was the man who was shot?"

"Mia's – Jesse's – fiancé. Mark Wade."

"How's his condition?"

She decided to tread carefully in case Kevin learned Mark was alive and sent someone else to finish the job. "I can't say at this point."

"You want me to help you but you won't share information." It was an accusation, not a question.

"He didn't make it," Ellie lied. If Kincaid was in cahoots with the Moons, let them believe that Mark was dead. He would be safer that way.

A strained silence fell between them before he responded.

"Are you certain this woman didn't just run off and now she came back for her daughter?"

"Yes. I knew her personally. She would never hurt Mark," Ellie said, irritated. "I found evidence that indicates Patty Lasso discovered something illegal going on with their business and the Moons were involved. Jesse left a journal stating that she was afraid of Kevin and had to get away."

Kincaid was quiet for a second. "What exactly did she say about the business?"

"I don't have all the details," Ellie said. She wouldn't share them anyway and she intentionally omitted what had happened when they'd found that warehouse. She still didn't trust that he wouldn't cover for the Moons. "I realize you're tight with the Moons, but if you know something, Sheriff, or if you find Pixie with them, you have to turn them in or I intend to arrest you as an accomplice."

"I don't like threats, Detective," he snapped. "If I find the child, I'll make sure she's safe."

He hung up and Ellie gritted her teeth. She hoped she hadn't made a mistake by calling him, but she wanted to make it clear that she would hold him accountable. Squaring her shoulders, she glanced at the Wades, who were clenching each other's hands in fear, then she headed toward Angelica. "I'm ready."

Angelica signaled her cameraman to begin then adopted her professional persona. "Angelica Gomez here with Detective Ellie Reeves and this late breaking story." She tilted the microphone in Ellie's direction.

"We are still searching for a missing woman, Mia Norman," Ellie began. "Tonight, Mia's four-year-old daughter Pixie was abducted during a shooting at the park in Crooked Creek. Pixie has blond hair and brown eyes." She paused, collecting herself. Angelica would run Pixie's photo for the story and the Amber Alert was going nationwide. They would find her. They had to.

A second later, she continued, "Mark Wade, Mia's fiance, was injured during the abduction. We have issued an Amber Alert for Pixie. If anyone has information about the kidnapping and shooting, or Mia's whereabouts, please contact the Crooked Creek Police Department."

She flashed a photo of Kevin from her phone. "We are also looking for this man, Kevin Moon, for questioning in both incidents. Please be advised he is armed and dangerous."

ONE HUNDRED THIRTY-SIX

SOMEWHERE ON THE RIVER

Kevin drove like a mad man to the riverboat where Mia was being held, Pixie's cries rattling his nerves. He'd turned on the radio to drown out the sound but that reporter and detective had plastered his name on the damn news.

Sweat exploded on his neck and he beat at the steering wheel. Dammit to hell – now every cop in the state would be looking for him.

His phone trilled with his father's ringtone and he cursed. But he picked it up. He had to. He might need his father's help.

"For God's sake, son, don't tell me you went and shot a man in public and kidnapped that child?"

"She's my daughter!" he shouted into the phone. "*Mine*. And that man cannot have her."

Pixie's sobs grew louder.

"I'll fix this," he said, although pure terror at getting caught seized him. "No one saw me. Now get me and Pixie a fake passport. I'll lay low at the river for a few days until the commotion dies down, then we'll go out of the country."

"You little selfish asshole," his father barked. "You're going to ruin our lives and land us all in prison. I told you to let me handle it."

"Just get the fake passports," Kevin said, so furious he was beginning to lose feeling in his fingers. He hung up and sped around a curve.

He knew what his father wanted him to do with Jesse.

He'd have to do it quickly. Get it over with. Or have someone do it for him. That would be easier.

He wanted to draw out her agony. Make her suffer the way he had.

As he sped toward the river, thunder rumbled and rain began to fall.

Pixie's cries grew more shrill. "I want Mommy!"

He adjusted the wipers to high speed as the downpour intensified, the fog thick and blurring the lanes on the curvy road. A pair of headlights flickered at him and the truck crossed the center line. He swung the wheel to the right, his tires churning as he swerved onto the shoulder. Losing control, he slammed into a boulder, metal crunching.

Pixie screamed so loud he thought his eardrums would burst. So angry he could feel his heart roaring out of his chest, he whirled in his seat to silence her.

ONE HUNDRED THIRTY-SEVEN

BLUFF COUNTY HOSPITAL

"I'm going to find out what other properties Kevin and his father owns," Derrick said. "If Kevin abducted Pixie, he may be carrying her to one of them."

"Mia could be there, too," Ellie said. "Get a list of properties Kevin has for sale, too. We'll divide up and have Deputy Landrum and Eastwood check them out."

He nodded and went to the car to retrieve his laptop. A tall thin woman in a doctor's white coat appeared before them. "Wade family?"

Mark's parents leapt up and hurried over. Ellie eased up behind them but out of respect allowed them a private moment.

"Your son is in recovery and will need time to heal. The good news is that the bullet missed his spinal cord so there shouldn't be any permanent damage."

Mrs. Wade burst into tears. "Thank God."

"And thank you, Doctor," Mark's father said.

"When can we see him?" Mrs. Wade said shakily.

"I'll give you five minutes," the doctor replied. "But he needs his rest."

Ellie stepped up beside them. "Doctor, Mark Wade was the

victim of a murder attempt by a man we believe to have abducted a child who was with him at the time. It's urgent that I speak to him. He might be able to identify the kidnapper."

"He's our son," Mrs. Wade said. "Can't this wait, Detective?"

Her husband touched her elbow. "Sylvia, whoever shot Mark is violent and that precious little girl is with him now. Let Detective Reeves go first so she can find Pixie."

"Oh, my lord, you're right." She gave Ellie a look of regret. "I'm so sorry. I'm just so scared."

"It's okay," Ellie said. "I promise I won't be long."

The doctor was silent, watching with a grim expression, then led her through double doors and down a hallway. "You understand he's still medicated and may be disorientated."

"I understand but he'll want to talk to me," she said. "He loved that little girl more than words."

The doctor smiled in understanding and paused at the doorway. "Try not to upset him."

She had a feeling that Mark would be upset, but not with her. With himself that Pixie was abducted while in his care.

She walked quietly into the room, the sound of machines beeping steady. He was hooked to a heart monitor, a machine to record his oxygen level, and an IV pumping saline and pain medication into his veins.

His eyes were closed, chest rising and falling. "Mark," she said softly as she stopped by the bed. "Mark, it's Ellie."

The sheets rustled as he tried to move, and she placed a gentle hand on his arm when he moaned. "You were shot, Mark, and had surgery. I—"

His eyes shot open, wide with panic. "P... Pixie... Pixie... Where is she?"

"We're looking for her. Do you remember what happened?"

His eyes were drifting closed again, but he fought it. "We

were at the park and... dark ... getting dark so went to the car." He coughed, one hand falling weakly to his chest.

"Is that when you were shot?"

He nodded slowly.

"Did you see who it was?" Ellie asked.

He winced in pain. "Behind... me. But..." He paused, seeming to be thinking. "Wait... I fell. Turned... saw his face."

Ellie pulled her phone and showed him a picture of Kevin. "Is this the man?"

Mark blinked rapidly to focus, then squinted at the photograph. He gave a weak nod.

"Did he say anything?"

He shook his head, his eyes fluttering. "Find Pixie..." he said in a pained whisper. "F... Find Mia, too."

"I will," Ellie said. She just prayed that they were alive when she did.

ONE HUNDRED THIRTY-EIGHT

Despair took root inside Mia as she crawled to the window of the cabin and looked out again. It was night outside, the shadows terrifying.

Where had Kevin gone? Would he be back?

Had he found Pixie? What would he do to her when he did?

He wants you to suffer.

Terror engulfed her. Kevin was tied to his father and the town. If he wanted to torture her, he could keep her locked here forever then take Pixie to Foggy Mountain or anywhere... if he had a paternity test done and confirmed she was his, a judge might even grant him custody.

A sob built in her chest and she struggled to breathe. The hum of the boat's motor buzzed in Mia's brain as the storm outside shook the cabin, and rain pinged the window just like it had the night her parents had died.

She screamed and clung to the side of the boat, shivering as her father raced through the choppy water. The force threw her to the side and Jo-Jo grabbed her hand to keep her from tumbling overboard.

Rain slashed her face and body. As her heart pounded, she heard another boat zooming up behind them.

Now, she closed her eyes and tried to block out the storm just as she had back then. But the storm in her heart could not be quieted.

She loved Mark. But by now he'd know she'd lied to him and he would never forgive her. He was such a good man. The opposite of Kevin. Kind and loving. His students and the kids he coached came to him with their problems and he listened with patience, guiding by example.

Kevin claimed he wanted children. But she'd never seen him interact with a child. When they encountered families with children at a restaurant, he'd complained that they whined and were noisy and messy.

When things had started to disintegrate between them, he'd replaced her birth control with a placebo without her knowledge. A child had meant a way to trap her, to sink his claws deeper and deeper into her. Anger at his deceit railed through her.

Now her sweet, precious, funny little Pixie was in danger...

She had to save her.

Blinking back another onslaught of tears, she dragged herself from the cot and searched the small dresser in the corner for something to use as a weapon. But there was nothing except a hairbrush inside.

The rocking of the boat was making her nauseous, so she staggered to the bathroom. Her reflection stared back at her in the small oval mirror above the sink. God, she looked like a ghost of herself. Gaunt face, bloodshot eyes, skin pale and splotchy.

Not that it mattered. She didn't care how she looked for Kevin. She was not Jesse anymore and she never would be.

She grabbed a washcloth from the towel rack, wrapped it around her hand and smashed the glass. Slivers flew into the sink, and a big crack formed down one side. She chipped it away until she pulled a sharp piece from the corner and carried it back to the cabin, hiding it beneath the mattress.

Before the Wades saw Mark, Ellie decided to give them a heads-up about her plan. She motioned Bryce over to explain.

"You heard the doctor say Mark is going to be okay," Ellie told Mark's parents. "But I think it's best that we don't advertise that fact. Let Pixie's abductor think that he died in the shooting."

Mrs. Wade gasped and Mr. Wade's face turned ashen. "Why would we do that?" he asked.

"For his safety," Ellie said with conviction. "He confirmed that Kevin Moon shot him and kidnapped Pixie. If he learns Mark is still alive and can identify him, he might send someone back to kill him."

Sylvia Wade slumped against her husband and he supported her with his arm, saying, "If you think he's still in danger, then yes, we'll agree."

Ellie directed her next words to Bryce. "Sheriff Waters will send a deputy here to guard Mark's room, won't you, Sheriff?"

He slid his phone from his belt clip. "Of course. He won't be left alone for a minute."

Fresh tears trickled down Mrs. Wade's cheeks as Bryce

stepped aside to make the call. "I can't believe this is happening," she said in a pained whisper.

"I know and I'm so sorry," Ellie said. "But we want to catch this man and bring Pixie home safely. When you see Mark, please explain our plan. He's asleep now, and I don't want to bother him again." She paused. "I know friends will be calling to check on him and the two of you, but for now please don't respond."

"Anything to protect Mark. Come on, Sylvia," Mr. Wade murmured. "Let's go see him."

Derrick returned as they disappeared down the hallway. "Kevin has several houses and properties for sale and rent."

"Forward them to me and I'll ask Deputy Eastwood and Deputy Landrum to start checking them out," Ellie said, then explained her plan to protect Mark. "Maybe we should return to that warehouse. Kevin could be holding Mia there."

"True," Derrick said. "But I found something else. The Moons own another riverboat called *Jesse's*. Kevin bought it after Jesse disappeared."

Ellie's pulse quickened. "We'll look there first."

"My partner at the Bureau is tracking Kevin's phone and his car to narrow down his location," Derrick said.

"Good." Ellie inhaled sharply. "Bryce, contact all law enforcement across the state, then reach out to bus and train stations, airports and the border patrols, and pass along Kevin and Pixie's picture. Kevin is probably desperate right now and may be planning to flee the country."

ONE HUNDRED FORTY

BLUFF COUNTY HOSPITAL

Mark drifted in and out of consciousness but even in his drug-induced sleep, he kept replaying the incident at the park in his head. He could feel Kevin Moon's gun jabbing into his back. Hear the zing of the bullet. Feel the sharp burn of the bullet splintering through him.

Hear Pixie's screams and see the tears in her terrified eyes.

Emotions choked him. Where was she? What would that monster do to her?

Guilt pummeled him. He loved her. He wanted to adopt her. Nothing about that had changed. He was supposed to protect her. And now she was gone...

And what had this sadistic man done with Mia?

The drugs pulled him back under, his eyes so heavy he couldn't keep them open. But on some level, he knew his parents were there. He'd heard his mother crying. His father assuring her he'd be okay. That he wasn't paralyzed as they'd first feared.

He lapsed into a drug-induced sleep again then sometime later stirred to beeping machines. As the drugs slowly wore off, his parents' voices drifted through the haze again.

"What did you do, Sylvia?" His father sounded angry.

"I... didn't mean for this to happen," his mother said, her voice breaking.

"Tell me," his father demanded.

A sob escaped her. "You know I thought something was off about Mia so I hired a PI to check into her."

"You did what?"

"I just wanted to make sure she wasn't going to hurt our son," she whispered.

"Mark is a grown man," his father countered. "You just didn't want to let him go."

"But I was right," she argued. "The PI discovered her name wasn't Mia, that she was lying. She'd gotten married and ran out on her husband. I... couldn't stand by and let her do that to Mark. Their marriage wouldn't even have been legal."

His father's sigh punctuated the air. "For God's sake, Sylvia. Tell me you didn't contact that man, Kevin Moon."

Mark forced his eyes open. Struggled to find his voice. It felt like he'd swallowed a mouthful of dirt. Finally he managed to push out a word. "Mom?"

He blinked her into focus and saw his father pacing across the room. His mother's eyes were teary, her lower lip quivering.

"Mom, did you call Kevin Moon?"

"Not exactly," she said, her voice shaky.

If he had the energy, he'd grab her right now and shake her. "Tell me what happened," he demanded.

Her sob rent the air but he didn't care. "Tell me, dammit. Pixie's in danger."

She pressed a fist to her mouth. "Before the ceremony, I went in and talked to Mia. I... told her I knew she'd been lying and that she had to tell you the truth or I would."

Mark forcibly swallowed. "What did she say?"

His mother wiped at her tears. "She started crying and then I left but... a man was in the hall."

"You mean Kevin Moon?" Mark growled.

"No, not him. Another man... He said he was looking for Jesse Habersham, that her husband wanted her found, and..."

"Good God. You told him where she was," his father cut in, his voice terse.

His mother nodded miserably and rubbed her forehead. "I... didn't know he was dangerous."

A deep ache of betrayal ripped through Mark's chest.

Mia had lied to him and now his mother had made things worse. "How could you, Mom? You put her right in the hands of a monster. And now that monster has Pixie."

ONE HUNDRED FORTY-ONE

Derrick's phone cut into his thoughts as he and Ellie stepped into the hallway. Lindsey. Surprised that she'd phoned, he immediately assumed she'd taken steps to overturn Rick's wishes regarding him and the children.

He motioned to Ellie that he needed to answer it.

Ellie nodded. "Okay, I'll call Cord and update him."

Braced for an altercation, Derrick stepped from the car and answered the call.

"Derrick," Lindsey cried, her voice near hysteria. "Evan's gone."

Derrick froze, heart pounding. "What do you mean *gone*?"

"We were talking about his father, and he ran to his room and closed the door. He was so sullen that I figured he needed some time alone. But when I checked on him later, he wasn't in his room. I've called all his friends and thought he might have ridden his bike to visit them but they haven't seen him." Her voice petered off for a second, then she continued shakily. "I drove around to the park and school and every place I could think of but he wasn't there. God, Derrick, what if he's hurt or if he's run away?"

Panic clenched Derrick's chest. Evan was just a kid. Out there alone somewhere. Missing his father.

Anything could happen to him.

"Is his bike at home?"

"It's in the garage," she said, frightened. "I'm... so scared. I can't lose Evan, too."

Guilt over his sister's death, the mission gone awry and Rick's suicide hit him like a sledgehammer. "You're not going to lose him," Derrick said firmly. "I'll be there ASAP."

Ellie was watching him when he hung up. "What's wrong?"

"Lindsey can't find Evan, Rick's little boy. He may have run away. Lindsey's hysterical."

Ellie squeezed his arm. "Then you have to go, Derrick."

He hesitated. He couldn't leave Ellie alone, not with Pixie missing and whatever the hell was happening in Red River Rock. "But the case—"

"I can handle the case," Ellie said firmly. "Sheriff Waters and the deputies will assist me." She kissed him on the cheek. "Go. You need to do this for Rick and those children."

Derrick was torn, but he saw the anguish on Evan's face in his mind and knew he couldn't let him down. He'd failed too often already.

"Seriously, Derrick," Ellie said softly. "That boy needs you more right now than I do."

His gaze met Ellie's and there was no doubt in his mind that she meant what she said. Still, he didn't want her facing a dangerous situation alone. He curled his hands around her arms. "Listen to me, Ellie. Wait until tomorrow and I'll go with you."

"We can't wait, Derrick. Kevin could be taking Pixie out of state or even out of the country."

Hell, she was right. His chest hurt just thinking about it. "Okay, but don't approach the Moons or go back to that warehouse until I get back or without back-up."

"Derrick—"

"Promise me," he said, his eyes imploring as her father's earlier accusations rang in his head.

Ellie gave a nod.

He had to go, he knew that. But Ellie had better damn well keep her promise.

ONE HUNDRED FORTY-TWO
SOMEWHERE ON FOGGY MOUNTAIN

Pixie was so scared, she covered her face with her hands so she couldn't see the big man's mean eyes. And his face... Blood covered his cheek and dotted his hands as he got out of the car.

He opened her door and she shrank away from him, screaming.

"Be quiet!" He grabbed her arms and shook her. "Stop crying and be quiet so I can think!"

"I want Mommy!"

He shook her again, this time so hard she bit her lip and tasted blood. His fingers were so tight on her arms, she whimpered in pain.

He looked like a crazy person from one of those horror movies her mommy wouldn't let her see.

"Listen to me, Pixie," he said, his lips snarling like a wild animal. "I'm your father and we're going to be a family."

"Mommy," she said, only she was so scared her voice came out like a baby whisper. "I don't have a daddy. Mommy told me."

"Your mother lied to you," he said, his breath so hot she felt it on her face. "You do have a father. Me. Only I just found out about you because your mother stole you from me."

She shook her head back and forth. She didn't believe him. Her mommy loved her and always said not to lie.

He loosened his fingers as a big black car rolled up. Headlights blinded her. Pixie wanted to scream for them to help her, but the man dragged her from the back seat. She kicked him and bit his hand and he howled. Tears filled her eyes.

Then he opened the door of the other car and threw her inside before he got in the front. The car jerked and sped off, tires screeching.

ONE HUNDRED FORTY-THREE

RED RIVER ROCK

In spite of her promise to Derrick, Ellie couldn't sit still and give Kevin time to disappear with Pixie.

She took an Uber to her house to get her Jeep; she planned to confront Kevin Moon's father and push him for the location of the riverboat.

But she did have to play it smart, so she made a quick call to Cord and explained about the boat. "Derrick had to leave town for an emergency. Can you stake out the Moon Stillery and keep an ear open for talk about Kevin Moon? Maybe someone there knows where he keeps the riverboat."

"I'll head there now," Cord agreed.

"Cord, don't do anything without calling me for back-up. These people are dangerous and we don't know who in the town is involved. Consider this a reconnaissance mission. Understood?"

"Yes, ma'am," he said with a soft chuckle.

"Keep an eye out for Ronnie and her boys, too. I think they're involved in this up to their eyeballs."

"Got it." He sighed. "And El, take your own advice. Call for back-up and don't rush in on your own."

"Of course." She hung up as the driver dropped her at her house. Moments later, she fired the engine of her vehicle and sped toward Foggy Mountain. Every minute that passed without Pixie meant Kevin could be getting further and further away with her.

The rain had slackened to a drizzle, the fog thicker as she drove up the mountain. Trees swayed and water spewed from her tires, the traffic thinning out with the bad weather.

Tension knotted every muscle in her body as she neared Armond Moon's home, pulling up the drive. The lights were dim inside, and she didn't see Mr. Moon's car, although the garage door was closed so it could be stowed inside.

She parked, checked her weapon, and kept her instincts honed as she walked up the drive and rang the doorbell. Seconds passed, stretching into minutes as she waited before ringing the bell again and banging on the door.

"Mr. Moon, open up, it's the police!"

Five more minutes and she walked around the house. Lights were off in the kitchen. No one was outside. The sound of rainwater dripping from the roof of the back porch blended with the whine of the wind and a flock of birds cawing above the pond.

Frustrated, she returned to her car then answered her phone.

"Ellie, my partner called," Derrick said. "He located Kevin's car. It's not moving. I'll send you the GPS if you want to head there."

"Will do. I'm at his father's house and he's not here."

"I told you not to go alone," he growled.

Ellie huffed. "I'm not at the warehouse and I'm armed, Derrick. Just find Evan and let me find Pixie. If I need back-up, I'll request it."

He muttered a choice word. "You'd better. Call me when you locate Kevin's car and be careful. He's dangerous."

"I know he is. Gotta go." Ellie hung up, cutting off the lecture she'd expected he was ready to give.

If she found Pixie and she was in danger, she'd do whatever necessary to save her. Back-up be damned.

ONE HUNDRED FORTY-FOUR

CROOKED CREEK

Cord replayed the conversation with Ellie in his mind. She'd warned him to wait for back-up and said she'd do the same, but he didn't believe her for a minute. Knowing Ellie, if she thought that little girl was in danger, she'd barrel straight into a blazing fire to save her.

It was one of the things he admired most about her. And the thing that drove him nuts.

Lola poured his coffee into a to-go cup. "Let me guess. Ellie needs you."

He knew he'd blown Lola off a few times for Ellie, but there were priorities. "I'm on the governor's task force," he said. The thought gave him pride. At least he was doing something important with his sorry life. "Mia's daughter Pixie was kidnapped. I can't sit here and not help."

Lola gave him a weary look. "I know. I hope y'all find her and Mia." She squeezed his hand. "Just be safe, Cord. You may not realize it, but you are important to some of us."

For a moment, his lungs tightened with emotion. She was still waiting on his answer about moving in together. But... he had to go.

"Thanks," he murmured, touched by her words. But his demons rose from the bowels of hell to taunt him, and he accepted the coffee, then headed out.

Maybe on the drive to Moon Stillery he'd make a decision.

But the minute he got behind the wheel, all he could think about was Ellie and finding the missing little girl.

ONE HUNDRED FORTY-FIVE

ROCKY BOTTOM

Ellie followed the GPS to Hog Mountain Road and realized Kevin had been heading to Foggy Mountain, but he hadn't made it. His black Range Rover was on the side of the road, nose into a boulder, front end crunched.

She pulled up behind it and parked, hand on her weapon, ready to draw as she surveyed the area. At first glance, she saw no movement. No one around.

Fear for Pixie robbed her breath as she approached. What if the little girl was injured?

A few raindrops continued to ping the roof of the car and the trees shook in the wind. At the rear door, she shined her flashlight into the interior, checking the back seat. No Pixie. She inched closer and looked through the front window but Kevin was not inside.

Panning the interior, she noticed blood on the front seat and steering wheel. A knot of fear burned in her stomach. Grabbing her phone, she called Bryce.

"I found Kevin Moon's Range Rover in a ditch."

"Any sign of him or the little girl?"

"No, but there's blood so one or both of them might be

injured. Send a team to process it and tow it in for analysis. I'll text you the location."

"Copy that. So far, no luck with the rental properties we've searched."

"Keep me posted." She sent the text, then opened the driver's door, surprised it wasn't locked, and looked for a clue as to where Kevin was going. No notepad or map. No phone.

She slipped on gloves, reached over and found the keys in the ignition. She started the engine and noted it had a built-in GPS system so she searched the entries.

Emily Nettles' address was one of them. The last one was for a place called Rocky Bottom, an isolated section of the river.

Her heart raced. If the boat was located there, Kevin might be on his way to it with Pixie.

She considered waiting on the forensic team and didn't want to leave the car unattended since they might find evidence inside.

Finding Pixie is more important. If she's injured, she might need medical attention.

Decision made, she locked the car, hid the key beneath the tire and texted Bryce where the team could find it. A minute later, she jumped back in her Jeep and entered the location for Rocky Bottom into her own GPS.

Every second counted.

ONE HUNDRED FORTY-SIX

NORCROSS

Derrick's tires peeled as he careened into Lindsey's driveway. She and Rick owned a house about thirty miles north of Atlanta in a quaint small town with railroad tracks in the heart of it.

He scanned the park as he passed, searching for Evan but it was dark and he didn't see him. Minutes later, he turned onto a quiet street lined with maple trees and oaks, keeping an eye out for the little boy. Lindsey had called again, desperate with worry, and said two neighbors were searching the neighborhood.

He parked in the drive, praying the boy had been found, but took one look at Lindsey's terrified face and knew he hadn't. Evan's little sister Maddie looked wide-eye and teary as she hugged a giant teddy bear to her chest.

"Any word?" he asked.

Lindsey shook her head, her chin quivering. "It's all my fault, he's gone. I shouldn't have let him stay in his room so long."

Derrick was tempted to give her a comforting hug but he doubted she'd welcome it. "We'll find him," he said with conviction. He'd lost his little sister years ago. He wouldn't lose Evan. "May I come in?"

She nodded, a shudder going through her as he followed her and Maddie to the den. Maddie climbed in her mother's lap and Lindsey rocked her back and forth, her eyes dulling as if she was lapsing into shock.

"Talk to me," Derrick said softly. "Tell me everything that happened today."

Lindsey rubbed her daughter's arm. "Evan's been really quiet and sullen ever since Rick... passed. I tried to comfort him, but he's so angry and wants to stay in his room by himself all the time."

"It's understandable that he's mad," Derrick said. "It's one of the stages of grief."

"I know, I know. But it's been so hard..." She struggled with her emotions and he waited, giving her a minute to compose herself. "I set the engraved plaque honoring Rick on the mantle and Evan got upset looking at it. I asked him if he wanted to keep it on his bookshelf but that's when he ran to his room and slammed the door."

Ahh, geesh. "That must have been difficult," he said, as an image of Rick formed in his mind. Neither of them had considered themselves heroes. They were both tormented by their guilt over their mission gone awry.

Lindsey's brown eyes were glassy with tears. "I tried to talk to him, make him feel better by telling him he was the man of the house now, but he wouldn't open the door. "She inhaled sharply. "But I think I said the wrong thing."

"There's no right or wrong thing to say at the moment," Derrick said. "You just have to love him. Give him time to grieve. To cry."

"That's just it," she said. "Except for the funeral, Evan hasn't cried since we heard the news about Rick."

So he was bottling his emotions. Damn, he was probably a

powder keg just waiting to blow. "You said you called all his friends. Was there some special place he and Rick used to go together?"

Lindsey worried her bottom lip with her teeth. "They enjoyed playing catch at the ball fields." She straightened. "I should have thought about that."

"I'll check there. Can I look in his room first?"

Lindsey nodded, then stood, carrying Maddie on her hip. The first thing Derrick noticed when he entered the room was that the bed was unmade and looked as if the covers had been ripped off in a fit of anger. Posters of the Atlanta Braves hung on one wall and two signed baseballs sat on a shelf along with a picture of Evan, Rick and Freddie Freeman between them.

Another wall held a photo of him and Rick at the train station in the small town, along with a map on the wall above it.

On the boy's desk, he found a drawing of the constellations. One star was bright and hung low over a sketch of a house which resembled the one the family lived in.

He turned to Lindsey. "I'll be back. Call me if he shows up."

A little boy alone out there... Evan had to be all right. He just had to be.

ONE HUNDRED FORTY-SEVEN

SOMEWHERE ON THE RIVER

The constant buzzing sound was driving Mia up the wall. As she drifted off, she was there again, at the place where Mama worked.

She snuck into the big room where all the sewing machines were, where Mama said not to go. But she wanted to see what Mama did all day long. Why she was so tired and cranky and complained about her shoulder hurting.

She crept through the rows of bundles stacked above her head and saw her mother hunched over a machine, stitching seams on long wool pants.

Mia was only seven, but she was fascinated by the rows and rows of machines and women working. The place was sweltering hot, the ceiling fan barely stirring the air. The room smelled like machine oil and sweat. Her mother looked tired and... miserable.

The shrill sound of the whistle blowing for the thirty-minute lunch break cut through the noise of the machines. Her mother jumped up, grabbed her sack lunch and rushed to join the other women to eat her sandwich. They sat in the middle of a pile of bundles, more work to be done, but didn't speak, simply ate in silence. She saw them looking around the room as if watching for someone else. Everyone looked nervous or scared.

One of the women whispered something then everyone went still, looking at the door and huddling closer together. Mia strained to see but she couldn't see past the piles of material.

Suddenly a noise jerked her from sleep. She stilled, confused by the dream. But she wasn't in the sewing room. She was still locked in this tiny cabin, boat bouncing back and forth.

The sound of Kevin's voice outside the cabin door sent her to her feet. Then... the sound of crying... A child... Pixie.

Pure terror consumed her.

"Sit down and be quiet, Pixie," Kevin ordered. "Your mommy is a liar. You're my little girl and we're going to be a family."

Pixie's wail echoed from the other side, shattering Mia's heart. Her sweet daughter must be so scared. She just hoped Kevin hadn't hurt her.

"Look, Daddy bought you a pretty necklace," Kevin said. "It's a gold moon-shaped pendant because your last name should be Moon. And it will be."

"I don't wanna be a Moon," Pixie cried. "I want Mommy!"

"But you are a Moon," Kevin hissed. "And you're going to wear this as a reminder."

Pixie started crying again and hate for Kevin mushroomed in Mia.

"Now this is your grandfather," Kevin said. "Isn't that right, Dad?"

Mia pressed her hand to her lips to keep from screaming. Dear God, she didn't want that man anywhere near Pixie.

"You said you were taking me to Mommy," Pixie said in a tiny voice. "You said that."

"Just put her in there with her mother and then we'll decide what to do," Armond Moon's voice boomed.

Mia pictured Pixie cowering in fear, then she heard footsteps and realized Kevin was going to open the door. Not wanting to scare Pixie with her frazzled appearance, she frantically brushed her hair down with her fingers and wiped at her eyes.

The door eased open, and Kevin stepped in, dragging Pixie by the arm as she whimpered. A gold moon-shaped pendant glittered on a gold chain around her small neck.

Damn Kevin.

Mia raced toward her. "Honey, I'm here. I'm right here." Pixie tried to run to her but Kevin held her back.

"Tell her the truth," he snarled. "Tell her I'm her father."

Pixie looked up at her with silver dollar-sized tears and all Mia could think about was getting them out of here. She had that piece of glass to use as a weapon. She just had to bide her time until she could use it.

"Kevin, please let her come to me," she said softly. "You're scaring her."

"She wouldn't be afraid if you'd told her about me," he said harshly. "It's your fault she's frightened."

He removed a small jewelry box from his pocket. "I bought you a matching moon necklace. Put it on so Pixie knows you both belong to me."

Her hate intensified but Mia did as he said, then Kevin allowed Pixie to come to her. She enveloped her precious little girl in her arms, vowing once again to save her from her father.

ONE HUNDRED FORTY-EIGHT

ROCKY BOTTOM

Ellie parked at a clearing by the river, her navigation system indicating she'd arrived at her destination. After leaving his car in a ditch, Kevin must have gotten a ride from someone – his father or the hired help. She scanned the dark area for another vehicle but didn't see one.

Don't go in alone, she and Derrick and Cord had agreed. But she just wanted to know if this was the right spot. If not, they'd search that warehouse next.

Pulling on hiking boots, she grabbed her rain jacket and a flashlight, secured her weapon and holster and headed into the woods. Tree frogs croaked around her as the wind hissed through the hemlocks and brush. She heard the sound of the river rippling to the east and headed in that direction, weeds clawing at her jean-clad legs.

Mosquitos circled her face and gnats swarmed in front of her as she wove through the trees. Storm clouds hung heavy, making the sky and woods seem even darker and more ominous.

She reached the edge of the river and looked in all directions for a riverboat. Directly north, she spotted lights. She ducked between the trees and followed the river until she spotted the boat nestled in a cove, a canopy of trees shrouding it.

She inched closer, watching for someone on the upper deck and finally saw two men emerging from below. Pulling her night binoculars from her jacket, she aimed them at the men, zeroing in on Kevin and his father. They were pacing and circling each other, and it looked like they were arguing.

She inched closer and heard Mr. Moon say, "I told you to get rid of that woman. Hell, I even tried to do it for you but you had to keep looking."

"What do you mean, you tried to do it for me?" Kevin barked.

"Before the wedding – your wedding. That little bitch and her friend Patty got too damn nosy. They were going to the cops," Mr. Moon yelled. "Someone had to stop them!"

"Jesse left because of you?" Kevin snarled.

"Because she knew too much. Saw too much. We had to put the fear of God into her or she would have ruined all of us." Mr. Moon's sinister laugh echoed in the wind. "Hell, once she saw her friend stuffed in that barrel, she knew what would happen to her if she talked."

Ellie eased her way to the boat, crouching down in the bushes. Just as she reached the stern, an arm's length away from where she was on the edge of the river, Kevin's father stalked to the pilot seat and fired up the engine. The boat puttered, then the motor roared.

Ellie couldn't let them get away.

She crawled onto the stern then crept around the port, peeking around the corner. The boat jerked into motion, blades chopping. She clawed for something to hang onto and grabbed a rope, holding it tightly to keep from being thrown overboard.

The wind brought Kevin's voice to her again. "Dad, where are you going?"

"To get rid of our problems once and for all since you don't have the guts to do it."

Ellie snuck around the side so she could see what was happening. Then Kevin pulled a gun and pointed it at his father.

"What the hell are you doing?" Kevin's father yelled.

"You can do whatever you want with Jesse, but the little girl is mine," Kevin shouted. "I told you, I'll take her out of the country."

"You'll take her nowhere," his father said. "I don't intend to have the law on my ass for the rest of my life, hunting for you, dragging my name through the mud accusing my son of being a kidnapper."

"Jesse took my daughter from me. I won't let you do the same." Kevin lunged toward his father and Mr. Moon used a right hook to try and knock the gun from his son's hand.

The gun fired into the air and the two men struggled, both grappling for control, before it went off again.

ONE HUNDRED FORTY-NINE

"Mommy, I'm scared."

Mia wrapped her arms around Pixie and hugged her tight, pressing her daughter against her chest. She could feel Pixie's little body trembling against her. "Oh sweetie, it's okay, Mommy's here." God, it felt so good to hold her again. Her little face looked terrified but so precious to her right now. She pulled back long enough to look into her eyes and search her face for injuries. "Did he hurt you?"

Pixie's chin quivered. "He pinched my arm and he was scary," Pixie whispered.

Fury filled Mia. "Oh, baby, that was so wrong." She hugged her again, reminding herself Pixie was alive and breathing. "I'm here now and I won't let him hurt you. I promise."

Heaven help her, she hoped she could keep that promise.

Suddenly the sound of a gunshot blasting above choked Mia with fear.

Pixie jerked and screamed, covering her ears with her hands. "Mr. Mark..." she cried. "He killed Mr. Mark."

Terror tore through Mia so intensely she nearly doubled over with it. An image of Mark's sweet face floated through her mind. Kevin had taken everything from her. Jo-Jo and Seth. Patty. Tori. And now Mark, the best man she'd ever known. She was pretty sure the Moons had had something to do with her parents' deaths, too.

She would not let them raise Pixie. She would die before that happened.

The second gunshot brought her out of her shock, the sound of the boat's motor panicking her. Where were they going now? Were they going to kill her and stuff her body into a barrel like they had Patty?

She rubbed Pixie's arms. "Listen, honey, I'm going to get us out of here. But you have to be really brave, okay?"

Pixie tightened her hold around Mia's neck.

She rubbed Pixie's back, soothing her daughter. "If I can get us out of the cabin we may have to take a lifeboat. I'll need you to listen and do what I say." She tipped Pixie's chin up with her thumb. "We'll call it our adventure. Now, I need to borrow one of your hairpins, okay?"

Pixie bobbed her head up and down. "'kay."

Mia removed the bobby pin then set Pixie on the bed, hurrying to the door. She jammed the sharp end of the pin into the lock and twisted and wiggled it until she heard the lock click.

Then she dug the piece of glass from beneath the mattress and slipped it into her pocket.

"Come on, sweetheart," she whispered. "Let's go. And stay behind me."

Pixie gave a small nod, and Mia clasped her little hand and led her up the stairs. Above, she heard a commotion. Shouts. Scuffling. Another gunshot.

She ducked her head above board and peered around, careful not to make a sound. Kevin's father gripped his chest and staggered backward. Blood soaked his white shirt and he collapsed in shock. Kevin stood gripping a gun, his eyes wild. He really was a monster.

Ellie burst onto the scene, throwing herself at Kevin. He pivoted, gun going off again, but he missed and he and Ellie rolled to the floor. Mia wanted to help Ellie, but she had to get Pixie to safety first so she pulled her little girl to the deck and ran with her toward the stern where the life rafts were stored.

She'd been terrified of the river when she was little. She was terrified now. But Emily had helped her overcome her fear enough to sign up for swimming lessons so at least she'd learned to swim.

Rain began to pummel them, drenching her and Pixie whimpered. Mia grabbed a lifejacket, helped Pixie into it then tugged one on herself and fastened it.

Ellie and Kevin rolled and traded blows, then Ellie lunged at Kevin again. This time he gave her a hard shove and sent her flying over the edge, plunging into the cold water.

Pixie screamed, and Kevin whirled around and charged her. Mia thrust the shard of glass at him and sliced him across the arm as he reached for her. He grabbed her wrist and shook her with a howl, but she kicked him then lifted the glass, jabbing it into his chest. He screamed and swayed, losing his grip on her. She snatched Pixie, threw the lifeboat over the edge then helped lower Pixie into it.

Kevin was shouting in rage and grabbed at her leg, but she kicked him in the face. He howled, grabbing his nose as blood spurted. Then she jumped into the lifeboat with her daughter and began to paddle with the current.

ONE HUNDRED FIFTY

NORCROSS

Derrick found the security team at the park where Lindsey said Rick used to take Evan, showed them the boy's photograph and explained that he was missing. They instantly issued an alert and officers started combing the park. Baseball was Evan's favorite sport and he loved the Braves. Derrick remembered Rick taking him to a game and talking about how excited Evan had been when he'd caught a foul ball. They'd never get to attend a game together again.

No wonder the poor kid was struggling.

The park was crowded with families waving flags and celebrating, awaiting the fireworks show. He didn't see Evan anywhere. A lone little boy was swinging at the far end of the park and Derrick hurried over, calling Evan's name. But when the kid turned around, disappointment crushed him. The kid wasn't Evan.

He had to keep looking. He walked past the splash pad, then down the steps to the ball fields, scanning the bleachers and fields but there was no Evan in sight.

He pinched the bridge of his nose, battling panic. An image

of Evan's room flashed into his mind and he pictured the maps, posters of the train tracks and the drawing of the constellations.

The train museum was only a few blocks away so he headed down the sidewalk toward it. A freight train blasted its whistle and the guardrails lowered, keeping people off the tracks as it passed. Kids lined up on both sides to watch in awe. He strained, hoping to see Evan's face among them. But he didn't.

The sound of happy families was both warming and unsettling. His family had been torn apart by tragedy when his sister was abducted. Little Pixie had been ripped from her mother and Mark, a man who loved her. And now Evan...

He had to find him.

The train museum slipped into view. It was busy today with families and he carefully checked faces for Evan, then decided to search the train carriages lined up for children to climb on and explore.

The engineer's car was a favorite, with kids waiting their turn to pretend to drive. No Evan there either. He went from one carriage to the next and came up empty again. Last, he climbed onto the red caboose at the rear.

A few children were exiting, chatting excitedly, but Evan was not in the mix. The ceiling was painted with stars, the constellations just as Evan had drawn.

A low sniffle came from somewhere and he eased his way deeper into the train car. He heard it again.

"Evan?" he said in a low voice. "Are you in here?"

The interior grew silent and his heart pummeled his chest. He heard another sound and stopped at one of the bench seats used for storage. Holding his breath, he opened the bench and breathed out.

There the little boy lay, curled in a knot, his cheeks soaked with tears.

ONE HUNDRED FIFTY-ONE
ROCKY BOTTOM

Ellie fought the force of the current, choking on water as the river tried to sweep her away. Gasping for breath as she surfaced, she treaded water in the pouring rain, shaking it from her eyes as she searched for Kevin. She spotted a life raft dropping into the river then saw Kevin climb into it.

A scream echoed through the wind, and she spun around and saw another lifeboat a few feet away bobbing back and forth.

Thank God. Mia and Pixie were inside. Mia seemed to be struggling to paddle against the strong current and wind and Pixie was huddled with her hands over her ears to drown out the sounds.

Summoning her strength, Ellie swam toward them, but the current flipped the raft over, dumping Mia and Pixie into the frigid water. "Hang onto the boat," Ellie shouted above the crashing waves and relentless rain.

Had Emily said Mia couldn't swim? That she was afraid of water?

Pushing herself to the limit, Ellie swam harder, seeing Pixie go under then pop back up, sputtering water. Mia surfaced again, spun around in search of her daughter then yelled her name in terror.

Ellie reached Pixie first, grabbed the child around the waist and crawled to the riverbank with her. She helped Pixie onto the shore and cradled her face in her hands. "Stay right here. Let me help your mommy!"

Pixie was trembling but nodded. The rain was falling in heavy sheets, so hard you could barely see, and thunder cracked the sky. Through the blurry haze, Ellie saw Kevin closing in. Ellie reached her hand to Mia, yelled her name and Mia swam toward her.

"Pixie!" she screamed.

"She's on the bank," Ellie called to her.

Mia frantically swam to her and Ellie helped her over to her daughter where she climbed on the shore and pulled Pixie into her lap. Kevin was only a foot away, barreling toward them.

Ellie dove into the river, then swam with all her might around the raft behind him, dragging herself into it. The wind was howling so loud it drowned out everything and she lunged on top of him. He spun around, eyes crazed, and shoved the gun at her. Ellie wrestled with his hand and twisted his arm, throwing him off balance. His face was bloody, and blood trickled down his arm and fingers. She squeezed his hand so hard he dropped the weapon. She snatched it and they fought again, but her finger slipped and it released a round. The whizz of the bullet sliced the air.

The bullet pierced his shoulder and sent Kevin flailing backward. Determined to keep him down, Ellie slammed the butt of the gun against the side of his head. He was thrown for a second but fought for the weapon again and this time when it went off, the bullet pierced his chest.

Blood gushed and his eyes rolled back in his head. His body convulsed then went slack. She knelt and checked for a pulse.

Seconds ticked by. Water surged into the boat. Kevin was not moving.

No pulse.

"Damn you for scaring that child," Ellie growled to him.

Breathing out in relief, she stowed the gun, grabbed the paddle and maneuvered the lifeboat to the riverbank. "It's okay, Mia, Pixie. You're safe now."

Pixie was clinging to her mother, shaking and crying. Mia stared in shock at Kevin, for a moment unable to move.

"He's gone, Mia. He can't hurt you or Pixie anymore. I promise." Ellie waved her over. "Come on, let's get out of here." Ellie extended her hand again to encourage her. "Please, Mia. We need to get Pixie out of the storm."

Lightning zapped a nearby tree, jolting Mia from her dazed state.

"Come on, Pix," Mia murmured to her daughter. "We're going home." Mia scooped Pixie into her arms, pressing her little girl's face against her chest to shield her from the sight of Kevin's bloody body.

Ellie took her arm and helped them climb on board. Mia sank onto the seat, turning away from Kevin and rocking Pixie as Ellie rowed them back to safety.

ONE HUNDRED FIFTY-TWO
MOONDOGGY'S

Cord stepped outside onto Moondoggy's dock and settled at a picnic table with a cold beer. He casually leaned back in his chair, a man simply enjoying his drink, as patrons imbibed and chowed down on Moondoggy's famous wings and chili burgers. With his jeans, T-shirt and boots, he blended with the locals.

Whitewater raft guides finished for the day, gathering to celebrate and a couple of truckers loped in for a dinner break.

He spotted Chester and Lloyd lumber outside then walk around the corner of the building, snarls on their faces.

Curious, Cord carried his beer with him down the steps and eased along the front of the dock, peering around the corner. There stood Ronnie's sons receiving a heated dress-down from Ronnie.

"You sorry shits," she growled. "We have to move the cargo for now. Too many pigs snooping around."

"We just done what you told us to," Chester mouthed off.

Ronnie lifted her hand and backhanded him across the face. "Don't give me no lip, boy."

Lloyd cowered backward as if he'd been hit too. "Where do we move it?"

Ronnie pulled a slip of paper from her pocket. "Here. And don't let anyone see you, you hear me?"

"Yes, ma'am," Chester muttered.

"Yes, Mama," Lloyd said.

Ronnie stomped toward the rear entrance and Cord set his beer on the dock edge, retrieving his keys.

As soon as the man got in his truck, Cord called Ellie. She didn't answer so he left a message.

"Ronnie told her boys to move the cargo. Didn't say what it was, only she knew the cops were getting too close. They're in a white utility van. I'll follow and see where they're going."

Derrick's heart ached as he studied Rick's son. Poor kid was suffering. He was only nine but he probably felt like he carried the weight of the world on his shoulders.

"Evan." He laid a gentle hand on the boy's arm. "Your mom is worried about you. Why don't you come out and talk to me?"

Anguish radiated from the little boy's lean body, but he climbed out then sat on top of the bench and stared out the window of the caboose. "I don't wanna talk."

Derrick gave a nod. "Okay, for now. But I need to text your mom that I found you."

He simply looked up at Derrick for a minute, his thick brown hair tousled, cheeks red from crying.

Derrick pulled his phone and texted Lindsey.

Found him. He's safe and sound. Will bring him home soon.

Lindsey: *Thank God. And thank you, Derrick.*

Emotions washed over Derrick as he turned his attention to Evan. He didn't know how to be a father figure but he could be

Evan's friend. "I know you're hurting right now, buddy. You miss your dad and... wish he was here. So do I."

Evan tensed his jaw, shifting angrily. He looked so much like Rick that it hurt to look at him. But he reminded himself that Rick lived on through Evan and that was a beautiful thing.

"Your dad and I were good friends, you know. Did he tell you we served in the military together?"

Evan cut him a sideways look then gave a tiny nod.

"He loved you, Evan. He talked about you and your mom and sister all the time."

"Then why did he leave us?" he said, teeth gritted.

Derrick put his hand on the boy's shoulder, giving him a gentle squeeze. "That's complicated. Sometimes things happen in people's lives that make them not think clearly. They're just so sad and confused..." Like Evan was now? Dammit, he was bungling this. "You've heard of PTSD?"

"Yeah, I may be a kid but I'm not stupid."

"Right," Derrick said with a small smile. "PTSD is kind of like a disease, only it's mental, and happens after a traumatic event. Like the things your dad saw when he was deployed." He paused, choosing his words carefully. "Some people just can't forget or get over that awful thing. It eats away at them and they're hurting so much inside that they can't live with it."

Evan scrubbed his knuckle across his nose. "They said he was a hero. Heroes don't kill themselves."

Derrick inhaled to control his breathing. "Listen to me, buddy. I understand you're angry and have every right to be. But your father *was* a hero. He fought to protect this country and everyone in it, including you."

Evan folded his thin arms. "If he wanted to protect me, he'd still be here."

Derrick had no answer for that. "I was angry when I heard what happened, too. Angry at him and at myself for not being able to help him."

"I didn't help him either."

Oh, boy. That was heavy. "Evan, that's not how it works. You're a kid. It wasn't your job to help your father. It was his job to help you." Now *he* had to help Rick's son. He couldn't let him down. "And he did try to take care of you." Derrick rubbed the boy's arms. "He told his lawyer he wanted me to be there for you, your mom and your sister." He paused. "Now, I'm not your dad and I never will be. But I'm here for you if you need me. You can cry or be mad or scream and yell – whatever you need to do. I'll always be here and so will your mom."

A long moment passed as Evan picked at a torn piece of the seating. Finally he spoke, "Mom says I'm the man of the house now." His face looked tormented. "But I don't know how to be a man."

Wow again. He'd felt the same way when his own father committed suicide after his sister's disappearance. Like he'd suddenly been thrust into an adult role he wasn't ready for. "That's a heavy weight to shoulder, isn't it?" Derrick said softly.

The boy nodded miserably.

"You aren't a man yet, Evan. You're a kid and you should do kid things." He folded his hands. "So how about this? Why don't you let me help with the adulting, be a friend that helps when big problems come up?"

Evan blinked and stared at him for a full minute, contemplating what Derrick said. Finally, his shoulders sagged slightly in relief. "My dad used to bring me here when I was little," he said, sniffling. "We pretended the train was taking us different places."

Derrick smiled, grateful to know a good memory was peeking through the sorrow. "Is that why you came here?"

Evan nodded. "At night you can see the constellations."

Derrick cleared his throat. "I used to watch them with my father, too, when I was young. My dad told me stars are bright lights of people who've passed, looking down to make sure their loved ones know they're watching." He nudged the boy to walk outside onto the platform and they leaned over the rail. His throat thickened as he pointed to a shining star in the distance. "That one belongs to my father."

Evan jerked his head at Derrick. "Your dad is dead, too."

Derrick nodded.

Evan scrunched his nose in thought as he searched above. A deep breath escaped him then he lifted his hand and pointed to the brightest star in the sky. "I think that one belongs to my dad."

Ellie called an ambulance for Mia and Pixie, a second team for Kevin's body and an ERT to process the riverboat. Medics were also on their way to check on Kevin's father.

Mia cradled Pixie against her and the little girl fell asleep, at peace now in her mother's arms.

"Are you okay, Mia?" Ellie asked while she waited on the ambulance. "Did he hurt you?"

"I'll be fine," Mia said. "Just so relieved you found me and saved Pixie."

"I'm glad too. We've all been so worried." Ellie wanted to know everything. "I learned your real name is Jesse Habersham and that you and your assistant Patty discovered the Moons were doing something illegal in town. That's why you ran?"

"They're money laundering," Mia said. "They killed Patty because she was going to the sheriff." Her voice cracked. "I was there. Saw them kill her and put her body into a barrel." She shuddered visibly. "They threatened to kill me if I said anything."

"Who were they?"

"Goons who worked for the Moons," Mia said.

"But they let you live? Why?"

"I don't know, maybe they were afraid of Kevin," Mia said. "By then I'd already wanted to call off the wedding. Kevin had become controlling and he hit me once, I was afraid of him. Then I learned I was pregnant and knew I couldn't raise a child with him." Pain suffused her eyes. "My sister and her husband helped me fake my death."

"By using the cadaver," Ellie said.

Mia's breath hitched. "You know about that?"

Ellie nodded. "Emily Nettles was keeping Pixie. She gave me the envelope with your instructions about the Penningtons. I tracked them down."

"But he murdered them," Mia said, her voice tormented with guilt. "They saved me and now they're dead."

"Your sister loved you," Ellie said. "Don't forget that."

"I won't," Mia said. "Not ever. I just wish I hadn't shut Jo-Jo out of my life all those months when Kevin and I first got together. She warned me not to get involved with him or to go to Red River Rock."

"You went there to ask about your parents' deaths," Ellie said. "What did you find?"

"Nothing specific. But I have this fleeting memory of my family on the boat the night of the explosion. And... I think they were running from something. That someone was shooting at us and we were trying to escape."

Mia rubbed her eyes, despair wrenching her voice. "Now I've lost everyone. Mark probably hated me when he found out the truth, and Kevin killed him, too."

Ellie gave her a sympathetic look. "Mia, Mark is not dead. He was shot but he survived."

Mia's face crumpled with relief. "Thank God for that. But he probably hates me. And I don't blame him."

Ellie had no answer to that. Mia and Mark would have to work out their personal feelings between themselves.

Sirens wailed in the distance and Ellie went to meet them. Mia and Pixie were safe.

But something was going on in that warehouse and she couldn't close this case without uncovering what it was.

ONE HUNDRED FIFTY-FIVE

Ellie met the ERT on the Moons' boat and found Kevin's father hanging on by a thread. The medics checked his vitals then carried him to the ambulance while another team recovered Kevin's body from the life raft.

She texted Bryce with an update and asked him to meet Mia and Pixie at the hospital, to take their statements and guard them.

Sheriff Kincaid arrived seconds after the medics, his expression stoic as he saw Mr. Moon's bloody body and the evidence of the struggle between him and his son on the deck. "What happened here, Detective?"

She explained about finding Kevin's car and tracking the GPS. "Mia – Jesse – and her daughter were being held in the lower cabin. Kevin and his father were arguing about what to do with them when Kevin pulled a gun. They fought and he shot his father."

Shock flared on Kincaid's face. "Kevin shot his father?"

"Yes," Ellie said. "I tried to subdue him but he pushed me overboard. Mia escaped the cabin and she and Pixie made it to a life raft. Kevin chased after them. I caught Kevin and he tried to kill me, but he was shot in the struggle and didn't make it."

"And the woman and child?"

"Are safe and on their way to the hospital," Ellie said.

"Well, you've certainly been busy," Kincaid said, his voice full of derision. "This is my county and you didn't bother to keep me abreast as things unfolded?"

No, she hadn't. "It all happened too quickly, there wasn't time."

His eyes pinned her with accusations. "Since you didn't request back-up, you have no witnesses to corroborate your story."

Ellie's heart thundered. "Mia will be able to confirm my statement."

His lips curled into a smile. "Why should I trust anything she says? She faked her own death, lied about who she was and planned to marry another man while she was already married."

"Because she was terrorized," Ellie said. "I think you know that and you were covering up for the Moons because they own you just like they own everyone else in this godforsaken town."

He threw his shoulders back. "I don't like accusations, Detective." He extended his hand. "Now give me your weapon. You're coming to the station with me for questioning and I intend to hold you until we clear up this matter."

Fury sizzled through Ellie. Damn him. She'd known he was involved and should have kept her mouth shut. Now he'd probably lock her up until he could find a way to cover his tracks.

Mia soothed Pixie as the doctors examined them and gave Mia IV fluids, then confirmed that she would be okay. She sent prayer after prayer to the heavens, thanking God that Pixie was alive and safe now. That Kevin could never get his dirty hands on her.

Thankfully Mark had survived, too. But he'd almost died because of her. She never should have become involved with him or allowed herself to fall in love. Everyone around her seemed to die.

But Mark was in this same hospital and even if he hated her, she owed him an apology.

Gathering her courage, she stroked Pixie's arm. "Honey, I think we should visit Mark. Mommy needs to tell him she's sorry for what happened." And for her lies.

Pixie's small hand tightened into Mia's as they found his room and knocked. She waited a second, then knocked again, and eased open the door.

The sight of him in that hospital bed made her heart throb with both love and fear. He was hooked up to tubes, an IV, his coloring was ghostly white, his breathing shallow.

All your fault.

Pixie tugged at her hand and halted at the door, trembling as she stared at Mark and the machines beeping around him.

Mia knelt in front of her daughter and rubbed her arms. "I know it looks scary to see Mark this way. But the doctor said he'll be okay. That tube is just helping him breathe for now and they're giving him medication."

Pixie clung to her hand. "Really?"

Mia lovingly tucked a strand of Pixie's hair back behind one ear. "Yes, honey, really."

The rustling of bedsheets broke into the silence. Mark lifted his head and looked over at her, his dark hair mussed from sleep, his eyes dazed slightly. Mia stood still, afraid to move forward. Although in spite of his pallor and the tubes, he was so handsome she wanted to run into his arms and tell him how much she loved him.

Instead, she remained frozen.

For a moment he didn't move or speak. He simply stared at her as if she was a stranger.

Seconds later, he blinked and pulled the oxygen from his nose, his eyes filling with mixed emotions as his gaze raked over her and Pixie. "You're okay?" he asked gruffly.

"We're safe now," Mia said softly. "Mark... I'm so sorry..." She tried to swallow back her tears but they spilled down her cheeks like rainwater.

He lifted his hand and motioned for her to come closer. Pixie took it as a sign and ran to him. Mia couldn't contain a cry as her daughter threw up her arms to Mark. He patted the bed, helping her climb up then she wrapped her arms around his neck, hugging him.

"Hey, sweetie, I'm so glad you're here," Mark murmured.

Pixie planted a big sloppy kiss on his cheek. "That other man was a meanie."

"He sure was." Mark stroked her hair gently. "I'm sorry he scared you, sweetheart."

"He scared Mommy, too," Pixie said, her lower lip trembling.

Mia's heart stuttered and she stepped up beside the bed and gave Mark an imploring look. "I'm so sorry," she whispered. "I... should have told you everything."

"Why didn't you trust me?" he asked, his voice thick with hurt.

"It wasn't that," she said in a pained whisper. "But he was so dangerous, so abusive, and I was afraid for me and Pixie." She twisted her hands together to keep from reaching for him. She wanted to touch him so badly it took every ounce of her restraint not to throw herself at him and beg for forgiveness.

She licked her dry lips. "I knew what he'd do if he found out about you, and I wanted to protect you." Her voice broke. "And look what he did. He tried to kill you."

Mark closed his eyes for a moment, inhaling and exhaling, then he opened them with a sigh. "I understand now, Mia. I'm just sorry for what he put you through."

"Oh, Mark..."

"Come here, you." He extended his hand in offering. "I love you, Mia. I always have. Always will." His eyes glittered with emotions. "I... still want you. That is, if you'll have me."

Mia gulped in surprise then clasped his hand and kissed his palm tenderly. "I love you, too. And of course, I'll still have you. You're the best thing that's ever happened to me."

Pixie placed her hand on Mark's cheek and turned his face toward her. "Does this mean you'll still be my daddy?"

"Yes, Pix, oh, yes. We're all going to be a family." Mark hugged her tight, then pulled Mia to him and kissed her.

ONE HUNDRED FIFTY-SEVEN
RED RIVER ROCK

On the drive back from Norcross, Derrick tried Ellie's phone a half-dozen times but she didn't answer. He called her boss, then Sheriff Waters but no one had heard from her.

"All I know is that she found Mia Norman and Pixie being held hostage on the Moons' riverboat," Sheriff Waters said. "They're at the hospital now and are safe. I spoke to Mia and she said Kevin and his father were arguing and Kevin shot his father. Ellie and Kevin fought and he was shot and killed."

"You said Kevin was dead. What about the father?"

"In stable condition at Bluff County Hospital and being guarded."

Then where the hell was Ellie? "Have you spoken with the sheriff in Red River Rock?"

"No," Waters said. "I called his office and left a message."

Derrick had a bad feeling in his gut. "I'm going straight to Kincaid's office," he said. "If he's in bed with the Moons, Ellie may be in danger."

"Copy that. Call me if you need back-up."

Derrick hadn't liked Waters from the get-go. But he'd suck it up and use him if it meant protecting Ellie.

"I took statements from Mia and Ellie filed one for Mark," Waters continued.

"Send those to me," Derrick said, following a hunch. Bryce agreed and Derrick hung up, then called Ranger McClain. "Have you heard from Ellie?"

"No, not in a while. Is something wrong?"

"I don't know," Derrick said, then relayed his conversation with the sheriff. "I'm on my way to Red River Rock now. Where are you?"

"I was at Moondoggy's and heard Ronnie tell Chester and Lloyd they had to move their cargo now because the police were closing in. I'm following them."

"McClain, listen to me. Stay back and don't let them know you're tailing them. If you see something going down, do not approach. Call me and wait, do you hear me? Ellie would kill me if I let anything happen to you."

A tense silence followed. "I can take care of myself, Agent Fox. And if Ellie's there and in danger, I don't intend to sit there and do nothing."

He hung up and Derrick heaved a breath. He knew the ranger cared about Ellie. But he was worried he was a hothead and would rush in, getting them both killed.

Derrick punched the accelerator and sped up, flying onto the mountain road toward Foggy Mountain. The mist was even thicker tonight, a red sheen rising above the ridges like red dust floating into the sky. Tree limbs sagged beneath the weight of what must have been a storm earlier this evening.

Hopefully, Ellie was at the police station tying up loose ends. But the closer he got, the more worry gnawed at him. If something was going down tonight and Kincaid was involved, things might be coming to a head.

And Ellie might be right in the middle of it.

"You have no right to hold me here," Ellie argued.

"Actually, I do, Detective." Sheriff Kincaid towered over her from the opposite side of the table in the interrogation room. "I'm following protocol. You shot and killed a prominent member of my town. You would do the same if I killed someone in your territory."

Dammit, Ellie hated to admit it, but she would. She forced herself to temper her attitude.

"You're right. But I have been consulting you, Sheriff. And a woman's and child's life were in imminent danger. I had to act quickly." She folded her arms. "Now, Sheriff Waters is taking Mia's statement and I already have a positive identification from Mark Wade identifying Kevin Moon as the man who shot him and abducted Pixie. No court in the world can deny that evidence."

His rapid breathing rattled in the room. For a moment, he stood staring at her, angry and frustrated and deciding what to do. "Sit tight, Detective. I'll call Waters for those reports."

Ellie pounded the table with her fists as he left the room. To what extent would he go to protect the Moons?

They hadn't hesitated to kill others who got in their way. Was she next?

ONE HUNDRED FIFTY-NINE

Derrick stalked into Sheriff Kincaid's office, every nerve cell in his body riddled with anxiety.

"Is the sheriff in his office?" he asked.

The receptionist looked at him warily. "I'll get him." She stood, hurrying through the double doors to the back.

Five minutes later, Sheriff Kincaid appeared, a cold steeliness radiating from him. "Special Agent Fox."

"I'm looking for Detective Reeves," he said bluntly. "Is she here?"

The man balled his hands into fists. "Yes, I needed her statement regarding the death of Kevin Moon and the shooting of his father Armond."

"Did you get it?" Derrick asked.

"Yes," he said. "But I was waiting for verification of the facts from Sheriff Waters."

"Do you have them now?"

Kincaid exhaled. "They just came through."

"Then release Detective Reeves or I'll call my boss."

Kincaid's scowl could send a bear running toward the woods, but Derrick held his own. The sheriff whirled around, disappeared through the back and a few minutes later, Ellie appeared.

A sigh of relief escaped him when he saw she was in one piece, although he did see fresh bruises on her face.

The sheriff returned Ellie's weapon and she tucked it into her holster, her glare of contempt toward Kincaid hot enough to burn rubber.

"Go back to Crooked Creek, Detective. And don't leave the state," Kincaid said with a warning in his eyes. "I might need to talk to you again."

Ellie lifted her chin in defiance. "Oh, you'll be talking to me again, I promise you that."

Anger humming through the air, she strode outside.

Derrick followed, giving her a moment to breathe before they reached his sedan.

"That asshole," Ellie said. "I want to nail him to the wall with the Moons."

"We will," Derrick assured her. "I talked to Ranger McClain. Something's going down tonight. Cord is following Ronnie's boys now."

Ellie's eyes flashed with concern. "He's going to call us with the location, right?"

"I gave him instructions to," Derrick said.

They reached Derrick's sedan and got in, then saw Sheriff Kincaid leave the police station.

Ellie fastened her seatbelt. "Let's follow him and see where he goes. If he's covering for the Moons, he may know what's in that cargo van."

Derrick agreed, started the engine and pulled away from the parking lot. He had a feeling the bastard was as deep and dirty as the Moons.

ONE HUNDRED SIXTY

SOMEWHERE ON THE AT

Ellie called Cord as Derrick tailed Kincaid.

"Are you okay, El?" he asked, his voice muffled.

"Yeah. Derrick and I are following Sheriff Kincaid. Where are you?"

"I'll send you the coordinates. Followed Chester and Lloyd past the docks to what appears to be a warehouse in a secluded section on the river."

"We know where that is," Ellie said. "We were shot at when we tried to get closer. Do not go in on your own, Cord."

"I'm outside," he said in a low voice. "They're about to unlock the door and—"

His voice was cut off. Ellie's heart raced. "Cord?"

Static sounded, then a rustling sound.

"Cord, what's happening?"

No response.

Panic rippled through Ellie. "Derrick, I think they have Cord. He's at that warehouse."

"Looks like Kincaid is headed that way, too," Derrick said.

Ellie gripped the edge of the seat. They had to save Cord.

Seconds ticked into minutes, her anxiety so intense she felt dizzy. Kincaid veered onto a winding dirt road into the woods, and Ellie realized Derrick was right. This was another route leading to the warehouse without having to go in on foot.

Her breathing rasped out as they crept behind Kincaid, every second filled with fear for Cord. He shouldn't be here. He should be home safe.

Kincaid slowed and Derrick hung back. But the road only led one direction, and two miles in, she saw him turn into a clearing. Then the warehouse slipped into view. Kincaid came to a stop and climbed out. A white cargo van sat near the doorway. Cord's truck wasn't in sight, but with his tracking instincts, he would have parked in the woods so as not to be seen.

As Derrick cut his lights, they pulled weapons and eased from the vehicle, maneuvering through the woods and keeping cover. Suddenly a noise drew her attention and she saw an injured Cord being dragged to the river.

Kincaid walked toward the van.

Ellie motioned to Derrick that she'd go after Cord and for him to track Kincaid, keeping an eye on the warehouse.

He signaled agreement and she gripped her weapon, slipped through the forest along the river and saw Ronnie nearing the edge of the riverbank with Cord. Cold fear clenched her insides, and she darted through the woods until she reached them.

His hands were tied, his feet bound, a bloody gash on his head. Ellie was so incensed she saw red and charged.

ONE HUNDRED SIXTY-ONE

As Ronnie shoved Cord into the river, Ellie stormed over. She lunged at the heavy-set woman but Ronnie fired a shot at her. Ellie dodged it, ducking sideways and rolling, using her feet to launch into a kick that sent Ronnie staggering backwards.

Terrified for Cord, she aimed her weapon at Ronnie, but the woman was as strong as an ox. Ronnie knocked it from her hand then grabbed her around the throat and began to choke her. She shook Ellie so hard her teeth rattled and she lost feeling in her limbs as the air was strangled from her lungs. A beefy slap to the face and her head snapped back, then Ronnie grabbed her like she was nothing but a sack of potatoes, hauling her into the barrel. Ellie struggled to fight her way out but the lid slammed on top. Then she heard a hammer pounding it.

She screamed and kicked with all her might. The wood cracked and she kicked again and again, then felt the barrel being thrown to its side and rolled. Claustrophobia and panic threatened to overcome her but she kicked again and again, using her anger to fuel her energy. She had to save Cord.

Finally, the wood splintered then she heard water splash as the barrel tumbled into the river. Fearing Cord was drowning, she pried at the splintered top, fingers bleeding as she pummeled it with her fist until the wood crashed and she managed to break the lid enough to escape.

Holding her breath, she dragged herself through, water pulsing around her as she fought its force and searched for Cord. She didn't see him anywhere. The sound of a motor rumbling, blades chopping through the river cut through the woods. Dammit, Ronnie was escaping.

But she had to get to Cord.

She took another deep breath then dove below the water's surface. She swam in circles, searching, then plunged deeper until she spotted him floating toward the bottom. She paddled faster, fighting the current until she reached him, then grabbed his arm and dragged him, forcing her aching legs to keep moving until she broke the surface. Holding Cord around the neck, she side-crawled to the dock and treaded water for a minute.

"Cord, Cord, hang in there," she said desperately through ragged breaths.

She swam, dragging him to the shallow side so she could stand, then pushed him onto the dock. A second later, she crawled on top of him, leaning close to listen for his breathing.

Painful seconds passed as she checked his pulse. God, she couldn't find one. Linking her hands, she started CPR and pressed against his chest, counting as she did compressions. One two, three... Her mind raced back to training. One hundred compressions per minute. "Come on Cord, breathe dammit." She pressed again, river water running down her face and into her eyes. Sweat beaded her skin. "Don't you dare give up, Cord," she ordered.

Seconds later, finally his body jerked. Coughing, he spit out water and opened his eyes.

She didn't realize she was crying until she laid her head against his and hugged him. "God, Cord, you freaking scared me to death. I thought you were going to die on me."

He lifted one hand and stroked her hair. "No... wouldn't leave... you."

Ellie lifted her head up and tried to compose herself but all she could do was soak in the fact that he was alive.

"You okay?" he said as he coughed.

"I will be once I catch that woman."

"Then get her," he ground out.

Ellie nodded. "I will."

"The warehouse... Go there first, Ellie. I'm fine. There are girls... They need you."

"What girls?" Ellie asked.

"Don't know, just heard Ronnie's boys talking. Hurry before they move them somewhere else."

ONE HUNDRED SIXTY-TWO

When Ellie caught up with Derrick, he was still surveilling the warehouse from a distance. As they hunkered in the bushes, he gestured to the right where Ellie spotted a guy holding a shotgun, standing guard. She filled Derrick in on the fact that Ronnie escaped but Cord was safe, then relayed what Cord had said about the girls.

Together they crept along the edge of the building, determined to get a look inside. Derrick went to the right, sneaking between the trees until he made his way up behind the guard. Twigs crackled, and the man jerked toward Derrick, but Derrick put the man in a chokehold, squeezing his neck until the man's legs buckled and he fell limp to the ground. Derrick snatched his shotgun and tossed it into the bushes.

Ellie inched nearer the old building. The windows were all painted over, concealing the interior. Derrick joined her and they flattened themselves against the wall as the door opened and Chester and Lloyd appeared, dragging several young girls from the building. They ranged in ages, anywhere from eleven to late teens, and looked dirty, malnourished, and terrified as the men led them at gunpoint to the cargo van. Some of the girls were crying and clinging to each other, some terrified, while others looked listless as if they'd been drugged or given up all hope of escaping.

Ellie's stomach plummeted. She'd thought the Moons and Ronnie were money laundering or running drugs, but these girls appeared to be human trafficking victims.

Chester and Lloyd shoved the girls into the van, then locked it and ducked back into the warehouse. Seconds later, they returned, hauling half a dozen more girls with them, piling them into the back of the van as if they were cattle. Ellie counted at least twenty.

One more trip and the count added up to twenty-five. Crickets and night creatures echoed in the tense silence as the van door slammed shut, trapping the young girls inside. Kincaid walked out then, and Ellie steeled herself not to shoot him on the spot.

"Stay here," Ellie whispered. "I want to see what's inside the warehouse." While the men stood with their backs to her in hushed conversation, she edged her way to the doorway and peered inside.

She expected to see cots for sleeping, that the girls might be forced to work at Moondoggy's, behind those closed curtains. The air was stifling and muggy and smelled of sweat and machine oil. Inside she saw a dark room full of rows of sewing machines, bundles of fabric piled high, boxing the workers in like sardines. With no central air, the interior was like an oven. It was so stifling hot you could barely breathe.

Dear heavens, it was a sweatshop. Anger and shock rolled through her. These girls weren't sex workers, they were being forced into child labor.

She walked through the inferno, imagining the injustice for the young girls. It was so horrific she vowed to make everyone involved pay. As she passed a room with steam irons, she choked on the hot air.

Another suffocating room was lined with mattresses on the floor where the girls must have slept.

They'd obviously been held prisoners, and no one in the town had known about it. Or if they had, they'd kept their mouths shut out of fear.

Heated voices lured her back to the scene at the van. Knowing she couldn't allow them to escape, she slipped up beside Derrick and they stepped from the shadows, guns raised. The van was locked with no windows, shutting the girls in again.

"This operation is over," Ellie said. "Raise your hands and lace them together above your head."

Kincaid and Ronnie's boys swung around toward her, stunned. The sheriff's steely gaze met hers. "I'm on your side, Detective."

"Sure," Ellie barked. "Damn you, you wanted to hold me at your jail to give yourself time to move these young girls so we wouldn't find them."

Derrick stepped forward. "I'll be taking *your* gun now, Sheriff."

The sheriff's jaw went rigid, but he remained still and allowed Derrick to confiscate his weapon.

Chester started to run, but Ellie fired a bullet at his feet. He jumped, squealing like a frightened pig and she swung the gun at his brother. "Don't even try it."

Lloyd threw up his hands, shaking in his boots.

"You lowlife coward," Ellie snarled. "Get on your knees. Now."

Chester dropped to the ground and so did Lloyd, both sweating and breathing heavily. While Derrick handcuffed the sheriff, she strode to Ronnie's boys and snapped cuffs on them.

"You're going to pay for this," Ellie said.

"We just did what we was told," Chester whined.

"It was all Mama," Lloyd cried.

"Shut up." Ellie bounded toward the van, then opened the door. Gasps of shock and fear rippled from inside. Knowing the young girls were traumatized, she holstered her gun, then eased inside, hands raised to assure them she wasn't a threat.

"It's okay now," she murmured. "We're here to save you."

Even as she said it, the girls looked at her with blank stares and whimpers.

"Just stay put and we'll take care of you." She lifted her phone. "I'm calling for help now."

ONE HUNDRED SIXTY-THREE

Ellie wanted to see Mia in the hospital but they'd issued a full-fledged hunt for Ronnie and she had matters to tie up. Bryce and his deputies had shown up to supervise the transportation of the victims and Kevin's body was on the way to the morgue, his father en route to the hospital.

The search team explored the area around the warehouse for miles and miles.

Her phone buzzed, a call from the helicopter team. "We spotted the woman down the river about a mile. There's an outbuilding of some sort there."

"Thanks," Ellie responded. "We'll check it out."

Hanging up, she told Derrick about the call. They rushed to one of the small motorboats she assumed had been kept by the property for transporting the girls in and out. They climbed in and Derrick started the boat. The blades cut through the choppy river, the sky black with the threat of another storm. The acrid odor of fear and death seeped from the dark moss and the horrible secrets that had been hidden there.

She kept her eyes peeled as Derrick maneuvered the boat, searching for the building. Finally, a metal structure, smaller than the warehouse and almost completely shrouded by trees and brush, slipped into view.

Derrick eased into a cove and they slipped off the boat then crept through the bushes, careful to keep their footfalls light. The garage door to the metal building screeched open and more whiskey barrels lined the inside.

A sense of evil permeated the air that made Ellie's chest tighten with dread. What was inside those barrels? Corn liquor? Drugs? Guns?

Patty Lasso had been found in a barrel just like those. Was another body inside one of these?

Staying hidden, she watched as Ronnie appeared, sweating and cursing as she rolled one of the barrels out to a ramp leading to the back of another cargo van.

She and Derrick moved closer, then when they were only inches away, she stepped from behind the bushes. Derrick inched the opposite direction so he could sneak up behind Ronnie.

"It's over, Ronnie!" Ellie shouted. "Put your hands above your head. Now."

Ronnie's harsh laugh boomed like thunder. "Honey, ain't nothin' over."

Gun aimed at Ronnie, Ellie eased closer. "Your boys are in custody and so is Kincaid. You're going to prison with them."

Suddenly Ronnie pulled a knife and lunged at Ellie. She fired a shot but Ronnie knocked her sideways and jumped her. The force of her two-hundred-pound body sent Ellie slamming against a rock and the world spinning. The woman was like a mountain, strong and tough, one beefy hand circling Ellie's throat, the other swinging the knife down toward Ellie's face. Ellie summoned every last ounce of her strength. She was not going to let this animal kill her.

Ronnie sneered at her, spitting tobacco as she traced the blade down Ellie's throat, drawing blood. Sucking in a painful breath, Ellie went totally still. The knife was too damn close to her jugular.

A tree limb cracked behind them, then came the sound of the chamber clicking in Derrick's gun as he placed it at the back of Ronnie's head. "Drop the knife, Ronnie."

The woman hissed like a rattle snake coiled to strike, then whirled around and tried to wrangle the gun from Derrick. It went off and the bullet pinged off one of the barrels. Ronnie jumped Derrick, using her bulk to knock him backwards, giving Ellie time to push herself up. She was breathing hard, blood trickling down her neck but she crawled to her weapon and retrieved it from the bushes.

Derrick and Ronnie rolled on the ground then Ronnie grabbed him by the shoulders and banged his head against a rock. He went limp for a second, and Ronnie twisted away to come after her.

Ellie didn't intend to let the woman get the best of her this time. She raised her gun, watching fear flicker in Ronnie's eyes for a second. It didn't last long. Ronnie bellowed and charged toward her. Ellie fired a shot and hit Ronnie in the shoulder. But the woman kept coming. Ellie pulled the trigger again and the bullet pierced Ronnie's stomach. She grunted, staggering as she gripped the wound.

"Go ahead and kill me, bitch," Ronnie snarled.

"No," Ellie said. "You kept those girls prisoners. Now you're going to know what it's like to be locked away."

Ronnie's eyes turned feral then she charged at Ellie again. Ellie fired at her knee and Ronnie went down in a blaze of agony.

While she howled, Ellie rolled the woman over and hand-cuffed her.

Derrick groaned and lifted his head, wiping away blood.

"You okay?" she asked.

A scowl darkened his eyes as he gave a nod, glancing at Ronnie wailing and cursing.

Ellie crossed to him and handed him her weapon. "Keep this on her. I'm going to see what's in those barrels."

His hand was shaking as he took it but he didn't argue. He trained the gun on Ronnie.

Seconds later, Ellie found a crowbar in the warehouse and carried it to the barrel Ronnie had rolled outside. Using brute force and the end of the tool, she wedged it enough to pry the nails loose, and then looked inside.

Shock and rage hit her as the stench of a charred dead body assaulted her.

Trembling with rage, Ellie rushed into the warehouse and found ten more barrels.

She held her breath, horrified as she opened one after another. Ten barrels. Ten bodies.

Heaving for a breath, she stumbled back outside and found Derrick still guarding Ronnie. The sadistic woman had stopped screaming and stared at her with the coldness of a psychopath.

"Those bodies... Who are they?"

Ronnie's yellow teeth were brown with tobacco as she grinned. "I told them girls what would happen if they tried to get away."

ONE HUNDRED SIXTY-FOUR

CROOKED CREEK POLICE STATION

DAY 5

It was the early hours of the morning and Ellie and everyone was dog-tired as Ellie tied up loose ends.

Ronnie was in the hospital under police guard while a recovery team transported the barrels and remains inside to the morgue for analysis. Since Ellie suspected most were undocumented immigrants, identifying them would take time.

Cord had been examined and Lola picked him up at the hospital; thankfully he'd recover.

Although Ronnie had clammed up and refused to talk, her sons spilled their guts. Their mother worked for the Moons, keeping the sewing factory thriving. In the beginning, other local business owners who couldn't pay their loans were forced to provide their wives and daughters to sew at the factory. The last six years, they'd promised papers to undocumented immigrants, in exchange for work. But once they were in Red River Rock, they refused to let the workers go free for fear they'd talk. Apparently the sweat shop made clothing and sold their products abroad, bringing in a small fortune by using free child labor.

She and Derrick kept Kincaid waiting, letting him stew in the consequences of his own sordid mess. Both faced him in the interrogation room, ready to seal his fate.

Ellie gave him a chilly stare. "You knew about this operation and covered it up for the Moons." Her temper soared at the image of those young innocent girls being forced to work in such horrendous conditions.

Sheriff Kincaid's mouth twitched. "It's not what you think. I was investigating the Moons for money laundering when recently I noticed they were hiding something in that warehouse. I planned to bust them for everything."

"Do you really expect me to believe that?" Ellie said between clenched teeth.

"Give me my phone call and you'll see I'm telling the truth." He leaned forward, his handcuffed hands folded on the table.

Ellie and Derrick exchanged a look, then she gave a nod, and Derrick handed him his phone.

"Is your lawyer on the way?"

"Not my lawyer," he said. "But someone you'll want to meet. Then you'll understand everything."

Ellie tapped her foot impatiently. "Go on."

"You'll find out when he gets here. I'm done talking until then."

"Fine. Suit yourself," Ellie said matter-of-factly. They had him dead to rights.

She and Derrick left the sheriff and found Angelica waiting in the press room. Already social workers and victims' advocates had been called to handle the care of the victims.

"You ready?" Angelica asked.

Ellie nodded. The people in Crooked Creek and Red River Rock deserved to know the truth, no matter how heartbreaking.

Hopefully the residents of Red River Rock would be free now to live their lives without fear.

She ran her hand over her hair, which was a rat's nest from her dive into the muddy river, then she delivered her statement, hoping to assuage the fears of the residents.

"Folks, I'm happy to say that we have not only found Mia Norman and her daughter Pixie, but they are safe and sound. During their recovery, we uncovered a money laundering scheme as well as a sweatshop utilizing child labor. Arrests have been made, the operation disbanded and the children being forced to work for free are now being treated and taken care of. With that in mind, hug your own children tonight and let's remember the soldiers who have worked to protect us and ensure our freedom in this country."

An hour later, Ellie and Derrick joined Kincaid in the interrogation room again. This time, a broad-shouldered man in his early forties stood beside the sheriff and introduced himself as Federal Marshal Clay Gibbons.

"What's going on?" Ellie asked.

"I'll let him explain," Sheriff Kincaid replied, his hands folded.

Marshal Gibbons took a seat and they joined him around the table. "Sheriff Kincaid has been working undercover with us for the past five years investigating the Moon family and the crimes in Red River Rock."

Ellie stared at Kincaid in shock.

Derrick shuffled in his seat, displeased. "If that's true, why didn't you fill us in instead of stonewalling our investigation?"

"Need-to-know basis," Marshal Gibbons said. "We have witnesses under protective custody whose lives would have been endangered if they were exposed."

Ellie tapped her foot on the floor and Derrick drummed his fingers on his thigh, obviously pissed.

"What witnesses?" Ellie asked.

Marshal Gibbons made a quick call. "Bring them in now."

Ellie and Derrick exchanged confused looks but waited. A moment later, the door opened and another marshal entered with a dark-haired man and a brunette woman.

Ellie swallowed hard. It was Jo-Jo Pennington and her husband. And they were very much alive.

ONE HUNDRED SIXTY-SIX
RIVER'S EDGE

Cord listened to a replay of Ellie's news segment as Lola drove him home from the hospital. She came inside to make certain he was okay, which was sweet, but the last thing he wanted was her fussing over him.

When he'd been half-unconscious in the ambulance, all he could think about was Ellie and the fact that she'd saved his life. Then he'd been worried sick about her, and now he'd been told she'd busted a child labor ring.

God, she was amazing.

His dog Benji met him at the door, tail wagging. But as he licked Cord's hand, he knew Benji sensed something was off. He nuzzled him then headed to the couch and Benji followed, climbing up beside him.

"Do you want some hot tea or a drink or something to eat before I go?" Lola asked.

He looked up at her and shook his head. "No, but we have to talk. Lola, I..."

"You don't have to say it," Lola said, sadness and resignation tingeing her voice. "I know how you feel. I even understand it. I think it's best we just move on."

Cord felt a pang in his chest. She'd been so good to him. And yet...

"You deserve better," he said.

"I know." She kissed him on the cheek and left.

ONE HUNDRED SIXTY-SEVEN
CROOKED CREEK

Mia had just gotten Pixie down for an early nap when the doorbell rang. For a split-second, panic struck her, then she remembered Ellie had given a press conference and the Moons were out of her life for good. Armond Moon had been arrested along with Ronnie and her sons, along with another hired hand who Kevin's father had paid to kidnap her from her wedding to Mark. With Mr. Moon in prison and Kevin dead, they would never get their filthy hands on Pixie.

Finally, she and her daughter were free and safe.

Not only safe, but Mark was amazing. He'd actually forgiven her. She'd lost so many people already, that she was grateful for that blessing. Her heart was full with love for him.

The bell dinged again, and she walked to the window and peeked out. Ellie's Jeep was in the drive. She must have come by to check on them.

Anxious to thank her, she answered the door.

Ellie stood there with a smile on her face. "Hey, Mia. How are you?"

"Good. Better now Pixie's with me and safe," she said. "And since I saw Mark."

Sympathy softened Ellie's eyes. "How did that go?"

"He's forgiven me," she said softly. "I can't believe it. I'm so lucky to have him."

"He's lucky too." Ellie shuffled from one foot to the other. "There's something else, Mia. Something you need to know."

Mia crinkled her forehead. "What? Did Mr. Moon get away? Has he hired a lawyer about Pixie?"

"No, he's going away for a long time. And he won't have any hold on Pixie, not after what he's done."

"Thank God," Mia murmured, breathing more easily.

Ellie turned and glanced at her Jeep. The car doors opened and a man and woman got out of the back seat. A woman with long brown hair and the sweetest face Mia had ever seen. A man with his arm around her, their faces eager. Faces she hadn't seen in five years. Faces she never thought she'd see again.

Shock stole her breath. She couldn't believe it.

Her heart thundered as she soaked in the sight. Her sister and husband Seth... They were alive.

"Mia?"

"Jo-Jo," Mia gasped.

Heart hammering, she ran toward her sister and Jo-Jo raced to her. They hugged and laughed and swung each other around just like they had as kids.

ONE HUNDRED SIXTY-EIGHT

Once they'd hugged and cried for a minute, Ellie followed Jo-Jo, her husband and Mia inside. "I don't understand," Mia said. "How is this happening? Kevin showed me your obituary."

They seated themselves in the living room and Jo-Jo clasped her husband's hand. "I'm sorry, Mia. We wanted to contact you all these years and let you know we were alive but it was too dangerous for all of us. Including you."

Mia swallowed hard. "I'm so sorry, sis. All this time I thought you were safe, still living in your house and that you were okay."

Emotions flickered in Jo-Jo's eyes. "It's not your fault, Mia. One of Moon's goons came looking for you and threatened us. We did what we had to do to protect all of us from that man and his family. I know how dangerous he was."

"You warned me from the start," Mia said, her voice catching. "I should have listened."

"I understand, you just wanted to find out what happened to Mom and Dad," Jo-Jo said softly. "When you called that night before the wedding about Kevin, and we came up with a plan to help you fake your death, I started having nightmares. Memories of when we were kids with Mom and Dad."

Mia nibbled on her lower lip. "What did you remember?"

"Mom and Dad owned a little restaurant in Red River Rock, but they were having financial troubles and accepted a loan from the Moons," Jo-Jo said. "When they couldn't pay it off, Mr. Moon told Mama she had to pay her debt by working at the sewing factory."

"That fits," Mia said, a faraway look in her eyes. "I remember sneaking in and watching the women sewing. But Mom didn't look happy."

Sadness colored Jo-Jo's face. "She wasn't. They still wanted more from her. When I turned eleven, they told her I had to work at the factory, too."

Mia gaped at her. "But you were only a child."

"They didn't care," Jo-Jo said. "I remember hearing their conversation. They threatened to make me stay at the sweat shop if she talked."

"Oh, my God," Mia muttered under her breath.

Jo-Jo nodded. "It was awful and I was so scared. Mama said she'd never make me do that. That's why they tried to leave with us the night they died."

"And they came after us and shot at the boat," Mia said, her voice haunted as the night replayed in her mind.

Jo-Jo glanced at Seth, then continued, "A few months after we faked your death, we noticed someone following us. They broke in once and trashed our house and left us a threatening message. The next time, they beat us. They said they knew you were alive and they'd kill us if we didn't tell them where you were."

Tears filled Mia's eyes. "Oh, God, Jo-Jo, Seth, that's horrible. I never should have involved you."

"Don't go there, sis. Of course, you should have confided in me. We're family." Jo-Jo paused, swallowing hard.

"She's right," Seth cut in. "We're fine now and are relieved you are."

Mia squeezed both their hands. "Then what happened?"

"By then I suspected they'd murdered our parents and wanted justice for you and Mom and Dad," Jo-Jo continued. "So... I turned to Sheriff Kincaid."

Mia's eyes widened. "Wasn't he working with the Moons?"

"I thought he was," Ellie interjected. "But he was actually undercover with the FBI. They were trying to expose the Moons' money laundering and investigating the sweat shop. When you were children, the Moons forced local busines- sowners who owed them money to work at the factory to pay off debt. But in the last few years, they've been forcing undocu- mented immigrants to work for them, holding them at a ware- house in the woods."

Mia shook her head in disbelief.

"Sheriff Kincaid connected us with federal marshals who placed us in witness protection," Jo-Jo finished. "We've been in hiding, waiting till he made arrests so we could reconnect with you." Jo-Jo's voice quivered. "It was agonizing not seeing you, sis."

"It was for me, too," Mia said. "I thought about you every day. Every holiday. Every birthday. I kept hoping one day it would all be over and we could be together again."

"Same," Jo-Jo murmured. "But I knew you went to Red River Rock to find the truth and I had to follow up. The marshal assured us you were safe for a while, so we waited..."

Tears gathered in Mia's throat. "It's my fault you had to give up your lives." She gave Seth a look of regret. "I'm so sorry I put you both through all this."

Seth curved his arm around his wife. "You're Jo-Jo's sister, that makes you my family, too."

Jo-Jo wiped at her own damp cheeks. "When I saw the

news about your disappearance in Crooked Creek, I was terrified the Moons had you."

Seth cleared his throat. "We contacted the marshal then and told him Kincaid had to do something to speed things up and end this. That he had to find you." Jo-Jo sighed in relief. "And now it's really over."

Mia pulled Jo-Jo into a hug. The nightmares about river monsters would hopefully end now. She had Ellie to thank for catching them and putting them away.

"It is over," she told her sister. "And we'll never be separated again."

ONE HUNDRED SIXTY-NINE

CROOKED CREEK

Two weeks later

A girl's wedding day was supposed to be the best day of her life. Ellie hoped this one would be for Mia. After all she'd been through, she and Mark deserved to be happy. The storms had passed, the sun was shining and flowers were blooming. It was a beautiful day to celebrate the beginning of their life as a family.

Ellie dressed in a dark blue sundress and shoved her feet into silver sandals, then hurried to answer the doorbell. A little makeup helped hide the knife wound Ronnie had inflicted on her, although it had been superficial and thankfully would not leave a scar.

Derrick stood on the other side, looking handsome in a gray sportscoat and khaki slacks.

His eyes lit with a smile when he saw her. "You look amazing," he said. "Isn't it against the law to upstage the bride?"

Ellie blushed. Derrick hadn't had a lot to smile about lately, so it was nice to see him in a good mood. "You're crazy," she said, surprised at how flirty she sounded. Maybe she was just enjoying a day away from the grueling cases they'd worked.

"How's Evan?"

"Grieving," Derrick said, his smile fading slightly. "But Lindsey's arranging counseling for both the children."

"That sounds like a wise move," Ellie said as she grabbed her wrap and clutch.

Derrick clasped her hand and they walked to his sedan. A light breeze was blowing, the air crisp and scented with flowers, the days since they'd closed the case sunny and bright.

Ten minutes later, Derrick parked at the Botanical Gardens outside of town where Mia and Mark had chosen to have the ceremony. Mia didn't want to be anywhere near the river. The gardens were a fiesta of colors with walking paths and benches for sitting and enjoying the scenery.

As they arrived, she spotted Lola in the gardens and she looked for Cord but didn't see him. Then Bryce appeared and Lola took his arm. Together, they laughed and walked to the seating area. Was something going on between them?

She hadn't heard from Cord since the night they'd discovered the Penningtons were still alive, when she'd called to relay the news personally. She couldn't help worrying about him.

A gentle breeze rustled the trees as she and Derrick seated themselves across from Lola and Bryce, and Ellie leaned across the aisle.

"Hey, Lola. Where's Cord?"

Lola gave a small shake of her head. "How should I know? I figured he was with you."

"I haven't talked to him since we finished the case," Ellie said, confused by Lola's terse attitude. "I called but he didn't answer."

"Maybe he went off to get his head straight," Lola said.

"Straight about what?" Ellie whispered.

Lola rolled her eyes. "Good grief, Ellie, you can't be that stupid."

Ellie jerked her head back in surprise. She started to ask Lola what she meant, but the music began, and Lola turned back to Bryce.

ONE HUNDRED SEVENTY

THE BOTANICAL GARDENS

"Mommy, Mommy, Mommy!" Pixie sang as she twirled around in her satin and tulle flower girl dress. "Today's the day we marry Mr. Mark!"

Mia smiled at Pixie's exuberance and her resilience. She'd tried to explain as best she could that Kevin Moon had technically been her father but she'd left him because he was dangerous. Pixie had learned that hard lesson herself and hadn't questioned her mother's story.

Guilt still plagued her for Tori's death. Liam had not been quite as forgiving as Mark. He'd packed his things and moved away from Crooked Creek, claiming there were too many memories of his wife here to stay. Mark's mother had visited her, apologized and cried when she'd admitted her part in leading Kevin to her. Mia told her she understood. Sylvia Wade was a mother protecting her son just as she'd protected her own daughter.

Her lies had hurt so many. There would be no more.

Jo-Jo waltzed over to her and adjusted Mia's veil, the two of them gazing at their reflections in the mirror. They'd been close as children and that bond was even stronger after the ordeal they'd endured.

"You look like Mom," Jo-Jo said softly.

Mia smiled. Now she understood the reason she'd had dreams of the sewing machine's buzzing and the reason Jo-Jo had had balked at the idea of sewing. "And you look beautiful, Jo-Jo," Mia said, her heart full of love.

Jo-Jo laughed. "Ready, sis?"

"I am." Mia stood. This time she knew she'd chosen the right man and her sister adored him, too.

She clasped Pixie's hand and Jo-Jo adjusted the train of her satin mermaid wedding dress. Together, they all walked outside.

The fading sun shimmered over the gardens, white bows and lilies adorning the rows of chairs for the guests. Just as before, she'd wanted a simple wedding with her closest friends and Mark's family. She spotted Ellie with that federal agent, and knew she owed them her life. Sheriff Kincaid slid into a seat in the back. She owed him, too.

As the music strummed and Jo-Jo walked down the aisle, joy filled Mia's heart. Pixie smiled and bounced up and down as she followed, scattering rose petals on the lawn. Mark stood at the end with his father, his best man, beside him. Sylvia blew her a kiss as the wedding march began.

Seconds later, she and Mark held hands and gazed into each other's eyes.

Mark spoke his vows first. "Mia, from the moment I met you, I fell in love with you." He squeezed her hands. "You are everything I've ever dreamed about – a strong, amazing woman, a wonderful mother, and my best friend. I love you now, forever and always."

Mia blinked back tears. "Mark Wade, when I dreamed of marrying as a little girl, I dreamed of you. I hadn't seen your face or met you, and I do think you're the most handsome man

I've ever met. But it wasn't your looks that stole my heart. I wanted a man with a kind heart, a loving soul, a man who loved family. You are all that and more. I love you, now, forever and always."

ONE HUNDRED SEVENTY-ONE

Ellie smiled as the wind whistled off the mountain, puffy white clouds dancing in the sky, and streaks of red, yellow and orange glittered over the gardens. The evil that had permeated the area was quiet for now, and peace had been restored to Bluff County.

"You may now kiss the bride."

Mark swept Mia into his arms and kissed her, with everyone clapping. Derrick clasped Ellie's hand and, for a moment, she pictured herself walking toward the altar in her wedding dress.

Only, in her mind, the face staring back at her and waiting at the altar was not Derrick.

A LETTER FROM RITA

Thank you so much for reading *The Girl in the River*, the seventh instalment in my Detective Ellie Reeves series! If you enjoyed *The Girl in the River* and would like to keep up with all of my latest releases, you can sign up at the following link. Your email address will never be shared, and you can unsubscribe at any time.

www.bookouture.com/ritaherron

I'm thrilled to continue this series and return to the Appalachian Mountains and the flavor of Southern small towns. This time, not only do you revisit the quirky characters of Crooked Creek, but the case of a missing bride takes Ellie to Red River Rock, another town full of secrets and mystery. A town set in an area called Foggy Mountain where rumors claim the red mist rising from the river is caused by the tears of those who lost loved ones. A town where nothing is as it seems and danger lurks around every corner.

I hope you enjoyed Ellie's journey in *The Girl in the River* as much as I enjoyed writing it. If you did, I'd appreciate it if you left a short review. As a writer, it means the world to me that you share your feedback with other readers who might be in interested in Ellie's world and her stories. I love to hear from readers so you can find me on Facebook, my website and Twitter.

Thanks so much for your support. Happy Reading!

Rita

www.ritaherron.com

 facebook.com/authorritaherron

X x.com/ritaherron

instagram.com/ritaherronauthor

ACKNOWLEDGMENTS

As always, thanks to my fabulous editor Christina Demosthenous. This series never would have happened without her encouragement and willingness to brainstorm and plot murder alongside me. Her faith, confidence, insight and inspiring titles have excited me beyond belief and made this series one I look forward to returning to with each book.

Thanks also to the Bookouture team for the beautiful cover, editorial support and marketing strategies so we can reach more readers.

Last but not least, thanks to all my readers for following Ellie and her adventures!

Made in the USA
Coppell, TX
14 April 2024

31266672R00260